Dark Enough to See the Stars

Beth Duke

For my mother, Patricia.
You read me the first words
and taught me to love them.

Everything I write is for you.

My beautiful daughter,

You are sleeping in a bassinet next to me,

and the miracle of you is almost more than I can bear.

How can I look at your tiny eyelashes,

your dimpled starfish hands,

your impossibly perfect rosebud mouth without crying?

I am overwhelmed with joy and gratitude.

You came into this world surrounded by love, and it will follow

you always.

Just like your namesake.

You are my world,

Mom

Part One

One

RONNI

FAIRFIELD SPRINGS NURSING HOME, ANNISTON, ALABAMA

FEBRUARY, 2020

"You're the girl who wrote that book." Mrs. Neely stared at her pale parchment arm, where I was desperately seeking a vein to insert her IV.

"Yes, ma'am, I am. But now I work here. I've been a registered nurse since last year. Not an author."

"You know what you should write a book about?"

I groaned inwardly as I found a home for the needle. This was going to hurt me more than it hurt her.

"No, Mrs. Neely, what should I write about?"

She laughed softly. "My grandma and grandpa each had a big gold tooth in front of their smiles. When PawPaw was a younger man, a mean ole dog bit off his weddin' ring finger. Just bit it clean off. 'Course, he shot that dog. But he couldn't wear his ring after that."

I nodded, wondering how she thought this would make a book. It was the tenth idea I'd heard this month.

"But my MeMaw, she had her weddin' ring melted down and made into a gold tooth, and got the dentist to surprise PawPaw with one for his mouth, too. Romantic, huh? Ever heard of such a thing?"

"I have not, Mrs. Neely." I put a bandage over her IV and stepped back. "That's a first for me." I laughed. "Maybe instead of betrothed, they were betoothed."

She cackled and patted her arm. "You did a good job. Hardly felt this." Her bright blue eyes followed me out of the room.

I stopped at the door and said, "You rest now. We need to hydrate you. You'll feel much, much better in an hour. You were trying to turn into a raisin on us."

"I love you, Honey," she said.

"I love you too, Mrs. Neely."

"You think about writin' that book, okay?"

"Yes, ma'am."

I wheeled my cushy desk chair into place and glanced at my computer, then the framed photo sitting next to it. Rick and I were bathed in red light (my co-workers never tired of asking if we were in an exciting part of Amsterdam), his arms wrapped around my waist, my head resting on his shoulder. He was sporting a camo baseball cap over his freshly-shorn hair. I was mad at the military buzzcut he'd gotten before coming home one Friday to announce I needed to pack a bag for a surprise trip.

Of course, I asked where we were going. Anyone else might have been more forthcoming, but Rick told me only, "Bring some shorts, a nice dress, and one outfit with long sleeves, jeans, and your running shoes." I stared at him, wondering what could possibly require long sleeves in July in the South. "It's only a couple hours away," he said. "An hour and a half if I'm driving."

"I'll pack all that if you'll pick out your favorite hats to bring so you don't look like you've newly arrived at bootcamp." Rick knew I hated the haircut, but I had to make my point.

When we reached the hotel in Chattanooga, Tennessee, a valet swung my door open and took my hand, helping me out of the car.

"How are you, ma'am? Welcome to The Read House." He lifted and lowered his black hat in salute and turned to Rick, who told me to go inside and he'd join me.

I'd never seen a place so beautiful.

I walked around, gawking at the towering chandeliers draped with ropes of crystal and the pearl-studded curtains; the velvet chairs and sofas in the lobby; the bowler-hatted bellmen with their brocade vests. The place had a 1920s vibe that made every woman wish she'd been a flapper—our room featured the graceful back of one in a giant portrait, seated at a piano, her dress scandalously low-cut with pearls draped over her shoulder blades. Even the hallway carpet had ropes of gleaming pearls in its design.

The Read House had to be the only hotel in the world that paired USB ports in its guest rooms and constant front-desk text communications with a big bank of gleaming, meticulously restored antique wood phone booths in the lobby. Elvis and Oprah and Prince had stayed there. I never wanted to leave.

I was lost in a reverie of that weekend when my computer dinged with an email notification on my author account. I ignored it and resumed my daydream, taking advantage of the lightly snoozing residents and my temporary freedom.

We'd eaten dinner in the hotel's elegant restaurant that first evening. Our server fussed over us constantly and brought the most delicious dinner of my life, from mini crab cakes to a fork-tender steak to a beautifully plated dessert of roasted strawberries atop brown butter cake with panna cotta and whipped cream. I sipped champagne and Rick drank a few of their smoked rosemary-maple old fashioneds. He stared into his empty glass and pronounced, "Imma need an Uber to our room." I told him in that hotel, I was pretty sure the staff would carry him on their backs if we asked.

Saturday morning, we walked to the riverfront aquarium, where we drank in the air conditioning at the penguin display. Rick pointed.

"You see her? That's Ronni." The bird in question had a major waddle issue and had just surrendered her fish to a friend lying on a rock. We also located Rick (that one bopped a smaller penguin on the head with his flipper). We decided Deanna was the one nodding her head at the tourists admiring her extra-round body, which could be wearing a black-and-white polyester pantsuit if you squinted. Kanye strutted back and forth in front of the window while Kim just stared at her reflection.

Rick started assigning tall and short penguins *Game of Thrones* identities, nodding at a tiny one in the corner. "I eat fish and I know things," he said.

I took his arm. "Look, the A/C is nice and we're facing a long walk, but you, sir, must be stopped," I told him. We trudged back in the July sun and collapsed on a sofa in the hotel bar. A margarita and another of Rick's fancy old fashioneds gave us the energy to get to our little corner of the seventh floor.

We spent the rest of the day and night in our room's bed, enjoying each other along with the champagne and cupcakes the hotel provided. I blushed a little thinking about it, glancing around to see if anyone was somehow seeing the images in my head, especially the ones involving cupcake icing. Later, we ordered a massive room service dinner—the same aged Wagyu steaks and fried potatoes we'd had the night before with crème brûlée for dessert.

Sunday morning I was instructed to dress in my warm clothes. Rick drove us to Ruby Falls, one of those touristy things I'd seen advertised all my life without paying much attention. We watched a brief intro movie about the guy who'd discovered the falls deep inside Lookout Mountain, his arduous struggle to reach them punctuated by predictable setbacks. He persisted because of his love for his wife—you guessed it—Ruby.

About twenty of us rode an elevator two hundred and sixty feet into the depths of the mountain, then walked a lengthy, chilly path that wound through stalactites and stalagmites and weird rock formations our guide kept pointing out, resembling everything from a turtle to angels' wings. It was dramatically lit and a bit cheesy, but we laughed our way through it.

Rick and I stayed close, my hand grasped in his as we made our way. When our group reached the waterfall's chamber, we stood huddled in near-darkness until the falls were suddenly illuminated by bright red lights. One hundred and forty-five feet they fell, thundering into a pool of frothing water.

It was gorgeous and impressive, far more than I'd expected. We all took turns standing in front of the waterfall for pictures. A sweet lady from California offered to take ours, the one that now decorated my desk.

Our guide, Russell, nattered on about tributaries and the level of magnesium in the pool and a hundred more things I didn't hear because Rick had pulled me away from the other tourists and into a dark corner. He kissed me long and slow. I looked up at him and giggled.

"What was that for?" I asked.

"It was because this is the place you're finally going to agree to marry me." Rick stole a look at the group and placed his hands on either side of my face. "It was because when you smile, my whole world is full of light, in a dark cave or at the breakfast table or sitting next to you on the couch. Because I treasure everything about you. Everything." He blinked and drew a deep breath. "Because if I hadn't met you, Ronni, I'd still be searching for exactly you and only you." Rick produced a ring box and fell to one knee on the damp cave floor. Twenty-one pairs of eyes were now upon us, ranging from Russell the tour guide to a ten-year-old with his family from India to a quartet of grinning Japanese women in their twenties.

Inside the box was an oval ruby surrounded by diamonds, glittering in a tiny built-in spotlight. Rick took the ring out and held it up.

"I am so in love with you, Ronni. Say yes and let me put this on your finger. It's cold and wet on these rocks. Have mercy."

I nodded yes and he kissed me again, in front of a multinational group treated to a little extra excitement on their tour. They all applauded. Russell the guide announced he'd known this was going to happen, and Rick had instructed him to leave me behind in the cave if I said no.

The group all laughed and came over to congratulate us. Most offered hugs, but the wide-eyed little boy from India solemnly shook my hand and said in heavily accented English, "I hope you will be very happy lady woman." His head bobbed as he enunciated each word.

I am, I mused, *very happy lady woman.*

In early 2018, my book royalties and Rick's savings had made it possible for us to buy a house in a leafy, upscale neighborhood. Our home had a luxurious kitchen for Rick to cook in, a lovely glassed-in breakfast nook, two stories of glossy walnut flooring and plush carpeting, a library that contained too many copies of my own book, a cozy living room fireplace, and a master bedroom balcony overlooking the cerulean pool out back. We talked occasionally about getting married, but we owned a house together and, as far as I was concerned, things were perfect.

The other photo on my desk was from that time, a month or two before he proposed at Ruby Falls: a grinning, shirtless Rick stubbornly pushing a lawnmower in a subdivision where every other family had a weekly lawn maintenance crew. He didn't sense their disdain, or he roundly ignored it.

Our wedding was simple. Rick and I were married by the patrol's chaplain at dusk on November 9, 2018, under a flower arch in the backyard of our home. Kaitlin and several of her friends strung lights and matching floral garlands into and between the surrounding oak trees, creating a softly glittering fairyland. We exchanged vows in front of Deanna, Kait and her new husband Mark; Rick's best trooper buddy, Brad, and wife Nita; and Rick's two sons, Josh and Jeremy. They were old enough to be artfully bored and lean on patio furniture, watching the fence gates for their mom to pick them up. I wasn't sorry to see Victoria arrive with their little half-brother and escort them away.

Our "reception" was an extended party during which Rick grilled steaks and everyone consumed a great deal of champagne. Our cake was a triple-tiered red velvet with cream cheese icing, appropriately Southern and accidentally ruby-themed. Well, it was accidental on my part. Rick might have sneaked that past me.

Neither of us could take much time off work. Our honeymoon was three days in a king suite at The Read House, where we emerged only to cross the street to The City Café and eat the best diner food in the world. I worried aloud about all the calories until Rick said the eight most beautiful words he'd ever uttered to me: "You could stand to gain a little weight."

I shook my head at all that had unfolded since. Rick was still with the highway patrol, though he was now officially a sergeant. This translated to more money and all the responsibilities he had before, plus some new administrative duties he hated.

My royalties had dwindled pretty quickly and it became clear I had only one book in me: the one Violet gave me. I'd gone back to school for my RN degree, and was now where I belonged, with my beloved patients. Unfortunately, my new job also included miles of medical red tape and management duties that kept me desk-tethered too much of the time. I was Head Nurse and Kaitlin was my Director of Nursing, occupying Donna's former rose-scented office. These days it smelled like whatever enticing wax melts Kait had discovered; last week was lemon pound cake. Today might be vanilla caramel sundae.

That office was my Happy Place during work hours. After my own, Kait still had the second-most wicked sense of humor at Fairfield, and had welcomed me back there with french-fry-scented wax melts and a brown glass wax-melter in homage to the late Audrey Marie Ledbetter and her potato vine adventures.

My "office" was the nurses' desk, with a dedicated computer for my personal joy. Kait routinely walked by and placed the brown

French-fry thing in front of my keyboard. I scooted it out of the way and read the email I'd ignored earlier. It was addressed to my public author account; I still had a website, even though only two (surely lost) people visited each month and Google was determined to bury me.

"Dear Mrs. O'Shea," it began. "My dad was the man you called Chet in your book. You called me Eric. It was real sweet of you to change all the names, but everybody knew who my family was. My mama died three months ago, and I promised her I'd never contact you, but she won't mind now. See, you made her life a living hell. She wouldn't leave her house after your book. Wouldn't even go to church. You made Dad out to be a killer, and told the world he was in love with another woman.

"And you were ALL wrong. That 'Violet' woman probably even knew what happened between my dad and the doctor you called 'Tolly,' and he was a damn hero to do what he did. I can tell you that. And he messed up some things as a kid, but not nearly all you think. That whole pitiful-Violet-at-the-train-station station thing wasn't his doing, either.

"I am asking you to meet with me. You should write about this for your next book. Tell the world you were wrong about 'Chet,' even if it's too late for my mama. Please email me back ASAP.

"Sincerely,

"Gary Harris (my real name)."

I read the email three times, and it took a while for me to close my gaping mouth. *Gary Harris, Son of Chet, I told the real story, whether it pleased you or not. You know what you should write a book about, Gary? Personal boundaries. But what if…*

I called my husband, who was somewhere beside an interstate, probably eating the lunch I'd missed earlier.

"You won't believe this, Rick. A guy claiming to be Chet's son just emailed me. Wants me to clear his daddy's name in a new book. He says Chet did nothing wrong, not even that whole train station thing with Violet. I don't know what to do. I guess I should at least email him back."

I heard him rustling in a paper bag, no doubt removing a barbecue sandwich from his favorite old drive-thru joint in Heflin. My stomach tumbled a little.

"Well, do you want to write another book?" he spoke in Garble-que.

"Of course not. You know that. Especially not with all we have going on."

"Don't answer him, Ronni. Delete that email right now."

"Aren't you the least bit curious about what he has to say?" I answered.

"No." I could feel his frown through the phone. "He's just a crank. A nut. How is our little walnut, by the way?"

"He or she is the size of a grape, Rick. Not a walnut. The baby is fine."

"Why is it always food sizes? Why not the approximate length of a AAA battery?" He munched thoughtfully in the background.

"Because that's weird, Rick. I'm taking good care of the grape. You keep yourself safe and come home to me tonight. And don't forget we're meeting Sam's son Max at Deanna's. Her new but ancient brother. She's planning to introduce him to turkey and dressing."

"I just got the weirdest bulletin about this virus in China," Rick segued. "Have you seen anything from the nursing home people?"

"No, I haven't. It's not a problem here and it won't be. I love you, Rick."

"I love you more, Ronni. See you about six."

TWO

ANNISTON, ALABAMA

1946

S am stood in the soft red glow, watching as three girls materialized
before him. Katie Ruth's dark dress appeared first, then Frances
with her auburn hair.

The girl in the middle—ah, she was all light. If Katie Ruth and
Frances were candles, Violet was a hundred-watt bulb. Three pretty
girls in full profile on a bench after school, the one in the middle with
her body leaning two feet behind the others, hands holding their
shoulders, head thrown back, her blonde hair liquid gold spilling to the
ground, looking at the camera like a publicity-still-starlet, laughing at
something Sam had said to amuse her. He couldn't remember what it
was. He was always too stunned by Violet's presence to remember
much of anything he'd managed to utter.

It was a perfect yearbook photo, but Sam wouldn't submit it. This
was a gift for his best friend, Johnny. Johnny Perkins walked the halls

of Anniston High School with the combined swagger of basketball captain and almost-certain valedictorian, a shiny DeSoto to drive occasionally, and the delicate ivory hand of Violet Glenn in his.

Sam had this, his passion for photography indulged by his parents into a ridiculously expensive twin-lens Rolleiflex camera and a custom darkroom in his enlarged former closet. He had a job working for his dad's department stores and a bright future assured whether he accompanied Johnny to college in Tuscaloosa or not. He had a spot on the basketball team and did okay, mostly because Johnny looked out for him.

And he had a girlfriend, Deborah. They'd been together almost as long as Violet and Johnny's two months. Sam reminded himself of that as he carefully hung the photo to dry, his eyes fixed on the girl in the middle leaning back as if she could never fall without someone to catch her.

Sam didn't hear the doorbell from his darkroom upstairs. He didn't see his dad accept a package wrapped in brown paper from the postman, nor did he watch Philip Davidson set it on the kitchen table and stare at it for a moment, checking his wristwatch.

Esther wouldn't be home for an hour.

Philip Davidson gently took his wife's family heirloom bronze Shabbat lamp from its display shelf. He also grabbed a bottle of bourbon and a cocktail glass, carrying these three things to the patio table in the backyard.

He returned to the kitchen for the parcel and delivered it to sit beside the bourbon, letting it witness the pouring of a generous slug into his glass. Philip settled into an uncomfortable metal chair and regarded the brown paper before him.

Esther would kill him for bringing her precious lamp out here. He glanced at the kitchen window and his son's upstairs, too. Sam was no doubt in his darkroom, his sanctuary from all things parental. It had originally been Philip's sanctuary during a brief fascination with photography, but it was Sam's these days with good reason.

After a few minutes and several sips, he peeled the package open slowly. He set the paper aside. It would serve as good kindling.

Philip put his prize upon the wrought-iron table and thought long and hard about what he was about to do. His bourbon glass was empty. He refilled it and took one sip, then carried everything to his new backyard grill. He placed the paper beneath the contents of the package and poured the paraffin oil from the lamp his wife used every Friday evening, dousing every burnable inch before him.

He struck a match from his favorite restaurant and tossed it onto the grill, backing away as he felt the heat reach his face.

Philip returned to the table and watched the tiny inferno he'd created. The flames shot satisfyingly high. Sipping his drink, he listened for any sound of a witness and heard none.

It was the first time he'd smiled in months.

Sam took the stairs two at a time, off to basketball practice. "Dad, I'm going!" he yelled. "Johnny's picking me up! I'll be back for supper."

Nothing. His father was probably in the bathroom.

Sam preferred to hurry up and leave before his mom got home. She hated his "skimpy" uniform and would have preferred he play with a trench coat over it.

She really was hopelessly old-fashioned.

Johnny pulled up to the curb with a grin, granted the rare opportunity to drive his dad's DeSoto to practice. They were usually stuck in Jimmy Lee Clark's rusted pickup truck for these trips, but Johnny's latest report card had earned them the shiny car.

Violet's trademark orange blossom cologne greeted Sam as he opened the passenger door. Johnny had driven her somewhere today.

"Here," Johnny said, handing Sam a folded white cloth napkin. "She made tea cakes this morning."

Mrs. Perkins' tea cakes were Sam's favorite thing in the world. He immediately felt bad for failing to grab the photo of Violet he'd meant to give Johnny.

"Amscray before my mom gets home, Johnny. A tea cake before supper is highly illegal in Estherville. And she thinks my uniform looks cheesy. I'm not in the mood to talk about it again." He turned around to scan the street for Esther's car.

"She just doesn't want you running around looking like a dreamboat, Red." Johnny laughed. "You're irresistible in shorts." He shifted into drive and punched his friend's bicep.

"You know I hate that nickname," Sam answered.

"Then lose that hair, buddy. Would you rather I call you Ginger? Actually, I kinda prefer that." Johnny took off a lot faster than the stately DeSoto was intended to, laughing at his own joke. "Oh, and by the way, Ginger, we're making a quick stop."

"What? To pick up Jimmy Lee?" Sam said. He noticed Johnny's turn signal indicating otherwise and figured things out pretty quickly.

"I'll only be a second," Johnny told him as they parked in front of a small house, its paint peeling in the Alabama sun. Standing alone on the front porch was Violet Glenn, who threw her arms around Johnny and kissed him longer than Sam thought necessary. She then gave Sam a tiny wave and floated gracefully through the screen door, leaving her smile stamped on his stubborn heart.

"This is not Violet's house," Sam informed Johnny, feeling stupid for saying it but unable to conjure anything better.

"No, it's some little kid she babysits. His name is Chet. I think he wants my girl." Johnny laughed as he turned the ignition key.

"Wh-why would you say that?" Sam asked.

"Well, Violet told me he has a crush on her. But that's where he's been since we drove up." He waved his hand low, indicating a not-so-little kid at the front window, staring out. "I know she told him she needed one minute of privacy on the porch, and look what he does." Johnny nodded toward the house. "But who wouldn't want her, right, Ginger?"

"Johnny, don't call—"

"As you wish, Red. As you wish."

Three

Ronni

February, 2020

Sam's eldest son, Max, began our dinner conversation with, "We just celebrated my seventieth birthday at Eleven Madison Park before I flew down here. And Deanna, everything you cooked tastes just as delicious as their food." Even I knew the restaurant's three-hundred-dollar-a-plate dinners did not likely include cornbread dressing. Max was a charmer.

He passed a platter of sliced turkey to me with a crinkly-eyed grin, and it was one of those old-man smiles that dazzled girls and women at any age. This polished New Yorker obviously got his dark hair and eyes from his mother, Deborah, and knew how to use them. Max looked like an older Patrick Dempsey, only taller. He did *not* look like my daydream version of Deanna's long-lost half-brother. This guy was something else, right down to his Italian suit and the three large diamonds in his wedding band. Of course I stared.

Rick didn't actually kick me under the table, but his eyes did.

Deanna should be my focus. I needed to remember that. She was a bit overwhelmed, trying to impress this supernatural being and find out more about him at the same time.

"Tell us about your dad, Max. I only knew him a little bit at Fairfield Springs. I'm sure Deanna would enjoy anything you could share." I nodded at Deanna, who was moving food around her plate and swigging wine with increasing urgency.

"My father—our father—was a businessman first and foremost. It was clear his parents raised him to understand retail and how to grow Philippe into a small empire of stores. We're up to seven in the state now. 'Philippe' is a tribute to my grandfather, of course. Dad thought it sounded chic-er in French."

I looked at Max in a way I hoped would convey *more personal*.

He continued, "Dad wasn't particularly religious. Didn't observe all the traditions like Mom wanted to. His favorite color was dark green, which was practically his entire wardrobe. Preferred a good cheeseburger over any steak. He loved his family. With three boys, I'm sure he would have been beyond thrilled to know his lovely daughter."

Deanna blushed at the compliment.

"He enjoyed Yankees games, but preferred the Knicks. Dad was really more into basketball. You know he played in high school, right?"

We nodded.

"That was our special time, just us boys. Dad took us to every Knicks game he could. My best memories revolve around that. But if I'm being honest, work was always his thing. Dad spent really long days at the office and traveled all the time. My mom hated it. She didn't really like life in the city, and they planned to move back to Alabama. After she died, Dad just burrowed deeper into work until he couldn't anymore. That's when we all decided Fairfield Springs would be best for him. He could be in Alabama, hear the soft accents he loved, and see some of his...umm...old friends. Like your mother, Violet."

The incredible awkwardness of my book was following me everywhere these days. Deanna smiled and nodded, reaching for the chardonnay and offering more to Max. All of us but Max knew I'd be halfway through my second glass if it weren't for the grape-sized baby in me. I smiled at Rick, who was quietly nursing an iced tea in solidarity.

"I am so sorry he never got to meet you," Max told Deanna. "I think it would have softened Dad a bit to have a daughter. And everything I've heard about your mother sounds…well, I can see how he loved her when he was a teenager. I'm so sorry things worked out the way they did for you. Of course, I wouldn't be here otherwise, would I?"

Okay, that dropped Max's charm points by at least a hundred. You could practically hear his remark clunk on the table. And surely The Grape wouldn't mind a tiny bit of chardonnay? Its mother needed it. Not for the first time, I thought: *See, Violet? See what your book has done?*

"I believe everything happens for a reason," Deanna offered, like the graceful sage she was. "My life turned out just fine. Ronni and Rick are family to me, and that's one of the greatest gifts I've received. Here I am living in Alabama, of all places, and my daughter and her children are nearby and thriving. My Sarah has a job she loves in Anniston, a paralegal at one of the best law firms. My granddaughter is now working on her master's degree at Auburn, and my grandson may even play football at Alabama, can you imagine? I love my life, Max. I had parents who were kind and loving to me, and they were always present." She smiled slightly and took a sip of wine, continuing, "I'm glad we got to meet. As we say in The South, I'm proud to know you." She stood to remove Max's plate and headed for the kitchen, promising to return with homemade pecan pie.

Rick, Max and I sat in polite silence, ignoring all the elephants herded into the dining room. But to my great surprise, Max saddled up one of the elephants as Deanna gave us each a slice of pecan pie with vanilla ice cream.

"This is so good, Deanna. I've not tasted pecan pie. Delightful." He set his fork down carefully and leaned forward, hands clasped. "There's something I need to say to you, long overdue. What my grandparents did to your mom was wrong. So very wrong. I can only hope you understand times were extremely different then, right after the war. There were many scars not even beginning to heal. All of that is no excuse, but you need to hear this about our father: he would never have left Violet if he'd known she was carrying his baby. I know that with complete certainty, and you should, too. I'm so sorry."

Deanna blinked and sat silent. I could tell she was at a loss for words.

After what was surely three minutes, possibly an hour, I was opening my mouth to say something, anything, when Deanna slid her chair back slowly and stood. She reached for Max's hand and pulled him to his feet. Then she wrapped her arms around him and held him for a moment.

"Thank you," was all she said. She sat back down and resumed her dessert like none of us were on the verge of tears and a single elephant hadn't been demolished before our eyes.

The rest of our dinner conversation was lighter: Broadway shows; weather; movies; Alabama football; fashion trends; working in a nursing home; being a Highway Patrol Sergeant; the cruise ship carrying people with this new virus; the heated debate over whether to allow those passengers to quarantine at a FEMA center a few miles down the road in Anniston. Rick and I did our best to remain the supporting cast behind Max and Deanna's leads. He was far better at silence than I was, though. Quiet rooms were an empty balloon to me.

Max smiled his lady-melting grin. "I really do have to get going back to the city. Thank you for inviting me to this wonderful dinner. I think I may love Southern food too much." He patted his non-existent belly. "I have one more thing to tell you; I'm not sure anything will come of it, but maybe. Our youngest, Samuel, doesn't like city life. Elise thinks he's an old soul; he's never quite fit in with his school friends or co-workers in Manhattan. It all seems to overwhelm him; it's too busy, too noisy, too much of all the things I think make New York the best place in the world. In fact, he loved that quaint old Victorian hotel we stayed in when we came down to visit Dad, the one in Anniston. He has this fascination with returning to the place his grandparents grew up, exploring the little town and area around it."

He paused when we all raised our eyebrows at "little town."

"Anyway," he continued, "as you know, Dad closed the stores here years ago, but we're thinking of buying the former location on Quintard and renovating it into a Philippe for Samuel to run. He seems to think he can live out in the country with a cow or something and commute to work. Could I bring him by to meet his aunt when we look around next month? We're meeting a real estate agent March 3. That's a Tuesday."

Deanna's smile was genuine, maybe even sisterly; definitely not just from wine. "I'd love that," she said. "How exciting!"

When she lit up that way, Violet was everywhere in her face. How I still missed her, and how proud she'd be of her daughter.

As Rick drove us home, he said, "Well, *that* was a lot of family bonding in one night. They've known about Deanna for years, Ronni, and Max and Elise have offered nothing beyond a distant, polite phone call here and there. I mean, Mel's come to see her, but he already knew Deanna. What made Max decide to descend from his glorious New York City perch to meet his half-sister? All because they might send their son down here? The kid's gotta be thirty or more. It's not like they need Deanna to watch a child."

"I don't really know," I said, watching the trees pass by. "But it makes sense he'd want a relative nearby, Rick, even if he doesn't know Deanna that well. Maybe this is how they'll all become closer, through this Samuel." I paused to consider. "She needed that apology, probably more than anything she's ever needed."

"Yeah, that was a good thing he did," Rick agreed. "So," he said, "what's this going to look like from now on, Deanna's relationship with the Davidsons? Are they going to give her a percentage of their business?"

I stared at him in the dashboard's blue glow. "That's a weird thought. I can't imagine Deanna accepting some kind of financial compensation, like it's going to make up for all these years."

"It's rightfully hers." Rick shrugged. "But I wouldn't expect that. I think it would probably be more like Max and his family visiting their son a lot if he moves here, but seeing Deanna only at Thanksgiving or Hanukkah or Christmas or whatever they celebrate. Drop off a nice gift, feel they've done their duty, fly off to The Maldives." He shrugged again. "But Ronni," he glanced at me, "why would they suddenly decide to send their son to Alabama? What if he's been in trouble? We know nothing about this guy."

I shook my head. "Stop being a cop all the time. You don't have any reason to be suspicious, Rick, honestly." I rolled my eyes at him. "Besides, lately there's been this strange convergence of people affected by my book appearing out of nowhere. I don't know what to expect next. 2020 has just started and it's already bizarre. Maybe it isn't going to be such a good year."

Rick reached over to pat my stomach. "Don't even say that. We have The Grape. This is going to be the most amazing year of our lives. Do you have any idea how long I've wanted a daughter? A daughter who looks just like you?"

I put my hand on top of his and closed my eyes with a sigh. "He may be a son who looks just like you."

"Ronni," he said, "that's a pink grape. I know that with all my heart."

FOUR

OXFORD, ALABAMA

1946

Deborah Leon turned to her best friend in the world, Sue, and held up a deep burgundy dress, its hanger folded down at her shoulders. She pirouetted while regarding herself in her bedroom's full-length dressing mirror, watching the soft folds of the skirt swing in time with her long black ponytail.

"Don't you think it's perfect for dancing?"

Sue turned the page of a magazine and sat up straighter on Deborah's pink canopy bed. "Since when do your parents let you go dancing?"

"They never have and probably never will," Deborah tilted her head at the mirror and wriggled out of her scratchy plaid skirt and white blouse, then tugged on the dress and zipped it. The color was perfect with her dark eyes, and she nodded at herself, smiling. "But they do let me go to movies with Sam, which is supposedly what we're doing tonight. I have to be dressed for that."

"Since when does Sam Davidson go dancing?" Sue laughed. "He's a dead hoofer if I've ever seen one."

"You barely know him, Sue." This was true. Sam didn't attend their high school in Oxford, and Sue had only accompanied Deborah to one Anniston basketball game to watch Sam run up and down the court. "But don't judge him by his athletic skills. Besides, he doesn't know he's going dancing." She giggled.

Sue placed *Vogue* on the bedspread and stood behind Deborah. "Hmm," she said, "dark red's good on you, but you'll clash with his hair. How are you tricking him into dancing? This should be good." Sue rolled her eyes in the mirror.

"We're going to Oxford Lake. He thinks we're gonna ride the carousel and play the carnival games. But I'm renting a boat for him to row me around in, and later he's going to discover we're near the dance floor when the music starts." She sighed. "It'll be so romantic."

"I thought Sam's parents wouldn't let him go to the lake at night," Sue said. "You told me they thought it wasn't safe, with all the soldiers and the fights that happened last year. Not to mention the alcohol." Sue's eyebrows shot up. "Those guys from Fort McClellan sneak that stuff in all the time. Everybody knows that."

"True." Deborah smiled. "But since the war ended, there aren't as many soldiers going to the lake and Sam convinced his folks it's perfectly safe at night. And it is."

"But not your parents." Sue smirked. "Your daddy would flip his wig."

Deborah peeled the dress off carefully and replaced it on the hanger. "I'm sixteen years old, Sue. I'd have been married with two kids fifty years ago, maybe driving a covered wagon across the West. They want me to be forever ten, pudgy in my sequined uniform at Zenobia King Hill's annual tap dance recital. Like I'm Shirley Temple or something. I'm not a child."

"Uh-huh." Sue nodded. "And what time is Sam picking you up for this adult adventure, Miss Ava Gardner?"

"Ooh, do you really think so?" Deborah's eyes lit up the mirror.

"No," Sue shook her head. "You're somewhere between Shirley and Ava in sex appeal, though."

Deborah swatted at her friend's arm. "He's coming at six, so we can not eat at Vic's before we *don't* see the movie at The Ritz. It's Ava Gardner, by the way, in *Whistle Stop*. That's a movie my parents would never go to, so it's a perfect plan."

"It certainly is." Sue nodded. "What could possibly go wrong?" She laughed as she left Deborah's bedroom with a wave. "Call me tomorrow, unless you're grounded for the rest of your life. Then we'll know if you're Shirley or Ava."

Sam knocked on the Leons' door at precisely six o'clock and Deborah rushed to greet him. Her mother's arm shot out like a steel guardrail, blocking Deborah and eliciting a groan from her daughter.

"A young lady never answers the door for a date. Your father will get it." Mrs. Leon nodded, appraising Deborah in the hall light. "You look very nice, honey."

"Thanks, Mom." Deborah forced herself to swallow a tiny, fiery speech about her parents' ridiculous rules as she listened to hear Sam admitted to the house. She did not want him alone with her dad. Sam couldn't lie without his face looking like an overripe beet. He'd been like that since he was a five-year-old in their shared Hebrew school class on Sundays and Tuesdays, her two favorite days of the week because of him and his shy smile.

When her dad finally called for her and she was allowed to make her grand entrance, she watched Sam drink her in, head to toe. As he closed her car door, Deborah tugged the neckline open to reveal the cleavage she'd smuggled under her parents' inspection.

"You look...wow," Sam said, sliding behind the steering wheel. "You are beautiful, Deborah Leon." He reached over and took her hand, holding it to his chest for a few seconds. Then he offered her a fairly chaste kiss, in case any parents were peeking out at the driveway. "Are you sure you're dressed to ride a carousel and watch me win you a stuffed animal with a baseball?" He laughed. "Or for you to win me a stuffed animal with a baseball, more likely?"

Deborah grinned. "How long since you've been to Oxford Lake, Sam?"

"Long time. Since I was a wee little Sam," he answered.

"Well, I plan on showing you a few other things we can do there," she said. Deborah attempted to raise her left eyebrow in a sultry Ava Gardner fashion, but the right one followed it up, dang it.

Sam answered, "Are you real sure you don't want to go sit in the back row at the Ritz and not watch a movie?" His eyes swept over her one more time before he backed his dad's Plymouth out of the driveway.

Deborah responded by pointing in the direction of Oxford Lake, not Anniston's downtown theaters. "Trust me."

"Oh, I do," Sam said, "but I might just make this car run out of gas tonight, the way you're wearing that dress."

The late-day sun scattered glitter across the lake. Sam took Deborah's hand and started toward the carnival booths in the distance, but she tugged him toward the giant boathouse instead.

"I'm renting a boat for you to row me around the lake in," she told Sam.

"You do know I don't like water much, right?" Sam stopped and nodded at the boats making their way to the island in the lake's center. "And these are new pants." He held the fabric out at the sides.

"There are plenty more pants where those came from, in your dad's store." Deborah dragged him to the attendant and paid for their two hours. Sam carefully climbed into the small, treacherous, rocking boat first and reached to help her board, as instructed. He tried to grab the oars in a manly way, managing to propel them thirty feet out into the lake in a fairly straight line. He found his rhythm; the oars sliced the water more easily than he'd expected. Sam breathed a sigh of relief.

Deborah turned her head to look across the water and he'd never missed his camera so much. She was a renaissance portrait, a study in light and shadow, and he longed to capture the moment on film. A strand of dark hair blew across her face and she brushed it away, smiling at Sam.

This boat thing wasn't so bad.

Deborah held her hand across her eyebrows and yelled over the noise of the wind. "Take me out to the island!"

He managed, somehow, to turn the damn boat. He was determined to look like he knew what he was doing. What if she wanted to walk onto the island? Was he supposed to tie the boat to something? He spotted a small dock where he guessed they were meant to pull up.

Oh, how much he'd rather be in a nice restaurant right now. In fact, he was starving.

"What are we doing about dinner?" he yelled.

Deborah fished a Baby Ruth from her handbag and waved it at him. "This will be your picnic snack on the island. There's food back around the lake."

Sam thought longingly of the rare, juicy porterhouse steak at Vic's, steaming buttered baked potatoes, some green beans, maybe. How had he let himself be talked into this? If he was lucky, there might be a decent hamburger stand at the lake, but that was doubtful. He pulled the boat up and Deborah threw a line to the waiting attendant, absurdly dressed as a sailor and obviously bored out of his mind. Sam watched her take the fake-sailor's hand and climb gracefully onto the dock. The way he looked at Deborah made Sam a little angry, plus he was clearly ignoring the boat's other passenger. He never bothered to glance at Sam, much less reach a hand.

Sam shot to his feet, irritated by the attendant's inattention, lost his balance, and plunged overboard into five feet of water. Soaked, head to toe, he stood and dripped for several seconds in humiliation. He refused to look at Popeye the Idiot and stared at Deborah, sputtering. His legs dragged through the water until he reached a shallow section.

All he said was, "Let's go sit down, Deborah," as if every ounce of his male pride hadn't flowed into Oxford Lake, dissolving forever.

They found a deserted strand of fake beach and Sam told Deborah to turn her back while he peeled off his clothes in the woods and wrung them out. That took several minutes through which she, admirably, still managed to hold in her laughter. He lowered himself to the sand beside her, realizing too late his pants were being crumb-coated like his mom's fried chicken, but beyond caring.

"I'm sorry, Sam," Deborah offered. "This is not what I planned at all." She gave him the candy bar, her face fighting between concern and stifled giggles. It startled him sometimes, how his five-year-old friend with freckles and a gap-toothed smile, the girl who handed him her precious lost baby tooth rather than cash in with the Tooth Fairy, had morphed into the woman beside him. "And I'm sure Gene didn't mean for you to fall in. He's probably more embarrassed than you."

"Oh, damn, I mean, dang, you know that guy?" Sam shook his head and slung little water droplets at Deborah's face. He liked seeing them land. "Why didn't you say? Why didn't you tell me? My experience could have been so much more complete, Deborah."

"You don't have to be sarcastic. I didn't really get a chance to introduce y'all." Deborah batted her lashes at Sam, swiping at her cheek. "And I don't know him much. He graduated Oxford my freshman year, that's all. I'm pretty sure he's embarrassed to be wearing a cheap sailor costume for a living. Last I heard, he wanted to go fight in Europe, but he finished boot camp just in time for the war to be over, and now he's back in town. I wasn't going to call attention to it."

"Well, that changes things a little, I guess," he said. "I hate boats. I hate water. Not crazy about your pretend anchor-clanker friend Gene back there." He waved a hand in the general direction of the dock. "But I'm glad we're together. I always have fun with you, Deborah."

If Sam had been looking, he'd have seen the shadow flit across her expression, just for half a second.

"I always have fun with you, too." Deborah patted his damp knee. "Can I laugh now?"

"No, and I will swim back to shore before I let that guy load us back into the boat."

Deborah drew a little design into the pretend-beach with her finger. "There were other things I wanted to do, when we sighted land again." With every second, she was having a harder time keeping a straight face. "But your clothes are ruined. I can't ask you to spend the rest of the evening like this. You'll…chafe or something." Now she allowed herself a giggle.

"Tell you what. I have the clothes I wore to basketball practice a few days ago in the trunk. Strictly against Esther's Laundry Rules, but I forgot them. So I'll change and we can stay. But, Deborah, I am not looking at your friend when we get back into the boat. You have to board first and reach for my lady-hand."

Now she let herself go, belly-laughing like he was Milton Berle. Sam grinned and decided he might as well join her, shaking his head and biting into the Baby Ruth.

"But I'm still going to be the man at the booth where you throw baseballs, and I'll win you the biggest teddy bear you want."

"Thanks, Sam," she sighed and leaned against him. Just loud enough to carry on the wind, she added a whispered, "When will you understand you're all I want?"

While Sam was five miles away in Oxford, hiding wet clothes in the trunk of his dad's car, Philip was alone in their Anniston home, removing Esther's lamp once again and heading to the backyard patio.

This was his third package, and he'd worked out a routine. He opened it with just as much care as the first two, according it the ceremony warranted. The contents did not disappoint. Philip smiled at them in anticipation.

This one, he told himself, was worth every last penny of the three hundred dollars he'd spent. Anyone else would think he'd lost his mind; it was enough for a decent used car. And he doubted he could explain it, but Philip found great meaning in what he was doing.

He walked over to the grill and set everything up just so. He'd discovered it took far less oil than he'd thought to make a fire, so he drizzled lightly with Esther's lamp, then took the time to refill it and place it back on its shelf.

Philip returned for one last look. He tossed a match and stood a few feet away, watching with his bourbon, relishing the flames. He was proud of the addition of the empty paint can next to him, awaiting the ashes.

No one would ever know.

Sam held Deborah's hand, dragging her toward a cheeseburger sign. He'd decided his wrinkled and only vaguely smelly school clothes were okay, since darkness had fallen over the lake and everything looked better in the soft light. They passed soldiers from Fort McClellan, most of them in groups, laughing.

He saw the way they looked at Deborah, appreciating her in a respectful way, though their glances lingered a bit too long to suit him. He ate two cheeseburgers with everything but onions—this was a date, after all—while Deborah devoured most of his fries.

"Now it's my turn to drag you, Sam Davidson," she told him, pulling him to his feet.

"Okay, skating rink? Bowling? Teddy bear for milady?" Sam asked.

"None of the above," Deborah smoothed her dress with her free hand. "They're just starting. Come with me."

Sam planted his feet, alerted by the opening notes of "Choo Choo Ch'Boogie" in the distance. "Oh no," he shook his head. "No. I'll go out in a stupid boat, I'll fall in the water to amuse you, I'll spend my hard-earned dollars to win you a stuffed animal, but I will not dance. No, Deborah—"

She stepped in front of him and placed her hands on the sides of his face, looking into his eyes. "This is the reason we're here, Sam. The least you can do is walk onto that dance floor with me. I come to all your stupid basketball games. You owe me this." She tapped his face lightly for emphasis. "Besides, this is race music! Our parents would be appalled. We have to dance to it." A stream of soldiers hurried around them toward the blaring jukebox.

"I don't know how to dance," he said miserably. "I don't want to. Please."

Deborah reached for both his hands and tugged as she stepped backward. "Don't worry. I'll lead."

By the time they got there, the dance floor was filled with more elbows and wildly swinging arms than any basketball game he'd played. Sam stepped his feet from side to side, staring at his girlfriend with a blank expression as she held his hands, moving in some sort of unassisted jitterbug. Deborah twirled, her coal-black eyes diamonds under the string of soft lights. He couldn't tell if that was joy on her face or more laughter at his expense.

He looked at all the couples around them. Most clearly knew what they were doing, jive-bombing along to the beat. Sam continued his stubborn shuffle. The song went on forever, all bass and horns and drums mixed in with words he didn't understand. Deborah danced on, happy as he'd ever seen her, refusing to acknowledge his awkward non-dancing.

When it finally ended, when the last horn tooted, Sam exhaled a breath he didn't know he'd been holding. He turned to leave the cramped dance floor, only to be grabbed again by Deborah as Eddy Howard began to sing "To Each His Own."

At least this was a slow song. Deborah wrapped her arms around his neck and he pulled her close to him, doing the box-step he'd learned for his bar mitzvah, his only move.

Deborah pressed closer to him, melted into him. Sam moved with her in a daze, dancing, it seemed, without even trying. When the song ended, he kept his arms around her, waiting to see what was next. The tinkly notes of Sinatra's "Five Minutes More" rang out.

Deborah leaned back and mouthed the words: five minutes more. Sam nodded and pulled her back to him.

When the music ended, Sam stood in place and threaded Deborah's hair through his fingers, gently tipping her head back. He kissed her softly, tentatively, barely brushing her lips. Then he deepened the kiss, not caring if everyone in the county was watching.

He pulled back and smiled at her, mouthing the words: five minutes more?

Deborah nodded, meaning yes with all her heart.

Five

RONNI

MARCH, 2020

I used to tell people, "I'm not even allowed in the same room as a carbohydrate."

I'd been in the habit of avoiding them forever, the only way I could continue to wear my favorite clothes. When Rick and I moved into our new house, I added a daily walk around our neighborhood, usually a mile or so at a fast pace. It was walker-friendly, and I was only passed by very slow-moving cars or golf carts full of parents and their kids.

These days I was eating a lot of previously forbidden fruit, tons of vegetables, extremely occasional hot fudge sundaes, and every single thing in the world made of cauliflower, including pizza crust. I was anxiously awaiting cauliflower crème brûlée, and by anxiously, I mean with terror. Cauliflower was taking over the world, in every form except the original. Did anyone actually eat cauliflower before 2020?

Even without potatoes and pasta and bread and all the things that made life worthwhile in the food world, I was determined to walk longer and faster each day, both for this baby's health and my fervent wish not to swell up like a newly-retired NFL linebacker with a restaurant chain. As I began walking today, I spotted the golf cart of Jinxie Tyler in the distance, easily identified by a jaunty Lilly Pulitzer flag at the end of its canopy. Jinxie drove up to me the first week we lived there, introducing herself and the three suntanned children in her cart I'd assumed to be hers. Turned out they were her grandchildren, and Jinxie was probably around sixty. She didn't look a day over thirty-eight. Definitely one of those women whose phone contacts included her Botox scheduler, chemical face peeler, expert hair colorist, and a personal trainer. I pictured him as a tall, sleek, dark-haired European with a ponytail, just handsy enough to gently guide Jinxie's skinny hips into place on a yoga mat with a whispered, encouraging, exotic accent of some kind.

Jinxie purportedly came from old money and was married to the president of a local bank. She was stylish and intimidating and endlessly cheerful. Why wouldn't she be? She drew closer and I slid my hands under my t-shirt and pushed it out in front, trying to stretch it enough to conceal my still-secret baby bump. I did not need Jinxie Tyler regaling me with terrifyingly accurate stories of her pregnancy discomforts and excruciating labors. I'm a nurse. I already know too much.

I spotted a man sitting up front with her, a young guy with a curly mop of hair who was definitely not her husband. Maybe this was the personal trainer? Nah, that was silly. They'd be running, not golf-carting around. A mental image of Jinxie and...Luca, I'd name him Luca...running around the neighborhood like bright-floral-clad gazelles, dazzling all the neighbors with their extra-white smiles, nary a drop of sweat on their fit brows, occupied me until Jinxie drove up beside me and stopped with a wave.

"Ronni! You look beautiful today," she greeted me.

"Thank you, Jinxie, so do you." And she did, of course.

"I want to introduce you to my son-in-law, Huel Love. He's married to our Muffy."

Muffy Love. I was going to die. Right here and now.

Jinxie patted the guy on the shoulder. He was even younger than I'd thought, maybe thirty-five, and had a huge grin under the mop of hair.

"Huel, this is Ronni O'Shea."

"It's so nice to meet you," I said, shaking Huel's hand.

"Likewise." He nodded, still grinning.

Jinxie continued, "Huel is an attorney, but he's really a musician who loves being on stage more than in a courtroom. He plays guitar and sings. Tell her, Huel." She jabbed him with her elbow.

"I'm in a little band and we play dates here and there. Just forget the attorney part. She's not supposed to tell people that." Huel was still grinning.

"So, you're not an attorney?" I asked.

"I am, but I don't want anyone to know. Especially not right off the bat." Now he was laughing and Jinxie mock-slapped his arm.

"You have one of the coolest names I've heard, Huel Love," I responded. "I mean, seriously."

"Well, thank you, ma'am. It's an old family name."

"Ronni, you should use his name in your next book!" Jinxie enthused. "Ronni is a writer, Huel. Ronni, you know what you should write about? You should write about Ruth Elder, who was a famous aviatrix back in the days of Amelia Earhart. I think she earned money for her flying lessons by winning beauty pageants. She was lovely, I've seen photos of her. Ruth attempted an Atlantic crossing, but she and her co-pilot crashed. They were okay, though. And then she went on to be a Hollywood starlet and got married a bunch of times. And Ronni, she was from Anniston! Did you know about her?"

"No, Jinxie, I've never heard of her, but that is extremely interesting." I nodded at Huel, whose smile was fading, likely from boredom. "Happy to meet you," I said. "I'll keep all that in mind, Jinxie, thank you. I'd better get back to walking."

"You could make Huel Love a character in the book! Nobody would care if there actually was one, I bet, and you said yourself, it's a great name. Huel could be a guy she meets in Hollywood. He could be a producer!" I watched his smile fade a tiny bit more. "Ruth's whole life was such a dramatic story; everyone would want to read it. You really should write about her, Ronni." Jinxie was on an unstoppable roll. "In fact, I don't think anyone has written much about Ruth Elder. I have a cousin whose husband's family lived near the Elders years and years ago in Anniston, I think. Do you want me to give you her number?"

"No, thank you, Jinxie, but I'm not planning on writing another book. I'm working as a nurse at Fairfield Springs."

She looked crushed for a millisecond, but recovered into her usual sunny expression. "Well, I think you'll write another book, I really do. You could even write it on weekends, if you're not working." Jinxie nodded, pleased with herself for solving my writing problems.

I knew what came next.

"Why, you wrote that first book while you were still working at Fairfield, didn't you? I just realized that. So surely, you could do it again. Oh, write another one, Ronni. I just loved your first book!"

"I'm so glad you did, Jinxie, that means the world to me," I said, and I meant it. "I'll think about Ruth Elder's possibilities for a novel," I added, and I did not mean it. It simply didn't work that way for me. People suggested ideas to me everywhere I went, and my brain refused to be inspired. Either a book would come to me on its own, or it wouldn't be written. There wouldn't be another book like Violet's.

"That's the spirit!" She beamed at me. "Now, I hate to rush off, but I'm taking Huel to look at a problem with the gazebo. I think the people who built it are going to have to be legally forced to come back out here and fix it."

Yep, that was the end of his grin.

I waved goodbye to them and took thirty good steps before I was far enough away to burst into laughter. I should write a very steamy book about Muffy Love; under a pseudonym, of course.

I had the news on in the background as I made a salad that evening. Someone in Washington State, literally across the country, had died of the new coronavirus. He was an older man with underlying health conditions. That tracked with what I'd heard about this disease: it would only affect elderly or the immunocompromised. And it was a world away from us.

The male newscaster continued from our living room. "At a nursing home facility in Kirkland, Washington, approximately twenty-seven of the one hundred and eight residents and twenty-five of the one hundred and eighty staff have some symptoms, health officials said during a teleconference with the Centers for Disease Control and Prevention. Authorities report that some among them have pneumonia—"

At that point, I clicked the television off.

I sat and wondered, not for the first time, if this thing could reach us. Surely not. Surely, I prayed to God, not.

I heard my cell dinging in the kitchen. "Hey, babe," Rick said. "I'll be heading home in a few. Want me to bring anything?"

"No, just you." And an extremely large bottle of wine and maybe a Xanax. "Just you, Rick. I made some salads for us."

"I'll grab a sandwich to go with that." He laughed. "Love you, bye."

"Love you more, bye."

I hit the red button and walked outside, taking a few deep breaths and cursing the squirrels that kept digging up my flower seedlings. They ruled the backyard like a tiny squirrel mafia, pausing occasionally to sit up and glare at me with a "whadda you lookin' at?" expression as they moved from oak to oak. It wasn't enough for them that it literally rained acorns out there.

"I'm coming back with a cat. A Maine Coon," I told them, a sudden heart-stab reminding me of my beloved Halle Berry. She'd been a fluffy black Persian, my roommate, writing buddy, and steadfast friend. It had been almost a year since she'd died in my arms at the vet's office, my tears streaming onto her fur.

Then I realized a cat would have to wait until I could scoop a litter box.

Pregnancy ruled my entire life.

Two minutes without my phone had rendered a frantic voicemail from Deanna. "Call me! Now!" was all she said. She'd texted it, too, for maximum effect.

"What's wrong?" I asked as soon as she picked up. "Are you all right?"

"They're coming here. Not just Max and Samuel in two days. Almost all of them, in three days instead. Elise and one of their other sons and his wife and their little boy!"

"What do you mean, coming here? Where are they staying? Why? What happened?"

"This coronavirus thing, that's what happened. Elise is terrified, said it's all over New York already and they just don't know it yet or aren't telling the public. They're basically evacuating to Alabama, because they think it's safer."

"And they're all going to a hotel, right?"

"For the first week. They bought a new five-bedroom house in Cider Ridge. Just…bought it. Cash. They're closing in several days, however that gets done. I have no idea." Deanna paused for breath. "Don't you think they're being over-dramatic? Hysterical?"

"Honestly, yes. Maybe they know something we don't know." I pondered the price of a five-bedroom house in Cider Ridge, which was an upscale golf community in Oxford. Could be anywhere from three-quarters of a million up, I guessed.

"They said if this all clears up like they hope, they'll move back to New York and then if Samuel starts the store here, he can live in that house. Max called it a 'long-term investment.'"

"Well, Deanna, he's not wrong. The real estate market is good right now."

"Lord, Ronni, can you imagine them all settling in here? They're used to really fancy stuff. They're used to Broadway and gala events and—"

"Deanna," I cut her off, "this will all be over soon. In the meantime, you can get to know your family. That's a great thing." And I meant that.

"It sure is a lot of family, all at once. I don't even know what to cook."

"Don't be silly. No one will expect you to cook for them. Don't you dare run off to the grocery store in a panic, Deanna. They're not coming to stay with you." I meant that, too. "I'm sure they'll settle in just fine, and love it here," I added.

I did not mean that.

SIX

ANNISTON, ALABAMA

1946

S am wasn't supposed to lock his bedroom door. The darkroom
presented his only opportunity for complete privacy; his mother
would never breach the door for any reason. He'd convinced her to do
so was to risk months of work, possibly destroying his entire yearbook
photography collection. It was his responsibility to deliver it. Esther
respected responsibility.

It was one of her favorite words.

So the darkroom was where he planned to hide the two "Tijuana
Bibles" his Cousin Mel had given him in Atlanta yesterday afternoon,
as their parents played bridge and sipped cocktails in the next room.
On the surface they looked like comic books, featuring well-known
characters like Dagwood and Blondie.

The pages inside contained the most shocking, awe-inspiring, mind-boggling introduction to sex in all its forms a seventeen-year-old boy had never dreamed of.

Sam frowned, thinking of Mel's awkwardness in his own parents' house yesterday. Aaron and Hannah Sobel could not have been more traditional and conservative in their tastes, right down to the Victorian wallpaper in the parlor. Their son was blazing a trail wilder and worse than Sherman. He'd married a Georgia peach named Katie O'Connor.

Katie was raised Southern Baptist and had borne one grandchild Aaron and Hannah desperately wanted raised in their faith. She was expecting a second. Katie and Mel were determined to introduce their children to both religions and allow them to choose.

Mel was older than Sam, sophisticated, married, visiting that day without his wife along. He'd slung an arm around Sam's shoulders and nodded toward the living room, their parents' laughter carrying into the kitchen in waves.

He handed Sam a slim brown paper bag that weighed almost nothing, telling him, "These did not come from me, buddy. If anyone finds them, you're on your own. Now use the back door to run hide them in the car."

Sam estimated his mom was halfway through her second daiquiri. She sometimes stretched the limit to three.

He glanced at the kitchen door, terrified Esther would wander in for a refill. He didn't dare take one second to look in the bag. Sam bolted into the backyard, scurrying around the house and ducking low to avoid any possibility of being spotted. He carefully placed the bag under the mat on the back floorboard, where he would plant his feet firmly on the way home and protect it like smuggled battle plans in WWII.

That night, he finally got the chance to examine the "Comic Sutra" Mel had joked about. This introduced so many glorious ideas, Sam could think of little else for hours.

He owed Mel a thousand thanks.

Of course, the torture of fully understanding what he could do with a girl, and that he probably wouldn't have the chance for at least a decade?

That was the worst.

It certainly wouldn't happen with Deborah, who had barbed-wire-strong ideas about what was unacceptable for a boyfriend to see, much less touch. This was especially unfortunate because his entire view of her had changed since that evening at Oxford Lake, kissing her under the stars on a dance floor as all the strangers around them disappeared and left only Sam and Deborah in their world.

He'd known Deborah Leon all his life, in a thousand different places and times.

He'd sat through movies with her; explored Noccalula Falls with her; stood twenty feet from a dressing room in his dad's store to approve a dress she wanted to try on; shared dinners with her and the Leons in his parents' dining room; held her hand when her beloved poodle died; escorted her to her school's homecoming game—and never, not once, had he felt the joy that bubbled through him like champagne when he thought of her now.

Maybe his parents were right. Maybe he and Deborah had been meant to be together since they were children, chasing each other from monkey bars to slides; throwing handfuls of the sandbox back and forth until Esther had to rescue a screaming Sam, his eyes full of sand and terrified because he couldn't see.

Sam's Monday morning was off to a good start. He shoved the secret books under a tray in the darkroom, yelling goodbye to his mom as he headed off to school. There, he did little but think about the many ways he'd like to explore Deborah's body, none of which incorporated the trigonometry and American Lit that buzzed the boundaries of his ears.

After school, his dad picked him up for Sam's shift at the store. It was the happiest time of his day, walking into Davidson's with Philip, even though his father was adamant everyone must treat Sam no differently from the lowliest stock clerk.

Because he was the lowliest stock clerk.

He spent two hours sorting through boxes of ladies' shoes in a musty stockroom, carefully checking and affixing the corresponding price stickers, placing each size and style on the proper shelf. When Sam emerged from the curtained room, blinking into the fluorescent store light, Mrs. Thomas offered him her brightest smile as she walked past to select some loafers for a waiting customer. She'd been working at Davidson's for as long as Sam's memory reached, and a number of ladies in town wouldn't consider anyone but Nola Thomas to outfit their feet in style.

"Thanks for straightening that shipment out, Sam," she offered, as though Sam weren't expected to do just that. "I really appreciate it."

"Happy to help, Mrs. Thomas." He walked past sales clerks in every department, noting how each one made solid eye contact and smiled at their customers. In Dresswear, Laura Deaton approached a man sitting on a velvet couch with a cup of coffee and a small plate of cookies. He'd probably been enduring a try-on session since noon.

Sam grinned at the man, recognizing him as the husband of his mom's friend, Betsy. "Hey, Dr. Blaylock," he said. "Mrs. B. finding everything she likes? We got a new shipment of silk shirtwaists last week in beautiful colors."

The man nodded as he bit into an almond cookie from Electrik Maid Bakery. "Oh, yes, she's already found one of those and a matching handbag, thanks to Laura here." He grinned at the salesgirl, who winked. "Today's my wife's birthday, which is why I'm here instead of filling molars." He brushed a few crumbs off his pants leg. "Laura is finding every blue thing y'all have ever stocked to match Betsy's eyes."

Laura was three years older than Sam and enjoying a nice sales career at Davidson's. Sam glanced at the fitting room door.

"Please tell Mrs. B. happy birthday for me!" he said to the dentist. "Laura takes great care of her customers. I'm sure she's making this visit really special." Sam shook Dr. Blaylock's hand. "Thank you for shopping with us today."

He pulled Laura aside, waving in the vague direction of Dr. Blaylock. "Here's a dime. Would you send Rita over to the bakery real quick, have her buy a cupcake for Mrs. Blaylock?" He nodded at Laura's counterpart in Sportswear.

"That'll make her really happy, Sam, thanks." Laura hurried off to conspire with Rita.

He continued to the best part of the store.

At Sam's insistence, his dad had commissioned a counter with large art nouveau mirrors situated atop it every few feet, each ready to frame a lady's face in gilt butterflies or daffodils or flowery dogwood branches. It was strategically placed near the store's entrance. Davidson's now featured the latest lines of cosmetics from Charles of the Ritz to Helena Rubinstein to their specialty, Max Factor. The overhead lights were a touch softer here; lady shoppers' diamonds sparkled in the multiple pinpoints.

So did the ladies.

Instead of spritzing those who passed with sample perfumes, Davidson's made sure their saleswomen wore generous applications of Rochas or Jean Patou or some other enticing fragrance. In the right circumstances, they might offer a lacy handkerchief misted with a lovely scent to carry away and consider.

A poster-sized photo of Lana Turner in a dramatic, upturned coat collar that showcased perfect, pouty lips and sculpted cheekbones gazed at every person who passed. A lesser but still beautiful human was always in attendance under Lana, both to greet customers and demonstrate how Mr. Factor created his movie-star looks.

Today it was Patricia, all blonde updo and sparkling brown eyes, working Cosmetics. Sam nodded and blushed a little, because Patricia made him stammer and fumble for words. He wasn't about to try to converse with a twenty-five-year-old goddess. She smiled and waved as he continued to the stairs leading to his dad's office, where he was expected to file vendor applications and then empty wastebaskets.

Over last night's supper, Sam's dad had announced, "Revenues in Cosmetics are up twelve percent over our best quarter last year. You did a good thing, son."

Sam beamed at his father's praise and watched his mom fork a piece of meatloaf to her smiling mouth. Esther would never tell Philip she and Sam had spent an afternoon dreaming the design of the department up together.

Better he should think it all came from Sam.

Later, Philip turned to Esther in bed, placing his hand on the book she was reading and gently lowering it. Without a word, Esther turned her full attention to him. A book interruption meant something important; Philip risked his life for anything less and knew it.

"I've...I've been doing something crazy lately," he began. "I wasn't going to tell you, but I always seem to." He took a deep breath and smiled reassurance at Esther, who was looking worried. "I'm fine, Essie, I truly am. But this thing..." he faltered and stopped for a few seconds. "After all we've lost in the war—your cousins and mine—it felt right."

She nodded, noting the tears forming in her usually stoic husband's eyes.

"It started with...I found a Nazi uniform in Austria and had someone buy it for me. It was expensive, and it took a long time, but—"

"It started with? What? Why in the world?" Esther interrupted. "Why in the world would you do that?"

"I burned it," he answered. "On the new backyard grill. With your Shabbat lamp oil to start the fire. And I drank two glasses of bourbon. I felt better, at least for an hour or so."

"We've never even cooked a steak there yet, Phil, and you...why would you do such a thing?"

Philip lowered his eyes. "I've bought and burned three of them now, Essie. And I won't lie to you, it's cost a lot of money. But each time felt...right. And I never let Sam see. He has no idea."

"With my family's lamp," Esther's eyebrows were sky-high, and she slapped the book in her lap with each word. "I don't understand, Phil. Again, why would you do such a thing?"

"Because," he answered, "I felt I was destroying evil. Maybe the memories connected to that cloth were gone from this world, whatever it witnessed. All I cared about was a Nazi heart once beat inside there. I felt such anger at…these pieces of cloth; they were so much more, Essie." He paused. "And the lamp, it just seemed perfect."

Esther leaned her head back and stared at the ceiling. It took her forever to say, "Are you going to burn every Nazi uniform left in Europe, Phil?" She turned to him, ran her hand through his hair and rested it on his cheek, whispering as she nodded her head. "Is that your plan? We'll need a lot of paraffin oil, husband."

"I thought it held meaning for me, Essie, but it's not an answer; it's part of a question, I guess." He shrugged. "It was stupid."

"No," she answered, "it wasn't. You're a kind and loving man, and found a way to honor those we lost, however strange." Esther frowned. "I found big flakes of ash a few weeks ago near the patio and wondered what they were. Thought maybe you tried to cook, bless your heart."

"I got better at hiding it all. The next two times, I put the ashes in an empty paint can. It's in the basement." Philip twisted his hands.

"Oy, Phil." Esther shook her head and sighed. "And you refilled my Shabbat lamp each time, so I would never notice."

He nodded, staring at the floral bedspread.

Esther bit her lip and looked out their bedroom window, at the tree branches silhouetted in the streetlight. "Do you know what the Germans did in Prague, Phil? They collected homes and possessions of the Jews. They were saving it all, artifacts for a museum of the vanquished race."

"No," he shook his head. "I didn't know that."

"So," she said, "maybe you make a museum of their evil here. Maybe you take back from them all the uniforms and guns and hate you can collect, and show people what they did and how they did it.

Maybe people visit and never, ever forget what happened." She shrugged and picked up her book.

"That would take many years and so much more money," Philip said, reaching for the lamp on his side of the bed. "I don't know, Essie. I could maybe talk to some people, try to develop interest, see if we could get funding together."

Esther smiled into her novel. "You have something better to do?" Her Yiddish accent always returned to escort this expression to his ears.

Philip smiled and closed his eyes. "You may have answered the question, Esther Davidson. The question I didn't know I was asking."

Seven

RONNI

MARCH 2020

Deanna and I stood outside the mini-mansion Elise and Max had bought, watching an army of movers unload and carry in two semi-trailer-loads of furnishings. Some of it was from their New York townhouse, but Deanna told me they'd bought roomfuls of new furniture and given the movers very specific diagrams for everything's placement.

"I didn't even know movers would do that," I said.

"These are no ordinary movers." Deanna nodded in their direction. "They are actually wearing white gloves in the house. Isn't that ridiculous?"

I shrugged. "Maybe it's because of the coronavirus."

"Maybe it's because Elise terrified them about fingerprints. Maybe it's because they can charge a hundred extra dollars per hour. Maybe it's because rich people can be really dumb." Deanna said. "Anyway,

I'd better get back in there. Thanks for bringing the mask. I probably won't wear it to the grocery store, but it's sweet of you to think of me."

"I'm being extra careful," I told her. "It's the nurse in me." I didn't mention that, at seventy-two, Deanna was at greater risk than any of us. The CDC hadn't mentioned masks yet, but we were wearing them at work and I wanted to protect Deanna the best I could. We still hadn't seen a novel coronavirus patient in Alabama. With any luck, we wouldn't.

I hugged her goodbye, promising, "Rick and I'll get here tomorrow night at six-thirty for supper. I'm bringing fried okra just to freak them out."

Deanna giggled. "I'll give you fifty dollars to make it boiled instead."

"Not even I am that cruel, lady. Let's see how this first meal goes, welcome them to The South, and then I'll decide if they deserve true okra punishment." I sped off to work, leaving Deanna waving the mask and blowing a kiss in my rearview mirror.

Kait called me into her office that afternoon. She waved for me to sit, wafting some lemon-cake-scented air my way.

"It's here," she began. "A man from Montgomery tested positive after a trip to Illinois. I got a call this morning." She rearranged the papers on her desk without meeting my eyes. "We're going to have to step up our PPE protocols, and I'm starting to worry about our mask supply."

I felt a tiny stab of guilt for the one I'd smuggled to Deanna.

"We need to monitor our residents constantly for signs of respiratory infection," Kait continued. "They'll have to be spaced apart in communal areas. Lots of hand sanitizer, everywhere. And we're supposed to start restricting visitors." She held her hands to her head and let it fall to the pile of paperwork on her desk, groaning miserably. "One visitor at a time, and we'll screen each one for exposure. No one who has traveled out of state within the last two weeks can come in."

Now she raised her head to meet my eyes. "You haven't been out of state, have you? Didn't you and Rick go to Atlanta one weekend?"

"That was nearly a month ago." Sheer paranoia made me add, "But Deanna's family moved here from New York less than two weeks ago. We're supposed to have supper over there tomorrow night."

"Oh God, why did you tell me that?" Kait's hands flew back to her head. "Okay, just be careful. I think there are only, like, a hundred cases in all of New York." She paused to think. "Ronni, if any of them look the slightest bit sick—"

"I know. I'm as worried about our patients as you are. The ones who are used to visitors will be fine with one at a time," I mused. "But it's going to be really hard to keep the people who count on dining together and afternoon social activities apart. How are we supposed to do that?"

"The same way we're doing all of this, Ronni. We're making it up as we go." Kait patted her paperwork and stood. "I have to see about setting up an isolation area, in case we have anyone test positive." She suddenly plunked back down into her chair. "I almost forgot, Ronni! How are you feeling? Still nauseated?"

"No, I feel pretty good. Just a little tired sometimes. Rick's been great about helping around the house, far less oblivious than usual. This morning he replaced the toilet paper roll in our bathroom. I didn't think he knew how."

"Men will do just about anything when you're carrying their baby," Kait said. "Enjoy it while you can." She stood again and resumed her management persona. "Please get word to everyone on your staff about these new precautions. I'll forward the CDC memo to your email, too. This stuff is likely to change daily for a while."

The evening of the following day, Rick and I stood in Max and Elise's living room, awkwardly maintaining a few feet's distance from them. No one shook hands. We smiled and nodded as we were introduced to Elise, careful to respect her well-known terror of the coronavirus, which had now assumed the name "COVID-19." She was dressed elegantly in head-to-toe black, of course, a stark contrast to her pure white hair, which was smoothed back from her forehead into a neat, low bun. The effect was striking; it was easy to see the cheekbones and brows that had made her a semi-famous model in the 1970s. The only color she wore was contained in the red and green Gucci stripe on her loafers. They had chunky heels embedded with large pearls that also screamed Gucci in gold logos.

"I'm sorry the boys and Jeannie aren't down yet," Elise offered. "Samuel is changing for dinner; Jeannie's had a terrible headache all day. I'm not sure she'll be joining us, but our son Ethan and grandson Oliver will."

I exchanged a quick glance with Rick. It took everything in me not to ask if their daughter-in-law had a fever, but then, Elise had probably been chasing her with a thermometer.

"Anyway," Elise swept her hand over the black leather and chrome sofas, "please sit down. Max is pouring some wine. Do you prefer red or white, Ronni?"

"Oh, I'm not drinking," I answered. "I'm pregnant, actually. The baby is due in September."

Rick reached for my hand and announced, "I'm not pregnant. Red, please." So much for solidarity.

Deanna chimed in her wine order from an animal-print divan in the corner of the room. It looked like she was sitting on a flayed cheetah, and I hoped it wasn't real fur.

"That's such wonderful news, Ronni," Elise said. She accepted a glass of white wine from her husband. "Isn't it, Max?"

"Yes, congratulations, Ronni and Rick." Max smiled warmly and handed Rick what looked like a clear soup bowl of Cabernet. He took a seat next to his wife, who was rubbing a spot on the glass coffee table between us with a napkin. She sat back and took a sip, her slender body almost disappearing into the sea of black.

"Chef prepared a wonderful dinner for us," Elise said. "I hope you like Branzino."

And I hope you don't call me "Nurse" and Rick "Policeman," I thought. I watched my husband search his mental archives for "Branzino" and come up empty.

"Oh, Rick and I love fish," I answered. "That sounds great. Did she grill it with lemon?" Score one for my cooking show obsession throughout pregnancy. I could speak Chic Fish with anyone.

"He," Elise corrected, assigning me demerits for gender assumption, possibly for gender as a concept, period. "Diego's been with us for twelve years. Keeps us healthy, right, darling?" She patted Max's arm.

Max was looking at Deanna, and I was betting he missed turkey and cornbread dressing. I wished I hadn't chickened out on my fried okra threat.

"Yes, he keeps us on a steady diet of every fashionable food that comes along, especially the ones that have to be imported. Tonight's European sea bass probably required a passport and a first-class seat." He took a swig from his glass. "I can't wait until you try Deanna's cooking, Elise. She's very good at it."

"Why, I could gain five pounds just thinking about it." Elise smiled at Deanna. "*Y'all* sure do know food in The South, don't *y'all?*" If she slowed that word with any more drawl, it would fall flat on the floor at her feet while trying to cross the room.

"We sure do," Deanna answered. "I can't wait to cook for you, Elise." She smiled sweetly and sipped her wine.

We all turned our heads to the thumping on the stairs, heralding the arrival of one miniature Spider-Man in the doorway. Only his eyes were visible; the costume looked far more detailed than pajamas. I wondered if the kid lived in it, just as he thrust a hand out dramatically and cast an imaginary web over all of us.

"Gotcha!" he screamed. "Everybody has to freeze!"

Max and Elise stopped moving for a good twenty seconds, eyes dramatically wide in exaggeration. Rick and I refrained from rolling ours, and I sensed Deanna did, too.

"Come here, Ollie darling, and meet our guests," Elise summoned. Ollie responded by grabbing a small crystal vase from the hallway table with another invisible web, then actually lifting it and jumping to the stairs, running back up in a series of thuds.

So *this* was Jeannie's headache.

A minute or two later, Spider-Man reappeared with his dad, who bore a striking resemblance to his grandfather, Sam, his red hair a throwback to every description I'd heard from Violet. Ethan replaced the vase and ushered his son into the living room, hands on his shoulders, forcing him to walk when I was pretty sure he'd rather leap.

He greeted Rick and me warmly with a germ-free wave, saying, "It's great to finally meet you. Jeannie says she's sorry. It's just been a day, with the moving and all." He accepted a glass of white wine from Max. "Oliver, this is Ronni and her husband, Rick. Say hello."

The kid nodded and crossed the living room in a series of superhero bounds.

We tracked him with our eyes, but neither Rick nor I stood and approached Oliver.

"It's nice to meet you," I said. "How old are you?"

"Almost five!" he yelled back.

"Ollie has attended a pre-school for gifted children since he was two years old," Elise informed us. "He can play violin and is learning the fundamentals of chess, aren't you, Ollie?"

No answer. Elise beamed a grandmother's adoration at him as he returned to grasp the back of our sofa for a minute, jumping up and down behind our heads.

Ethan settled in next to his parents, his pink shirt and jeans a stark contrast to Elise's column of darkness. He stared his son down long enough for Oliver to bound closer to Deanna, then turned his attention to us.

"Ronni, I've heard so much about you. Of course, we're all dying to know what you're going to write next. Do you have a book in progress?"

"No," I answered simply. "Not right now."

"Well," Elise replied, because Ethan had stood to take a look at Ollie, "I'm sure you'll find inspiration soon."

"Ollie! You mustn't do that," Ethan said to his son, who was busy crawling under the divan where Deanna sat. He pulled at the long skirt she wore, pretending he'd caught it in a web. Deanna locked eyes with me, and I knew we were both thinking it was going to be a long night.

Ollie ignored his father; we tried to ignore Ollie as he plotted the best ways to irritate adults, most of which involved jumping and landing in a crouch, one hand planted on the floor, directly in front of whoever was speaking at the time.

Then Samuel appeared and we forgot Ollie for a blessed minute. He walked in with a smile and extended his hand to Rick, who'd decided he was too manly to ignore the custom, virus be damned. Samuel was every bit the tall, young, dark-haired clone of his dad, Max.

Ollie ran to his uncle and jumped in front of him, obviously waiting to be scooped up. Samuel obliged and placed the kid on his shoulders, sparing us all a few minutes of aggravation.

He said, "I see you've met Spider-Man and his dad already. Oliver is actually the greatest kid ever without the costume. Ethan is just meh." He laughed at his brother good-naturedly; Ethan raised his glass. "I'm happy to finally meet you, Ronni and Rick. Happy to be in Alabama, too." Ollie continued to reach for faraway things and people with his Spidey-hands. Deanna tugged at her skirt, clearly happy to have him across the room.

"We're glad to have you, Samuel. I hear you might open a Philippe store here, where your great-grandfather started out," I said. "I think that's a wonderful idea."

"I'm excited about it," Samuel answered. "Granddad used to tell us all about that store when we were little, and he made it sound magical. I guess when he worked there, in the 1940s, it was really something else. Serving cookies to customers, pampering everyone who walked in. I can't recreate all that, but I'd like to come close. Maybe Dad didn't tell you," he glanced at his father, who nodded, "but we're closing on the property in a couple of weeks. There's a ton of renovation work to be done. Can't wait to get started." He reached up to stop Ollie from pulling his hair.

Elise said, "Excuse me, I'm going to check on dinner." She set her glass on the coffee table, and I noticed Max refilled it immediately. She paused briefly to kiss Ollie's dangling foot and told him, "Goodnight, sweetheart, Glam-ma will tuck you in later."

Ethan stood and crossed the room to extricate Oliver from his uncle's shoulders. "Wave goodnight, big guy," he told him. "Chef is bringing some chicken nuggets up to your room, and you can have all the iPad time you want." The child waved one last web over us all and pantomimed pulling us closer. Elise hopped backwards from her path to the kitchen like a netted fish, and Ollie giggled all the way up the stairs.

As we sat for dinner and unfolded our napkins, Rick and I stared at a giant, bright pink-and-blue painting that dominated the room, elaborately framed in gold, illuminated by an almost-hidden museum light peeking over the top. It was mostly blobs of color on a white canvas, but there were two figures who were unmistakably policemen in the forefront. They were almost amorphous, sort of oblong-ish, and wore crudely-drawn hats. One seemed to have sharp teeth in his gaping mouth.

Rick, quite innocently, asked, "Did Ollie draw that?" I knew he meant it; the painting looked like a kindergarten experiment in garish color and dark slashes.

I watched Elise hesitate before answering, "No, that's a Basquiat, from the early eighties. Are *y'all* familiar with his work?"

"No, we're not," Rick answered for us. He was squinting at the painting. "It's certainly different."

"Well," Elise said, "let me tell you about it. Max and I acquired this painting at auction several years ago, and we were lucky to buy it. It's a museum piece, you see?" Now she stood to walk over and fully introduce us to the art on her wall. "These," she swept her hand at one of the blue blobs, "are New York City policemen. Basquiat painted this work in response to the death of Michael Stewart, a young Black man who died after being arrested for writing graffiti on a subway wall."

"He died how, exactly?" my husband asked.

"Officially, it was cardiac arrest," Elise said, taking her seat. "But he died from the unlawful arrest, period. He suffered greatly at the hands of the New York City Police. He's one of many."

Rick's jaw tightened like a marionettist had jerked a string upward. He glanced at me and said, "That's awful, and I'm sorry to hear it. Sounds like a bad cop was involved."

"I know you're a law enforcement officer, Rick, and you'd see all this differently," Elise offered, her face arranged into a polite hostess smile.

"I might and I might not," Rick said, "but I'd like to know both sides of the story."

"The details can be debated endlessly, of course," Max told Rick. "Let's all take a moment to enjoy our carrot bisque." He nodded gratefully at Chef, who had entered and started placing artful bowls of soup before us, each topped with the tiniest swirl of crème fraiche, pumpkin seeds, and sprigs of parsley.

It was creamy heaven in a bowl and I never looked up from mine, savoring the soup and grateful to Max for ending the discussion with grace. I wondered if the baby and I could ask for seconds, eyeing Chef Diego as he silently padded back into the room. He clearly possessed magic.

Elise said, "Isn't it delicious, Ronni? This is my favorite dish."

I wondered if I'd involuntarily groaned a spoonful or two ago. Everyone was looking at me and my empty bowl.

"I thought you might like to take some of that home, Ronni. Chef will box some up for you," Elise said.

I might have cried a little in joy.

My husband had decided he needed the last word, ruining my bisque bliss. As Diego served us kale salads, Rick said, "You know, there are bad cops. There are evil people in every profession, but mine is the one you hear about. And Elise, no one hates a bad cop more than a good cop. No one." He stabbed a piece of kale with a little more force than necessary. He chewed politely and smiled, even though I knew he'd rather eat anything else on earth. Tofu ranked higher on Rick's food list than kale.

Elise returned the smile and nodded.

"So, a new store for Anniston, huh? That'll be great, Samuel," I said, determined to swoop in with a new subject.

Samuel grinned. "I think it will. Feels kind of full-circle to me. I'd like to think Granddad would be proud of what we're going to do. My great-grandfather Philip, too."

"I am absolutely sure they would be," I said, wondering how long it would take for a local girl to fall hopelessly in love with Samuel's shining eyes and the smiles that reached them. Not long. I had a feeling Philippe would be a huge success, especially with female shoppers.

Elise said, "Ronni, you know what you should write a book about? Basquiat." She waved her hand in the direction of the painting. "He worked with Andy Warhol, can you imagine? Warhol used to frequent Studio 54, and he brought him along once. I saw them. Basquiat danced with Madonna. Well, near her. We all used to dance like one giant organism." She sipped her wine. "I can tell you all about that era in New York City. There will never be another like it. You could write about that."

I was tired of giving my not-an-author speech. "Maybe I will someday," I answered between bites of kale. "Sounds fascinating. I've heard about discos like Studio 54 and what they were like then." I looked at Ethan and Samuel. "You have a very cool mom," I told them.

"Oh, the coolest," Ethan answered. I couldn't tell if he was being sarcastic or not, but Samuel just smiled at his kale salad, listening.

"Of course," Elise took Max's hand in hers, "that was before I met my handsome husband."

I consciously willed Rick not to say anything about Studio 54 debauchery, or the documentary he'd half-watched with me about its heyday. He stayed quiet for the rest of dinner, except to compliment

Diego on the fish as he removed our plates for a dessert of berries with honey.

I also willed Rick not to ask for whipped cream, and he didn't.

He stayed quiet all the way home after we offered our thanks and awkwardly waved goodnight. No one was willing to touch, much less shake hands or hug. Rick walked Deanna to her car and turned the radio on in ours as soon as he sat behind the wheel, loud enough to prevent one word from me. I knew better than to reach for the volume. He needed time.

When we climbed into bed, he laid his head on my stomach. "Is she still a grape?"

"He or she is a plum," I said, stroking his hair.

"You're not going to give me a drop of that soup, are you?" Rick kept his ear to my belly, listening, his arms wrapped around me.

"No, I am not."

"She probably did cocaine at Studio 54 with Bianca Jagger, you know."

I laughed. "Rick, you wouldn't even know who Bianca Jagger is if we hadn't watched that documentary, and no one ever said she used cocaine. That's a false accusation."

"Well, I'm a cop. That's what we do, right?" He rolled over and lay next to me.

"I know that discussion was hard for you, babe. I'm sorry the subject came up." I reached to turn my bedside lamp off. My eyes traced Rick's profile in the moonlight as he stared at the ceiling.

"Ronni," he said, "you have no idea. We get this stuff everywhere we go. When I'm in uniform, I get all kinds of hateful looks. I've actually had kids shepherded away from me in a restaurant."

"Most people don't feel that way, Rick. I've seen so many thank you and hug you—"

"For every one of them," he interrupted, "there are ten who assume I'm a racist. I wanted to say so much more to Elise, Ronni. I wanted to tell her about Jordan Sims, who went through Parris Island with me, who saved my life twice in Iraq. I want her to know Jordan was Black, that his favorite candy was Snickers, that he despised country music, that his grandma mailed me cookies when she sent his, that I went to his family's house in Memphis on leave, not mine. That they love me and I love them." He paused and threw an arm over his eyes. "That he was killed three weeks before our tour was up and it wrecked me. They let me accompany his body home, did you know that? I was a pallbearer. And there are others, guys who mean a lot to me. You can't fight alongside men every day, your life in their hands, and care about their color, Ronni."

"I know, Rick."

"I'd like to tell Elise Devonte Green's mom sends me a card every year on his birthday, thanking me for pulling him out of a burning car. That I've been close to Devonte since he was eight, gone to his ball games, tried to give him good advice. Hell, he wrote his college application essay about me and my place in his life. I'd do anything for him."

"I know, Rick, how much you care about Devonte, and that you still miss Jordan. And I know," I turned his chin toward me with a finger, "you love and treasure those friendships. But that's the thing, babe: you can tell Elise or anyone else all of that and it proves nothing. The only way you prove you're not racist is the way you live your life and do your job. Elise may never know, but you will in your heart, and Rick, you lead others. So many look up to you. Never forget that."

I could see a faint smile on his face. "How did I marry such a smart woman?"

"Well, honey, it took you three tries." I patted his cheek and we both laughed, then I rolled off the bed and announced, "I'm going to have some soup."

"And so am I." Rick jumped up. "I've never been so captivated by carrots. Diego has a way about him that makes me want him to live with us."

"I think Chef is pretty busy where he is," I said. "Apparently, Ollie eats nothing but chicken nuggets for all three meals, and they must be freshly fried."

"Our little plum will never be spoiled rotten," Rick said.

"One tiny finger around your pinky and you'll be buying her a pony, Rick."

"So we agree she's a sugar plum and not a spice plum, then?"

"That's vaguely disgusting." I wrinkled my nose. "But yes, I'm starting to think this is a little girl." I patted my belly as we walked down the stairs.

"So, little Violet, then?" Rick asked.

"Absolutely Violet. The woman who changed my life, who's the reason we met, who basically handed me a family, who made me a writer—"

"Ahh. Thank you for remembering, Ronni. You are a writer. And when it's time, you'll write another book and people will love it," Rick said. "You can't force it, babe, but it will come to you."

Eight

ANNISTON, ALABAMA

1946

Sam blew out the candles on the chocolate cake Esther had baked, then opened a series of photography-related gifts from his family and a wallet stamped with his initials from Deborah. He rounded the room with a series of brief hugs for the females present: Aunt Hannah, his mom, Mel's wife Katie, and a slightly lingering embrace for Deborah. In the wake of his mother's final admonitions for her nephew to drive safely, Sam settled into the back of Mel's new Ford Super Deluxe with Deborah at his side.

He took her hand and told Mel, "Please go before Mom comes to check my face for chocolate icing." Sam glanced at the front door of his house and swiped his mouth with a thumb. "And do not drive safely. Burn some rubber as you drive off."

Deborah swatted his arm. "You're her only child. Of course she worries."

Katie regarded the two of them from the rearview mirror. "Do not speak ill of your mother, Sam. That woman is the reason I can leave my feral two-year-old here and enjoy a night out with y'all. Mel's mom is only interested in a game of bridge, but I think Esther wants grandchild practice." She turned around to wink at Deborah, who responded with a nervous laugh.

"Whoa there, Katie. We're barely going steady." Deborah looked at Sam, whose face was now a light shade of crimson. He was staring out of the window and trying to ignore the conversation.

Katie turned her focus to Mel. "Where are you taking your pregnant wife who's been locked up with your wild spawn for weeks?" She patted her small belly with satisfaction. She had on one of her favorite skirts, and wondered how long she'd be able to wear it.

"Wherever Sam wants to go," Mel answered. "It is *his* birthday, honey."

Sam glanced at Deborah, knowing what she wanted him to say. "Let's go to Oxford Lake," he said. "We can walk around and maybe go skating. Sometimes there's music and dancing. There's a bowling alley, too. But I will not get into a boat."

"And I will not get into a roller skate," Katie said. "I'll be happy to watch all of you, though. My husband is very entertaining on wheels, especially when he's trying to stop."

Mel rolled his eyes. "She's trying to tell you I once lost control in our driveway and sailed toward a tree, cartwheeling my arms and Katie thought it was hilarious. I was just a child."

"It was three years ago, Mel. You were twenty-six," Katie said. "And you screamed," she added. "Like a banshee."

"Okay, birthday boy," Mel reached across his wife into the glove box. "Here's one more gift." He handed Sam a brown paper bag with two bottles of beer inside. "You're old enough for a sip or two of this. But go slowly and don't get sauced. I'll kill you if you spew in the back seat of my new car."

Sam saw Deborah's eyes widen. "What?" he said. "You think I've never had beer?" He used the opener Mel had provided and handed the cap to Deborah. "Here's a souvenir for you." Sam took a long pull from the bottle and blinked at the label. "This is great, Mel, thank you."

Deborah shook her head and stared in the opposite direction. "Hey," she said, "isn't that your friend Johnny?" She pointed to a tall boy on the sidewalk across the street, about twenty feet ahead.

"Yeah, he's probably sneaking over to see his girl," Sam said. "She babysits somewhere around here." As he spoke, Violet Glenn stepped from behind a tree and wrapped her arms around Johnny's neck, bestowing a kiss on him for God and everyone to see. She took Johnny's hand and they walked off in the direction of the Wilsons' house.

Mel had slowed the car to a crawl, partially because of the blonde beauty on the sidewalk. Sam asked him to stop and park. He guzzled the rest of his first beer and hopped out, running to see his friends. Deborah watched as he grabbed Johnny's shoulders from behind, yelling something that was likely basketball-related. Johnny swung around, grinning, and Violet offered Sam a smile that could only mean happy birthday, because she followed it with a hug and a pat on Sam's back. Deborah had never seen Violet, though Sam mentioned her often as Johnny's girlfriend.

Violet offered a little wave in the general direction of the car, but didn't walk over. She took Johnny's hand and tugged him forward. Sam jogged back across the street and climbed in beside Deborah.

"You should meet Violet sometime. You'd love her. Everybody loves Violet. She's a real sweetheart."

Deborah met Katie's eyes in the mirror. "I look forward to it," she said. She kissed Sam's cheek and tried to ignore the beer on his breath, a smell she despised.

Katie Sobel kept her eyes trained on Violet as the car passed. She had her arm around Johnny's waist now, pulling him closer, gazing up at him as they walked along. Katie remembered when she used to look at Mel that way. She smiled to herself. Obviously, there was one man in the world for Violet, and that was Johnny.

"She's going to babysit, like I thought," Sam said. "This kid named Chet and his little sister, CeeCee. Violet says she's the only babysitter Mrs. Wilson ever wants, and her mom makes her go every time. Says they need her help. Mr. Wilson works at the train station, running everything in the office. He's never home."

"Where does the mom go?" Katie asked, clearly intrigued by the idea of hiring a babysitter and taking off on her own.

"I have no idea," Sam answered. "But Violet feels really sorry for those kids because Mrs. Wilson's always going out. She has a soft spot for Chet, says he's a nice boy and his mom doesn't seem to pay attention to him or his sister. There are no grandparents anywhere near Anniston, or I guess they wouldn't need Violet so much."

"Why does Violet's mom make her go every time Mrs. Wilson wants to hire her?" Deborah asked.

"Violet says it's mostly because her mom knows the Wilson kids, especially Chet, love having Violet there and it's practically the only time they're well taken care of. That boy, Chet, has a massive crush on Violet. Drives Johnny crazy, the little twerp. Anyway, Mrs. Glenn sends cookies and stuff over there sometimes. I think maybe Mrs. Wilson used to go to their church."

"Well, that's sweet of them," Katie said.

"Yes," Deborah nodded, "very sweet of them." She snuggled up to Sam, despite the second beer he'd begun sipping.

"Well, maybe not. Violet keeps saying her mom makes her go babysit to keep her from spending so much time with Johnny." He chuckled. "I'm pretty sure she doesn't know they meet up before Violet goes, or right after sometimes."

"Sounds serious," Katie said. "I wonder if they'll get married someday."

"Without a doubt," Sam answered. "Johnny's been determined to marry Violet since eighth grade. And she's crazy about him. Just like Deborah is about me."

Deborah sighed and prayed there was no more beer in the glove box.

As promised, Mel delivered his cousin home by midnight, walking into yet another game of cards. Mel noted his mother and Aunt Esther seemed tipsy; the two beers he'd brought for Sam's eighteenth birthday didn't seem like such an infraction. He kissed the top of his mom's gray head as he passed. Hannah automatically reached up to smooth her hairdo.

"Did y'all have fun?"

Sam collapsed into a wing chair across from Mel and Katie on the couch. "Yes, ma'am, we did. Deborah did, too."

"Such a nice girl, Deborah," his aunt offered. "She's very pretty, Sam." She stole a glance at Katie and Mel. "Your son is fast asleep. Little Sammy, cute as his cousin; he even looks like you, Sam." She played a card with a small whoop. "His Great-Aunt Esther gave him a bath and read him a story at bedtime. We put him in the middle of your bed in the guest room."

Katie said, "Thank you for watching him. I'm going up to join him now. I'm so tired."

Mel nodded at his wife. "I'll be up in a bit. Sam and I are going to sit on the patio and enjoy the air."

Mel popped open a beer from the Davidsons' refrigerator and offered Sam a drink.

"No thanks," Sam said. He leaned back and looked at the sky. "Thanks for driving us tonight, and for bringing me a couple of birthday Ballantines. I really appreciate it."

"Happy to be here for your birthday," Mel said, setting his beer down. "I've been wanting to talk to you, anyway. You're the little brother I never had, Sam, and I hope you know how important you are to me. We wouldn't name our son after just anybody."

Sam smiled at the stars. "I know. I'm glad I have you, too. And Sammy is adorable. If your next one is a girl, I want you to name her Samuella."

"Yeah, we'll consider that. Anyway, Sam, Katie and I were wondering about your plans after high school. You'll graduate next spring, and when you're thinking of colleges, I want you to think hard about Emory. We'd be happy to show you around. Or Tech. Either one would be close by. Katie and I would love that."

"Oh, I won't be going away to school. I'm going to take business courses at Jacksonville State. I'll work at the store at the same time. But Mel, I've been taking classes all my life, in the store. At the dinner table. Basically, all the time. Dad didn't go to college. I don't think he considers a four-year degree important. I mean, for someone like you, yes. But I'm not going to be a lawyer. My whole future is going to be Davidson's Department Stores."

"Your whole future?" Mel's brows were raised high.

"You know what I mean," Sam said. "Everyone assumes Deborah and I will be together, and I want that, too. It's just—I don't know— hard sometimes. I'm only eighteen and it seems like my whole life has been planned out for me, including a wife. I love Deborah, of course I do." Sam patted the patio table. "But it's not always great between us. For one thing, you know those books you gave me? The dirty comics?"

Mel looked behind Sam to be sure they were still alone. "Shh, Sam, don't mention those out loud."

"Okay, well, nothing in them is going to happen with Deborah." Sam shook his head.

"It's not supposed to! What did you think, you fathead? Sam, I gave you those to answer questions for you, that's all. That stuff is for when you're married." He took a long drink of his beer. "I'm sorry if you misunderstood. You should never expect Deborah...oh, Sam—"

"I get it, Mel, I do. I don't expect much of Deborah, but she barely lets me kiss her. Anything beyond that just isn't allowed. Ever. And it gets...frustrating. Johnny and Violet have done a lot of things—"

Mel threw up his hand. "I don't want to know what Johnny and Violet have done. And Johnny shouldn't be telling you about it, either. What kind of guy is your best friend?"

Sam sighed. "He's a good guy, Mel. A lot of it, I've assumed."

"Well, there's your problem." Mel checked again for parents and continued, "Look, I know you can't ask your dad about these things. You're always welcome to talk to me. I'll tell you what you need to know, and I'll be honest and up front, okay? But Sam, not Deborah. Not the woman you're going to marry."

Sam cringed. "Don't say that, like it's all decided. And besides, if not Deborah, who? She's my girlfriend. What am I supposed to do?"

"You wait, buddy. You wait for that part of your life, that's what."

"Easy for you to say," Sam said. "You've been with Katie for years and years."

"First of all, that's not something—look, Sam, what's between Katie and me is personal and for us only. But if you think it's been easy for us, think again. You know we went through a lot to get married in the first place. It's especially rough on Katie."

Sam bit his lower lip and shook his head. "I know what you mean, Mel. I think it's just…I don't know; now that the war is over, everyone is in a rush to go forward. My parents want Deborah and me to get engaged soon, I know they do. I just want to have some fun, experience life. Why do I even have to think about settling down?"

"Honestly, Sam, we lost so many good young men in the war. We lost millions of Jews, our people, to Hitler. It's not hard to think why we all want to go forward, is it? Surely you can understand how your mom and dad feel."

Sam looked thoughtful. "I know, and I love Deborah. We probably will get married, eventually. It's just, when I think of the future…" he trailed off, shaking his head.

"When you think of the future, what?" Mel asked.

"I just see myself building our business. It's what I've been focused on forever. Dad's always made me look at the store like this living entity, and we're all responsible for its health, you know? I've worked in every department, Mel, bottom to top and back down again, and now he's teaching me about all the financial stuff, too. We're already opening a new lower-priced store in Oxford and Dad wants a flagship someday in Atlanta or New York. He wants to create a whole chain of stores. Being part of all that is the future I've worked so hard for, Mel. I'm ready, so ready."

Mel checked his watch, drained his beer, and stood. "I understand, and I love your enthusiasm, kid. If you ever change your mind, Katie and I would love to have you close by. I think it could be good for you to spread your wings a little bit." He yawned. "It's 12:23 a.m., and your birthday is officially over. I'm going to bed. I hope this year is your best yet, Sam." He patted Sam's shoulder and looked out at the backyard. "Do y'all ever actually use that grill?"

"No, I think my dad's afraid of it," Sam answered.

Nine

RONNI

APRIL, 2020

Mrs. Reed sat in the hallway, staring into space. I knew she was missing her afternoon companion of the last two years, Mrs. Colley, who was now confined to the isolation ward along with four others exposed to COVID-19. Two of Fairfield Springs' residents had been transported to a local hospital. They would not be coming back.

I stopped and gave her shoulder a squeeze, knowing my mask would make it impossible for her to understand anything I'd say. Mrs. Reed's hearing loss caused her to read lips more than listen. She looked up at me, eyes smiling, and I felt another piece of my heart chip away. I held up a finger and walked back to my desk to make a sign to hold up for her.

"Mrs. Colley is still doing okay."

Mrs. Reed nodded and started to reach for my gloved hand, which I had to draw away. I did my best to make my smile reach my eyes. I hoped she understood, but how could she? Everything about the world we'd so carefully constructed for her comfort and wellbeing had fallen away. I was feeling bitter, on her behalf and my own.

And now Kait had summoned me with an ominous email.

She swiped a tear from her eye as I entered her office. My heart plummeted to my knees.

"Who?" I asked. "Not Mrs. Colley, please. She was fine this morning, didn't even have a fever."

"No, it's not that," Kait said. "Please sit down, Ronni."

I collapsed into a chair, noting the absence of any wax-melt smell of the day. Then I panicked, wondering if I had COVID-19. Why couldn't I smell anything?

Kait saw me sniffing for lemon pound cake or chocolate pie fragrance and smiled gently. "You're fine," she said. "I skipped it today."

"Are your nostrils on a diet?" I picked up a souvenir paperweight featuring Rock City painted on a barn. Kait loved her kitsch.

She placed her clasped hands on her desk, and I knew she was about to tell me some awful thing. Every day was a hailstorm of bad news, pelting us at every turn.

"Ronni, I've been notified of a decision by corporate. I'm so sorry, but you have to go home. Only temporarily, just until the virus is gone." She leaned back in her chair, shaking her head with a frown. "They're concerned," she glanced at her computer screen, "about your safety."

"I don't understand. What do you mean, go home?"

"You're four months pregnant, Ronni. We have no idea how COVID-19 affects pregnant women or their babies. Fairfield doesn't want to risk your further exposure. That's how they put it. And Ronni, we're afraid this is only getting started with our residents. It'll be impossible to keep the virus away from you here."

I rolled my eyes. Rick had been saying the same thing, and it had caused more than one fight.

"First of all, there's no evidence I'd be any sicker than people with minor cold symptoms. I'm twenty-nine, Kait. I'm healthy. You need me here. I can't just walk away from our patients. They need me more than ever." I realized I was turning her paperweight over and over in my hands, and replaced it on the desk. "And where am I supposed to work? We have mortgage payments—"

"You can work at Dr. Aronson's office. I already called them, and they'll take you on part time doing workups and BP checks and urine samples and all the stuff pregnant women need. You'll be safer in an OB/GYN's office. You and the baby both."

"This is ridiculous." I smacked her desk with my palm. "And you know it, Kait."

She leaned forward, chin on her clasped hands. "Actually, honey, it's not. The most important person in your life is that baby, Ronni. He or she comes before everything."

I glared at her. "When do I have to 'go home'? In a week?"

"At the end of your shift today. Corporate is transferring someone here tomorrow. I'm so sorry, Ronni. Maybe this will all be over in a month or two."

"I belong here, Kait. You know that better than anyone." I stood to leave. "This is so unfair."

"None of it's fair, Ronni. We're all doing the best we can. Please call Aronson's office soon and let them know if you want the job. They're waiting to hear from you." Kait didn't stand to hug me the way she had a hundred times before in our years of friendship. She was firmly ensconced in the new, distant, contactless world we'd entered.

"Well, bye then, *Boss*," I shot at her. "I'll be gone by five and I'll leave a detailed list of things your new nurse will need to know."

"It's temporary, Ronni. I want you and the baby safe. I love you."

"I love you, Kait, but slightly less than usual," I told her. I shook my head slowly, my mouth open. I still couldn't believe I was about to be separated from those who needed me most, at the worst possible time.

She made a mirthless little chuckle. "Understood and noted. Call me every day. I'll miss you so much."

I couldn't answer or I'd cry, and I really didn't want to make things worse for Kait. She was just following orders. I tapped my hand against the doorway a couple of times and nodded.

I kissed the top of Mrs. Reed's curly white hair as I passed her, waving my gloved fingers as I backed away. She looked at me with so much love in her blue eyes, my mask was tear-soaked by the time I reached my desk.

I stared at the mountain of work I'd have to complete in two and a half hours. Packing wouldn't take too long, though. I dried my eyes and replaced my mask.

Seeing my patients was more important. I went from room to room and found many of them sleeping. Mr. Roberts was watching Fox News, shaking his head at the latest pandemic statistics. I squeezed his foot through the cotton blanket and told him not to worry; this would all be over soon. I stood and watched Mrs. Henderson snoring softly. I put fresh gloves on and moved the candy her grandchildren had sent to her bedside table.

Mrs. Delaney, who'd been at Fairfield five years, needed the bathroom. Rather than call an aide, I helped her myself. I asked her for the hundredth time about her experiences as a third-grade teacher in Georgia, the only subject she'd discuss.

"Those kids acted up a lot today," she murmured. "But they're mostly good children. We're working on times tables." She turned to stare out her window.

I didn't tell her I was leaving. I told none of them, because they were already trying to understand too many changes. Many were aware enough to worry along with the rest of us; some didn't really register fear. Mrs. Ruth Delaney was one of them, spending her days in a long-gone classroom.

How many of them would be here when I returned?

I dried my tears again, wondering if hormones were going to make me cry nonstop for the next five months. After finalizing staff scheduling and miscellaneous administrative details, I started typing personal notes on all the patients I knew: everything from former occupations to possible visitors to TV shows to talk about. I made sure each medical chart was updated and left my phone number in a note on the desk, asking my replacement to please call with any questions.

I made a quick mental inventory of all the trinkets and photos surrounding me, trying not to think about the ones given to me by patients. I sighed and started gathering the non-crushables for the bottom of a cardboard box. First, a small, battered stuffed toy monkey with a homemade tag proclaiming him "Mikey." Mikey had huge surprised eyes and looked like he'd been loved half to death and was scared of more. His fur was missing in lots of places. Despite myself, I thought about Mr. Matthews presenting him to me after lunch years ago. His great-granddaughter had left the monkey for him. He said Mikey gave him the creeps sitting in his room, staring.

As I placed Mikey in the box, a tiny fluttering-butterfly ballet began in my lower belly. I'd never felt anything like it before, but knew instantly my baby was making herself known, reminding me why I had to leave. I smiled, despite the day and all it had hurled my way. I placed my hands on my ever-growing stomach and the movement stopped.

I decided to place Mikey next to Rick's dinner plate tonight to stare at him, thinking he'd either throw him at me or rush to hide him away somewhere. It would be a perfect introduction to telling Rick about feeling our baby move for the first time.

Then I'd let him know he'd gotten his way, and I wouldn't be working at Fairfield until COVID-19 was over. And I'd cry all over again.

I called Deanna on my way home, both to check on her and tell her about Fairfield and my possible part-time obstetrics career.

"Oh, honey, I've been so worried about you in that place. You remember that Zika mosquito thing a few months ago? I was so glad that all seemed over before you got pregnant, and now this. You really shouldn't be around the people most likely to get it, Ronni."

"I know, I know," I said. Deanna had been only slightly quieter than Rick about her concerns in the last few weeks.

"I was talking to Max before you called," she segued. "Jeannie's family in Westport, Connecticut is sending someone to pick her and Ethan and Oliver up. Her dad said they'll be better off there on the estate—he actually used the word *estate*—and they can continue Ollie's violin education while Ethan and his family are staying. I mean, they have some huge place on the water. They could all go days without seeing each other, Max said."

"How are they continuing the violin lessons?" I asked.

"I don't know. Maybe they keep a violin teacher in the basement. Elise is livid, but there's nothing she can do about it. They're leaving tomorrow."

"Someone's driving down to pick them up that fast?" I tried to imagine hours in a car with Ollie. Benadryl might be required. For both of us.

"Her dad is sending their *private jet*." I could picture Deanna, eyes wide, nodding her head, bestowing this amazing news. "He's some kind of corporate raider or something. Owns companies around the world. And they know all these celebrities and I think Jay Leno bought a car from them. And their house is the size of a mall." She paused for breath. "Anyway, I'm sorry you never met Jeannie. She's really pretty, tall with long blonde hair and blue eyes. She worked for some fashion designer before she married Ethan. They got married on a private island."

"Are you sure you're not talking about Carolyn Bessette?" I rolled my eyes as I turned into our driveway.

"Who is that?" Deanna asked.

"She was married to John F. Kennedy, Jr., and they died in a plane crash, remember? I was a little kid, but it was all over the news."

"Ronni!" Deanna yelled into my ear. "Don't say plane crash! They're flying out tomorrow. And Jeannie did say to tell you she's sorry she didn't meet you that night, and we've all been isolated since. She said she was sorry they couldn't see more of Alabama."

"Well, I'm truly sorry I didn't get to meet her." And now she would look like Carolyn Bessette in my head forever, staring at me from a *People* magazine cover. I glanced at the box of memories on my passenger seat, picking up a photo of Kait and me at work back around the time of what we now called 'The Ledbetter Vine Incident'. "I guess I'd better get my stuff toted inside and get something going for dinner. Rick's been on a long shift and he'll be starving. It's my turn to cook."

"Bye, I love you," Deanna said.

"I love you, too," I answered. "Stay safe." It struck me that had become part of our regular vernacular in 2020, on every occasion. *Stay safe. I'm going to pick up groceries curbside: Stay safe. I have to put gas in the car: Stay safe. I'm watching Netflix: Stay safe.*

Rick called at 6:30 to say he was running late, and I decided I wouldn't wait to tell him about my job. I'd had time to digest it. I was feeling logical, and proud of myself for that.

"I'm glad you finally listened to me," Rick said. "You have to think of the baby first."

"I didn't listen to you. My boss sent me home, Rick." I stirred the spaghetti sauce hard enough to splash it onto the stove, irritated at his attitude. "And I do think of the baby first."

"And she is the size of...?" he said.

"I have no idea. I'm kind of tired of fetus-fruit-sizing, honestly. But I do have something about her to tell you when you get home. Will you be here by seven?"

"Are you okay? Is the baby okay?"

"The baby is fine, Rick. I'm fine. Will you be here by seven?"

"I will now," he answered. "I'll see you soon. I love you."

"I love you," I answered. "Stay safe."

I placed Mikey the Monkey next to Rick's water glass, and a fresh wave of sadness passed over me. I tried to reassure myself this would all be over soon, and I'd be back with my patients.

The ones who make it through, my brain added.

Twenty minutes later, Rick sat down, held the monkey up and said, "I hope you did not buy this for our daughter."

"No," I took a sip of water. "It was given to me by a patient, and I'm sentimental about Mikey there. Even more so since I was holding him the first time I felt our baby move this afternoon."

"You did?" He jumped up and knelt next to my chair, hands on my belly. "You felt her, really? Can I feel her kick?"

"No, it's too early for that," I told him, patting his hand. "It's just a fluttering sensation sometimes. But it's very cool." I kissed the top of his head. "Now eat your spaghetti. It'll get cold."

"You didn't make flaming garlic bread?" Rick would never let me forget the first time I cooked dinner for him and started a fire in the process.

"No, I skipped the garlic bread," I said. "I have to sleep next to you, and garlic breath seemed like a very bad idea. Did you know I can detect smells from miles away now? I can pick up Jinxie Tyler's gardenias as I'm driving up to our house. It's a pregnancy curse."

Rick chewed his spaghetti and set his fork down. "Yeah. I have some bad news," he said. "Jinxie's in the hospital. She tested positive a couple of days ago and they took her in last night. She's not doing well."

"Oh, not Jinxie, Rick. She's so healthy. She's the biggest fitness fanatic I know. Surely she'll be fine."

"I hope so," he said. "But she's sixty-eight, Ronni. And her husband is seventy-eight. He's home alone and the hospital won't let him see Jinxie. His daughter can't even go in his house, so she's dropping meals off at the front door. I saw her this morning."

"God, I hate this." I set my fork down, too. "What can we do? Can we take food over there, or would that be a bad thing? He might worry if it's from anyone else."

"You're right," Rick said. "Better not to. Just pray. That's about all we can do." He reached for my hand. "And I'm sorry about your job, babe. I know how much you love your patients and want to be there for them."

That started the tears all over again. Without another word, we decided to save the spaghetti for later. I took our plates to the kitchen, grabbed Rick a beer, and we settled on the couch together. I leaned against my husband and listened to his heartbeat, trying to shut out the world as the sun sank behind the oaks in our backyard, softening the light streaming into our living room, wrapping us in a temporary blanket at sunset.

I woke the next morning as Rick emerged from a shower, shivering as he walked into our warm room.

"I think I might be sick," he told me. "I mean, I really don't feel that bad, just achy." I automatically held my hand to his forehead. His temperature had to be over a hundred degrees. The thermometer measured 101.7.

Training overtook my panic. I grabbed the N95 mask I'd been wearing yesterday and put it on. I resisted the urge to give him acetaminophen, knowing the fever might be beneficial in fighting off what I prayed wasn't this new virus. I made him lie down as I walked away, searching my phone for the soonest testing site appointment we could get.

"I'm supposed to work a shift at one!" he yelled. Then he coughed: a dry, hollow sound that slashed through my calm like an arctic wind.

Part
Two

Ten

ANNISTON, ALABAMA

1947

"I despised that movie," Deborah said as Sam closed her car door. "Didn't you, Violet?" She glanced in the rearview mirror to find Violet and Johnny kissing in the back seat. She cleared her throat and practically yelled, "Don't you think it was dumb? The woman followed her husband to the middle of nowhere to become a chicken farmer. Who would do that? And the title, *The Egg and I*, is so stupid."

Even after Sam slid behind the steering wheel, Violet and Johnny didn't come up for air. Deborah hoped Violet's bright red lipstick would be smeared to her eyebrows. Sam ignored her, too, and shifted the car into drive. She decided then and there she'd never subject herself to another double date with Violet Glenn.

She glared at Sam as he navigated downtown traffic. "You know, I feel kind of sick from the popcorn, Sam. Will you just take me home?" she asked.

Sam didn't hesitate, bruising her feelings. "Sure." He nodded, his face a blank. "I think I'll head home, too." He glanced at Violet and Johnny over his shoulder. "I'll drop y'all off on my way and you can go on to the lake or wherever, okay?"

Johnny unlocked his lips from Violet's long enough to say, "Sounds good."

Violet managed to find the breath to speak, at long last. "I have to go home right after the movie. My parents made a big exception, letting me out on a Thursday night."

"You know we have a history exam tomorrow, Johnny, right?" Sam continued. "You wanna come over and study for a while?" Deborah noted he seemed as irritated by the back seat display as she was.

"Nah," Johnny said. "I'm fine for history. I'm going to spend Saturday morning with my *Algebra II* book, though. And we have practice, Red, don't forget. I have to take Kimmie back to Tuscaloosa Saturday after supper."

"But we still have our date tomorrow night," Violet whispered, loudly enough for everyone in the car to hear. "Don't forget that." She kissed Johnny's ear and giggled. Deborah knew from the immediate silence that they were making out again. She willed the car to reach Oxford faster.

When Sam walked her to her door, leaning in for a kiss, Deborah pulled him away from the porch light and did her best Violet-in-the-backseat imitation.

"Wow," Sam said, breathless. "Where did that come from?"

Deborah lowered her lashes and stepped back. "I know you want more from me. You're a guy and it's different for you, and..." she trailed off.

Sam glanced at the car. "It's fine, Deborah. We're fine. We don't have to talk about this now." He offered a brief brush of his mouth against her cheek and turned to go. "I'll call you after practice Saturday afternoon, okay? We'll do something, just us. Maybe a picnic at the lake Sunday."

She nodded and placed a hand on his arm. "And Sam? I don't want to go anywhere with Johnny and Violet again. I know he's your best friend, but the double-date thing isn't fun for me. Those two are in their own little world and don't even notice we're there."

Sam looked at his car and the back of Violet's moonlit blonde hair. He swallowed hard and answered, "You're right. They don't even know we're with them half the time." He shrugged and sighed. "No more double dates, okay, I promise. Well, good night." He pecked Deborah's cheek once more and left her staring from the porch, wondering why Sam ended their evening with two kisses that seemed appropriate for a grandmother, not a girlfriend. She smoothed the skirt of her dress and opened the door to find her parents pretending not to notice she'd been home for a few minutes. As long as it was Sam, they didn't mind.

It occurred to her the Leons and Davidsons had done all but erect a chuppah and throw a veil on her. Everyone was waiting for Deborah to marry Sam.

Except, it seemed, Sam.

Sue had said more than once Deborah needed to make Sam jealous. Maybe she'd tell him about Timothy in her chemistry class, who was practically failing because he looked at her for fifty-five minutes instead of the periodic table on the wall. Maybe Sam needed a reminder she wasn't guaranteed to be his, like some ancient girl traded for three goats. Deborah called goodnight to her parents from the stairs, carefully planning what she'd wear and say the next time she saw Sam, on Sunday.

Saturday afternoon, Sam delivered Johnny to practice and went to change into the shorts and t-shirt his mother despised. He emerged to find Johnny grinning idiotically and waving from the school's office, stealing some time on the phone before practice. He had no doubt Violet was on the other end of that line; it was plain from Johnny's face.

Sam told himself for the hundredth time he was happy for what Johnny had with Violet; that the guy's best friend shouldn't look at her the way Sam did. He tried not to, he really did, but Violet was everywhere: passing him in the hall with her friends; three seats down at the Cool Kids' Table at lunch; two rows away from him in American Lit at the end of every day.

He could never confess how often his mind wandered to his fingers woven into her hair, his thumbs framing her face, asking her for one kiss, just *one*; telling her it was all he'd thought about for much too long, all he asked of her. One kiss. Then he would know if the way she constantly pulled him to her, a fish on a line she didn't even know she'd cast, meant something.

Sam heard Coach yelling for the team to assemble and motioned to Johnny, who nodded and took another full minute to hang up the phone, long enough for Sam to shake his head clear of Violet. He focused on basketball with his steadiest friend since third grade, who'd soon go off to college and leave such a hole in his life in Anniston. Sam threw a playful arm around Johnny's shoulders and they headed to the gym, Johnny whooping and clapping as they entered. Coach stood in the corner, knowing nothing he could do or say could rally his team for practice like the captain they all loved and respected.

Sunday, Sam watched his mother place peanut butter and jelly sandwiches, cheese and crackers, potato chips, four cupcakes, and two bottles of Coke into a woven hamper on the kitchen table. He hugged her side and leaned his head against hers.

"Thank you, Mom. That's pretty much my idea of the perfect picnic basket."

She smiled and patted his arm. "I'm glad you think so. You'll eat some real food when you get home. This is for you to pretend to Deborah you took the time to make it so nice. I couldn't exactly make it look like you cooked a brisket."

Sam rolled his eyes. "Like you wouldn't worry about food poisoning." He reached for the basket and dropped it as the phone rang in the hallway. "I'll get it, Mom. Probably Deborah saying she's running late."

Esther listened to her son answer the telephone in the polite way she'd taught him as a six-year-old, smiling to herself. Sam stopped talking right after that, so she went to the hall to find him sitting slumped on the floor against her rose-print wallpaper, palm to his forehead. Sam raised his eyes, brimming with tears, to his mother. He muttered something Esther couldn't make out and hung up the receiver.

"That was Dr. Perkins. Johnny's been in an accident and he's in the hospital in Birmingham. It was bad, Mom. Kimmie died. His car went off the road last night—"

"Oh, son." Esther wrapped her arms around Sam. "I'll take you. Or your father will. Is he awake? Can he have visitors? How can we help?"

"He's not awake yet. I want to go by myself." Sam straightened and rubbed his eyes. "I told Johnny's dad I'm coming, even if I can't go in his room right away. Johnny will want me to be there. I'll wait in the hall if I have to. I promise I'll be careful." Sam reached to the hallway hook for the keys to the '38 Plymouth Coupe his parents had given him last December, knowing his mother would be terrified at the idea of him driving to Birmingham alone.

Esther's eyes went wide, but she stifled the urge to stop her son. "I'll call Deborah," she said. "Go. Go and be with your friend. Your father and I will be waiting to hear from you. I'm sure Johnny will be all right, Sam. My heart hurts for Dr. and Mrs. Perkins. I can't imagine what they're going through."

"They admitted Mrs. Perkins to the hospital. She's in shock about Kimmie. Dr. Perkins is going back and forth between the two of them."

"Oh, that poor man." Esther shook her head and looked at the floor.

Sam took a deep breath. "I'll try to help, even if it's just making sure Dr. Perkins gets some food or whatever. It'll be good for Johnny if I'm there when he wakes up. He'll be okay." He nodded, as if reassuring himself.

"Has anyone called Johnny's girlfriend?" Esther asked. "Surely they have."

A flood of guilt washed over Sam. He hadn't even thought of Violet, and now every daydream he'd had for months made his stomach churn.

"I don't know, Mom. Will you call their house? They may be at church."

"Right," Esther nodded. "of course. I'll keep trying until I reach them. Don't forget to telephone us from the hospital."

Sam hugged his mother and removed the car keys from their wall hook, rushing toward the front door. He paused for a second and waved, the way he had when the school bus had arrived to pick him up every day of first grade. Esther felt her heart shift in its space.

"I'll be praying, Sam," she called after him. Then she went upstairs to tell Philip everything she'd just learned.

Sam found Violet and her mother sitting in the hall outside Johnny's room. Violet ran to him and he wrapped her in a hug, determined to comfort her no matter how horrible the news she had about Johnny. But there was nothing; a blank canvas to paint all their most awful worries on. Johnny still hadn't awakened.

Violet said, "My dad's upstairs with Dr. Perkins. Come sit with us."

He took a place next to Mrs. Glenn and waited with them in awkward silence, punctuated only by Violet's occasional reassurances—mostly to herself—that Johnny would be fine. They couldn't bring themselves to discuss Kimmie's death or Mrs. Perkins' hospitalization. It was a tidal wave of sadness they tried to ignore while focusing on their hope for the young man lying in the room in front of them.

Sam checked his watch. As minutes crawled past, the tension in the hallway erupted into a fight between Violet and her mother. They argued about future hospital visits; about Violet stepping back and allowing the Perkins family to take care of their son; about Violet's need to concentrate on school; about everything a mother and daughter could under the circumstances.

Sam watched Violet gather herself and announce to Mrs. Glenn that she and he were taking a walk. They passed the nurses' station on their way to the glass doors, Violet's eyes desperately trying to connect with one of the women coming and going from patients' rooms. Sam steered her gently away, knowing no one there could or would be able to tell them anything about Johnny.

They settled on a bench under the broad canopy of a mimosa tree, its fuzzy pink blossoms hanging above them and carpeting the ground. Violet immediately began complaining about her mother, which Sam had suspected was the entire point of their walk. Then he felt a gut-punch as Violet informed him she and Johnny were to be married. It wasn't official yet, but he had to get better so they could begin their lives together as husband and wife after graduation.

Sam pondered his response. His mother had told him from the hospital's pay phone Deborah was hurt Sam hadn't thought to take her with him to Birmingham.

"We'll get Johnny through this. Deborah wanted to come with me, but I told her it would be better to wait until later in the week to visit him."

Violet tilted her head to one side, as if calculating how many times she could get Sam to drive her to the hospital later in the week. They chatted for a few minutes; Sam even made her laugh once or twice. Then it was time to go back and face whatever waited in Room 168.

In the hallway, a small crowd had gathered: Dr. Perkins, Mr. and Mrs. Glenn, and a tall man who introduced himself as Johnny's doctor. After a brief discussion, Violet negotiated her way into Johnny's room, promising simply to hold his hand as he slept. Sam felt, rather than heard, his dismissal.

He drove home with a long-forgotten prayer from Hebrew school, *Mi Shebeirach*, running through his mind. *Bless Johnny with the renewal of his body, the renewal of his spirit*, he prayed.

The next day, Violet begged him, exactly as he'd expected, to drive her to the hospital. He took her along for a brief shift at the store, then sneaked off to Birmingham in the hope news there would be so good, his parents might forgive him.

Violet asked him to give her a few minutes alone with Johnny, waving her hand at the hallway bench they'd occupied the day before. Sam nodded and smiled, catching a glimpse of his best friend, sitting up in bed, eyes open, as Violet entered the hospital room. He placed his head in his hands, rubbing his temples, exhaling a slow *thank you* as he strained to hear their quiet conversation.

The door burst open suddenly, Violet sobbing hysterically, Johnny with his face turned to the wall, his jaw set. Sam stood and she ran straight into his arms.

"What's wrong? Violet, honey…"

Between gasps for breath, she managed to tell him Johnny didn't want to see her. Didn't want to see Sam. Didn't want to see anyone.

"It was so horrible," she cried into his shoulder. "He says he wants to die."

"What? Why? Because of Kimmie?" Sam pushed her away gently, trying to search her eyes as he held Violet by her shoulders.

"Because of Kimmie," Violet gulped for air, as if trying to calm herself, "and because he thinks he'll never walk again. But he will. I know he will."

Sam threw an arm around Violet, glancing back at the door to Johnny's room. He guided her down the hall, determined he'd come back soon and talk some sense into Johnny. He'd be fine with therapy. He had to be. They just had to get through this.

A nurse eyed them walking together and stopped Violet with a light hand on her arm. "Miss, give him time. He needs to adjust to all this. Dr. Deason has arranged for a psychiatrist to see him tomorrow morning."

Violet summoned a smile. "But he will walk again, won't he? He can get better with therapy. I know there are things you can do."

He watched the nurse harden her features and shake her head. "No, there is no possibility. I'm sorry," she replied. The nurse glanced at Sam, who was struggling to process all he'd just been told. She patted Violet's shoulder and added, "He's young and strong. He'll find his way. Pray for him."

Sam swiped at a tear he hadn't been aware was running down his face. Violet watched the nurse enter Johnny's room, and then they walked out to the mimosa tree.

"I don't want to go home," she announced, taking a deep, raggedy breath. "Could we get a cup of coffee? I don't think I could eat anything. The truth is, I could use a cigarette."

She closed her eyes and sighed as Sam produced a pack of Marlboros and lit one for her. That was the day Sam discovered Violet smoked, that she took three sugars and cream in her coffee, and the day he found the courage to ask her to stop using Johnny's nickname for him. "Red" was banished forever in favor of "Sam."

He would come to the hospital in a few days' time, by himself, and talk his best friend back to sense. He'd have Violet back by Johnny's side, and she would help heal and inspire him. Sam didn't care what the nurse had said, he knew there was hope.

There was always hope.

On Saturday morning, Sam located a favorite photo in his yearbook collection, of Johnny and Violet pretending to be jitterbugging between the arches of Anniston High School's entrance. He placed it carefully on the passenger seat and set out for Birmingham, anxious to see Johnny and remind him of all the good in his life, the wonderful things that lay ahead.

The same nurse he and Violet had spoken with earlier in the week spotted Sam and stopped him. "Your friend has been moved to Room 322," she said. "He's in a special unit to help him recover from his injuries."

Sam's face broke into a grin. "So he's doing better? He's going to walk, after all?"

Her mouth fell open. "I'm so sorry, no, I didn't mean that. But Johnny is going to need and receive good treatment to restore his health overall. We learned a lot about spinal cord injuries during the war, and how to help patients with them." She smiled gently. "Go see him. I'm sure he'll be happy for the company. His dad took his mom home this morning."

"Room 322?" Sam said, and she nodded, pointing the way to the elevator.

Johnny looked up and tried to arrange his face into a smile as Sam entered, but it was clearly not authentic. He pushed himself up to a better sitting position.

"Hey, this is a surprise, Red," he said. "Have a seat."

"Whole team says hi," Sam said. "How do you feel?"

Johnny waved his fingers in the air. "Like I look, Red. From the waist up. That's about it." Johnny sighed. "Look, I'm sorry. I don't know what to say to anyone."

Sam swallowed hard. "I am so sorry about Kimmie," he said. "My parents and I went to the funeral. It was very nice."

Johnny blinked. "They wouldn't let me go. I'm not even sure when I'll get out of this place. Thank you for being there. And your folks, too."

Sam wondered if he should say more about the funeral, which was the saddest thing he'd ever sat through. Instead, he offered, "I brought you a photo I thought you might like." He handed Johnny the 8x10 print he'd made.

Johnny took one quick look and tossed it in Sam's direction. "That part of my life is over. I'm not even sure what I'm doing now *is* life. The shrink says it is. He's so much help." Johnny rolled his eyes. "I keep telling him how much I love basketball and running and all kinds of fun things a person with working legs can do. And he tells me I *can* and *will* have a useful life and I *will know joy again.* It's all bullshit. At least admit that to me, Red. You know it is."

"No," Sam said, "I don't. You have a beautiful girl in love with you who wants to be your wife. There are a million things you can do, Johnny, so maybe try to stop thinking about all the ones you can't."

Johnny stared at him.

"Violet wants to see you. I'll drive her over here. I'll do whatever I can to help you, Johnny. Any of us will, in a heartbeat. Whatever you need."

"I don't want your help," he answered. "I want you all to leave me alone. Including Violet. Especially Violet."

Sam shook his head. "Did you have to be so mean to her? She came out of your room with her heart shattered. She didn't stop crying for an hour, Johnny. She cries at school. She—"

"... and I will never be together again," Johnny interrupted. "Look." He drew a deep breath. "Violet is not going to spend her life taking care of me, and before you say a word, that's what it would be. She's seventeen years old, don't you get that? Her whole life is ahead of her."

"Johnny," Sam said, "she wants to be with you. She loves you."

Johnny slapped his palms on the bed. "Damn it, Red, you can't be that stupid. Just stop. I'm not me. The Johnny you knew is most definitely not in this room. I don't even know if I can...if I can have kids." He muttered something under his breath Sam couldn't make out.

"Just let me bring her to see you. I told her I'd talk to you, make you understand—"

Johnny's eyes flashed dark. "No. Don't you dare. I'll make her cry harder than before. I won't have anything to do with Violet. That's over." He bit his lower lip. "And I'd appreciate it if you wouldn't come here, either. I need to be alone. I need time." He turned his face to the wall.

Sam picked up his photo and left without another word, his insides fighting between hurt and anger. By the time he reached home, he'd decided to frame the photo and give it to Violet, a gift to soften his news from the hospital.

When he handed her the box with the photo in it, expertly gift-wrapped by his mother, Sam reminded Violet of a quote from *You Can't Go Home Again,* which they'd both struggled to read in American Literature two months ago.

"Remember what Thomas Wolfe said, Violet. The human mind is incredible in its ability to adapt. Johnny has unlimited capacity to self-heal. He'll be all right, we just have to give him time."

She nodded, tears running down her face as she saw the framed photo. "I really want to believe that, Sam. I remember reading somewhere about how people who are in love dance to the same music in their hearts for a lifetime. So maybe that's what Johnny and I can do instead of this." She ran her fingernail down the jitterbug picture and brought it back to Johnny's smiling face. "I hope he'll let me back in soon. I miss him so much."

"I do, too," Sam said. "We'll all be together again. I'm not sure how long it will take, but I know it'll happen, Violet."

Eleven

RONNI

APRIL, 2020

"I'll be home soon," Rick said.

"I know you will, baby. Everything is fine here. You just concentrate on getting better, and only speak to the ugly nurses." I scratched at a spot on the kitchen table, a tiny drop of chocolate from lunch.

"There's just one ugly one, but I'll do my best," Rick replied. "The rest of 'em, I'll hold signs up for. I'll explain my wife is a jealous and dangerous woman who's inclined to confront them in the parking lot." He coughed a little.

I held up Mikey the Monkey to my screen. "I'm saving this for our daughter's first birthday, and I'm going to tell her you bought him for her, Rick. She needs to understand the taste and refinement she inherited from you."

"I think that'll be pretty apparent the first time she sees me out of uniform, Ronni." I could hear the nurse come into his room. Rick added, "I'm going to put Angelina on the phone. She's fresh from a beauty pageant and holding a bouquet of roses she won along with her sash and tiara."

I could practically see him winking and grinning at her. I missed that smile so much. Rick handed his cell over with a series of bumps and thumps in my ear. My view was suddenly ceiling tiles and fluorescent lights.

"Hi, Mrs. O'Shea," an older woman's voice said. "My name's Tanya and I'm about twenty-five years older than your husband, with six grandchildren, but he's a mighty flirty man. I can only imagine how devastatingly handsome he is in his state trooper uniform."

"Well, he thinks so. Please call me Ronni."

"Ronni, Rick's doing much better. His oxygen level is staying around ninety-two with support. We'll take the cannula out tomorrow and see how he does on his own. He's looking and feeling stronger than his first three days here. Dr. Lehman thinks the dexamethasone is helping him most, and we're carefully monitoring that. But you saw for yourself: he's much friskier today."

I heard Rick laugh, then cough, in the background.

"I'll hand you back to your husband," Tanya announced. I strained to hear her check the machinery in place to treat and monitor Rick, mentally walking through each step as though I were there.

"I wish you could visit," Rick said. "I miss your face. And FaceTime isn't the same. I miss your touch, Ronni. I mean, everyone here has been great, and I appreciate it, but..." he glanced toward the sound of his room's door closing, and shook his head. "I feel so alone in this place. I need you with me."

"I'd give anything if they'd let me in, Rick. I've considered stealing a nurse's ID badge, sneaking in dressed as maintenance crew, or wearing your baggy uniform and trying to look official. I don't think any of that would work."

"Don't you dare. You just stay there and take care of yourself and our baby and let me ride this out. Like I said, I'll be home soon. And," my husband grinned at me, "I'm working on a playlist for when you're in labor. Gives me something to do."

"Shouldn't I be the one deciding what I want to listen to as I endure the agony of bearing your enormous child?" Rick's vinyl collection was a testament to his horrible taste in music: nothing but oldies. He could be downloading anything from the sixties to the nineties. If he was choosing the playlist, I was definitely requesting drugs.

"You *will* thank me. I'm graciously including some newer stuff, and you can't even think of listening to any of it or looking at the titles until it's time. This is all a surprise," Rick said.

I heaved an exaggerated sigh. "I'll stand under your window in a few hours and call you then. I love you so much," I told him.

"I love you more," Rick said, and hung up.

Rick's room was on the second floor of the hospital. I stood in the parking lot, carefully distanced from the eighty-year-old man trying to spot his wife in the array of small, grimy windows above. He was here with me daily, though we'd never exchanged a word. Today he leaned on his cane and stared upward, dejected, as I watched for my husband's face to appear.

Rick walked into view, the most beautiful sight I'd seen in days. He held his phone up and kissed it.

"They let me take the oxygen out for this special occasion. I'm dragging an IV pole around, because Tanya demanded it."

"You listen to Tanya. I can tell she knows her stuff."

"I feel like my butt is hanging out of this gown," Rick said. "I don't want the nurses to see me naked. It'll spoil them for any other man."

"Uh-huh," I answered. "They won't see you naked unless you have them shave your back."

"Very sweet, my wife. You know my back is muscular and devoid of hair. Kinda like Vin Diesel." This led to a coughing spell and I saw the nurse who must be Tanya appear at his side. She waved at me, her eyes above the mask steady on mine as she nodded.

"Just please tell me how you feel, Rick," I said. "All the numbers in the world mean nothing if you're not getting stronger and breathing easier. What did Dr. Lehman say today?"

"He basically said what he says every time. They're giving me all the best-proven treatments and my prognosis is good. And I feel myself fighting this thing off, Ronni. I'll be out of here soon. My biggest problem right now is a headache like you can't imagine. I'm going to ask Tanya here for some morphine." He laughed and started coughing again. "Your next appointment is tomorrow, right? The ultrasound at Aronson's?"

"It was supposed to be, but I have to stay away from their office an extra week, until I'm out of isolation. One week won't make any difference, and we'll have you home in time to go with me."

"I can't wait for that. Can we confirm it's a girl then?" Rick asked, though I'd told him the date a thousand times.

"Yes. But she's a girl, and she has your eyes and your smile and her name is Violet. I know that in my heart. You're going to love her more than me."

"Impossible," he whispered. Rick's voice was getting raspy, and Tanya shook her head at me.

"Okay, well, I have to get home and you need to get back in bed. Go use your charm on Tanya. I like her." I waved and blew a kiss, encouraged to see my husband walking and standing on his own. *Thank you, God.*

I called Deanna and invited her to meet me at the hospital the next day. We could stand six feet apart and Rick would be happy to see her there.

He and Tanya appeared at the window and Rick answered Deanna's surprise call, sweeping his eyes to her. She was wearing her annual Halloween costume, some sort of hideous oversized Mother Goose thing she'd bought long ago to amuse her grandchildren and now donned to hand out candy each year. The old man with the cane stared and broke into laughter, pointing Deanna out to his wife.

I could hear Deanna say, "I know you've always loved a good goosing, and this was as close as I could get." I was so grateful for Deanna's crazy side and the way Rick laughed and shook his head at her from his wheelchair.

But the coughing that followed scared us both. Deanna hung up and I dialed Rick's number.

"I promise to wear my sexy nurse costume out here next time," I told him.

"Save that one for next week when I can fully appreciate it, okay?" He grinned and waved goodbye as Tanya wheeled him backward.

The old man yelled to Deanna and me, "Thanks for the laugh. My wife enjoyed it very much. She's coming home tomorrow." Joy was written all over his face. "Stay safe," he called out, closing the door of his ancient Buick.

For the next three days, I watched my strong, healthy husband fade before my eyes through a dark window with streaks of yellow pollen running down the outside. True to his word, the old man with the cane never returned. It was just me and Rick, separated by thirty feet and a million miles.

On the fourth day, I'd been told our "visit" must be very brief, a minute or two at most.

Rick's breathing was labored; I wanted to cry as he whispered, "Hi, baby" into his phone and waved his fingers. An unfamiliar nurse stood behind Rick and nodded at me; I automatically began to worry for Tanya.

"Hey, you," I answered, glad he couldn't see the anguish on my face through the mask I wore. "You look great. I love you."

"I look like shit, Ronni." He shook his head. "But I feel better after seeing you. How's our little Violet?" he rasped.

"She's fine and can't wait to meet her daddy." I rubbed my swollen belly and smiled up at him. The nurse shook her head, indicating Rick needed to get back in bed. "Rick, you'll be home soon. Keep fighting, baby, for me and your daughter both. You have to be there for this ultrasound. I put it off for a few more days. I'm not doing it without you."

"I'm badder than any bug. You know that," Rick said. Then I heard him struggling to catch his breath.

I blew a kiss at his window as the nurse pulled the wheelchair back. I watched as his face faded from view, willing myself to walk to the car before I collapsed into sobs, banging my palm on the steering wheel.

Everything that led to that moment in my life was faded scenery behind the white-hot anger that blazed in front of it. I'd spent years worrying about Rick being shot with his own gun or ambushed in his patrol car or struck by a speeding vehicle while he stood on the side of a highway. My nightmares never included a virus someone brought to him from across the world, delivered as innocently as the morning mail. His captain said Rick was probably exposed while standing next to one of the myriad drivers he encountered; knowing Rick, he'd been changing a tire or helping someone arrange a tow.

My heart knocked at my ribs as I drove away, forcing deep breaths for the sake of our baby. I glanced at the hospital as I pulled out of the parking lot, praying through my tears for God to save my husband. I'd felt sick ever since the latest telephoned medical update this morning.

"But he's only forty-three!" I'd told Rick's doctor.

"Yes, but he's not responding to the treatments we're giving him anymore, Mrs. O'Shea. Are you aware of any heart issues in his past?"

"No, of course not; we would have told you, Dr. Lehman. There's nothing to suggest a cardiovascular problem. There's no family history."

He paused, and I could practically hear him searching for an easier subject as he consulted Rick's chart. "So, I see here you're expecting a baby. About three months along?"

"Four. Look, doctor, I'm a nurse. I understand your concern about Rick's heart, but there's nothing to indicate a problem. Nothing he or I know of, anyway."

"I promise you, Mrs. O'Shea, we're doing all we can. Your husband is being given dexamethasone, high doses of vitamin c, zinc—"

"What about antivirals?" I interrupted. "Surely there's something you can use to combat COVID-19."

"We're giving him antibiotics, but we don't have approval for any antiviral drugs yet. It could be very dangerous for him if we administer an antiviral that hasn't been tested for this," Dr. Lehman answered.

"What about hydroxychloroquine? I keep hearing that's been successful in COVID patients," I said.

"We can't use it yet. I'm not sure it would have any therapeutic value, anyway. We're following all the standard protocols, the ones that have proven to work, Mrs. O'Shea. I promise you, we're doing everything we possibly can. Hopefully, he'll turn the corner soon. I'll update you tomorrow, okay?"

Driving home on empty streets, I tried to focus on the hurt I felt. The hurt was easier for me to breathe through than the anger. I didn't know if that would ever leave me. Deanna kept reminding me the baby I carried took priority over anything, that her health and safety had to come first. So I prayed to calm myself, to find and hold onto something stronger than me, because nothing in my life felt in my control anymore.

Our bills were piling up on the kitchen table. I spent my time staring at the television, uncomprehending, answering the phone only for Rick, the hospital, or Deanna. Stuck in a surreal routine of tasteless food and restless sleep, waiting for the next time I'd see him through that grimy window.

Eventually, when I stopped answering Deanna, she showed up at my front door and banged her fist until I responded. She backed away quickly, hand to her mask.

"What the hell, Ronni? You have to answer your phone. I have no way of knowing if you and the baby are all right."

"I'm a grownup, Deanna. I'm a nurse. You don't have to keep checking on me. I know everything there is to know about pregnancy and how to take care of myself. Please just go home."

"You look like a month-old wet dishrag, Ronni. Are you even eating? When's the last time you showered?" She stood with hands on her hips, her head tilted, so much like her mother it hurt.

"I'm eating fine. I'll get to the shower thing soon. I really have to go, Deanna." I started to close the door and she yelled loudly enough for my neighbors to hear.

"If you won't take care of yourself, I'll move in here and do it for you!"

I automatically scanned to see if anyone's head was poking out to listen. Our pristine little neighborhood was the gossip capital of the county, and the last thing I needed was a masked, distanced visit from someone down the street. I bit my lip and swallowed, lowering my voice.

"You're not welcome here right now. I need to be alone. Rick isn't any better since yesterday or the day before or the day before that. Nothing else matters to me, and I don't want company." I watched her face fall and added, "I love you, Deanna. Just give me some time. I promise I'll take care of myself and the baby." I closed the door and returned to my place on the couch to watch the latest COVID-19 press conference. Rick's nurse was due to call in another hour.

I jumped at the ring of my phone, startled out of a nap. Rick's nurse Dahlia said, "Hey, Mrs. O'Shea. I want your husband to speak to you for a minute."

As soon as I heard his faint and broken voice, I knew. Every bone in my body froze. Dahlia wouldn't immediately hand Rick the phone if the medical staff weren't planning to put him on a ventilator.

"Ronni," he rasped, "I love you, and I love our little Violet. They're going to hook me up to something to help me breathe better, so I can't call for a day or two."

I closed my eyes and let the tears fall. "I love you more. And you'll only be hooked up for a little bit, babe, you'll beat this thing. You'll come home to us soon."

"You have made my life, Ronni Johnson O'Shea. My life."

It was the last thing he ever said to me.

The funeral was held on a wet, gray day, with Deanna, Rick's captain, his best patrol buddy Brad, Victoria, and Rick's teenaged sons in attendance. We all stood six feet apart, holding umbrellas, watching as my husband was lowered into the ground. No one hugged. No one could grasp another's hand. No one could offer comfort in this hellish landscape; the minister didn't even try. He read some solemn words and made a hasty exit.

I nodded at everyone and thanked them for coming. As I turned to leave, I saw a lone figure standing in the rain, twenty yards away. It was Devonte Green, all the way from Auburn. I watched him dry his eyes and walk to his car. I didn't try to speak to him. I had no encouraging words for him or anyone else, and I was afraid a dam would burst in me if I tried to form some.

Deanna was waiting in my driveway, despite my protests at the cemetery. "Ronni, let me move in with you for a while. I'll wear a mask. I'll stay away from you in the house until we both know we haven't been exposed. But honey, you need someone here with you. You shouldn't be alone right now."

I took a deep breath. "I'll be alone whether you're here or not, Deanna. I can't see anything through this wall of grief. All I want is to climb into my bed. I promise I'll eat, for the baby's sake. But don't ask me to have you or anyone else around right now. I love you, but I can't do it. Please understand."

She looked down. "I wasn't going to burden you with this before the funeral, but Max called and said Elise is sick. They don't have any idea how she might've been exposed, but he's going to take her to be tested tomorrow. Her temperature is running about 101.5 and has been for two days. Of course, she's worried out of her mind; you know Elise."

"She has good reason to be." I turned my back on the dearest friend I had and walked into my house. Deanna deserved much better, but I had no politeness in me.

The stupid, grinning stuffed monkey was sitting on the kitchen table where Rick had left it so many long days ago, where I'd held it up on FaceTime. I threw it into the trash can, heading for the only sanctuary I knew: my bedroom. Making sure the drapes were tightly closed against what little light remained in the day, listening to the rain fall, I kicked off my uncomfortable shoes and fell into bed clutching Rick's favorite shirt, inhaling him, drifting off into a deep sleep where my husband was still with me in this world.

"That key was for emergencies only," I snarled, blinking at Deanna. She had appeared at the foot of my bed in a tan polyester pantsuit that screamed *concerned old lady*.

She sat next to me, scooching me over. "This is an emergency, Ronni. It's been eight days. I know you haven't left this house; haven't gone to your new job—"

"I quit. I called and told them I can't right now." I closed my eyes and wished she'd disappear. "I didn't go to my ultrasound either. I don't want to see anyone or go anywhere. And I most definitely am not going to sit in an office and smile at pregnant ladies while I check their vitals. I can't."

"That's one of the reasons I'm here," Deanna said, smoothing hair back from my forehead. "There are things you need to know, and you refuse to answer my calls and texts. I had no choice but to show up." She cleared her throat. "First off, when's the last time you ate?"

"I ate an entire pizza last night. Helps me sleep."

Deanna heaved a motherly sigh. "I'm going to bring you some vegetable soup. It'll be ready by the time you get out of the shower. Your hair is due for an oil change, Ronni." She shook her head and I surrendered.

I took my place back in bed, my hair dripping on the pillowcase Deanna had replaced. She'd left Rick's shirt beside it, at least. The soup was just hot enough and I found myself truly hungry for the first time in over a week. I slurped a spoonful and nodded a silent "thank you."

"I've been tested for COVID. I made sure I'm negative before I came here," she began.

I shrugged. "Wouldn't really matter to me."

"Stop it, Ronni. I know you're hurting, honey, and none of this is fair, but you have to think of—"

"No, *you* stop it. I don't care about this baby, Deanna. I don't even want it. I don't want to live, honestly." I was satisfied to see her mouth drop open. "I'm a twenty-nine-year-old widow with a baby coming in less than five months. I have no job and no way of knowing when I can return to work. The government is talking about sending me a few hundred dollars to help. How, exactly, is that going to work? Will my mortgage payment magically drop to ten bucks?"

I watched her twist her hands in her lap. "I talked to my cousin, Ronni. Mel's going to arrange for the early release of funds from the estate my mother left you. Your thirtieth birthday is only two months away."

I placed my empty bowl on the bedside table and crossed my arms. "I told you a long time ago, that money is yours, Deanna. The book deadline money and the thirtieth birthday inheritance. If Violet had a way to ensure you'd inherit, she would have. That's what she'd have wanted."

Deanna smiled and patted my leg under the covers. "You're wrong about that. She'd want to help you out of this situation, Ronni. She'd make sure you and the baby were taken care of. And that's what I'm going to do. Max and Elise added me to the trust my father left. I'm doing fine, financially. So you're going to respect my mother's wishes and take this money, to help you along until the world returns to normal."

"The world is never going to return to normal, Deanna." I couldn't hold back my tears any longer. She leaned over and held me as I sobbed into her shoulder. "I can't do this without him. I have no idea what to do with a baby. Rick's experience was supposed to get me through it.

He kept telling me he knew all we needed to know; he'd changed hundreds of diapers and suffered runny oatmeal thrown into his eyebrows…" I couldn't say another word. Deanna just held me tighter for a minute, then leaned back and tilted my chin up with her finger.

"I know how much pain you're in. It won't get better today. It won't be much better next week. But it will get better, Ronni; that ache in your heart will ease with time, I promise you. You'll put one foot in front of the other, as women have always done. You'll be a wonderful mother. There's so much love in you, honey." Deanna grabbed my hand and stroked my fingers with her thumb. "Ronni, think of it: this baby is a part of Rick, a part of him to cherish and nurture and teach and tell all about his dad. Rick will always be here with you. Always."

I sniffed. "I'm pretty sure this is a girl."

"Then you'll see Rick in her beautiful little face, and a host of other wonderful genes from him. She's your future, Ronni."

I took a deep breath. "What else did you have to tell me?"

"Elise got better. She wasn't terribly sick. But Max isn't doing well at all, and I think he's going in the hospital soon." Deanna finally allowed tears to her eyes.

"I'm so sorry, Deanna."

She shook her head and stared at the floor, her voice low when she said, "Please let me stay here with you, Ronni. I can't be alone during all this anymore. Sarah won't come to my house or allow my grandchildren near for fear of exposing me. It would be the best thing in the world for me to take care of you. Let me have that." Deanna reached for my hand again, and I waited a few beats before answering.

I looked at anything in the room but her. I didn't want to see her eyes when I said no. Somehow, though, my mouth formed the word "okay" before I could stop it.

Deanna walked over to a corner chair and picked up a pillowcase. She drew out and held up Mikey the Monkey, tattered and now stained with something that looked like tomato sauce.

"I found him in the trash and fished him out. I know everything in your heart that's tied to this monkey, Ronni, you told me all of it. I'm going to put him in the washing machine. Then I'll store Mikey until you want to see him again."

"I won't. Ever."

"You will, honey," she replied, "I promise you will."

Twelve

ANNISTON, ALABAMA

THREE MONTHS LATER: JUNE, 1947

Sam sat in uncomfortable silence next to Deborah on Jerry Payne's parents' couch. His girlfriend had spent much of their time tonight telling him about the boys who'd asked her to Oxford High School's Spring Formal dance the previous week. Sam wasn't oblivious to Deborah's attempts to make him jealous; he just took a lot of satisfaction in ignoring them.

Now, Deborah was alternately glaring at the beer in his hand and searching the room for someone, *anyone* at this Anniston party she might know. The answer came through the front door in the worst possible form Deborah could imagine: Violet Glenn in a pink sundress, her white heels making her look tall, slender, and more like Lana Turner than Deborah's patience could handle.

She locked eyes with the big lug who escorted Violet into the living room and nudged Sam, asking, "Is that Violet's new boyfriend?"

Sam said, "That's Hugh Parker. He's a linebacker for the Bulldogs and may have a scholarship to Alabama next fall. He's a good guy. I'm sure Violet likes him a lot." He looked from Hugh to Violet and back again. Hugh acknowledged Sam with a slight nod and put his arm through Violet's, preparing to walk over. Sam said, "I'm going to talk to Violet about Johnny, see if she's heard anything from him." He jumped up before Deborah could protest and made a beeline for the queen, who hugged him and stepped back, glancing toward the couch.

Hugh said a few words, no doubt about Johnny, then stood awkwardly as Sam and Violet talked.

Deborah waved to Hugh Parker as if she'd known him all her life. She was rewarded with a return wave and a grin, but Hugh disappeared from view and her stomach churned at sitting alone on the couch in a room full of people she neither knew nor liked. It took two minutes for Hugh to reappear by her side, offering a paper cup of beer, which she pretended to sip. Clearly, he wasn't feeling very attached to his date for the evening.

Deborah did her best to attract Sam's eye to the two of them, Hugh now occupying Sam's seat and reciting a list of all the Oxford High School football players he knew. She hoped Sam thought he was making a declaration of love at first sight instead of blathering about sports. She did her best to look flattered as Hugh described a tackle he'd made at last year's regional playoff game at her school, responding by smoothing her dark hair back with one hand and tilting her head in fascination. Sam turned his eyes from Violet to her and she seized the opportunity to laugh and place her hand on a bewildered Hugh's arm—he'd been telling her about a minor ankle injury that still bothered him from time to time.

Sam was still across the room, talking to Violet, a small group of couples slow dancing between them. Deborah took Hugh's hand and tugged him to his feet, pulling him toward the makeshift dance floor. She didn't notice Sam's immediate decision to walk Violet outside for some fresh air until she was doomed to a gorilla-sized football player box-stepping her to Vaughan Monroe's "Ballerina," an irony not lost on her occasionally trampled toes.

Though she had no way of knowing it at the time, while Deborah was suffering through the dance, Sam was summoning courage from a starlit night and a glass of wine to tell Violet Glenn he'd loved her since sixth grade. He was explaining that, while he cared deeply about Deborah, it was his parents who were *in love* with her. As Deborah and Hugh took their place back on the couch, Sam was confessing he'd asked Hugh to convince Violet to come to the party. As Deborah found an arm casually thrown around her back and a meaty hand rested on her shoulder, Sam was telling Violet her smile was the last thing he saw when he closed his eyes to sleep.

And as Deborah glanced around, wondering why Sam was taking so long to discuss Johnny, he was allowing himself the kiss he'd dreamed of: Violet's soft lips under a canopy of oak limbs as old and gnarled as time itself.

Sam walked back into the party alone thirty minutes later, smiled at Deborah, and motioned to Hugh for a private conversation. They stood out of earshot, but Deborah saw Hugh nodding and was thrilled at the thought Sam was declaring she was his. Sam took her arm and walked her down the street to his car, not uttering a word as she gazed at his profile under a full moon.

When they neared the car, Sam said, "I'm going to drive Violet home, too. Hugh's had too much to drink tonight."

That was when Deborah realized Violet Glenn was already sitting in the back of Sam's Plymouth, where she'd been waiting all along.

She would remember it as the night she lost Sam for months, but not forever. It was a detour he had to make to realize how much in love he was with Deborah. This, she believed and treasured in her heart the rest of her life.

Sam's own mother confirmed it.

Three days after the party, when Deborah was sure Sam wouldn't be home, she called Esther Davidson.

"Sweetie," Esther told her, "Mr. Davidson and I are sure Sam is being rebellious, this thing with Violet. Let me tell you a story. When Sam was ten years old, he wanted a new bicycle more than anything in the world. We told him we'd buy him the fancy Schwinn he'd picked out for his birthday, but that was months away. This is when our store was downtown, and Sam worked in stockrooms even back then for a little pocket money. One day, he left the store and walked over to Western Auto, where he paid the owner all the money he'd saved for a used bike, a bright red one he'd seen in the window. It wasn't the fancy one he'd picked out and dreamed of, but he just had to have the bicycle right then and there. It was flashy and he couldn't resist it."

"Am I a Schwinn in this story?" Deborah sighed.

"Not really," Esther said. "But I want you to know this about Sam. He doesn't always think things through. He can be headstrong and impulsive. Anyway, the owner of Western Auto called Mr. Davidson and asked him to pick the bicycle up and take it home. And my husband told him no, let Sam ride it all the way there. He watched for Sam to leave and followed in his car, just to make sure he was okay. And three blocks from our house, the chain fell off the bike for the first of a thousand times. Mr. Davidson drove up and waved at our son, then continued home in his car. Sam showed up thirty minutes later after managing to put the chain back on. He lived with that red bicycle for three and a half years, replacing the chain and dealing with a bunch of other aggravations, until it wore out beyond use. He got the Schwinn he'd wanted only on his fourteenth birthday. I think he learned a lesson there, but he seems to have temporarily forgotten it."

"I appreciate all that, Mrs. Davidson, but it doesn't make me feel any better," Deborah said. "My heart hurts all the time."

"I know it does, *bubbeleh*. This won't last, though. Sam loves you, and he's been taught from a very early age he'll marry within his faith and raise his children in it."

"I've always known that. It's why I didn't worry too much about Violet. I've seen the way he looks at her," Deborah was crying now, "but she was his best friend's girl, and I thought Sam would be faithful to what you taught him, what we've believed all our lives. I should have known. I feel like an idiot. I never dreamed he'd have anything beyond a friendship with her."

"Deborah, he *will* do that. Staying true to our faith is more important than ever after what just happened to our family in Europe. Sam will choose you. He'll get past this flashy red bike sooner than you think. Give him a few weeks. He'll come back to you, there's no doubt about it. You will be my daughter, Deborah, and our entire family will cherish you. Especially Sam."

Sam and Violet visited his cousin's house in Atlanta weeks after the party. He loved introducing his new girl to Mel and Katie, noting Katie's warm acceptance of Violet as a friend. It was a relief, because Katie had always been so crazy about Deborah, just like the rest of his family.

Mel and Katie watched Sam's car drive away from their house, waving the obligatory Southern see-off until the taillights vanished on the horizon.

"What do you think?" Mel asked his wife.

"He's definitely crazy about her. I told Violet I wish them the best. That's the truth," Katie answered. "But there isn't a chance in hell they'll be happy together. And you know Esther and Phil won't stand for their only son to be with her. They'll tolerate it for a short time. I think Sam will come to his senses when he's through being dazzled."

Mel nodded. "Yeah, maybe. But I have a feeling Sam won't stop being dazzled anytime soon."

Katie frowned. "He's meant to be with Deborah, and you know it. Speaking of whom, I'm going to call her tonight and see how she's doing."

"Katie, don't tell her about this. She doesn't need to know Sam brought Violet here." Mel crossed his arms, a sure sign she was in for a lengthy lawyer debate. Katie smiled at her husband and put her hands on the sides of his face, kissing him lightly.

"Let's go feed the kids and put them to bed early."

"You shouldn't interfere," Mel said. "It isn't fair to Sam. And Deborah's only going to be more upset than she already is. What good would that do?"

Katie pulled the screen door open. "I wouldn't dream of interfering. Deborah's almost like a kid sister to me, Mel. We've spent a lot of time together. It's only natural for me to check on her."

"Checking on her is one thing. Spying and reporting is a completely different one," Mel said, picking his infant son up from a circle of bright plastic building blocks. "Look, Little Mel made a tower." He pointed at three red blocks in a haphazard stack. "This one is smart like his daddy."

"I'm sure he'll grow up to be a lawyer and marry a wonderful woman, just like you," Katie replied. "Sammy, go wash your hands for supper," she yelled at her elder son's room. "And Mel, it's not spying if it's brought into my own living room and paraded around."

"He didn't *parade* Violet around, Katie. That's not fair. Is Deborah even dating anybody?" Mel asked.

Katie looked serious for the first time. "No. She says she only wants Sam."

"Katie, please don't—"

"I'm not interfering! I'm calling a friend for some girl talk. I can really use that, after being locked up with three males all the time. Let's drop the subject, honey." Katie took the baby from her husband and placed him in his high chair. She smiled brightly at Mel and said, "What's meant to be is what will be."

"I agree with that, Katie. You and I were meant to be. But Deborah and Sam…well, that's more complicated. I know you care a lot about Deborah. I do, too. But you have to stay out of it, sweetheart. You'll only upset her with news of this visit. Leave Deborah alone for a while. Let her find someone new. She will, in time."

Katie nodded thoughtfully, biting her bottom lip. "Of course, you're right, Mel. I won't tell Deborah, I promise. But mark my words, this thing with Violet will lose its shimmer and Sam will go back to Deborah. He's infatuated, that's all. When he gets past the blonde hair and the body it's adorning, he'll find there's not much else." She helped little Samuel into his chair and ruffled her son's hair. "Be careful who you fall in love with, son," she told him. "It's the thing that will determine your happiness for the rest of your life."

"He's five, Katie," Mel said, rolling his eyes. "Give the boy some peace."

Samuel reached for the rarely-allowed potato chips next to his turkey sandwich. "When I grow up, I'm going to fall in love with a lady who can cook," he announced.

Mel stopped laughing when he met Katie's eyes, but he added, "Your mother has many other talents, son."

Samuel nodded. "And she is the most prettiest lady in the world."

Mel hoisted his glass of iced tea. "That, Samuel, we can agree on. By far, the most prettiest."

Thirteen

RONNI

June, 2020

"Ronni, you need to eat the blueberries, not just the watermelon," Deanna said. I stifled the urge to thrown one at her.

She and I'd fallen into a daily routine. We'd both get up late, she'd force me to eat fruit for breakfast, we'd sit by the pool in the mid-morning sunshine, and then she'd allow me to go back to bed. It was still the only place I wanted to be. Deanna indulged me until noon or so, when we'd swelter together through a walk around the neighborhood, always with a mask at the ready in case we got close to anyone. Occasionally a golf cart would pass at a strategic distance with children waving cheerlessly, their little faces solemn when they should have been excited about summer vacations and camps.

This was followed by something Deanna deemed a "healthful lunch," usually some kind of grilled chicken breast salad and her idea of dessert, which was more fruit with the tiniest dollop of whipped cream. On Sundays, and only on Sundays, we'd go to the drive-through of her choice for ice cream. None of her efforts kept my pregnancy weight down, probably because of the Snickers bars I devoured for peanut protein.

I was a month late having the ultrasound that confirmed the baby was a healthy girl. We called her Violet from that day on and Deanna was far more excited than I was. She shopped online while I slept; our daily UPS delivery included every lacy, delicate-floral early-twentieth-century-looking pink baby outfit the original Violet might have worn. I was pretty sure Deanna would purchase a Victorian perambulator if she could find one. She wanted to paint the nursery a color called Peony Petal.

All I wanted was my husband back. I saw him in every room of our house. Reminders of our life together surrounded me, bringing me to tears over his favorite spot on the couch; his starched uniforms in the closet; the smell of his cologne; the Valentine's Day cards from me he'd saved in his bedside drawer. Sympathy cards arrived in the mail, and like every delivery, Deanna dutifully wiped the envelopes with disinfectant. My home smelled like a sterile operating room and held just as much warmth for me.

I was a swollen, sad six-month-old incubator. I started spending more time on my phone, scrolling through social media, alternating between the few photos on Rick's Facebook page and spying on other people's lives. There were many who'd been heartbroken by losses to the pandemic. I followed their sorrow with a hunger that embarrassed me. I made Rick's page into a public memorial and checked the messages there hourly; there were plenty from those whose lives he'd touched, which invariably made me cry. Two posts appeared on that page from Gary Harris, "Chet's" son, asking me to get in touch, even listing his phone number for the world to see. I deleted them and blocked him from my account and Rick's, too.

Max spent seven weeks in the same hospital with the grimy windows where I'd last seen my husband. Three of those weeks were on a ventilator. None of us expected him to survive, and Deanna worried constantly on the phone with Elise, but he did.

He was released two months to the day after Rick's death. What had not been apparent to hospital staff was immediately noticed at home: Max would never be fully healthy again, even though he'd had almost a month of physical and occupational therapy. His heart rate soared every time he walked across a room. He was exhausted all the time, always out of breath.

Deanna held her phone up on speaker for me to hear Elise say, "All the doctors tell us the same thing: he needs to rest and build up his strength and lung capacity. But he's not getting better. He can't do anything without his heart racing. I'm terrified. And all they say is that he needs time. The truth is, they don't know anything with this damn disease. It's just that none of them will admit it. I'm trying to get him in to see someone who's studying post-COVID 'dysautonomia,' as they call it, at the University of Alabama hospital in Birmingham. He's not up to making any longer trip than that. But I have to do something, Deanna. I'm watching and nothing is changing."

Deanna looked at me as if I might hold some secret medical truth that would help Max. I shrugged and shook my head. She took her phone off speaker and held it to her ear.

"He'll get better, Elise. The doctor at UAB will probably have some good ideas for Max. I'm sure he's far from the only patient experiencing this." I wandered off to take a nap and missed the rest of their conversation, though I was certain Deanna would tell me every bit later as we shared one of her special "fetus-and-feed-us" nutritional dinners.

Instead, I found I'd left her too much time to think, which was a bad thing. "Ronni," she waved a roasted Brussels sprout at me with her fork, "I think I have a good idea for both you and Max. He needs a nurse. You need a job—"

"I do not need a job," I interrupted. "You have generously seen to that, and I'm grateful."

"Not for money," Deanna said, "although it wouldn't hurt for you to start setting aside for Violet's college. You need a job to occupy you. You're moping around this place all day long, sneaking candy bars and burrowing down a Facebook rabbit hole. It's bad for you, and it's bad for Violet. And Max and Elise have more than enough room for you to move in. I could stay here and take care of your house."

My eyes widened. "*My* house, exactly. Why would I leave my house, Deanna?"

"Because Rick is everywhere you look here, Ronni. You think I don't see the sadness each time you walk through this place, sweeping your eyes over every memory? The way you run your hand over the fabric of the sofa where he used to sit? The way you still glance up with that expectant look on your face when I enter a room, only I watch it dissolve into disappointment when it's me, not Rick?"

I pushed my corn into a pile, refusing to look at her. "I do not. I know my husband isn't going to walk into any room in this house, and that hurts my heart all day long. You said I need time. I'm trying, Deanna. But there isn't enough time in the world." I placed my fork on my plate and stood. "I need to go for a walk. Alone." I struggled to stand, trying to balance my belly with a hand on the table. "And as you can see, I'm in no condition to take care of Max or any other patient."

"That's ridiculous," Deanna said. "Women all over the world work right up until they deliver babies. It's not like you'd have to pick Max up and move him around. He needs a nurse to monitor his blood pressure and heart rate and oxygen levels and all the other things you can do properly. Elise and I already talked about it. You'd be perfect for the job, and she'd feel better having a medical professional in the house. I'm sure Max would, too."

"I'm glad you and Elise enjoyed planning my life for the next few months, Deanna," I called over my shoulder. "I won't be participating, though." I slammed the kitchen door to the garage, angry at the thought they'd talked about me at all. I could only imagine Deanna's whispered worry over my grief—my perfectly legitimate grief at the loss of the love of my life. How dare she minimize it into something she and Elise could cure by keeping me busy?

I stalked down the road to the abandoned gazebo, noticing the fresh wood recently used to repair it at Jinxie Tyler's demand. Had that only been three months ago, when her smile beamed at me from her golf cart as she introduced her son-in-law? I said a prayer for Jinxie's family, sorry she never got to see the finished carpentry on the neighborhood gazebo, the purple hydrangeas blooming next to it, her grandchildren's high school graduations, the entire world stolen from her.

As if my prayers meant anything anymore; as if they were heard anywhere but in my own shriveled heart.

I stood to walk home but sat back down as I spied a girl on a bicycle, her neon-green helmet familiar from visits with her grandmother. She drew toward me and stopped, carefully making sure she was at least six feet away. I saw her glance down the street at Jinxie's house and then she removed and hung her helmet on the handlebars.

"Hi," she said, "I'm Maddie. I met you with my Nana, remember?"

"Yes, I remember, Maddie. I'm so sorry about your Nana. She was a wonderful lady."

Maddie nodded, her eyes shiny with tears. "Yeah, she was. My mom sent me and my little brother over here to stay with Papa. She thinks it will cheer him up. He's so sad all the time."

"Is it working?" I asked, my head tilted.

"Well, Donnie made him laugh when he asked us if we wanted to make something today, like cookies or art projects, and my stupid brother said 'money'. Papa thought that was pretty funny."

I smiled. "Well, he is a banker. That's a kid after his own heart."

Maddie turned her eyes heavenward in an exaggerated roll. "Donnie is a kiss-ass." She paused to see if her language had shocked me. This was definitely Jinxie's progeny, and I couldn't help smiling a little.

"How old are you, Maddie? Fifteen? Twenty?"

"I'm twelve. But I'm precocious."

"I can tell. I can also tell you like big words, as I always have," I told her.

Maddie smiled. "I'm a logophile. My teacher taught me that one last year. And you're a writer. Nana told me. I haven't read your books, though." She looked almost apologetic.

"Well, there's just one book. I went back to nursing after it was published—"

"What was your book about?" Maddie interrupted.

"It's about a lady who was a big part of my life; she was like a grandmother to me. Her name was Violet. That's what I'm naming my daughter, too."

"So, you know it's a girl?" Maddie asked. She nodded at my belly.

"Yes, it's a girl. This is my first baby, and that's about all I know at this point."

Maddie said, "You know what you should write?"

"Please don't tell me what I should write a book about, kiddo. Most authors kinda hate that, Maddie, if I'm being honest."

She summoned another dramatic eye roll. "I wasn't going to. I was going to say you should write a letter to her, right after she's born. My mom did that for me, and it's so sweet. I'll keep that letter forever. She wrote one for Donnie, too, although I've never read it. It's probably full of regrets."

I laughed. "I'll do that. Sorry I jumped ahead of you there. It's just, I hear it all the time, even from patients when I was still nursing. 'You should write a book about whatever,' and it drives me crazy. Writing to Violet is a beautiful idea. I like that a lot."

"Why did you quit nursing?" Maddie locked her blue eyes on mine.

"I loved my job. I didn't quit. I was sent home because—"

"You're going to have a baby," she supplied, nodding her head. "And no one knows what the virus does to pregnant women or their babies. You do look like you might have yours any minute," she blurted. Maddie stood astride her bike, casually swinging the handlebars back and forth and catching them.

I suddenly felt fifteen candy bars gathering at what used to be my waist.

"Feels like it, but I'm only twenty-five weeks along, out of forty. Don't let anyone tell you a baby comes in nine months. It's forty long weeks, sometimes forty-two. With my luck, it'll be forty-five."

Her face went solemn. "I'm sorry about your husband, Mrs. O'Shea," she said, taking my breath away. I hadn't expected her to know.

"Thank you, Maddie. He was a very good man. Seems like we've all lost someone."

She cocked her head to one side. "My mom is having a really hard time. I think that's why she sent us over here, because she still cries all the time about Nana. Donnie and I are a lot to keep up with, especially since we haven't been to school in forever, and Mom probably needed a break. I didn't want to come, because what are we going to accomplish for Papa, right?" She glanced back at her grandfather's house again.

"Right. But I'm betting it's good for him to have you two around."

"Well, Mom left it up to us, the way she does when she wants us to *choose what will make me proud*, as she loves to say. Donnie wanted to come anyway, because Papa will order pizza for any meal we want, even breakfast. But I said yes because it still hurts so much when I think of Nana, and I remembered one of her favorite sayings, something she told me I should never forget." She drew a deep breath and exhaled. "When you're hurting, the best way to make yourself feel better is to help someone else. So I'm here, trying to help Papa, like she'd want me to."

"Jinxie was a smart and beautiful woman, Maddie, and you're going to be, too. Gosh, you remind me of her a lot. I wish I could give you a hug."

"Yeah, me too. I miss hugs. But this pandemic isn't going to last forever, and you should focus on that," she announced, replacing her helmet. "I'd better get back and see what Donnie's up to. I have to keep a close eye on him. He's only eight, but he has the destructive power of ten boys."

"Hold on," I said. "Wait a minute. I just realized your name is Maddie Love. Mad Love. Seriously? That's a show business name, maybe a singer or rap superstar."

One last eyeroll. "Muffy and Huel are my aunt and uncle. My mom is Darcy Tyler Reid. Maddie Reid. Not nearly as exciting, huh?"

"No," I replied, "but if your brother encounters any student of ancient TV history, they might tease him about Donna Reed."

"Believe me, there's much more to tease Donnie about than that." She wheeled her bike around and took off, waving back down the street as she pulled into the distant driveway.

Deanna met me at the door. "I'm sorry, Ronni. I didn't mean to push you."

I hugged her. "I know you didn't. You mean well, and Elise does, too. I'm just not ready. I can't help Max or anyone else until…" I stopped mid-sentence and looked out the window at the quiet street beside my house.

"Until what?" Deanna said.

"Nothing." I shook my head and started toward the stairs and my bedroom sanctuary.

"Ronni, will you at least think about it, honey? I hate to see you like this."

I paused on the landing, halfway up.

"You know," Deanna said, her eyes looking into mine, "the best way to heal is to help someone."

I sighed. "Sometimes it's like I'm being bombarded with messages from beyond."

Deanna smiled. "I'm not sure what you mean by bombarded, but maybe you should listen to them."

I nodded. "Maybe. Right now, I'm going to lie down."

Fourteen

ANNISTON, ALABAMA

1947

Violet stared at the ceiling of Sam's bedroom, suddenly too shy to meet his eyes. What had just happened—the things Sam had done to her body; the earthquake he'd summoned from her—was nothing like her brief experience in the back seat of Johnny Perkins' car.

She glanced at Sam, whose eyes were fixed on her, an amused smile on his face. She couldn't know he was silently thanking his cousin Mel for a stack of books full of ideas he'd never have conjured on his own. He was also silently thanking his parents for their trip to New York this weekend, their second in as many months. They wouldn't return until Tuesday, which meant he and Violet could be together as much as they could sneak past Mr. and Mrs. Glenn.

"You really are the most beautiful woman in the world, Vi," he told her. It's what he'd said the first time they'd been alone in this house, when his parents left the month before. "But that's only what drew me to you. Now I know all there is to love in you. I know the way you treat that poor kid you babysit, the ways you try to help him out. I know how you hug Corinna as often as your own mom, probably more, and that you baked cookies for her grandchildren last week. I see the way you listen to your friends when they come to you with their problems, really listen to them, and go out of your way to make them smile. You may be Homecoming Queen for the way you look, but you should have a tiny tiara for your heart, Violet Glenn."

There were tears in her eyes. "I love you, Sam. I only wish we hadn't hurt Deborah with all this. She's a good person. She deserves better."

"And better is what she'll get. Deborah will be much happier with someone else. She just doesn't know it yet."

Violet sat up, clutching the sheet to her chest. "I think I know someone Deborah might like. I could tell him to give her a call. He's actually my cousin, Randy Glenn, and he loves to dance. He graduated from Heflin a couple of years ago, but he lives in Anniston now, working at Bynum. He has a great job there. And he's really cute—"

"Violet," Sam placed his hand on her arm. "That's very sweet of you, but Deborah won't go out with anyone who's not Jewish."

Violet frowned. "But you're with me, and I'm not. Mel's married to Katie, and she's not. I don't understand."

Sam sighed. "I'm going to have to talk to my parents soon. They think you and I are only a fling, probably over by the end of summer; that we'll go our separate ways when I start college this fall. I know my mother, especially, believes I'll go back to Deborah. They don't realize I'm already…" he trailed off, closing his eyes.

"Already what?" she asked, her hand reaching for his face.

"Thinking about marrying you, Vi. I've never felt this way in my life. I sure didn't expect to, at least until I was thirty. You've messed up my bachelor years completely."

She lay back down and rested her head on his arm, snuggling against him. "We're so lucky, Sam. We were two feet apart for much of our lives without ever knowing we were supposed to move closer. You make me so happy."

He kissed the top of her head. "You make me delirious," he said. "And hungry. Let's go raid the kitchen naked."

Violet laughed. "I'm not delirious enough for that. Not yet, anyway. This is your parents' house. Maybe in our own kitchen someday."

"Deal." Sam stood and hurried into his clothes. "I'm going to cook for you, madam. How do you feel about scrambled eggs?"

"Less than delirious, but fairly cheerful about them," Violet answered. She hesitated a few seconds before adding, "Sam, did you really mean that? About marriage?"

"When I've made up my mind, Vi, you'll be the first to know. I'll get on one knee and beg you for your perfectly exquisite hand, and promise to buy you a ring worthy of it someday. Because I sure can't afford it now."

"So, you'll ask my dad first?" Violet nodded as she pulled on her skirt.

Sam shook his head, thoughtful. "Probably not. If you and I marry, it might be best if we elope. Your dad may not be as enthused about me as you are, Vi. Katie and Mel eloped. Then they had a party later, with people from both their families. And actually, that might be a better plan than talking to my parents about you. I'd rather just introduce you as my wife."

"Are you serious about all this?" Violet asked. "Because if you're not, it'll be the worst thing that's ever happened to me. And that's saying a lot, Sam."

Sam paused for a minute. Then he threw his arms up with a small laugh, dropped dramatically to his knees, and crossed the room on them in a comical shuffle. He reached for Violet's hand.

"Violet Glenn, will you promise to marry me, as soon as I can arrange a surprise trip to a romantic place where you'll find it impossible to change your mind?"

She fell to her knees and hugged him, then answered with a long, deep kiss.

"You really mean it?" Violet whispered. "How soon?"

"Soon. I'll look into tickets and places to stay. Maybe in a month, two at most. Is that soon enough for you to be Mrs. Sam Davidson?"

"I already am, in my heart."

Weeks later, Philip and Esther Davidson stood in their living room, folding German military uniforms carefully, inserting sheets of tissue between each crease.

"I think this is the right thing to do," Philip said. "His collection is already extensive, and someday it will all be in a magnificent museum. I don't know Farley Berman well, but he and his wife seem like great people. You should see their basement, Essie. It's packed full of all kinds of weaponry and uniforms. They have a silver tea service that belonged to Hitler, can you imagine such a thing? He has personal photographs from Mussolini's collection; two he says were on the dictator's bedside table. When I saw all that, I knew it's where the uniforms should go. I'm proud to donate them."

"Who would want to own Hitler's tea service? He should melt it down and make Kiddush cups." Esther frowned and shook her head. "I'm proud of you for doing this, Phil, but I still think you could put the museum together yourself."

"I could never do it on the level this man will. Do you know he and his French bride were spies in the war? At least, that's what people say. He won't talk about it, but I know he was a colonel in the Army. Before that he was a successful lawyer in Atlanta. Then after the war, he brought his new wife to his hometown, Anniston. If they hadn't opened that ladies' wear store on Noble, I might never have met him. Everyone, in fact, calls him 'The Colonel' in Berman's. It's a nice place, too, Essie. You'd like their fashions."

Esther looked at the ceiling. "As if I'm allowed to shop anywhere else."

Philip shrugged. "You're my best model, what can I say?"

"Sure," Esther said. "So, have you told your son why we keep going to New York?"

"No. I'm waiting until the final papers are signed, and I'll introduce it gently. Sam still thinks he's going to start his career in the Anniston store, where everything is so familiar, it's practically a part of him. But Essie, we weren't even sure until yesterday whether this deal would go through in New York. So, when it's absolutely solid, I'll talk to Sam. I'll tell him we have a few months here, and soon after he and I will be hosting the grand opening of our flagship location on Fifth Avenue. I can hardly believe it myself. Sam will be so excited. And this will give him an opportunity to study business at Columbia or NYU while he's working in Davidson's. We can't match that in Anniston."

Esther's frown returned. "He hasn't even applied to those schools, Phil. This is all so rushed. And it's a lot to surprise him with, however gently you think you're introducing the idea."

Philip nodded at his wife. "We talked about this. If Sam wants, he can stay here and attend Jacksonville State, live there in the dorm. He's already accepted for this fall. He'll have that choice; I just don't think he'll pass up New York." He took her hand. "And whose idea was this rushing, Esther? Whose idea was hiring Andrew Leon to be our chief financial officer for the new company?"

She shrugged. "We trust Andrew, and he's an excellent accountant. But I agree that part was serendipity. We had no idea the Leons had relatives on Long Island."

"For that matter, we had no idea this store, which is so perfect, would come on the market. We'll never find another deal like this, Essie. And if Sam doesn't get into business school at either of those places, there will be others all around us. He can even wait a year, get his feet wet at the new store. And maybe he just learns on the job, after all. Sam doesn't necessarily have to go to college."

"It's just," Esther sighed, "I feel like you're ignoring the elephant in the room. The blonde, teenaged elephant. Sam may not want to leave for New York in three or four months. He seems crazy for this girl."

"I think when Deborah moves away with her family in two weeks, it's going to wake Sam up. He loves her, Esther. He always has."

Esther shook her head. "I know he'll come to his senses, but I think it's going to take longer than you expect. He hardly notices anything in the world but this Violet right now. I think it's one of the reasons Deborah immediately said she wanted to move with her parents. He's made her miserable."

Philip sat down next to the last of the uniforms. "And what about you, my darling? We've lived here all our lives. Will you truly be happy, moving so far away?"

"Only if Sam comes with us; if he doesn't choose to stay and go to college here, which would kill me." Esther took a deep breath. "I can't imagine him deciding on that, though; he's been hearing you talk about opening a flagship store in Atlanta or New York since he was little. It's become part of his dreams, too."

"You'd be all right in a week or two. Mothers have been sending their sons off to be educated forever, Essie, you'd adjust." Philip patted the uniform next to him. "We should be grateful we're not sending him off to war." He paused after seeing the storm brewing on his wife's face, then added, "But I feel sure Sam will want to move with us."

She waved her arms at their living room furniture, looking wistful. "We'll still have this house. We'll travel back and forth. I'll definitely miss some people, but we're taking the Leons with us, and we've been friends forever. All those vacations over the years, all those dinners, all those hours on the beach. This will be the biggest adventure we've ever shared." Esther paused, thoughtful. "I'm excited, honey, you know I love New York. I think the change will be wonderful for every one of us. But if it isn't, our Anniston store will be waiting. It'll be in good hands with Gene Stewart running it. We can always come back here to live. We could leave someone in charge of the New York store."

"That's true. You know, it's been a long time since we've discussed the possibility of a store in New York. I hope Sam will be as enthusiastic as we think." Philip raised his eyebrows.

"A few months ago, I'd have said he'd be ecstatic. Now, he's so focused on this girl, he may not think moving is so wonderful. But Phil, we have at least three months before we go. We can fly him up there, show him the new store, the bright lights, the restaurants, Broadway, the apartment…I think Sam will be more dazzled by that than this Violet. He'll see that's his future, the one he's been working for all his life."

"What if she wants to move to New York to be with Sam? Have you thought of that?"

Esther collapsed onto the sofa next to her husband. "No, I hadn't." She folded her hands in her lap and sat staring at the uniforms neatly piled on a floral armchair. "I don't think she would do that. This is her home. She's a popular beauty queen in Anniston. Her parents are here. Her entire life is here. New York wouldn't be appealing to an eighteen-year-old who's used to being worshiped in her Southern hometown. Too scary, too uncertain, too big a pond for that pretty little fish. Even with Sam. They've only been dating for a couple of months, so I don't think it'll be that big a deal to him. She's…an experiment. A detour, is what I told Deborah."

"Well," Philip sighed, "I guess we'll find out when we tell him, after the papers are signed next week." He got up and placed the pile of Nazi uniforms into a cardboard box, happy to be rid of them. How long ago it seemed since he'd sat in the backyard watching flames consume the first one. He'd thought it made him feel better.

Now, Philip Davidson felt genuine happiness. He'd worked hard to secure this future for Sam. His family would grow and prosper in New York, but they'd always have their Southern roots, the warmth of this smaller town waiting for them whenever they needed it. He had strength and hope, things lost to him during the war.

The next day, Sam visited Anniston's train station to purchase two coach class tickets to New Orleans for the coming Friday. He reasoned a relatively brief trip in coach would be redeemed by the three-night stay he'd arranged at the Hotel Monteleone, the poshest place he could find in the French Quarter.

He and Violet had seen the movie New Orleans at the Ritz Theater when they'd first become a couple. Violet had giggled at the movie's "Torchy! Scorchy!" posters as they'd walked up to the ticket booth.

"Are you trying to ruin my reputation?" she'd asked, tucking her arm into his. He'd watched her tap her feet along to Louis Armstrong and his band, excited as a little kid. Her eyes lit up with the first beats of every jazz song in the movie.

Best of all, Mel recommended New Orleans as the place he and Katie had eloped and honeymooned for a week. That was all Sam needed to hear to forget Charleston, Tampa, and Memphis, his other choices.

By the time his parents found out, it would be too late to stop him from marrying the girl of his dreams.

Fifteen

RONNI

JULY, 2020

The nurse, Kristin, asked Max questions about his symptoms for a solid twenty minutes, then placed her tablet computer on the exam room's counter and checked his blood pressure and pulse rate for the second time. I couldn't see the numbers she recorded. I knew they were high, but her face betrayed nothing.

"Dr. Garland will be in to see you soon. Please make yourself comfortable, as comfortable as you can be in that mask, Mr. Davidson." Kristin swept her brunette bangs back and seemed to realize she'd touched her face, moving to wash her hands after the fact, offering a hidden smile that reached her dark brown eyes. "Do you feel like you're breathing okay right now? We can get you a clear face shield if you'd prefer it." Her scrubs featured tiny magnolia blossoms and glasses of sweet tea. I wanted an opportunity to ask where she'd bought them, but Max spoke.

He pulled his mask down and rewarded her with one of his trademark grins, still undimmed by illness. "Are you married, Kristin?" he asked, replacing the mask quickly before she could scold him.

Elise shook her head slightly and her mouth flattened into an unamused line. If her husband wanted to flirt with a pretty nurse in her twenties, I thought it was a great sign. He'd lost eighteen pounds and a great deal of muscle mass in the hospital. This was the first glimmer of the old Max I'd seen since picking them up today.

"I'm not," she said.

"You're a stunning girl." Max glanced over at Elise.

"It looks like you already have a beautiful wife," Kristin said. Her tone was kind and warm. I suspected patients asked about her marital status all day.

"Oh, I'm not asking for me. We have a son about your age. He hasn't had a girlfriend since we moved down here. Of course, no one is dating during the pandemic. But I'm sure he'd like to meet you when all this—"

Elise jumped in. "You'll have to forgive him, Kristin." She patted Max's shoulder. "He's been cooped up too long."

Kristin laughed and closed the door. We began listening for footsteps approaching, the way you do when shut into an examining room. There were no magazines, no reading material of any kind, I noted.

Do not touch, do not breathe without a mask, do not relax.

Elise turned to me. "Thank you so much for coming along. I'd never have found this place without you. And I'm counting on you to understand whatever this Dr. Garland says and translate it later. Forgive me for telling them you're Max's full-time caregiver. It was the only way they'd allow both of us to come back here."

I shrugged. "I understand. I'll try. I don't know much about post-COVID syndrome, so I'm hoping he has answers." I stood and held my fingers to Max's wrist. "His heart rate is about a hundred and ten beats per minute now, but it was one-ninety after we walked down the hallway. Surely there's a way to control this." Max blinked at me and looked away.

"But what's causing it? That's what I want to know. The doctor in Anniston sure couldn't tell us." Elise settled into a hard plastic chair near the door and crossed her arms.

"Well, in the short time doctors have been treating post-COVID patients, there've been a lot of inexplicable symptoms. This guy has been studying it at UAB. I'm sure he'll have insights to offer. I'm hoping for medication to help."

Elise said, "The doctor in Anniston gave him something called Tenormin, and it made Max so nauseated we had to stop it after two days." She glanced at her husband, who looked like he was on the verge of falling asleep sitting on the exam table. "Max? Max, honey?"

"Yeah," he answered, his eyes still closed. "I'm fine."

Elise's face showed how little she believed that. She smiled at me across the room, trying to look calm. "It means the world to have someone we know and trust to help process all this today. And I know you're still hurting so much. I wish there were something we could do for you."

I sighed. "Deanna's usually right, and she was about this. It's better for me to be here than wandering around the house all day between naps. Today's good for me, too, Elise. Yesterday I found an old note Rick wrote, stuffed in the kitchen junk drawer, telling me he'd be back from the store in twenty minutes. It was on the back of a business card from some plumber. I needed to get out of there."

I could see her fighting the urge to cross the room and hug me, which would have been the most natural thing in the world a few months ago. Now, we sat six feet apart, friendly hugs a distant memory.

Max began to cough. After several seconds, I could see the fear in his eyes; the first time I'd considered the memories he carried from the hospital and the terror that accompanied them.

He's like me. There's no place to hide except sleep.

He managed to catch his breath as Dr. Garland knocked perfunctorily on the door and swept in. He was a short, heavyset fireplug of a man in his forties, bald head shining in the overhead lights, wearing a bright pink and orange flowered mask that looked very seventies-retro over his N-95.

"Hey, Mr. Davidson, I'm Dr. Garland," he said, removing gloves and washing his hands before he donned a new pair. "I hear you're looking for the most handsome doctor on our staff. I'm sorry to keep you waiting." He plopped onto a stool and wheeled himself over to Max, his head tilted as he looked at Max's face. "Your chart says your heart races often. Is it the mask my daughter made me or these blue eyes making it race now?"

I liked him immediately.

Max offered a half chuckle with no mirth behind it. Dr. Garland immediately assumed a more serious tone, glancing at the laptop he'd carried in. He placed his gloved fingers to Max's wrist.

"I want you to lie down for me, Mr. Davidson, while we chat for a few minutes." He eased Max's head and shoulders back and continued, "I'd like to ask you a few more questions, and I know Kristin already asked a million, but it's important. I also know you're tired, and this visit is taking a lot out of you. I'll get through it as quickly as possible, okay? First of all, have you noticed any pattern to when your heart seems to speed up?"

Max looked confused and glanced at Elise. She shook her head.

"I'm not sure," she said. "It happens all the time. The other doctor gave him Tenormin. We never found out if it worked because it made my husband nauseated. He already has no appetite as it is."

Dr. Garland nodded. "Food tastes funny?"

Max shrugged and nodded. "More like food doesn't taste at all."

"Other than that, any gastrointestinal problems?"

"Not really," Max said.

"I'm prescribing milkshakes and sundaes for you, then. That's what I wish someone would prescribe for me." Dr. Garland drummed his fingers on the exam table, studying Max.

He turned back to Elise. "Did the other doctor suggest a different medication, instead of the Tenormin?"

"He suggested we come to UAB. He said he wasn't sure what would be best for my husband." Elise crossed her arms. "We haven't gotten much help."

Dr. Garland scooted away from Max, who had closed his eyes and might be napping, as far as I could tell. "You're Mr. Davidson's home health nurse, right?" He nodded at me. "It said 'Ronni' on his chart, I think."

"Yes, Ronni, but I just started," I answered. "I'm not familiar with his history. All I can tell you is, his resting heart rate was about a hundred and ten before you walked in." *And I'm only here because Elise begged me to come along.*

Dr. Garland bit his lower lip and scooted back to Max. "Mr. Davidson, I know you're still fatigued. You've been through a tough battle many didn't survive. I'm not gonna lie to you, we're still figuring out how to treat 'long COVID' patients with symptoms like yours. And please understand, when you hear people on the news talking about 'long COVID,' it doesn't mean you still have the virus. Some patients have symptoms after they recover. The insomnia and anxiety, I can help with that. There are prescriptions. The sweating and chest pain may improve when we address the anxiety. Have you had dizziness? Do you ever feel like you're going to faint?"

Max's eyes snapped open. "I *did* faint last week. I was getting out of bed and—"

"Max! Why didn't you—" Elise caught a glance from Dr. Garland and stopped.

Dr. Garland continued. "Some of my colleagues are treating the dysautonomia—the malfunction that's making your heart rate go up and down—with traditional drugs like Inderal or Lopressor. In my opinion, that can hurt more than help."

Max shook his head. "I already feel weak all the time. And the confusion, it's like I can't remember what I'm saying halfway through a sentence. Scares the hell out of me. I really don't want to add to all that with drugs." He looked at Elise, with whom he'd clearly not discussed much of this. "I just want to know when it's going to end," he added quietly, "*if* it's going to end."

Dr. Garland put his gloved hand on Max's arm. "We'll get you through this, Mr. Davidson. I don't have an exact timeline, but you *will* get better."

"Why the cardiovascular stuff, though?" Max asked. "My heart's always been strong. I ran the New York City Marathon twelve years ago. I've never had high or low blood pressure. I just want someone to give me a straight answer. How badly is my heart damaged?" His eyes were shiny with tears. He looked down at Dr. Garland's hand holding his wrist.

"No one's talking about heart damage, Mr. Davidson. Let me explain," Dr. Garland said. "When the typical person stands up for a while, blood tends to pool in their legs and lower abdomen. The body detects this and their system releases epinephrine to speed up the heart and increase blood flow." He reached for Max's other arm. "That works perfectly. But in some patients after this virus, the epinephrine and other things are off kilter and too much, so the heart rate soars. Now, I'm going to pull you into a standing position and ask you to stay there for three minutes, okay? I'm not letting go, and I'm stronger than I look." He turned to me. "Ronni, would you please get your phone out and set a timer for three minutes?"

Dr. Garland pulled Max up and held him in place. He looked fine at first, but after a minute or so, Max closed his eyes and frowned.

"Your heart rate is already up," Dr. Garland said. "Are you having chest pain?"

"Yeah," Max gasped, "and I can't catch my breath. I need to sit down."

Dr. Garland eased Max back onto the exam table. "You're going to be okay, Mr. Davidson. Your heart is still strong; I have the recent medical records from your cardiologist to prove it. But, as you just saw, your body is overcompensating when you stand up, especially after you've been in a prone position. That's why your heart is racing. And

I know it's as scary as a six-year-old's walk to the principal's office. But there are some things we can do."

"The other doctor told me to rest, and drink a lot of fluids," Max said. "That hasn't helped."

Dr. Garland patted Max's arm. "The fluid part is spot-on. And you do need to take it easy. But bedrest isn't good for you. We're going to get you into some high-waist compression stockings that won't look very manly, but they'll serve a purpose. We'll give you some exercises that Ronni can help you do. You don't have a recumbent bike available, do you?"

I opened my mouth to protest, but remembered I was only in the room on the pretense I had a job as Max's caregiver. Elise smiled at me and then Max.

"We can get a recumbent bike," she said. "I'll have one delivered and set up downstairs."

She and I exchanged glances, and I knew she'd be shut in her bedroom when this delivery happened, probably directing the young and healthy Samuel to admit the person doing the setup. She'd likely produce a hazmat suit for him, though.

"Ronni," Dr. Garland turned back to me, "monitor his heart rate and chart it for your next visit, please. And keep an eye on his pulse ox. Blood pressure, too. Anything too wild, call me immediately. I'll need you to see how he responds to the alprazolam, but it's only a quarter milligram. Should be fine. I'll get Kristin to bring you a written prescription. We might try fludrocortisone if we're not making progress, but I'd like to hold off on that."

I blinked.

"Okay," Dr. Garland nodded at Max, "no alcohol, and I'd rather you not drink coffee for a while. Lots of water, and healthy food to go with those milkshakes. I don't really care about your salt intake; it might actually do you some good, so have some potato chips here and there. Sleep with an extra pillow for a little elevation, and keep some water by your bed. Drink as much as you can, especially before you get up in the morning." He paused to watch Max nod his head in understanding.

"When you go to stand up," Dr. Garland continued, "do it slowly and make sure there's something you can grab nearby if you need to. You'll have this chart of isometric exercises," he pulled a piece of paper from a drawer, "and you need to do them every day. Every single day, no matter what, all right? It's simple stuff, but it'll help you.

"Kristin will be in soon with paperwork explaining the schedule for the recumbent bike, which will increase slightly with each session. After two weeks of that, I want you to start walking short distances, preferably in the sunshine, and always with Ronni at your side. You'll also leave here with a list of local places to buy the high-waist compression stockings, which are usually black. You'll wear them until you feel like you're ready to star in a cabaret, but put up with it. Fight the urge to pose dramatically with a bistro chair and sing with a German accent."

Max laughed and coughed. "You really think all this will help?"

"Give it two months. I'd bet my youngest child on it," Dr. Garland said. "But he's the one I don't really like." He grinned and patted Max on the back. "You've been through a lot. Be gentle with yourself. And be grateful you're still here with your beautiful wife." He nodded at Elise. "I'll see you in eight weeks. Let me know if I'll be surrendering Geoffrey. He's two and a screamer."

It was the first time I fought back tears that day, watching Dr. Garland joke his way out of the room. Rick would have loved him. It was also the first time I saw a path forward. I wrapped my arms around my belly and hugged Violet.

Maybe this is where we're supposed to be.

Two weeks later, as Deanna had known I would, I was living with Max and Elise in Oliver's hastily redecorated room. My twin bed had an ivory comforter and still sported Spider-Man sheets when mine were being laundered. I would have preferred Ollie's posters to the pastoral scenes and *Live, Laugh, Love* décor Elise hastily ordered online.

Max was a compliant patient, eager to do the exercises Dr. Garland had ordered. He grumbled constantly that "nothing is changing," but I could see the tiniest improvements in both his vitals and stamina. When he was finally ready to begin walking outdoors, it was only a few yards up and down the level sidewalk. Even that, without chest pain and shortness of breath, was a huge victory.

"Thank you, Ronni," he said. "It's so good to feel the sun on my face again."

I nodded at him, opening the front door to go back inside. "Best medicine there is."

"I think it may be working for you, too." Max's grin was still beautiful. It faded as he looked at me closely. "Ronni, like me, it'll take time. Give yourself time."

"That's what everyone says. And it's good for me to be here with you, I know that. I needed a purpose, something to get me out of bed every morning. I've missed my patients, too. I still do."

Max laughed. "I'm not old enough for you? Insufficient decrepitude?"

"They were all sweeter." My phone rang and I answered it automatically, because Deanna was the only person I could imagine calling. Max settled onto the black living room sofa and blatantly eavesdropped.

"No. How did you even get my number?" I said.

Max's brows shot up.

"Don't call me again. I'm not interested." I shoved the phone into my pocket and reached for Max's wrist, dutifully recording his heart rate for the app on my phone.

"Damned telemarketers," Max said. "I hate 'em."

I sat opposite him. "Not a telemarketer. You read my book, right? That was Chet Wilson's son, trying to get me to clear his daddy's name, which was a pseudonym in the story, anyway. It's ridiculous. I thought he'd have given up by now. Rick told me a long time ago not to answer his emails. Now he's gotten ahold of my cell number. I'll have to change it."

Max nodded, thoughtful. "Know what you should write a book about?"

"Don't make me poison one of your milkshakes, old man."

Max laughed. "I know how much you hate that. But seriously," he took a big gulp of water. "it's about time you learned the truth behind some things in that book you wrote. Maybe it wasn't as fair to that guy's father as you thought."

I stared at him.

Max offered his trademark grin. "We have weeks to spend together here before the baby's born. Lately I've had a lot of time to think." He smacked his palms on his knees. "What the hell," he said, shaking his head. "Ronni, I know a lot from both my parents and even my *Zayde* Phil. They all loved to reminisce about Alabama. Maybe it's time to tell their stories, even the ones that aren't so pretty."

Sixteen

ANNISTON, ALABAMA

1947

The call came as Esther was cooking breakfast for Philip; Sam was already off to the store. She would always remember she was frying eggs and had to turn the stove off to grab the wall phone and cradle its handset against her shoulder, knowing the cord wouldn't reach far enough for her to continue cooking.

"Mrs. Davidson?" a boy's voice asked.

"Yes, this is Mrs. Davidson."

The kid cleared his throat. "This is Chet Wilson at the Anniston Train Station ticket office. My dad runs the station here. He asked me to call because Mr. Davidson's secretary said y'all needed the schedule for your son Sam and his passenger to New Orleans tomorrow. It's the Southern Crescent at 5:15 p.m., on Track 2. They'll arrive in New Orleans at 7:38 a.m. Saturday."

Esther stood with her mouth open.

Chet filled the silence with, "They'll come into the Southern Railway Terminal on Canal Street, ma'am. It has a beautiful lobby for y'all to meet them."

Esther said, "I'm sorry, I believe you have the wrong number," as Philip entered the kitchen and picked up *The Anniston Star*, unfolding its pages and shaking them into place as he settled at the breakfast table. She heard him mutter, "King George's daughter Elizabeth is marrying that Greek guy. Hmm."

"No, ma'am," the kid persisted, "your son Sam and his passenger have tickets on that train. And I double-checked the schedule for you. The *Crescent* should be on time. It almost always is."

Esther held her hand over the mouthpiece and hissed at her husband. "Phil, come here and talk to this boy." She handed the phone to Philip and turned to resume her egg frying.

"Are you sure?" she heard Philip say. "And who is this passenger?"

She glanced at him and her eyes grew wide in understanding. The eggs were forgotten before she turned the stove's burner on.

"All right, thank you," Philip said, hanging the phone up. He took a deep breath. "It appears our son is planning to elope. That's the only reason I can imagine him buying train tickets to New Orleans for himself and Violet Glenn."

Esther lowered herself onto a kitchen chair and stared at her husband in disbelief. "But they only started dating a few months ago," she said. "Why would he do such a thing, Phil? Without a word to us?"

Philip sat next to her. "Because we would object. He's going to elope with this girl because Sam knows we won't agree to his marrying her."

Esther sat, stunned, and considered the situation. She began to sob and put her head in her hands.

"He can't do this to me. To us. To our family. His whole life, he's known he's going to marry a nice Jewish girl." She lifted her head to look at Philip, swiping at tears. "Millions of our people are dead. Lost forever. He's supposed to preserve our traditions, not destroy our future."

"Essie," Philip said gently, taking her hand, "he's not thinking about that."

She shook her head, her mouth a tight line. "She smokes cigarettes. Did you know that? And Deborah told me every time they were with Violet and Johnny, she was all over him like a cat in heat. It was embarrassing to watch, for Sam, too…oh, Phil, you don't think they've—"

"Oh, no, no Essie. I'm sure they haven't." Philip took his hand back and looked away.

"All the plans, all the things I've been so excited for. *Aroysgevorfen.* Wasted. He's thrown it all away."

Philip shook his head. "No, he hasn't. We'll still go to New York."

Esther drew herself up, sniffing. "Not with her we won't. If he marries this girl, I won't speak to her. And Sam can stay here. I won't want to see him for a long time. I won't have a son if he goes through with this."

Philip's brows shot up. "You would disown him?"

Esther shook her head and took a shuddery breath. "No, but disinherit him. He can get a job like everybody else, make his own way. He's not going to do this and still be the spoiled prince." She paused and thought for a few seconds, twirling a glass salt shaker between her fingers. "Our estate can go to this Berman man's museum to help preserve what should never be forgotten. What Sam seems to have forgotten already."

"Esther, you don't mean that," Philip said.

"Actually," she answered, "I do. I'm so angry at Sam right now. He knows what this would do to me—"

"Essie, he's a good young man. He thinks he's in love with this girl. Sam wouldn't deliberately hurt or anger either of us—"

She shook her head, clearly not finished. "Sam's a boy, an impulsive child. He doesn't know what he's doing. This is the red bicycle all over again. Violet Glenn will never make him happy. You've seen her, Phil, she can't walk past a mirror without admiring herself. She isn't ready to be a wife any more than he is to be a husband."

Esther ran her hands through her gray hair, smoothing it away from her face. "No way will we allow this. I won't let him ruin his life. I won't let him do something all of us will regret forever."

"Essie." Philip reached for her hand again.

Esther sat lost in thought for a minute.

"We'll get him out of here," she said. "We'll put him on a plane to New York with the Leons. They'll be happy to make an advance trip up there and even happier we're buying the tickets and hotel for them. Sam can stay in our new apartment until we join him this weekend. He won't have a telephone…" she looked off into the distance through her kitchen window. "He'll get over it, Phil. It'll take a few weeks, but he'll see she's wrong for him."

"And how are you planning to pull this off, Esther? You think Sam will listen to reason right now?"

"I think he'll listen to reason if he hears he'll no longer be our son with this woman as his wife. If he knows he would give up his future with the stores, the bigger future he doesn't even know is unfolding for him yet." She shook her head. "She'd ruin his life, Phil. She's not right for him and you know it."

Philip sat back and crossed his arms. "He'll no longer be our son? You would say this to him?"

"Yes, I would. It's the only way he'll take us seriously, Phil. And I think he'll know we mean it. It's wrong, what he's planning with her. It's the opposite of everything he's been raised to respect and believe. He can get a job on a loading dock somewhere instead of taking over the family business."

"He's our only son, Essie," Philip said quietly.

"Which is exactly why he can't do this," she answered. "We'll tell him we're moving to New York and his only option is to come with us and enjoy everything we've planned for him."

"The minute he tells her it's off, or that we want him to wait at least, she'll change his mind, Essie. It's young love."

She looked thoughtful. "We'll get him out of here and you and I will meet her at that train station instead of Sam. We'll explain to her that marriage to Sam is not possible, that he made a mistake, that he forgot who he is."

"Esther,' Philip nodded at her, eyes wide, "Sam is eighteen years old—"

She began to cry again. "I won't let him do this, Phil. I'll never accept that cheap shiksa as family. Think of your Cousin Sophia. Think of all we lost in Germany." She put her hand on her husband's arm. "And think of the grandchildren Sam can have with Deborah. He loves her, you said it yourself. This Violet is a temporary fascination, that's all."

She stood and said, "I have to get busy. You can finish the eggs if you want them. But how could you eat?" Esther sniffed as she untied her apron, threw it on the kitchen table and exited. Philip stared after her, wondering what to do. He walked over to the stove and regarded the gelatinous mess that was to have been his breakfast. He slid it into the trash can.

Esther returned to poke her head back in the kitchen. "I'm calling Diane Leon, and then you'll call the travel agency. We have to hurry."

"Essie," Philip said, "why did the train station contact us in the first place?" He rinsed the spatula in the sink and scrubbed at the egg remnants. "It doesn't make sense."

She sat back down at the table, her chin resting on her fist. "They said your secretary requested they call with the train schedule for Sam."

"Mrs. Marsh?" Philip said. "There's no reason Leila Marsh would have made that call. Not unless someone told her about Sam's plans, but that makes no sense. Why would she interfere? I think the kid made it up. But why would he make that up, and call us?"

"I don't know," Esther said. "Not unless the boy knows Violet or Sam and wants to mess things up for them. I, for one, appreciate the call whether he meant well or not." She patted the table with her hands. "Now, we have to get busy, Phil. I'll use the phone first."

Hours later, Sam saw his dad approaching the stockroom where he was discussing dress sale prices with Laura Deaton. Something about his face told him Philip had learned of his plans for tomorrow. He left Laura's side without another word and met his father in the main store aisle.

"Not here," Philip told him. "Come upstairs to my office, son."

When they got home, a tearful Esther was waiting for Sam on the living room sofa. He spent thirty minutes trying to convince his mother Violet Glenn was going to be his wife, no matter what his parents had to say about it. He was a grown man, capable of making his own decisions. His parents would grow to love Violet as he did. They had to give her a chance. It wasn't fair. None of this was fair.

Esther played her final card. "Sam, I know how you feel right now," she told him, "but you're not thinking right. You marry this girl, and I won't speak to her. She'll be miserable. You'll be miserable. And you won't work for the stores any longer. We've made big plans for you, Sam, in New York. If you walk away with this Violet, you walk away from all of it. You walk away from us. Permanently." Esther locked eyes with her son to be sure he understood her fully. She stood and reached over to hug Sam, then left the room.

"Dad," Sam turned to Philip. "Please—"

"She's made up her mind, Sam. This is very important to your mother. Her beliefs are strong, and what you're trying to do is unforgivable to her. And honestly, Sam," he placed his hand on his son's shoulder, "it's unforgivable to me, too." He looked at the floor, anywhere but Sam's face. "You'd better go pack your things. I'll be driving you to the airport in an hour."

Sam decided he'd go along with his parents' diversion to New York but come back to Violet soon, after they'd had a chance to calm down. He went to the kitchen telephone and called the Glenn house to tell her their plans had been delayed, but he'd return to her.

Corinna answered the phone. "Glenn residence."

"Is Violet home, Corinna?" Sam asked.

"No, she's gone to her friend Katie Ruth's house," Corinna said. "She told her folks she's spending two nights over there. I think this afternoon they went to Rainbow Springs, though. You can try to call her over at their house in case they're back already."

Sam held the receiver out and banged it against his forehead. "Okay, Corinna, I'll try her at Katie Ruth's. But if I don't get her, tell Violet I had to go out of town suddenly, but I'll be back."

"Okay, Sam. I won't see baby girl until Monday. I'll tell her, though."

The following day at the Anniston train station, Esther stayed in the car and watched her husband swing the lobby door open, disappearing into the building. Several minutes later he emerged looking as distraught as she'd known he'd be. Philip had a tender side, and would hate to hurt anyone. But Violet would be okay. Beautiful girls like her always were.

Philip eased into the driver's seat and turned to his wife. He gripped the steering wheel.

"Essie, she thinks—"

"She thinks she and Sam are in love and would have a perfect life after a glorious trip to New Orleans behind our backs. I know what she thinks." Esther stared at the train station. "This is best for both of them. They'll see."

Philip swallowed hard and turned the key in the ignition. If Violet was right, she'd soon leave town to have a baby. His own grandchild, one he would never know. The guilt spread through his belly like a black liquid.

When Corinna saw Violet's tear-stained face Monday, she knew it was best to say nothing about Sam's call. Mrs. Glenn told Corinna Violet and Sam had broken up, and her daughter was not taking it well. She was going to stay at the beach with her aunt in Florida.

Corinna had seen her share of broken hearts. Let the girl go and heal.

In Atlanta, Katie Sobel sipped sweet tea and watched her young sons play on the living room floor. When Mel told her Sam's plan to elope to New Orleans with Violet, all breathlessly excited for his cousin, she'd known she had to do something.

Posing as Philip Davidson's secretary had been easy. It went better than planned, because Mr. Wilson's son answered the train station's phone. Katie remembered the kid was the one Violet babysat, who had a crush on her. All she had to do was ask Chet to check reservations for the coming Friday and discover Sam and Violet's names, then explain Mrs. Davidson would like to have her son's travel confirmed. He said he'd check with his dad about calling, but Katie told him that wasn't necessary; Mrs. Davidson was waiting to hear from him right away, and it was important because Sam's parents wanted to surprise the happy couple in New Orleans Saturday morning.

Katie smiled, knowing she'd accomplished all she could to ensure a future for Deborah and Sam.

They belonged together.

Seventeen

RONNI

AUGUST, 2020

I woke and blinked at the wood and metal Live Laugh Love script that was hanging beyond the foot of my bed, rolling my eyes and then rolling my heavy body sideways to land my Goodyear Blimp feet on the floor. The baby had kicked me awake almost every hour of the previous night.

I was not feeling Elise's sign today, not at all. If I didn't have to put Max through his exercise paces and then drive myself to the obstetrician's office, I'd have stayed in bed. It occurred to me Deanna was right: I'd have had a soft pillow under and a blanket over my head for my entire pregnancy if she hadn't pushed me to take care of Max.

I turned the word "push" over and over in my mind, hating its new meaning in my life. I had about one month to go before enduring what I was pretty damn sure would be unendurable. Rick wouldn't be there for me to crush his hand in mine, to play my favorite music, to smooth my hair back, to hold the baby for the first time…

I shook all that from my head and slipped my feet into the only shoes that really fit now: some giant fuzzy pink slippers Elise had ordered online.

Apparently, people did not go barefoot in the Davidson home.

I passed Samuel's closed door and would like to think I padded, rather than thundered, my way down the steps, but Max and Elise clearly heard me and had smiles pasted on when I entered the breakfast room. Chef delivered a plate of fruit and the bran muffin Elise insisted I eat daily, because we were all being septuagenarians together now at meals. She insisted fiber was as important to me as it was to her and Max, but I noticed she didn't insist Samuel ingest cardboard muffins.

I failed in my attempt to scoot my chair forward and decided to eat at belly-distance, then muttered a thank you to Chef, who smiled and nodded. I wondered if the poor man had a family somewhere, was waiting for COVID isolation to end so he could be released from captivity and get a restaurant job feeding normal people. I'd never seen inside his bedroom near the kitchen, a former den Elise had fashioned into his chef cell. It probably had Live Laugh Love all over it.

She really could not have chosen more ironic COVID-19 décor if she'd tried.

"How are you feeling this morning, Max?" I asked him, unwrapping my raisin-date-pecan bricklet.

"Not bad," Max replied. "Heart rate is still up, but I think that may be for the rest of my life."

"Max," Elise patted his hand, "don't be so negative. We knew your recovery would take time. You're making progress, honey." She tapped the phone beside her and used a finger to scroll down. "Oh, the Benjamins have gone to the Hamptons. Lucky Deb."

Max raised his eyebrows and took a bite of today's bowel-blessing-muffin, which really wasn't bad.

Elise turned to me. "You've heard Max talking about the Leons? Deb Benjamin is their granddaughter from their son, David, Deborah's baby brother. She got married last year. Thank God before all this virus stuff."

"What happened to your Leon grandparents, Max?" I asked. "Did they stay in New York?"

Max glanced at Elise. "No, our families had a falling out a few years after they moved up there. My *Zayde* Phil didn't speak to my *Zayde* Andrew ever again. I don't really know the details of their feud, but our grandmothers continued to talk secretly now and then. They came back to Anniston. My Leon grandfather retired very young. The stores did well for him."

Elise jumped in. "But as soon as David was old enough, he went back to the city for college and stayed there. Max remembers his Uncle David well. He's been gone for a long time, though. Heart problems." She looked stricken, as though she'd uttered the worst blunder ever.

"It's fine, Elise. I'm not my Uncle David." Max placed his napkin on the table. "I'm going to start the torture on the bike, Ronni. Take your time and join me whenever you're ready."

I swallowed the last of my breakfast in a gulp and said, "No, you don't. I'm coming with you." I grabbed my phone to record him. Now that he could keep his breath better, Max shared the juiciest stories while he was pedaling. They were beginning to find their way into my laptop, like yesterday's revelation about his cousin Katie's part in encouraging Chet Wilson to call Esther Davidson from the train station. It was Max's opinion that, had Katie not alerted Chet so far in advance, Sam and Violet might well have boarded that train to New Orleans. Deborah had confided this to her son in her old age, as a way of relating what a sister-friend Katie had been to her.

I was toying with the idea of contacting Chet's son after all. Maybe I owed him a slight apology. Maybe he had some information about his dad I could incorporate into what might be a sequel to my book someday. But it would have to wait until after the baby.

Today, though, Max didn't seem inclined to reminisce. I set my phone aside and asked him questions about his favorite subject: his wife and sons. I'd become especially curious about Samuel, who stayed closed in his bedroom almost all the time. I saw him only for meals. He was a perfunctory eater, always in a hurry to get back to whatever it was that kept him behind that door.

This, Max was happy to discuss. He was proud of his family. "Samuel has a master's degree from Cornell in computer science. I don't understand a damn thing he says about any of it. He's doing a magnificent job keeping the stores afloat during this pandemic, though, even the one that was damaged and looted during the riots. He's developed this wrap that people can put onto their phones and order merchandise to be picked up. He's even working with our New York people to arrange delivery service for much of the city. It'll all be at their fingertips within weeks. Already our sales are bouncing back."

I stifled a laugh. "You mean an app?"

"Yeah, not a wrap, an app or whatever. All I know is, our customers are happy. I think a lot of them are enjoying being able to shop again, even if it's not in person. You know, Philippe is one of a kind; all our stores have a pianist or harpist to perform soft music while people shop. We don't pipe anything in, none of this electronic crap. Lots of fresh flower arrangements everywhere. Dedicated fitting rooms with lighting and mirrors specifically designed for each department. We even try to continue the traditions my *Zayde* Phil started, with fresh-baked cookies and drinks for some customers, especially the ones assigned personal shoppers. And we don't stock this cheap stuff our competitors have turned to, either. Our margins are lower, but we maintain the kind of quality we've been known for all these years. Ethan has been a big part of that. He's a great negotiator, that one." Max stopped pedaling and sighed. "How much longer?"

I looked at my phone. "You have eleven more minutes to go."

He winced, so I tried to distract him. "Do you have famous customers in New York? I bet you do."

"I don't say the names, but yeah. Several movie actresses you'd know. A major politician or two, one comes from Washington. And a bunch of stylists who work for these people. There's one morning show co-host you see all over the country. She's not wearing our clothes on camera, but Philippe is *all* she wears in her private life. Her kids, too." Max laughed. "Also a certain very famous lady chef and hostess. I think you'd call her a 'lifestyle guru'."

"Wow," I said. "I promise, I won't tell."

"That's how I met Elise, you know. Elise Lilly was becoming known as a model in New York, and our ad agency wanted to hire her for a campaign. I didn't usually get involved with that stuff; we had people better suited to those decisions. But I sure did that day. Don't you dare tell her I said this, but Philippe made her famous. Elise on a billboard in Times Square wearing nothing but diamonds and a short sable coat. Of course, that was in the days you could wear real fur. Now it would have to be ethically sourced diamonds and neon-pink sustainable recycled fake fur from plastic bottles or something." He drew a deep breath and clenched his teeth. "Not that there's anything wrong with that. How long now?"

"Seven minutes. You don't have to talk anymore if it's difficult. I'll just sit and stare at your pretty face," I said.

Max nodded. "That's what Elise said when I met her. I'd be the pretty one." He looked toward the breakfast room. "She married me anyway."

"You two make a striking couple. It's pretty disgusting, you both could easily grace a magazine cover together. *Age*, already," I said.

"You're beautiful yourself, Ronni. I noticed that when we met, before you grew this enormous baby," Max glanced at my belly and coughed. "I'll loan you my torture bike to get back in shape after your Violet is born."

I raised my brows at him. "This bike is going to be part of your life for a while, Max. It's doing you a lot of good. That and your Liza Minelli stockings." I ran my hands across my huge stomach. "I'll lose this by walking my neighborhood. It's easy to get a lot of good exercise there. And maybe I'll take a month's worth of Chef's muffins to flush out my system."

Max looked into my eyes. "I'm going to miss having you here."

I blinked and tried to swallow my tears. "I'm going to miss you, too. You and Elise will have to come visit. Deanna will be staying with me. And we've all been isolated; we should be fine. It's like we've been on an island together through this."

"Gilligan's Island, with no radio and little hope after what was supposed to be a three-hour tour," Max mused. "You probably don't know that show."

"I do, Thurston Howell III," I said, my fingers on his wrist. "Now let's get your cashmere sneakers on and go for a walk. We'll cut the bike time short in favor of more distance today."

Hours later, I returned from Dr. Aronson's office (*you've gained six more pounds since your last visit, Ronni*) to find Max and Elise napping, according to Samuel, who'd magically emerged during my absence. Probably because of my absence. He was sitting on the black sofa watching CNN.

"Now," he told me, "they've had reinfections in Hong Kong. That means you can get this more than once. No immunity. Not like we all thought." He crossed his arms in front of his faded gray Cornell t-shirt, which I noticed for the first time.

I plopped onto the opposite sofa with way too much gravity assisting me. If Samuel noticed the sofa creak, he was too kind to say so.

"That's bad news," I offered. "I can hardly stand to listen to it all anymore."

Samuel clicked the TV off. "Me neither. I wish I hadn't even turned it on. God, it's been, what, six months in this country already? We thought it would be another MERS and just go away. What the hell is this virus? Do you understand it, medically?"

"Not really. I don't think the medical community has a handle on it, and I'm afraid we're going to see new strains of it sooner or later. Viruses mutate, that's what they do. Until we have an effective antiviral drug, we're going to keep losing people. I know they're trying Remdesivir now, but it doesn't seem as effective as hoped. And even with a good antiviral, COVID-19 can create collateral damage we're only beginning to understand."

Samuel nodded, his face flat. "Like my dad. But he's getting stronger, right?"

"Yes, he is, he's doing better. It's gradual, but he's recovering a lot better than some patients I've heard about with similar complications."

Samuel frowned. "God, I'm sorry, Ronni. You lost your husband to this thing and I'm sitting here going on and on like it hasn't touched your life."

"It's okay. Everyone I know has been impacted by this one way or another. And I think it helps to talk about it clinically, instead of personally. I don't know if I'll ever be ready to talk about it personally." I clamped my eyes against the tears.

"I just wish the medical community could be more promising about what's coming, how we're going to end this. It has to be soon," Samuel said.

"Well, I know Pfizer and Moderna are working on developing vaccines, but that'll only be really effective if everyone gets them, like smallpox vaccination was done. And my understanding is that it'll be voluntary. It could be a very long time before this pandemic ends." I returned my eyes to Samuel's. "Oh, wow, I am a ray of sunshine, huh? It'll be okay. I'm naturally pessimistic about it after all that's happened." I stopped and searched for encouraging words. "Look, viruses and other germs have been trying to kill humans forever. Since the beginning of time. We'll overcome this one."

Samuel offered a small, polite laugh. "Is that you being optimistic? It's not exactly miles away from Pessimistic Ronni."

"Yeah, I guess not. What are you doing out of your room, anyway? This isn't like you at all. Chef didn't prepare afternoon snacks, did he?" I leaned over and looked toward the kitchen.

"I'm waiting for QA to finish testing the app. It'll be a while. First break I've had, and I hardly know what to do with myself. On the other hand, it's not like we can go anywhere and do anything, anyway."

"Your dad's really proud of you," I said. "Your wrap has saved the stores."

He grinned. "It was my rap, Ronni. 'Get it from Philippe—drive up and go beep—we'll bring it out—that's what we're talkin' 'bout—our merch is so fine—come help our bottom line...'"

"Gah," I laughed. "You are horrible at that."

"You know many computer geek rappers? Young Binary? Lil' Modem?" He held his hands up, gangsta style, mock-tough.

I couldn't stop giggling. "You're more like Young Cheesy."

"Very gouda, Ronni." Samuel glanced at the stairs, listening for his parents. "I hear Dad's been telling you all the old stories. I know a few, from my granddad."

"Not *Zayde* Sam? Granddad?"

Samuel chuckled. "He always wanted to be called Granddad or Granddaddy when we were little. He said it was an Alabama thing. I think he missed living here. Well, I know he did. He practically begged us to move him to Fairfield Springs after Grandma Deborah died. She missed Alabama, too. I'm not sure why they stayed in the city all their lives. Maybe he was too caught up in his career, that's what Dad thinks. And they just got used to it there."

He paused, thinking. "Granddad made it all sound wonderful: the warmth of the people; the beauty of the scenery around the state. The summer I was nine, he took me and my brothers on a trip to Little River Canyon and DeSoto Falls. We stayed in an old lodge in Mentone a few days and then drove on to Anniston. I remember him introducing us to everyone in his store on Quintard Avenue. It was so beautiful then, not like that empty building you see now. Oh, and he took us up on Cheaha Mountain. That was really beautiful, especially for a city kid. We swam in the pool up there, surrounded by the mountains and green valleys in the distance.

On the way back to our motel, Granddad bought some tomatoes from a roadside stand and fixed us tomato sandwiches for dinner. I fell in love with Alabama that day. It took me a long time to convince Dad to look into buying and re-opening the old store here. And then all this happened."

"Your dad says you have a master's degree in computer science. But you want to run a department store?" I asked.

"I learned a lot working in our stores in New York, and from my dad. He probably didn't mention I minored in business," Samuel said. "I have some ideas I want to try here, like letting customers use the app to make appointments for alterations or personal shopping assistance. Our service really sets us apart, and we can capitalize on that with a generation using smartphones for everything. You know how some restaurants give their servers handheld computers and they can process checks at the table? Like in an Apple store? I want to do that; completely eliminate checkout counters. They would only be stations for our employees to wrap things up nicely and quickly for customers to take home."

He drew a breath. "But aside from technology, I like the idea of designing and running a Philippe of my own, putting my stamp on it. I want coming to our store to be an experience shoppers won't forget, unlike anything they know. I want to get people away from ordering online and make shopping fun." He shook his head. "Well, I wanted to," he added.

"You think Anniston is the market for that?" I said. "I mean, why not Birmingham or Atlanta?"

Samuel smiled. "It's perfect. It's nostalgia, where it all began. There are people here who remember what the store was like. I want to do it old-style, kind of art deco inside. But we'd market to Birmingham and Atlanta; Chattanooga, too. I plan for the store to be a destination."

"Well, it sounds wonderful to me," I said. "And it'll happen, Samuel, the time will be right before too long." I smiled at him. "Does anyone ever call you anything but Samuel? Sam? Sammy?"

"God, I hate 'Sammy.' And Sam was my granddad. My full name was always used to differentiate us. My mom says it suits me because I was born an 'old soul' and my name is downright ancient. Biblical. I mean, it's a bit formal, but I'm used to it. There's no good alternative."

"What's your middle name?" I asked.

Samuel laughed. "Lilly. My mom's maiden name, and there was a semi-famous Samuel Lilly in her family back in the 1800s. Isn't that cruel?"

I nodded, my face grave. "Yes, it truly is."

"Anyway, I'm going to go check on the app testing. I forced myself to leave my phone up there so I wouldn't keep looking at it every other minute. Nice talking with you, Ronni." Samuel offered a little wave and headed for the stairs.

"Nice talking with you, Lilly," I called after him.

"Let's stay with Lil' Modem," he answered. "It sounds much manlier."

Eighteen

New York, New York

1947

T he elevator doors opened onto a hallway of softly lit brass sconces shining on plush burgundy carpeting. Mr. Leon walked Sam to the door of his parents' apartment, telling him, "Don't worry, son, this'll all work out. You'll have people you know around you, people who care about you a lot. Your mom and dad get here Sunday. I'll pick you up for breakfast in the morning. Diane, Deborah, and David get here before then, but I'm not so sure…well, I'm not sure you'll see them right away. Oh, I almost kept your key," he said, pulling it out of his pocket. "I'm sorry. It's been a long day." Those were more words than Andrew Leon had spoken on the entire flight from Atlanta.

Sam felt sorry for Andrew, a quiet, shy, unassuming man who'd been placed in a painfully awkward position. A man whose daughter Sam had upset along with all the other daughters in the world, it seemed.

"I understand, Mr. Leon. Thank you. I'll see you in the morning."

Mr. Leon turned to leave, then reached his hand to shake Sam's. "Look, son, I know things haven't been good between you and my Deborah lately. She doesn't talk to me about that stuff, and her mother doesn't, either. I hope it'll all work out, now that I've come up here to work with your dad. Y'all have always been close friends."

Sam wondered briefly if Andrew Leon had any knowledge of his daughter's life *at all*. "Umm, thank you, Mr. Leon. I appreciate that." He felt his stomach bottom out as he shook Andrew's hand. *What a mess.*

Sam closed the door and locked it, then crossed the room to pull back the heavy draperies and scan the foreign landscape sixty feet below. More people were walking past the San Remo Apartments than Sam had seen gathered in one place, even at nine o'clock at night. He could make out the trees of a park nearby and a lighted bridge in the distance. He located a lamp next to the brocade sofa and switched it on.

The apartment his parents rented had soaring ceilings, the same plush carpeting in the living room as the path from the elevator, and ivory walls hung with a gold-framed painting here and there. The carpet led to a polished wood parquet floor that reflected the overhead light in the hall. Sam discovered two bedrooms, both of which were furnished with a bed and dresser each—he figured the smaller was his, especially since the bedspread featured basketballs. What was his mother thinking? He found an empty room he supposed was intended to be a library, and a den next to it.

The kitchen was tiny compared to his mother's at home; he spotted a bowl of fruit and snacks someone had placed on the wood counter. The refrigerator featured chilled Cokes. He grabbed one and returned to the living room, which boasted the best view of the park through its tall windows.

The apartment was nice, and had every single thing he needed for a comfortable night except the most important one: a telephone. Sam suddenly realized he was in one of the largest cities in the world, one that surely boasted pay phones on every corner. He gave Mr. Leon a few minutes to catch a taxi to his hotel, then grabbed the apartment key and took the elevator to the building's bottom floor.

He stepped into the softly lit lobby, where he was greeted by a uniformed attendant who'd been missing when they arrived. "Hello, sir, I'm Edgar," he said. "And you must be young Mr. Davidson."

Sam stood a little taller. No one had ever addressed him as "sir." He offered a tentative smile to Edgar.

"Yes, I am. Nice to meet you, Edgar. I don't think my parents will call, but if they do, would you tell them I went to get a sandwich after Mr. Leon dropped me off?" Sam nodded at the phone sitting on a marble desk. "And can you tell me where the nearest phone booth is?"

Edgar grinned. "You're more than welcome to use this phone, sir. Even for long-distance. I'm guessing you're calling a pretty girl down South. That's where I'm from, too. West Virginia."

Sam nodded. "Thank you, Edgar, but I'm gonna want some privacy for this call. I'll be back in a little bit."

Edgar held up his index finger, then rushed from behind the desk to sweep the massive glass door open for Sam. "I'll be right here, Mr. Davidson. Just go about half a block to your right. You'll see the pay phone."

Sam passed fifty people on the way down the block, not one of whom met his eyes. He opened the phone booth and asked the operator to dial the Glenns' number. He deposited four quarters and two dimes, then waited a full minute for her to put the call through.

Mrs. Glenn grabbed the phone on the first ring. "Hello?" she said in a low voice, as though she were afraid of waking someone. Sam glanced at his watch. It was eight-twenty in Alabama.

"Hi, Mrs. Glenn, it's Sam—"

"I'm going to say this to you one time," she hissed into the phone. "Don't you ever call this house again." She hung up before Sam could say a word. He trudged back to the apartment, out of quarters and too sick to his stomach to smile back at Edgar.

His first night in New York was a restless one, tangled in his ridiculous basketball bedding, tortured by thoughts of Violet sitting in that train station, bewildered and alone. Sam stared at the wall, light and shadows filtering through the curtains.

How long did she wait before giving up on me? Did my parents show up to talk to her, or just leave her there?

He jerked his head to the window, startled by a loud siren. Sam padded over and parted the sheers to see the taillights of an ambulance round the corner a few blocks away.

Surely Violet will forgive me once I explain. We'll still get married. I just have to get my parents to understand. It will take time, but they'll come around. I'll spend every quarter I have to get through and get Corinna to put Violet on the telephone come Monday. Corinna will help me.

He was still considering, planning, plotting at three o'clock the next morning, when he finally drifted off to sleep.

Sam woke to sun streaming through his window and the honking of multiple horns on the street below. He hurried to shower before Andrew Leon arrived to pretend everything was okay over eggs and toast, or whatever people ate for breakfast here. It turned out to be bagels and lox. Sam made a mental note to grab a box of Cheerios and some milk from the small grocery store near the apartment.

His parents arrived Sunday, sweeping in with gale-force enthusiasm to show him the local sights. They took a taxi to view the Statue of Liberty, an elevator to the top of the Empire State Building, walked through Chinatown, and Esther had her portrait drawn by a sidewalk artist. They had dinner that night at Barbetta, an Italian restaurant recommended by friends Philip and Esther had met on a previous trip. It would become Esther's favorite, a place the family would gather over the years for birthday celebrations and anniversaries.

Through it all, Sam could only think of finding a telephone.

On Wednesday, Sam looked around him, trying to block the noise from passing cars and excited tourists from his ears. Even inside the phone booth, which was suffocatingly hot, he could barely hear the operator. He stuffed a finger in his free ear after depositing all the coins requested and waited through three rings.

"Hello?" Alice Glenn said.

"Hi, Mrs. Glenn, it's me again, I was just wondering if I could speak to Violet. Please. I need to tell her some things. It's really important, Mrs. Glenn. Please don't hang up this time."

"Sam," Alice said, "I told you not to call again. You don't get to talk to our daughter. She cried for three days after you left, Sam. And she's gone to stay with relatives in Florida, at least for the fall, maybe longer. Before you ask, I will not give you the telephone number there. Leave Violet alone."

"I promise you, I won't upset her, I just need to explain—"

"There's nothing you can explain to her, Sam. You left for New York. Violet's devastated. Don't you think she's been through enough already this past year, with Johnny's accident and the way he treated her after? And then you made out like you cared about her and pulled this stunt, running off with Deborah. It doesn't matter what you want to say to her. Forget Violet. She's going to forget you. Do not call this house again."

Sam heard the receiver click on the end of the line. "*What?* I didn't…Mrs. Glenn? Mrs. Glenn, please." But Violet's mom was gone, and so was his hope of talking to Violet. *Florida.* Who did she know in Florida? Sam had no idea. He rested the back of his head against the glass wall of the booth, eyes shut, trying to think, sweat beading on his forehead. The three occasions Sam had managed to break free and get to a pay phone, Mrs. Glenn answered and slammed the receiver down as soon as she heard his voice. His attempt today was the first time Mrs. Glenn bothered to speak to him, and that was only to let him know Violet was gone. There was no way to reach her by phone. Her mother would probably tear up any letter he mailed without opening it. He didn't know what to do next.

A gray-haired man holding a briefcase banged his palm impatiently on the door. "You're not the only guy in the city who needs to make a phone call, fat head," he yelled. Sam startled and nodded at the angry man, blinking his way into the late-summer sun.

"I'm sorry," he said.

"Sawreee," the man mocked, shaking his head.

Sam waited for the guy to finish his call, glancing at his watch as he paced back and forth beside the booth. The gray-haired man scowled at Sam and walked off muttering something Sam couldn't make out. It didn't matter. He'd figured out how to locate Violet.

Sam stepped inside and asked the operator to look up the number for the Jennings residence on Knox Avenue in Anniston, Alabama. After he'd surrendered the last of his quarters, a familiar voice drawled, "Jennings residence, this is Katie Ruth."

"Katie Ruth! It's Sam. Sam Davidson. I sure am glad to get you on the phone. I'm trying to find Violet and her mom won't tell me where she is—"

"And you think I would?" Katie Ruth shot at him. "I wouldn't tell you for anything. No one will. You've got a lotta nerve asking about Violet after what you did to her. Get lost, Sam. Enjoy your life in *Newwww Yorrrrk.*"

Once again, Sam was dismissed by a slammed phone receiver.

He was due back at the store soon, and he knew his dad would send a search party if he didn't return with the sandwiches he'd promised. Sam made his way to Katz's Delicatessen and back to Davidson's, eighty thousand square feet of space being designed to look much like its smaller sister store in Anniston, Alabama.

It was the only place Sam felt at home in the city.

He wanted to launch the store, to be a part of everything his father was building, to achieve the success they had in Anniston on a New York City scale. Sam and his dad had nosed around Macy's and Saks Fifth Avenue, massive marble spaces offering fine merchandise and well-trained salespeople. But Sam knew they had a secret ingredient: the personal attention afforded everyone who walked through the doors of Davidson's. It was going to be beautiful; their display designer was coming in two weeks to duplicate much of the cachet in the

Alabama store. A few other key employees were making the trip up, including Laura Deaton. Patricia Hollis was coming from Cosmetics, a softly-chiming blonde Southern Belle sure to charm the women of the city and also inspire their husbands to buy the most expensive perfumes. Edward Geist from Men's Suits and Mrs. Herring from Accessories would accompany them.

Their missions were temporary; they'd train new hires in the store's products, procedures, and philosophies. Sam thought some of them might even decide to stay. Patricia had always wanted to be an actress. Maybe she'd get her start in New York. She was strikingly beautiful; even Violet thought so.

Violet.

He knew the store would succeed, but it didn't feel like he'd ever find the space in his heart to fully enjoy it.

Sam unlocked and entered the employee entrance and made his way to the break room on the ground floor. His father hadn't come down yet. He placed the bag of sandwiches on the table and handed one to Mr. Loudon, saying, "Pastrami, right?"

Hank Loudon nodded and put down his newspaper, creasing it neatly in half. "I could get spoiled with this. Thanks, Sam. I have exactly thirty minutes before I have to pick up that paintbrush again." He took a huge bite and chewed. "How are you liking the city?"

"Honestly, Mr. Loudon, I haven't been here long enough to decide. It's an exciting place for a vacation, but I'm a little overwhelmed at the thought of living here for good. I mean, you were born in New York, right? It must be different when it's the only place you've known."

"Call me Hank, kid. And yeah, born and raised in Brooklyn. Inherited my dad's painting business at twenty-two and had four sons within five years, Nancy and me, so I ain't traveled much. This place must seem real big and noisy to you, coming from down South and all. And we're not exactly known for our gracious politeness on the streets."

Hank took another bite of sandwich, musing for a minute as Sam ate his Reuben and swiped sauerkraut juice from his chin. "Here's the thing, kid: New York is always more than anyone expects, and I mean that in the best way. Nancy says this city is the most hope-filled place on the planet. There's excitement, electricity in the air, ya know, every single day, like what's gonna come next? The whole city is hurrying, busy, watchin' to see what happens. It ain't peaceful, exactly. You can go to the mountains or the beach for that. New York, she keeps you dreamin'. She makes you think anything is possible. And every new day, she proves it to folks who come here from all over the world."

Philip Davidson entered the room and sat next to Sam, reaching for his own pastrami on rye.

"What are y'all talking about?" he asked.

"The wonders of New York." Hank winked at Sam. "Your boy here is going to discover all of 'em. I envy him, just startin' out. And you and Mrs. Davidson, too. Greatest city in the world, that's a fact." He took another bite of sandwich as Sam wondered where he'd ever fit in outside the walls surrounding him, their colors and sights a little island of home amid the constant buzz of excitement Hank Loudon loved so much.

The most hopeful thing he could grasp was the arrival of old friends from the Anniston store in two weeks. He needed to hear their accents, their stories of home. Andrew Leon spent his days behind the closed door of his office. Sam barely saw him, and Mrs. Leon, Deborah, and David had yet to make an appearance.

Sam wouldn't blame Deborah if she avoided him in some corner of New York for the next thirty years. He deserved it.

Nineteen

RONNI

SEPTEMBER, 2020

D r. Garland spent fifteen minutes examining and talking to Max. Then he scooted his wheelie stool over to me and patted my arm.

"Well done, milady. Max is looking much healthier than two months ago, and you look like you're about to give birth in my office. It's time for you to go home, draw the shades, and enter your confinement." He slapped his knees, chuckling softly. "Sorry, I've been reading a lot of Tudor history. I recently discovered I have an ancestor beheaded by Henry VIII. Cool for me. For him, not so much."

He slid back to Max on the exam table. "You just keep doing what you're doing. We're releasing you into the wild. I'm sending these records," he waved at his laptop, "to your cardiologist's office in Anniston. I know you'll miss me, but that's the heartbreak of being a success story. And you are, Mr. Davidson. Remarkable improvement."

"Call me Max since I almost got to raise your youngest child," Max answered.

Dr. Garland scrunched up his face. "I'd forgotten about that bet. Wanna go for two out of three?" He stood and washed his hands as Max cackled into his mask. "Always leave 'em laughing if you can. My ancient great-grandfather should've tried that with Henry, but he was apparently a humorless bishop with a grudge. I'm pretty sure we Garlands survived by developing our comedic side. I'm probably related to Mr. Bean." He wiggled his eyebrows and winked at me as he exited.

I automatically reached to help Max up, but he waved me off.

"I should be helping you up, Ronni. Sad as I am to say it, you need to go home this afternoon and let Deanna fuss over you. Also, you should sleep like it's going out of style. Because it is." He nodded at my huge belly. "She'll change everything about your life, Ronni. Don't tell anyone, but I always wanted a daughter. You're the closest thing I've known."

"You have a daughter-in-law named Jeannie, Max," I said, swinging the door open.

"That is correct," he replied, nodding. "How do the kids put it? I said what I said."

Cars are not designed for pregnant women, particularly tearful pregnant women with blurry vision. I waved goodbye to Max, Elise, Samuel, and Chef as they stood on their front porch—it seemed they had adopted the Southern tradition of sending car passengers off like they're making Atlantic crossings—and tried to wedge myself behind the steering wheel. After an embarrassing pause to step out and power the seat backward, I drove away with my arms extended Formula One driver-style.

As I'd known she would, Kait called before I rounded the first corner. "Are you okay? Does Max seem all right?"

"Yeah," I sniffed. "I'm fine and he's doing great. I'm just dreading going back to my house. It was easy to pretend Rick was off somewhere else while I was living with the Davidsons. Now his absence will follow me into every room."

"I'm sorry, honey." I heard Kait tapping a keyboard.

"Hey, I know you're busy," I said. "You don't have to babysit me on the way home."

"No, it's delightfully quiet right now. We only have one patient who's currently positive and isolated, and so far she's doing well. A newbie you don't know, before you ask. Anyway, this thing seems to be slowing down. Please God."

"I hope so. It can't last much longer, can it?" I made a left, heading for ice cream. Chef had kept my diet remarkably healthy during my tenure with Max, and I intended to fix that. "I mean, are you hearing much that's encouraging? I've been avoiding the news."

Kait's silence was eloquent. Then she said, "There are mixed opinions. We'll see."

"Well, I'm going to get a hot fudge sundae and then do a grocery pickup for Deanna. And then I may drive around aimlessly until the frozen stuff starts to thaw."

"Maybe it won't be so bad, Ronni. Hey…know what you should write a book about?"

This had become Kait's favorite way to make me laugh since she'd heard everyone else constantly told me ridiculous ideas. It was our best-friend equivalent of knock-knock jokes.

I pulled into the Dairy Queen drive-thru behind six cars. "No. What should I write a book about, Kait?"

I pictured her biting her lower lip, eyes widened as she struggled not to giggle. "A post-apocalyptic story about lesbian sheep who develop human-level intelligence through AI. They take over the world and make it better. It's called Ewe-Topia."

I couldn't help but cackle and roll my eyes. "How long have you been saving that gem?"

"It's been super busy at Fairfield, as you know. I wrote that down two weeks ago and decided to offer it when you went home. Maybe their Christmas greeting is Fleece Navidaaaad."

I shook my head and suppressed a giggle, glad there was at least one person in the world as weird as me. "I'm sure readers would flock to that. You gotta stop reading sci-fi, Kait." I paused as I inched my car forward. "I actually might write another book, though. Max and Samuel both told me a lot of interesting things about their father and grandfathers' lives here in Anniston and in New York. It could make a nice sequel to my other book; maybe tell another side people don't know."

"Hmm." Kait said. She was probably blowing her blonde bangs up off her forehead as she considered, then leaning back with a frown. "After last time, are you sure you want to bring more revelations into the world? Are they good or bad for Deanna?"

"Good, I'm guessing," I answered. "I have to think about it. And I don't know when I'm going to actually get a chance to write, anyway. I just have piles of notes in my laptop."

"I can picture you with the baby papoose-style on your back, banging away at the keyboard. The baby, of course, will be silent and softly snoozing, careful not to interrupt you."

"That would work," I told her, "with a drugged sloth on my back. No chance this baby will give me any peace. She's already treating my ribs like a dance floor, 24/7." I shifted in my car seat, wondering what the Ford Explorer driver at the window could possibly have ordered to take fifteen minutes. I rarely experienced road rage, but drive-thru rage was a thing. I imagined a massive plow for my Acura's front bumper, clearing my path to desperately needed ice cream.

Kait said, "I gotta prepare for a Zoom call that should be an email. Call me later, okay? Let me know how you're settling in. I love you."

"I love you, too."

Deanna ran her finger back and forth on my bedspread's chenille pattern as I unpacked. "I've really missed you. I have whole conversations with the squirrels in the backyard."

I smiled at her, noting she'd lost weight and begun wearing clothes that echoed my wardrobe. Or maybe it was my wardrobe. My clothes were a distant memory. If my long bohemian skirts and t-shirts could get Deanna out of polyester pantsuits, she could have them all.

"You look really pretty," I told her. "Love your lipstick, too."

"Thank you," she answered. "Playing dress-up and modeling for the squirrels has been my favorite pastime." She stood and handed me a ginormous pair of floral maternity overalls—my current favorite outfit—to hang up. When we'd finished, she said, "You take a nap and I'll get supper ready in a bit. Don't forget we have Dr. Aronson tomorrow morning."

I would rather think about anything than another obstetrical visit. Taking care of Max had allowed me a fantasy world with only one responsibility. I'd been live-laugh-loving a pretty easy two months.

I rolled over and contemplated the blackout drapes Deanna had drawn for my "confinement." Rick's shirt was bunched up under his pillow and I held it to my face, inhaling the tiny bit of scent that remained. Deanna heard me crying and swung the door open, standing quietly in the light from the hall.

"I can't do this. I could pretend it wasn't happening when I was staying with Max and Elise," I blurted. "I can't pretend anymore. It's all too real here. It's just wave after wave and I feel like I'm drowning." I inhaled a shaky breath. "I miss him so much."

Deanna leaned against the door jamb and shook her head at me. "I'm sorry, Ronni. I knew coming home would be hard for you."

I watched her cross the room to perch beside me on the bed, trying not to cry harder. She began running her hand in circles on my back.

Deanna exhaled and nodded, like she'd reached some decision. "It's been almost half a year, and I know it's not any easier yet. But honey, you can do this, and you have so much to look forward to. You have a baby on the way. You have light and laughter and joy in your future." She stopped the circles with a back pat and rested her hand on my shoulder. "Ronni, your memories of Rick will never go away, but you can't move forward with them crushing you, honey. You're supposed to climb the mountain, not carry it on your back. You can't breathe under the constant weight of your grief."

"So, I'm supposed to act like I didn't just lose my husband, the center of my world, my rock, my anchor, my…as much as I hate the phrase…the love of my life?" I dragged my sleeve under my nose.

"You know that's not what I'm saying, Ronni. I'm saying *you're* still *here.* You have reason and purpose and a whole lot more than many have been left holding. As hard as it is, try to appreciate that."

She stood and walked to my bedroom door. "I'll come get you in about an hour," she said. "We're having grilled chicken salads and some cantaloupe. I'm not Chef."

"I hate cantaloupe," I sniffed. "It's mushy."

"I'm not Therapist, either. You'll have to deal with it."

"Elise told Chef how I am with food textures, and he was really accommodating." I gripped the bedside table and made my way to a reclined position.

Deanna said, "I knew we shouldn't have sent you to Versailles."

I made a sudden decision to tell her my secret. "Something interesting happened there, Deanna. I think I'm going to write another book. Max and Samuel both told me all kinds of things about your father and his life here and in New York. He was a great guy."

She frowned. "Well," she answered, "you couldn't prove it by me."

"There's so much of that story you haven't heard—"

"Maybe I'm not ready to." She cut me off and shrugged. "I keep telling you, let's look ahead, not into the past. Besides, you're not going to be in any position to write for a while."

"I can write while the baby's sleeping," I told her.

Deanna laughed. "Baby sleeps, you sleep. You'll see. It's the law."

She closed my door and left me to contemplate. I'd suspected she wouldn't welcome the idea of learning more about Sam. Deanna made it clear she'd never stop resenting the way he left her mother. In time, though, I felt sure she'd love hearing things weren't as black and white as she'd thought.

As any of us had thought.

I took my laptop out and sat it on my belly-desk, opening the folder of notes I'd compiled. The baby kicked hard enough to shake Google Earth, so I closed it with a sigh.

"Already, you won't let me get anything done." I rubbed my belly and stared at the ceiling, surrendering to the insistent thumping as I grimaced.

The Grape was loving and cute. *The Parasite* was not. Yet that word kept running through my head, over and over. I was afraid I'd overheard it when I was little, that it was a fragment from a dark motel room or back seat.

Iron bands of dread tightened around my chest. I hadn't told Deanna or Kait or anyone my worst fear: I didn't know *how* to be a mother. My own had been practically non-existent. I had no memories of her holding me as an infant or toddler, no lullabies, no story books, no love. Jocelyn was the kind of mother who'd eat her own young.

The mountain Deanna kept telling me to climb, not carry? It was much more jagged, steep and slippery than she imagined. I rolled myself off the bed and made my way downstairs to find Deanna seasoning chicken strips on my cutting board.

"Hey," she said. "That wasn't much of a nap."

"Baby's trying to take out a rib." I reached for a grape from the bowl she kept on the table. Deanna put down the paprika and washed her hands carefully, then leaned against the counter and regarded me with her arms crossed.

"You know, a lot of first-time moms are anxious about labor, and a thousand times more anxious about taking care of an infant."

I shook my head. "How did you know?"

Deanna shrugged and laughed. "First of all, I'm a woman. But I met Jocelyn, remember? I can't imagine she set much of an example for you as a mother. That won't matter. When that baby is placed in your arms, she'll become the center of your universe. And you'll know, instinctively, a lot of what to do. The parts you don't know, I'll help with. You're going to be a great mom, Ronni."

I stared at the squirrels leaping from tree to tree outside, unwilling to meet her eyes. "I'm not ready."

"Of course you are. You know why God made a pregnancy last forty weeks, Ronni? Because it's *exactly* the amount of time it takes a woman to prepare to be a mother." She went back to her chicken. "Your biggest problem is you've never fully appreciated the kindness, the innate sweetness and frankly, intelligence in yourself. I can't wait to see you discover it."

"By birthing a baby who feels like she's wearing cleats in my uterus? That's how I'll make this stunning discovery?" I finally looked at Deanna, who was rummaging in my refrigerator, ignoring my sarcasm.

"Not exactly." She closed the door and smiled at me. "When you meet this little girl, she'll be the most wonderful mirror you can imagine."

Twenty

New York City

December 30, 1947

"No one could have predicted this crazy storm, Essie. The paper said the weather pattern was opposite the usual, so they never saw it coming." Philip stood at their living room window, staring at the towering piles of dirty snow that still crippled much of the city. The Great North American Blizzard of December 26, 1947 had literally frozen everything in Manhattan. Seventy-seven people were dead in its wake. Businesses shut down, including Davidson's, though Philip was grateful the holiday retail season had ended successfully before they had to close. No subway service ran for days. Busses were stranded in the streets. In a city that depended greatly on public transportation, it was a devastating and historic event.

Esther joined him at the window. "A thousand miles we had to move, to experience this—what did they call it?—*cataclysm*. A little snow is nice. Not drifts the size of blue whales. I'm sick of it already.

Not to mention New Year's Eve being cancelled. It all feels like a bad omen." She pinched the bridge of her nose and sighed.

"New Year's Eve is happening whether we eat at a fancy restaurant or not, Essie, or whether we see the ball drop in Times Square. It'll still be 1948 in two days and we'll still sip champagne and kiss at midnight tomorrow. Look at that," Phil pointed at a group of men who'd come into view. "They're shoveling snow into the sewers."

"Where it belongs," Esther replied, taking her women's magazine and heading to the bedroom. She'd spent days alternating between the living room fireplace and snuggling under the pile of blankets on their bed.

Philip joined his wife. She put the magazine down with a sigh as he lay atop the covers beside her.

"What's on your mind?" he asked her. "I know being shut in here is bad, but it doesn't account for this much Essie Gloom."

"Would you please stop calling it that?" Esther rolled her eyes upward. "Just because I don't share your rose-colored glasses doesn't make me gloomy. I'm a realist, Philip. There's a lot you don't see. I think you try *not* to see."

Philip closed his eyes. "What is it now, Essie? This snow mess is temporary. The city will be back to near-normal tomorrow or the next day. We'll re-open the store and people will be so excited to get out and shop, we'll probably set a new record."

She rolled onto her side to face him. "Do you know Deborah has a boyfriend? He lives in their building, Phil. Which means they're together, right now. Diane is probably serving them lunch. While your son is sitting in his room thinking about that *shiksa*."

Philip blinked at his wife. "He's over Violet, Essie. It hurt him for a long time, but you're wrong about that. He's a little glum right now after days locked up with us, sure. But I see him at work. He's the old Sam. He's happy, smiling, even. Our son is finally enjoying this place."

"And this is why I say you don't see what you try not to see. I'm not talking about Violet. I'm talking about that *Patricia* selling cosmetics. You think he's thrilled to go to work to look at a shiny shipment of shoes or old Mr. Nussbaum measuring for suits? It's *her*. *Oy!* My husband is blind." Esther shook her head in disgust.

"I am not, Essie. He likes her, sure. She's from home. They have a lot to talk about. That's all. Patricia Hollis is *way* out of Sam's league." Philip chuckled until he saw his wife's face. "I mean, she's older. More sophisticated. And, my darling wife, she has a boyfriend. I've seen him pick her up after work. Nice suit. Looks like Wall Street. So stop your worrying."

Esther held up a finger. "One: she is a blonde Alabama girl built a lot like Violet Glenn." Esther's eyebrows shot up near her hairline. "You think she doesn't remind him of her? Two: she's smart enough to schmooze the owner's son, all day long, when you're not looking. Because you *don't look*, Phil. Three: Sam's a *mensch*. He's an innocent, good-hearted kid. He doesn't understand the first thing about ulterior motives."

Philip sighed. "I do look, Essie. I see them talking. That's all. Like I said, she has a boyfriend. You're making an evil mountain out of this platonic molehill. And what am I supposed to do about all this? You want I should fire the girl? For being nice to our son?"

Esther lay her head back on the pillow and studied a spot on the ceiling. "No, of course not. But we have to find him a girlfriend, someone who will capture his attention. And I know the perfect one. You say she's from home, and that's a big deal? So is Deborah. And they have a lot of history already connecting them, to each other and to Alabama."

Philip shook his head. "You just told me she has a boyfriend. A boyfriend who's with her even as we speak, hiding from this storm. So how does that work, Esther Davidson?"

"This Alex, he goes with her and the Leons to Shabbat services at their new synagogue. As soon as they clear Siberia out of our street, we're taking Sam to B'nai Jeshurun."

"I thought we agreed on Temple Emanu-El, Essie. I love that place. Besides, taking Sam to temple isn't going to accomplish anything with Deborah. Let the girl enjoy this new boy in her life. Sam wasn't exactly good to her." Philip laid his arm over his eyes, closing them against the headache he felt coming on.

"You understand nothing about teenage boys, Phil. It's hard to believe you ever were one." Esther stood and tossed her heavy blankets onto her husband, leaving him cocooned to nap in the afternoon dimness. She went to check on Sam, knocking softly before she opened his door. He was sitting on his bed and waved from behind a book called *East Side, West Side*. The cover looked trashy to Esther. She opted not to mention that.

"Are you hungry?" she asked him.

"No, thank you, I made a sandwich for lunch." Sam never moved his face from behind the book, obviously waiting for her to leave. Esther knew how it felt to be disturbed in the middle of a novel. She closed the door silently and moved to the living room windows to mentally encourage the crew of men feeding snow to the sewers.

Sam threw the book he'd been reading onto the bedspread—mercifully a tasteful gray after he'd protested the basketballs—and crossed to the new desk his parents had bought him. He was going to lose his mind if he was trapped here much longer; the blizzard had made that abundantly clear. Last week he'd approached his dad about the possibility of taking some business classes. Now, after five days of living elbow to elbow with Esther and Philip, he'd decided that wouldn't be enough. He would enroll full-time this fall and live on campus.

He slid the application to Columbia out of the top drawer, where it was nestled among the promises of freedom and parties and girls. In months, he'd be in a dorm room, working in the store around his class schedule. Sam began filling blanks in his precise block letters. He'd already decided the subject of his essay: the impact an automobile accident had on his best friend and everyone around him.

Sam's mother had a call from Mrs. Perkins last week. Johnny was enrolled at The University of Alabama; he wanted to be a lawyer. He had a new girlfriend named Rose. Johnny was using his wheelchair well; he even played basketball in it in Tuscaloosa. But it probably wasn't a good idea for Sam to call him. Not yet.

And no, no one had heard anything about Violet.

The next Saturday, the Davidsons navigated the foothills of slush that remained in the city to attend services at B'nai Jeshurun. Neither Philip nor Esther told Sam anything other than they were still trying to decide on a synagogue.

Because Sam knew his parents well, he was surprised, not stunned, to see Deborah Leon sitting with her mother and father a few rows ahead. He turned to make a face at Esther, who promptly thumped him hard on his upper arm, the way she'd done when he acted up in public at the age of five. Sam shook his head and squirmed, wondering how he could avoid Deborah after the service.

As Andrew, Diane, and David Leon walked toward them, Sam noticed Deborah trailed behind with a tall man who looked older than she was. He guessed early twenties. The guy was handsome: his hair dark and on the longish side, his brows framing bright blue eyes. Sam's jaw dropped a little when the stranger casually draped his arm around Deborah's shoulders as he made a point of meeting Sam's gaze. As they drew closer, he dropped the arm before the Leons saw and settled for holding Deborah's hand.

Deborah greeted Sam with far more grace than he deserved. "Sam, this is Alex Goldman. Alex, meet Sam, a childhood friend of mine from Alabama." She gazed adoringly at this Alex person as she spoke.

The guy extended his hand. "Debbie's mentioned you, Sam. Welcome to New Yawk."

Debbie. Sam gripped Alex's hand a little more firmly than necessary.

Sam noticed both sets of parents had scooted away to give the three of them some space, as one would before a nuclear explosion.

"I hear you live in Mnnnhattin' by the pahk," Alex continued.

"Yeah, we do. It's very nice there." Alex's accent was grinding into Sam's ears like a rusty drill, but he was determined to be polite for Deborah's sake. He owed her that and much more. Sam briefly studied the laces of his shoes, trying to think what to say next. The words he planned were not the ones he heard coming from his mouth.

"Deborah, could I speak with you privately for a minute?" He indicated a nearby place to sit. "Alex, would you mind? Won't take long at all."

Alex looked at Deborah. She shrugged and nodded, so Alex said, "Nice to meetcha, Sammy." He ambled off to join the Leons and Davidsons, standing near the doors.

Sam bit his tongue. No one had ever called him "Sammy" more than once. He'd have to fix that.

Nice to meet you, *Allie*. He stared after Alex and shook his head.

Deborah sat carefully, fanning the full skirt of her blue dress and crossing her ankles. Sam maintained a respectful two-foot distance.

"Look, I've known this day would come, and I've been dreading it. Definitely a bit sooner thanks to the puppet masters over there." He nodded at Esther, who was gesticulating wildly about something to Diane. "Anyway, I just wanted to say how sorry I am. I was miserable to you, Deborah. I hope you don't hate me, but I'd understand if you did."

Deborah's face blossomed into a soft smile. "Of course I don't hate you." She waved at Alex and turned her eyes back to Sam. "I did for a while, yes. Breaking up with me by sneaking off at a party with Violet was about the crassest thing you could've done. But I'm over it, and everything worked out for the best." She directed a brighter smile at Alex, who was shuffling from foot to foot, obviously bored.

"Okay, well, I wanted you to know how sorry I am. I truly apologize, Deborah. It's taken me a long time to realize it, but Violet was probably wrong for me—"

"Probably? *Probably* she was wrong for you? *Oy*, Sam. You haven't changed a bit."

"I never set out to hurt you, Deborah. In fact—"

Deborah stood abruptly and cut him off. "Like I said, it all worked out for the best." She smoothed the skirt of her dress and Sam noticed a tiny diamond ring on her left hand.

"Is that?" He frowned the question at her.

"No, no, of course not. Not yet. This is a promise ring from Alex."

"A promise ring?" Sam asked. "What exactly does that mean?"

"Remember the class ring I mailed back to you? It means *that*. Only for grownups. Alex is twenty-two. He's studying at NYU to be a dentist. His dad has a practice in Brooklyn he'll take over someday. And they live on the third floor of our building." Once again, she sent a smile sailing to where Alex stood, her eyes shining softly in the dimly lit building.

Sam stifled the impulse to touch her face. Deborah had never looked like this. She'd never *shone* like this. He guessed the entire transformation was due to her happiness with the impossibly handsome tooth fairy by the doors.

"I'm really happy for you, Deborah."

"Call me Debbie. Alex says it suits me better."

Sam laughed with the slightest tinge of acid and said, "I'll call you Deborah. It suits you perfectly."

"Up to you." Deborah gathered her handbag and turned to leave. "I accept your apology, Sam. I'm happy and there's nothing to be gained by dwelling on what you did. In fact…" She paused and started digging in her small handbag. "Do you have a girlfriend here? I can only assume things are over with you and Violet Glenn."

Sam was almost certain Deborah knew Violet was no longer a part of his life, but he let the remark go. "They're over. And no, not really. I've been working a lot. Haven't had a chance to meet many people. Really, nobody outside the store. I'm hoping to when I start classes at Columbia this fall."

Columbia. Take that, NYU Boy.

"You got accepted? Congratulations, Sam!" Deborah seemed genuinely thrilled for him.

"Yes," Sam lied. In fact, he'd heard nothing from his application and wouldn't for weeks.

"Well, I was going to say, we could go on a double date. I'd like that." Deborah took a pen out and scribbled her family's phone number on the back of a crumpled receipt, handing it to Sam. "If and when you do meet somebody, give me a call. Alex and I know a lot of people here, and we'll introduce you. Oh, wait, what am I thinking?" Deborah feigned slapping her hand to her forehead. "Alex has a sister your age. She graduated high school last year. She's adorable. Her name is Anna. Alex calls her Sissie."

Of course he does, Sam thought. Deborah was dating The Lord of Nicknames.

He cleared his throat and pocketed the piece of paper. "I'd like that. I think. Does she look like you?" Sam swept his eyes up and down Deborah appreciatively.

"Sam Davidson, are you flirting with me? I am a promised woman. Besides, I'm crazy about Alex. Not to mention you poured kerosene all over the bridges between us and tossed a match." Deborah glanced toward the doors.

"I am not flirting with you. I just want to know if she looks more like John Wayne or Vivien Leigh. That guy is very tall and big-boned." Sam nodded at Alex.

"She's beautiful," Deborah answered. "Give me time to talk to Alex and call me in a day or two." She swept past Sam in a cloud of *Miss Dior*, which he recognized from Patricia.

"Hey, Deborah," he said. "I'm glad we kept the friend bridge."

She met his eyes. "Me, too."

Twenty-one

RONNI

SEPTEMBER, 2020

"Should I open it now?" Deanna extracted Rick's phone from her purse and held it up. "I'd say you're plenty far enough along for us to listen to the playlist."

I clenched my teeth against the pain of a contraction and nodded. Deanna chuckled as the opening strains of "Let's Get It Started" by Black Eyed Peas filled the room. My husband had actually given me something from the current century, and it was so perfect, I found myself laughing as tears rolled down my cheeks.

"I can't wait for you to hear the rest of this," Deanna shook her head as she scanned the list. "He outdid himself, God bless him."

My laughter stopped as I began sobbing. "He should be here. This is so fucking unfair." I inhaled a ragged breath. Deanna crossed the room to squeeze my shoulder.

"He *is* here, honey," she said. "The way I believe, he's always with you. Rick's watching from somewhere, maybe in this room. There's so much around us we can't discern. I believe that with all my heart."

I shook my head at her and willed myself to stop crying and breathe as normally as I could between contractions. The tears weren't helping me or the baby.

"You know what I mean."

"I do," Deanna nodded, biting her bottom lip. "I know and I understand. I'm sorry, Ronni." She returned to her chair.

I closed my eyes and waited for the next song, intrigued and counting on my husband's sense of humor to carry me through. "Don't Stop Believin'" began to play as I felt the strongest contraction yet. "Got to Get You Into My Life" came next. I giggled at Deanna.

"He was something else, wasn't he?"

"I think 'amazing' is the most overused word in the English language, but Rick was amazing," Deanna answered.

The first notes of "My Girl" just about killed me. All I could do was squeeze my eyes tightly shut and swipe at the tears. *Did he mean that song for me, or the girl he was so sure we'd have?*

Deanna paused the music as the door swung open and a nurse walked in, asking me to recite my name and date of birth. She examined me briefly and crossed to the sink.

"You wrote a book a few years ago, didn't you, Ronni? It took place in Anniston?" she asked. I glanced up at the whiteboard listing the names of my medical attendants in Labor and Delivery. This was Sharee stripping off gloves and washing her hands, her back to me. She was wearing enough PPE to climb through a hazardous waste dump. And if Sharee was about to tell me, as I reclined on an uncomfortable bed with my teeth clenched, enduring seismic contractions that were breaking my body apart, what I should write a book about…I would strangle her with my IV line and leave. I would—

"Yes," Deanna answered from the corner of the room. "She did."

"I thought so," Sharee said. "It was a good story. My mom and I both enjoyed it."

I nodded and tried to shift into a more comfortable position. "I'm glad you liked it," I told her.

Sharee continued, "I've always wanted to be a writer and I would love to pick your brain someday about my ideas. But I mentioned it because my mom's neighbor told her a long time ago it's his father in your book, with a different name. Drove her crazy talking about it. Said he needed to straighten out the story, that you got it wrong and you wouldn't discuss it with him. *Gary*, that's it. Gary something." Sharee made a few notes on her tablet, presumably about my stubborn cervix and not her writing aspirations. "I told Mama it's fiction, and it makes no difference what you wrote, right?"

I glanced at Deanna and back at Sharee, blinking in frustration. "How dilated am I?"

"We're up to seven centimeters. You're doing great. Hang in there, Ronni, and I'll be back in about forty-five minutes."

"I haven't talked to your mom's neighbor, but if you'll get this baby out of me, I'll—"

Deanna cut me off. "Thank you, Sharee. We'll see you soon." She came to the side of the bed and smoothed my sweaty hair off my forehead. "How bad is it, on a scale of one to having your fingernails pulled out?"

I winced. "Right now it's five fingers and a toenail. Why do women go through this? I want drugs. *All* the drugs." I closed my eyes and panted.

"You don't want drugs. You want what's best for the baby. Just breathe, Ronni."

"Pretty weird Sharee's mom lives near Gary Harris." I took a deep breath, trying not to think about the next contraction about to attack me.

"Not really," Deanna replied. "This is a small town. It's not even the first time I've heard something like that. Apparently, Gary shares his frustration occasionally with patrons at the public library."

I grimaced. "Why didn't you tell me?"

"Rick told me not to. He thought Gary might be dangerous."

"Rick thought everyone might be dangerous. He would've taken his pistol to a meeting with the Dalai Lama. He'd...AAAAAARGH."

"Bad one, huh?" Deanna said, as my fingernails dug into her palm. She tapped Rick's phone and informed me "Orinoco Flow" by Enya was next. "You need this to calm you down some now," she told me over the soft music. "Perfect timing."

"That pain was ten times worse. I can't stand this, Deanna. We've been here hours and I've dilated exactly one more centimeter. Something's wrong."

"Nothing's wrong, honey. Everything will be okay." Deanna smiled her best reassuring smile and ignored the way I mutilated her hand.

But everything wasn't okay. By the point I was listening to "Push It" by Salt-N-Pepa for the second time, that much was very clear.

"Ronni? Mrs. O'Shea? Ronni, can you hear me? Hey, I'm Helen. Your baby girl is doing fine."

A pair of wrinkly blue eyes hovered over me in the bright light. I blinked and tried to swallow. My tongue felt like it had been baked.

"Here, honey, you want to sip some water? Your throat may be a little sore from the anesthesia." The blue eyes smiled over a mask and an arm supported my head as I tried to raise it.

A flame of pain blazed across my lower belly. "Where is my baby?"

"She's under some lights for a bit, then I'll bring her to you. She's gorgeous. Looks like her mama."

I sipped a drop or two from a straw and closed my eyes. "Under lights?" I mumbled.

"She's the tiniest bit jaundiced. Nothing to worry about. We'll take her out of the blue lights soon."

I nodded. "Bili-lights."

"That's right. Are you in the medical field?" Helen fussed with my IV as she asked.

"Yes, I'm a nurse."

"Well, then you know she's fine. Such a pretty baby and I'll bring her to meet you before too long."

"What happened? I was supposed to get an epidural." I frowned and tried to catch a memory. It was a fuzzy mishmash of voices, all sounding like they were from another planet, lights on the ceiling rushing by overhead.

"We ran out of time for that. The cord was tangled and Dr. Aronson had us get you to the OR. But Ronni, you're fine and your baby is, too. Get some sleep and I promise I'll bring her soon."

"Where's Deanna?" I opened my eyes and squinted at Helen, who stood in the doorway.

"She's fine, too, honey. We sent her home to rest. You were in labor for hours and hours."

I thought I was dreaming the first time I held her. Between the anesthesia and painkillers, the impossibly perfect little face nestled in the crook of my elbow seemed like a doll, not a human I'd grown inside me. She gave a tiny yawn and my heart surged with something I'd never be able to fully define: a mix of inordinate pride in my daughter's ability to yawn and a sudden panic over the idea of something, anything, hurting her.

"Don't try to do too much yet, Ronni," Helen said. "You're going to be really sore." She took Violet from my arms and I pulled my gown down, exposing the nipple as instructed, holding my breast the way she'd shown me. Helen placed the baby next to it and I watched her tiny mouth root around, eyes still closed, and try to latch on. My baby managed to do it on the third try.

"That hurts," I told Helen.

"Only at first. You're a natural, Ronni. So is your little Violet. Look at her, nursing like a pro. That's such an old-fashioned name, and I love it. Is she called after someone in your family?" Helen's eyes were kind and warm as she looked at my baby girl.

"Yes," was all I said. It was true as far as I was concerned.

"Well," Helen told me, "she's as beautiful as her name. Really. I know you think I say that to all the moms, but I don't." She chuckled. "Sometimes it's more like, *what a sweet baby she is* or *oh, he's all boy!* Your Violet is truly exquisite."

"Like her namesake," I said, nodding.

"Well, you keep that pillow there to support her and mash that call button if y'all have any problems. I'll be back in a little bit."

I looked down at my daughter and wiped my tears off her head as she nursed. "Sweet girl, your daddy would have been crazy about you," I whispered. "He would've said you look exactly like me…" Violet opened her dark eyes as I spoke: Rick's eyes. She stopped nursing for a few seconds and resumed for a while until she seemed to drift off, a bit of milky dribble on her tiny mouth. I waited a minute or two and moved her cautiously to my other breast, amazed she seemed to know what to do better than I did.

"How's it going?" Helen poked her head in about twenty minutes later. "Did she get enough to eat?"

"I think she did. Should I be worried she hasn't cried at all?"

Helen laughed. "Thankful is the word you're looking for, not worried. She'll cry for you when she's ready. You both need to sleep now." She came to the bed and gently extracted Violet into her arms. "We're going to put her under the lights just a tiny bit longer. I'm sure they'll bring her bassinet in your room tomorrow morning to stay with you."

I felt like part of my body was being dragged away from the bed, some vital organ. "Are you sure? Does she really need it? She doesn't seem at all jaundiced to me."

Helen looked at me the way she'd no doubt looked at a thousand new mothers, calmly and patiently, probably stifling the urge to argue or smother me with a pillow.

"Let me check. I'll bring her back if the doctor says it's okay."

Fifteen minutes later she wheeled a clear plastic bassinet into my room. "Dr. Aquaro says all right; we've been through a couple of diapers and her bilirubin level is down. Violet can stay in here. But when she wakes up to nurse, you'll need to call one of us. Tomorrow we'll have you on your feet, but you shouldn't lift her on your own just yet. Understand?"

"Yes," I smiled at her tiny form, bundled inside a white and pink blanket. "I understand. Thank you, Helen."

"They'll let your friend back in tomorrow after ten. Deanna, right?"

"That's right." I closed my eyes.

"Is she a relative?" Helen asked, a bit nosily for my taste.

"Yes, she is. I'm going to try to get some sleep."

That first night, I must have pressed the call button six times. Violet slept for the first hour, then began wailing. She was fine once I'd fed her, but then she'd startle at something and cry again. The nurses came and changed her diapers. They handed her to me to breastfeed. They muttered reassurance. Lather, rinse, repeat.

Still, Violet cried. She cried so much I began to worry there was a physical cause. In the early morning light, I grilled Nancy, the day nurse assigned to me, about Violet's health. I wanted to know about any concerns the pediatrician had. I demanded every bit of minutiae from her chart.

Is this colic? Are her little internal organs working properly? Is she possessed by demons?

It was all normal. My baby girl was a crier, apparently, and I would have to figure out how to listen to her scream without losing my mind. Even the painkillers Nancy gave me didn't dull the edge of Violet's shrieks. I felt completely incapable of doing anything but producing milk for her greedy little mouth. I was a giant udder with no maternal skills, too helpless to pick up my own baby. Within a few minutes of her return to the bassinet, she'd cry. It was hard not to take it personally.

I'm doing everything I can. I'm new to this, too.

My belly incision felt newly slashed by a machete, but I was forced by Nancy and her aide, an unsmiling girl who looked about twelve, to carefully ease myself off the bed. They made me walk the hallway hunched like Quasimodo.

A quasi-mama, that's what I am, a stooped wannabe. I stared at the sad shuffle of my feet in slipper socks, firmly convinced I'd never stand up straight again.

And, in a moment that felt like a completely new low, I asked Nancy to take Violet back to the nursery for a few hours. I was desperate for sleep. My daughter wailed her sentiments all the way out of the room.

Deanna breezed in fresher than ever a few minutes past ten. I still couldn't figure out why she looked so different lately. Maybe it was new makeup. She'd begun to resemble her mother more and more.

She took my hand. "How do you feel, honey?"

"The pain is dulled, kind of like it's in another room. Unfortunately, so is my daughter, because she won't stop crying." I shook my head at her, a little angry at her grin. "Why is this amusing to you?"

"She's fine, Ronni. She has a set of healthy lungs and she's using them. She'll quiet down when she gets used to being in this strange place. It's a big shift from her home for the last nine months."

"Uh-huh. I guess. It's so weird, because she was almost too quiet when she was first brought to me. She nursed easily and never fussed one bit. It worried me, how silent she was."

Deanna shrugged. "Maybe leftover anesthesia? I don't know. But stop worrying. She's healthy and so lovely, Ronni. She's a ridiculously beautiful baby. It's almost embarrassing, how much better she looks than the other babies in the nursery window. A few parents have filed complaints. One said to move her to the back."

I clutched the pillow held to my belly tighter. "Do not make me laugh. Gah, that hurts." I waved up and down at her. "Is that a new dress?"

"It is. I went shopping a few days ago. Trying to fix myself up a bit."

"What is going on with you, Deanna? You look younger than when I met you." I narrowed my eyes. "Are you in love?"

"Of course not. Who would I be in love with, besides that guy who plays Loki in the movies my grandson watches? When I met you, I was going through an old patch, that's all." Deanna turned her palms up and lifted one shoulder.

"An old patch, huh?" I smiled, wary of the tiniest chuckle and the pain it would deliver.

"I'd been dealing with a divorce, Sarah's pill problems, taking care of my grandchildren full-time, and then suddenly finding out about my own adoption, showing up too late to meet my birth mother…it was a lot. I'm feeling more like myself these days."

I heard the nurse call out to someone down the hallway and my milk let down as soon as my ears registered Violet wailing her way to me. Nancy placed her on my lap pillow and Deanna sat, watching the baby breastfeed. When she finished, Deanna took her from my arms, nestling her expertly by her own neck, patting and rubbing her tiny back with her three middle fingers. She jiggled the baby up and down in a motion as timeless as mothers themselves and paced away from me.

Violet opened her dark eyes and peeped over Deanna's shoulder at me, silently telegraphing, *This is what I wanted. How hard could it be, seriously?* She didn't make a peep. I realized, with more than a twinge of guilt, my c-section meant I'd probably be asking Deanna to stay at my house longer than expected.

She read my thoughts, as usual, and called the words over her back. "I'm not planning to move my stuff back to my house anytime soon. We'll get you and Violet settled when they release you in a few days, and I'll do the heavy lifting, okay? It feels so wonderful to have a baby in my arms again."

"What about Sarah? What about your grandchildren?" I blurted. "Do they ever think it's weird that you spend so much time with me?"

Deanna returned to the bedside chair, still bouncing the baby up and down slightly as she sat. "Sarah's all wrapped up in her job and volunteering at Lacey's school, which is perfect. She should be Lacey's mom, not me. Kevin and Charlotte are old enough they only want to be with their friends these days. Nobody's missing me."

"But *she's* your daughter—"

Deanna held a finger to her lips and whispered, "Baby's almost asleep." She rubbed Violet's back and smiled. She continued in a low voice, "DNA is far from the only thing that holds people together, Ronni. The strongest bonds are formed by love, not genes. If anyone on the planet knows that, it's you." She bit her lower lip. "She does have his eyes, doesn't she?"

"The nurse said they're such a dark blue, they'll turn brown. So yes. Definitely Rick's eyes." I looked at my sleeping baby on Deanna's shoulder. "She's every bit as patient as he was when she wants food, too. When Rick was hungry, he could scare a herd of cattle with a look. Actually," I grinned, because laughing would kill me, "the night we went to Max and Elise's that first time for dinner, Rick stopped on the way and stuck his head out of the window at a roadside pasture in Oxford. He stared at the cows and they stared back for about a minute. Then he licked his lips and sure enough, they all scattered like he'd thrown something at them."

"He did love a steak," she said, giggling softly. "I miss him too, Ronni."

"I was thinking last night how he would have cradled Violet in his huge paws and studied her face. I could practically see him doing it. And it occurred to me that it's a different Rick I'm grieving now: the father he would have been to her. The man I can only imagine trying to make her say *Daddy*; the one holding his arms out for her first steps to him."

Deanna nodded without a word. She stood and placed Violet in the bassinet Nancy had optimistically rolled into position nearby, then reached into her handbag and produced Mikey the Monkey. She nestled him next to Violet and whispered to me, "I washed him twice."

"I can't believe you brought that thing here," I told her, shaking my head.

Deanna smiled. "You're not crying, though, Ronni. And neither is she."

We watched Violet peacefully dream whatever dreams a newborn can conjure, her rosebud mouth mock-nursing every once in a while. She slept a full three-and-a-half hours next to a tattered stuffed animal that held a tiny moment of her dad's life.

Twenty-two

New York City

1948

S am slid the thin envelope out of his family's mailbox, glancing around to see if anyone was watching before he opened it. Columbia University regretted to inform Sam they could not welcome him for their fall semester. He was encouraged to re-apply. Sam crumpled the paper into a ball, depositing his hopes for a dorm life full of people his own age into the lobby's trash chute. He hadn't applied anywhere else; his heart was set on Columbia and he'd honestly thought his essay would gain him entrance—and exit from Philip and Esther's home.

He loved his parents dearly, but living with them as an adult was becoming more and more difficult. His dad continued every business conversation they'd begun in his office at the dinner table. Sam's mother seemed to think this was great, hanging on Philip's every word, eager to contribute her own ideas. Worse, Esther had begun to experiment with new recipes inspired by her women's magazines. They'd suffered brown sugar meatloaf and lima beans suspended in some horrifying clear tasteless Jell-O last week.

Sam dug out his abandoned Rolleiflex, eager to pursue anything besides work. That camera became his best friend in the New York spring, capturing buildings that tickled the clouds and dinner-plate-sized pink magnolias in Central Park. He located a place to develop his photos and clutched the packet as he walked home to examine his work in the privacy of his room. As he placed each print on the bed, Sam held up a few he'd consider framing: his favorite views of the city and an occasional tourist who'd captured his eye. He would definitely order an enlargement of the Indian woman in a blue and gold sari pointing at the Empire State Building, her arm decorated with an impossible number of bracelets.

Waiting at the bottom of the pile was a series of photos he'd forgotten were on the roll: Deborah blowing him a kiss at Oxford Lake, dark hair tangled across her face in the wind. Deborah reading a book, her legs curled together on her parents' sofa as she leaned toward a lamp. Deborah laughing at something he'd said, her head thrown back in the passenger seat of his old Plymouth. Deborah sipping a milkshake at Woolworth's counter, pretending to be unaware of the camera.

A close-up of Deborah's coffee-brown eyes, soft, looking at the lens as though it were Sam's own heart. He remembered taking that one on a fall afternoon after Johnny's accident.

After Johnny, before Violet. When Deborah still adored him.

Esther knocked on Sam's door to announce dinner and he surprised himself by saying, "Come in." His mother walked to the bed and picked up the photo of Deborah laughing.

"Oh, look at her. Why did you never call Deborah, honey?" Esther glanced up from the picture.

"I didn't want to go on a double date with that guy's sister. He's barely tolerable, and I doubt I'd like her," Sam answered.

"Or maybe," Esther raised her gray eyebrows, "you don't want to see your Deborah with him."

"She's not *my Deborah*, Mom." Sam gathered the photos into a pile. "After what I did to her, she won't be. She deserves better."

Esther put her hands on her hips. "Oh, I agree. But you can *be* better, Sam. And this…whatever his name is…Alex…he's not so great for her. He bosses her around. He tells her how to dress, how to act, what's acceptable for a *hillbilly* in New York. He actually used that word, thought it was a funny joke. He's a *schmuck*."

Sam glanced at his mother. "I know Mrs. Leon told you all that, but it doesn't change the way Deborah feels about Alex. She's head over heels. You've seen the way she looks at him."

Esther reached for the close-up of Deborah's eyes and handed it to her son. "It's nothing like the way she looked at you. It never will be." She walked to the door and paused with her hand on the knob. "And Sam," she said, without turning around, "I know you miss her. She's everything you could want in a girl. She's beautiful; she's Alabama *and* New York; she's your past and your future. Not that I'm trying to interfere."

Sam threw his hands up at the door closing behind his mother. *Interfere* was her middle name. He was pretty sure she chanted it like a mantra.

He lined up the photos of Deborah and swept his eyes over them, reliving each of the moments they captured. Sam sighed and allowed his heart to whisper: *You miss her. The way she sighs after you kiss her; the way she giggles in movies and clamps her hand over her mouth; the way she brushes her hair behind her ears when she's about to say something; the way she feels in your arms when you dance.*

He opened his desk drawer and located the piece of paper with Deborah's number. Sam bit his lip and headed to the living room to arrange a date with Anna, Alex's "Sissie."

What's the worst that could happen?

Three nights later Sam paced near the front of the Roxy Theatre, squinting at the marquee's bright lights surrounding the feature's title, *The Miracle of the Bells*. Deborah, Alex, and Anna were supposed to arrive at 7:15; it was now almost 7:40 and the movie had already started. He was stalking off to a phone booth when their taxi disgorged them half a block away, Deborah and Alex hand in hand and Anna hidden behind them at first.

Alex strolled nearer at a leisurely pace as Deborah stared at the movie palace, her mouth a small 'o.' The Roxy seated nearly six thousand, dominating an entire street corner, decorated with enough lights for five Ferris wheels. It was billed as "The Cathedral of the Motion Picture." Sam was irritated he wouldn't be seeing inside it, unsure if they'd return for the later showing.

Sam waved hello with only the slightest hint of annoyance, his practiced politeness taking over. Alex shook his hand and introduced his sister. Anna was as pretty as Deborah had promised, with long, wavy brunette hair and large blue eyes. She smiled and reached for Sam's hand.

"Are you as embarrassed as I am by this set-up?" she asked, chuckling a little. "Only for my stupid brother would I do this. You like the theatre?"

Sam noted the pronunciation of "thee-TUH" and nodded. "It's huge," he said. "I've never seen anything like it."

"I bet you haven't," she said. "But *y'all* had movie theaters, right?" She looked back and forth between Sam and Deborah.

"Yes," Sam nodded. "We were hoping talkies would come to Alabama soon." He reached over to hug Deborah quickly and continued, "The hardest part was trying to eat fried chicken in those folding chairs. Used to be out of napkins by intermission—"

Deborah caught Anna's expression and jumped in. "He's kidding, Anna. Sam's a bit of a cut-up."

"Just like you, Debbie," Alex said, grinning at her.

"Just like me." She smiled and kissed his lips lightly, right there in front of God and everybody. "I love to make you laugh, honey."

Sam wondered how often Alex was laughing with Deborah, not at her. He cleared his throat.

"Anyway, bad news. We're too late for the movie and the next showing isn't until 9:45. Would y'all like to grab some dinner somewhere?"

Alex and Deborah nodded without a single word of apology or explanation for being late. "I know a place down the street," Alex said.

Anna said, "That's so cute, how you say y'all. I'm starving, so let's go." She looped her arm through Sam's. "Say it again."

"Say what?" Sam asked.

"Say 'y'all,' of course. Oh, and then say 'bayou.' And then say 'watermelon.' Please. I could listen to you pronounce things all night."

Sam shook his head. "Not right now."

He and Anna followed Alex and Deborah for a couple of blocks to a small Italian restaurant, the kind with red-and-white checkered tablecloths and candles dripping down the sides of chianti bottles. Alex chose a booth and settled in as close as humanly possible next to Deborah, his arm draped around her shoulders and his hand just a little too close to her left breast. Sam met her eyes and smirked the tiniest bit, knowing she was uncomfortable.

"Whew," Deborah fanned the air with her hand. "It's already pretty warm outside, and I think they still have the heat on in here. Would you mind, honey?" She looked at Alex, who obediently scooted away an inch or two and took his arm back. Deborah held her menu up to read and whispered something to Alex behind it. He laughed and Sam turned his attention to Anna. She promptly pointed to "cannoli" on the menu.

"Say that," she insisted.

So he did. She giggled. Sam entertained her with his most exaggerated Southern accent until their dinners arrived.

"So, Sam," Alex said, "you a Yankees or Dodgers fan?"

"I'm not much of a baseball fan at all, Alex. Basketball or football, those are my games. But I guess if I had to choose, it would be the Yankees. I'm not much for underdogs."

Alex chuckled. "They are that, my Dodgers, but we love 'em." He folded a piece of pizza in half and paused with it mid-air. "Of course, you would go Yankees because of Jackie Robinson." He took a bite and nodded.

Sam shrugged. "What are you talking about?"

"The Dodgers just signed the first Negro player ever to take the major league field, that's what. Only natural you'd feel that way about them." Alex glanced at his sister, who raised her brows.

Sam put his pizza down and sat back, crossing his arms. "So, I'm from Alabama and that makes you think I'd be against Jackie Robinson playing, that's it? The guy's an incredible athlete. You've got some cockeyed ideas about me, Alex, and you should apologize."

Deborah placed a hand on Alex's arm. "Honey, he's right. You owe Sam an apology. Don't make assumptions about him or anyone else. It's not fair."

"Yeah, I'm sorry, Sam. I thought you'd agree with what I've read in the news about that one." Alex nodded slowly at Sam as he said it.

"First of all, I have no idea what you've read in the news," Sam said. "Second, Robinson is talented enough to actually help your Dodgers finally win the World Series for once. I think he's great. Third, baseball is boring as hell."

Anna jumped in. "Our dad likes the Knicks. He went to their first home game a couple of years ago."

Sam took a bite of pizza and chewed. He thought for a few seconds and said, "Chicago at Madison Square Garden. They tied 2-2. Beat Pittsburgh in their next game, though. I think it was 3-2. Ralph Kaplowitz was amazing in that game."

Alex laughed. "You're a basketball encyclopedia, huh?"

"Just a fan," Sam said. "I played in high school. Love the game. I'd like to go to a Knicks game sometime."

"Oooh," Anna said, "say 'sometime' again."

Sam rolled his eyes and ignored her, hoping someone else would order the cannoli they'd agreed on. He wasn't about to say it out loud.

As soon as dessert was finished and their checks were paid, he told Anna, "I'm so glad to have met you. Y'all please excuse me, but I have to be at the store tomorrow early for inventory. I don't think I can stay for the next showing of the movie. I'm so sorry."

"Inventory?" Deborah asked. "On a Saturday? Since when would Esther allow that?"

"Things are pretty different here," Sam said, shrugging. "The store's growing fast, and there's a lot to keep up with, so sometimes we have to work on the Sabbath. Mom's learned to make peace with it." He stood and took Anna's hand, kissing it as elegantly as he'd seen Cary Grant do in movies. It was the least he could offer after deciding he never wanted to see her again.

"Okay then. Well, goodnight and thanks for a nice time." Sam waved as he backed away. "Deborah, give me a call sometime, huh? We should catch up on things at home. Some of the restaurants have indoor plumbing now." Alex and Anna laughed, but Deborah just shook her head, watching him walk away.

She called the next day, as he'd known she would. "You're not doing inventory. You're not even at the store," she said without preamble.

"Of course not. It's the Sabbath." Sam sank back into the sofa cushions and nodded at his mother, who'd been trying to eavesdrop in the hall but retreated to her room. "It's just like we did in Anniston. We're open, but the only employees there are non-observant." He said it loudly enough for Esther to hear, then lowered his voice. "Umm, first off, thanks for setting me up with Anna." He took a deep breath. "Look, I haven't said it enough: I'm still sorry about the way I treated you in Alabama—"

"Sam," she interrupted, "that's all ancient history. I am so tired of talking about it. I have Alex now, so everything turned out for the best. I accepted your apology. Enough, already. How did you like Anna? She's gorgeous, huh?"

"She's beautiful." Sam nodded into the phone. "I'm not sure she's right for me, but thank you for trying."

"Oh, come on, Sam! How can you not be crazy about her?" Deborah said. "She has boys chasing her all over the city. You're lucky to get a date."

"Do you never get tired of the condescension, Deborah? *Debbie?*" Sam turned his eyes to the ceiling.

"I don't know what you're talking about. Just because she thinks your accent is cute. Alex thinks mine is, too. What's the big deal?"

"Did he really call you a *hillbilly?*" Sam twirled the phone cord around his finger and looked at his mother's closed door.

Deborah laughed. "He was joking. I can't believe my mother's telling people about that. It's ridiculous."

"Maybe," Sam answered, "she didn't hear it as a joke."

"Look, your mother and my mother will find what they're determined to find with Alex. I'm ignoring it."

Sam laughed. "That's not far from the truth. So…can we talk a little here and there?" He shouldered the phone. "To tell you the truth, all I do is work and come home to my parents. I could use a sympathetic ear."

"Anna is sympathetic," Deborah answered. "And you know darn well I'm calling to see if you like her enough for a second date. She likes you."

"I'm sorry, Deborah, but no. Anna would make me recite the Pledge of Allegiance for her amusement. I'm not *that* lonely yet."

She paused for a beat or two. "Okay. You can call and *kvetch* about your parents every once in a while. As long as I get to complain about mine. I don't think Alex would mind."

"Deal," Sam said. "Bye for now."

Deborah hung up the phone and walked to her building's elevator, pressing 3 to reach the Goldmans' apartment. Anna swung the door open wide and grinned at her.

"Did you call him?" she asked, giggling.

"Yep. It all went perfectly. He thinks you're obnoxious, but very pretty," Deborah said, following Anna to her bedroom.

"Does he think Alex is obnoxious but pretty, too?" Anna laughed. "I mean, he is completely obnoxious, my brother. Not ugly, though."

"Where is he?" Deborah asked.

"Out with his other girlfriend, presumably," Anna said. "Alex will not be tied down."

"Well, he's played his part perfectly. Even my own parents think we're the real deal. And my mom finds him fairly obnoxious, too, as an added bonus." Deborah twisted the tiny promise ring on her finger. "I'll be able to give this diamond back to you in a week or two, I think, when Alex and I officially break up."

"Are all Southern girls this devious, like Scarlett O'Hara?" Anna said. "I want to learn your mysterious ways."

Deborah laughed. "There's nothing mysterious about it. We're just helping Sam to wake up. He's way past due."

Three days later, Sam stopped at his favorite lunchtime phone booth and dialed Deborah's number.

"Guess what?" he said. "Patricia's getting married. I forgot to tell you."

"Patricia who?" Deborah replied.

"Come on, Deborah. You know her. Patricia Hollis from the store in Anniston. She works here now. Met a guy named Ronald Carpenter and fell madly in love with him. Now they're getting married at Trinity Church. It's gorgeous, Deborah, one of the most historic buildings in Manhattan. Surely you've seen it?"

"No, I haven't. I mean, what kind of church is it?" Deborah closed her eyes and gripped the receiver a little more tightly.

"It's Episcopal, Episcopalian, whatever you call it. And I'm invited to the wedding this Sunday afternoon, with my parents, of course, and I was just wondering if you might go with me? Please? It would be a real act of kindness. You could maybe tell Alex Patricia's an old friend from Alabama, so you're tagging along with my family."

Deborah bit her lip and forced herself to pause before answering. "I guess it would be okay with him. She is an old friend, after all. And we'll be with your folks. So yeah, I'll go."

"Great," Sam said. "I'll pick you up at five. Oh, and Mom thinks you might have to cover your head with a lace thing for the church. She's still trying to find out. Do you have a lace thing?"

Deborah chuckled. "I'll bring something in my handbag, I guess. I think Catholic women have lace caps. Maybe Episcopalians do, too."

"It's a strange new world for us," Sam said. "It'll be fun to see how they do it. There's gonna be a reception at a restaurant, too, and Patricia says there will be canapés, whatever they are. Champagne and dancing, too."

"Sounds great. I'd better call Alex and tell him, but I'm sure he'll understand. Bye, Sam. I'll see you Sunday." Deborah hung up the phone and danced around her parents' living room, arms wrapped around her own body.

Diane Leon stuck her head out of the kitchen, holding a carrot she'd been peeling. "Was that Sam?" she asked.

"Yes, it was." Deborah beamed at her mother.

"Sounds like you're going to have to call Alex and break his heart, if it can be located."

"Mom, really. Alex is a nice guy. And all I'm doing is going to a wedding with Sam and his parents this Sunday."

"Uh-huh," her mother nodded, "and all I'm doing is watching your plan unfold. I'm not stupid, Deborah. Your dad and I have noticed you've barely seen Alex lately."

Deborah laughed. "Just as you'd hoped."

"Just as we'd hoped. But Sam had better never hurt you again. I mean that." Diane shook her carrot for emphasis.

"I don't think he would, Mom. And there's no guarantee this will work out, anyway. Maybe Sam just really needs anyone who's not a stranger to escort to this wedding. Have you ever been to an Episcopal one?"

"No, I haven't," Diane answered. "I doubt the reception will be as much fun as ours. Nobody's getting carried on a chair while you dance the hora." She waved her carrot as she sang a brief verse of "Hava Nagila."

Deborah sank into the couch, sighing. "I wonder if I'll ever get carried on a chair." She scratched at the nubby green fabric and then picked up the novel she'd been reading.

"You're eighteen, Deborah. Enjoy your life. Someday you'll be peeling carrots for a pot roast instead of reading a good book."

Sam stood at the Leons' door, waiting through an excruciating silence as Mr. Leon looked him up and down. "Deborah will be out in a minute," her father said. He didn't invite Sam in. They stood awkwardly until Deborah showed up in a pink chiffon shirtwaist, its full skirt swirling around her ankles.

"It's not too much, is it?" She smiled at Sam's appreciative grin.

"I don't think so, but who cares? It's beautiful on you," Sam answered. He offered Deborah his arm and nodded to Mr. Leon. "We'll be home by midnight, sir."

"You'd better be," Andrew Leon answered. Deborah looked puzzled, like she wondered how a six o'clock wedding could stretch into a reception that late. Maybe there were more traditions than cake-cutting.

Esther scooted to make room for Deborah in the back of the taxi; Philip was riding up front. He turned around and complimented her dress. Sam half-listened to the women chatter from his seat on the other side of his mother, watching the skyscrapers roll past. He closed his eyes and hoped he'd made the right choice by inviting Deborah. He wasn't sure about anything anymore.

The church looked like a massive European cathedral, a stalwart Gothic Revival landmark with graceful spires soaring hundreds of feet into the sky. Sam wished for his camera, thinking he'd have to come back and capture it. The inside was elaborate and majestic, cavernous with flying buttresses, nothing like any synagogue he'd seen. Sam couldn't help but admire the roses adorning the ends of the pews, each large bouquet held by satin ribbons. Patricia would never be crass enough to discuss money, but it was apparent to Sam she was marrying a well-to-do man. Her parents ran a country store and had never traveled beyond Alabama as far as he knew. He glanced at Deborah, who was studying a program they'd been handed. Her hair curtained her face and she swept it back to look at him.

"We're gonna be here a while," she whispered, running her finger down the order of the service.

Sam smiled and nodded. He glanced at his watch, expecting things to get started at any moment.

He recognized Mrs. Hollis on the arm of an usher he didn't know, but was pretty sure was an Oxford cousin of Patricia's. The guy walked her to a place near the front and deposited her in the pew, then went to stand next to Ronald and two other men. Sam noticed the groom shifting his weight from foot to foot, his hands clasped in front of him.

A hush fell over the murmuring crowd as Patricia's sister Gina walked up the aisle, her dress a deep emerald set off by the pink roses she held. Two more bridesmaids followed before the organist played the opening notes of "Here Comes The Bride" and everyone stood and faced the back of the church, where Patricia entered on the arm of her father.

Sam had never seen a more incandescent bride. She was beauty itself, her white lace dress prettier than anything a movie star ever wore. Sam smiled to himself, glad the store had ordered and tailored it as a gift to "their" bride.

He listened as the rest of the congregation sang hymns and the wedding ceremony meandered its way to the vows. He heard Patricia say "I do" and saw Ronald Carpenter swipe a tear away after he kissed his bride.

Good. He'd better treat her the way she deserves.

He met Patricia's eye as the newlyweds made their exit. She smiled back at him and winked, clutching her husband's arm. The congregation clumped into the aisle and began the five-minute walk to Fraunces Tavern for the reception.

"Everybody walks everywhere here, don't they?" Deborah said, matching Sam's stride behind his parents. "It's so different."

"I kinda like it, though, now that I can find my way around a bit," Sam answered. "I want to bring my camera back to that church. It's amazing. This restaurant we're going to is really historic, too."

"I never knew you cared so much about history," Deborah said. "These heels are killing me. Slow down, Sam, please."

Sam glanced over his shoulder. "We'll get run over by hungry people." He pulled Deborah aside and leaned her against a building as his parents sailed on, unaware. He pointed to Deborah's feet. "Are you wearing stockings?"

"That's kind of personal, Sam," she answered. "But yes."

"Okay, take your shoes off," he said.

Deborah stared.

"Just do it." Sam removed his own shoes, and then peeled his socks off, handing them to Deborah. "Put these on over your stockings. We're only a minute or two away from the restaurant."

"I'll look like an idiot." Deborah looked at all the people passing them on the sidewalk.

"No one cares, Deborah. It's New York. There are stranger things than a girl in a fancy dress with black socks strolling along." Sam waved for her to hurry.

Deborah hesitated, but took her high-heeled pumps off and handed them to Sam.

"There. You look perfect." Sam stifled a laugh. "And you'll be able to dance later without your feet bleeding."

They rejoined the crowd and Sam was right: no one blinked at her weird socks.

"It's architecture," Sam said. "Not history so much. I love taking photos of the buildings."

"Oh, you've started using your camera again? That's great." Deborah smiled up at him. "Have you gotten any good ones lately?"

"Yeah. Yeah, I have," Sam said. "I found some real beauties in the latest batch I had developed."

Deborah stumbled and grabbed Sam's arm. "These socks are big enough for clown feet," she said. "I can't walk in them."

Sam took her arm and threaded it under his, clutching her to his side. "Here. Just hang on and we'll get there."

Just outside the restaurant, he held her shoes out and guarded the space around Deborah as she slipped them on, handing his mutilated socks back.

"I guess they're better than nothing." Sam shrugged and slid the socks back into place, picking a piece of paper from the bottom of one. He opened the restaurant door and a hostess directed them to a private room, where they found themselves seated at a table blissfully far from his parents. They were near the back with the younger people, none of whom seemed particularly eager to talk to Sam and Deborah. Sam lifted their place cards and moved them to an empty table nearby.

"Is this okay?" he asked a passing waiter. "It's so noisy in here, and we'd like to talk."

The guy nodded. "Sure. It's not dinner service; we're just passing around appetizers. Would you like a glass of champagne? They're toasting soon." He held out a tray of coupes and Deborah snatched one like a raptor, taking a big swallow before anyone was supposed to.

"What?" she answered Sam's stare. "I'm thirsty and my feet have been abused."

"I've never seen you willingly drink alcohol," Sam said.

"You've never seen me offered champagne."

They raised their glasses to Mr. and Mrs. Ronald Carpenter, then sat at their table. No one moved to join them. Sam pretended to listen to the speeches and tributes and jokes at the front of the room while Deborah finished one and a half glasses of champagne.

"You might want to slow down on that, Deborah. You're not much of a drinker," he told her.

"Are you really telling me what to do?" she answered.

"Are you really not used to it, after months with Alex, Debbie?"

She surprised him by answering, "Touché." She set her glass down. "Alex is a little bossy."

Sam said, "General George S. Patton was a little bossy. Alex is a Sherman Tank."

"That's not fair, Sam. You barely know him." Deborah's eyes flashed dark at Sam. "Alex is a good guy."

Sam nodded and looked at the crowd. They were backing away, creating a circle so Patricia and Ronald could begin their first dance. He noticed a trio of musicians and a singer in the front corner of the room.

The room went quiet as the opening strains of "For Sentimental Reasons" played. The wedding singer said, "Ladies and gentlemen, Mr. and Mrs. Ronald Carpenter" as the bride and groom walked hand in hand to the dance floor and wrapped their arms around each other. "I looooove youuuuu," he crooned as they swayed to the music.

Sam turned to Deborah. "Are you allowed to dance?" he asked, as she drained the last drop from her champagne glass and grabbed another from a passing waiter.

Deborah took a less-than-dainty sip. "Don't be ridiculous. I'm allowed to do anything I damn well please. I'm a grown woman with my own mind."

Sam laughed. "Remind me never to give you champagne." He held out his hand and pulled her to her feet.

"The question is," Deborah said, "are you able to dance?"

"Hahaha. I do okay. Come on." Sam pulled her to the dance floor and caught his mother grinning and elbowing his dad as they passed.

Sam held Deborah close, remembering dances to this very song in Alabama. Her head was on his shoulder. He wondered what expression was on her face. *Happiness? Gloating? Revenge?*

"Hey, maybe we should be a little further apart," he suggested. "You belong to someone else."

"Has that ever stopped you?" she said to his chest.

Sam shook his head. "I guess I deserve that. But can it be the final shot, Deborah?"

She nodded into his shoulder, pulling away slightly. Now she looked up into his face and Sam found it much harder to talk.

"You'll find someone who's right for you, Sam." She blinked and smiled at him.

"I already have," Sam said, before he could stop the words. "I was just too stupid and stubborn to realize it."

Deborah laughed, a small titter he felt like a dart hitting his chest. "It's too late. I'm sorry, Sam. I'm going to marry Alex."

"He proposed?" Sam said. "He actually proposed?"

"Not yet, but he will."

Sam nodded and swallowed, his mouth a tight line. He saw his mother across the room, smiling at him as though she knew some secret he'd been denied.

"They were of you," he said.

"What are you talking about?" Deborah answered.

"The beautiful photos I found when I developed that roll of film. There were pictures I'd taken a long time ago. And there you were, smiling at me and laughing and reading a book and drinking a milkshake. I keep looking at them—"

Deborah stopped dancing and stepped backward. Sam followed as she hurried to the back of the room and grabbed her handbag.

"I think I'm going to be sick," she told him, darting for the door.

Sam waited ten minutes before knocking on the ladies' room door. "Are you okay, Deborah?" There was no response. An older lady he recognized as an Alabama relative of Patricia's opened the door and walked out.

"She's okay, son. Just a little too much champagne. The attendant in there got her a toothbrush and toothpaste. She'll be out in a minute."

"Thank you," Sam answered. "Aren't you Patricia's aunt? I remember you coming in the store. I'm Sam Davidson."

"I'm her daddy's sister, Imogene Davis. Beautiful wedding, wasn't it? Patricia is so happy." The woman swiped at her eyes, trying and failing to wipe away some errant mascara. "I remember her when she was the prettiest baby I'd ever seen."

"Now she's the prettiest bride," Sam said. "Here," he extended his thumb near her face, "may I?"

Imogene Davis nodded and Sam swiped the black mark from the old lady's cheek.

"Thank you, honey. You're a nice boy. Don't you let New York City change you. Keep those Alabama manners, hear?"

"Yes, ma'am." Sam smiled at her retreating back and waited a full two more minutes before Deborah emerged, looking fresh as a slightly tipsy daisy.

"I'm sorry," Deborah said. "Clearly, I'm not used to drinking."

He took her hand to lead her back to the table. "I could've told you that. And your favorite flowers are hydrangeas. You read trashy romance novels and hide them from your mom. You love vanilla ice cream more than any other flavor. You have a tiny scar on your right knee from falling off your bike when you were five." Sam pulled out her chair for her. "And you want three sons, because daughters are too difficult."

Deborah gazed at him and said nothing. Sam watched as light entered her eyes, a distant sunrise that brightened as he spoke.

"I'm going to get you a glass of water," he announced.

When Sam returned, Deborah was fumbling in her handbag. She took tiny sips of the water as Sam watched.

"Do you remember that night at the lake when I fell in?" he asked. "Because I do. You were wearing a dark burgundy dress, and you looked like a genuine Hollywood starlet, Deborah. You leaned back in that boat I was trying to row to the island; I was trying so hard to get the damn thing to go where I wanted it to, and the wind blew your hair across your face and you laughed and you looked absolutely perfect, beautiful beyond words. I wanted my camera so bad. And then I plunged into the damn lake and got soaked and all my pride just floated away. Remember how I had to run and wring my clothes out in the woods?"

Deborah started laughing, the color returning to her cheeks. "I peeked, you know. I saw you hopping on one foot, fighting to get your other foot out of your pants. But that's all I saw, I swear."

"And then you dragged me out there to dance and I hated dancing but I didn't hate it with you. I loved that night. I'm sorry I screwed everything up so bad. I lost my mind for a little while. I was like a kid, all confused. I mean, it's no excuse, but—"

Deborah stopped laughing. "I told you. Enough with the apologies already."

Sam looked at the couples, young and old, moving across the dance floor.

"You thought I didn't hear you," he said.

"Hear me? When?"

"That night at the lake when you whispered, *When will you understand you're all I want?* But I *did* hear you, Deborah. And that didn't just go away, I know it didn't. Please go out to dinner with me tonight after this. And again another night. Maybe we could go to Coney Island sometime and I could win you the biggest stuffed animal if they have a basketball game. And back to the Roxy so we can explore it together. I don't even care what the movie is. Look, I...I'm not gonna sit here and run Alex down, but I think he's wrong for you. I'm asking you to try again, at least see what happens."

Sam paused his torrent of words for a breath.

"We can leave right now if you feel like it. How's your stomach?"

Deborah shrugged. "I could eat."

She didn't tell him until years later she'd been tucking Anna's tiny ring into a safe corner of her handbag as he delivered that glass of water.

Twenty-three

RONNI

FALL, 2021

(ONE YEAR LATER)

If you took Shirley Temple's golden ringlets and dimpled face at the age of five and reverse-engineered them to baby size, you'd have the picture of Violet at one. Her eyes were huge and brown like Rick's, shining at anyone who'd meet them, and she'd inherited his thick hair (apparently, natural curl from someone, too). She was the kind of plump little cherub people stopped and stared at, even as we hurried along, separated from masked strangers in the grocery store. All Rick's distrust of strangers came back to me, and I began to be wary of the attention. We traded leisurely shopping for curbside pickup whenever possible.

Her first ten months or so were a flurry of sleepless nights, arbitrary crying, two terrifying times she ran a fever (it was a cold, then a mercifully brief stomach bug), one awkward fall backward that left me monitoring her for a concussion, more crying when she started teething, and a mysterious rash that came and went quickly. I was very, very grateful for telemedicine in those days.

Now she was the most cheerful kid I'd ever seen. She directed a sunny two-toothed smile at anyone in her orbit. She took her first tentative steps just before her first birthday. Violet's discernible vocabulary was initially limited to three words, starting with "mama." She called everyone but me "honey." If I said "NO!" to her, she'd drop whatever she was doing and throw her tiny hands in the air. Usually she'd say "OKAY." The rest was a unique jumble of alienish sounds only Violet understood, unless she was pointing at something.

I promised myself we'd have a first birthday party later, when everyone stopped worrying about the Delta variant. Violet, Deanna and I shared an old-fashioned strawberry cake and an absurd number of presents for our girl. Elise had gone fashion-overboard, not for the first time *("You have no idea how exciting it is to shop for a girl! Davidsons have nothing but boys, generation after generation.")*. I held up a teeny long-sleeved pink velvet dress and matching fringed ankle boots for Deanna to see. Violet was disinterested by that point, focused on her jumbo wood puzzle with brightly colored geometric-shaped inserts. She was slamming the yellow triangle into the red circular opening and growing more frustrated by the moment.

"Here, honey," I said, taking the piece from her and placing it correctly. "It goes here."

Violet nodded. "Heeeeere," she said. We had a new word. "OKAY." She picked up the red circle and immediately tried it in the green square space.

"I mean, it's cute, but where's she going to wear fringed ankle boots? And by the time I can take her anywhere, they'll be way too small," I said to Deanna. Deanna shrugged and smiled at Violet, who was crawling toward her favorite electrical outlet, determined to remove its cover. "Violet, no!" I hollered at her.

She sat on her plush little bottom and held up both hands. "OKAY." She spotted a long-eared white stuffed rabbit I'd given her, hoping to lure her away from the bedraggled Mikey the Monkey she still slept with. Violet pushed herself to her feet and toddled toward it. She plopped down and began trying to remove the pink bows atop its ears.

The next package contained a leopard-print jumper with matching fedora, black turtleneck and tights. The tiniest black patent shoes were at the bottom of the gift bag. Then Elise's *pièce de resistance*: a silver sequined disco-looking skirt and top.

"For her budding stripper career?" I laughed. "Geez."

Deanna examined the tag. "Well, it's a 3T, so clearly intended for when Violet is more mature."

"Speaking of mature, Maddie was here four afternoons this week," I said. "I got a lot done." The convergence of several miracles had allowed me to start writing my book. First and foremost was Maddie Reid. Her family moved into a house in our neighborhood so they could be closer to her grandfather, Lee Tyler. Maddie said her mother had worried constantly about her dad and insisted they relocate near him. She was homeschooling Maddie and Donnie. They were usually finished by around 2 p.m., when Violet would begin a nap and Maddie watched over her.

"What are you writing?" Maddie had asked me the day before, balancing a newly awakened Violet on her leg in the corner of my room. "I mean, if you don't mind me asking."

Violet patted the sides of Maddie's face and said, "Honey."

I glanced up from my laptop. "It's the sequel to my first book. Actually, it's the long-overdue novel my original contract called for. It was supposed to be completed three years ago. My publisher has been somewhat understanding because of COVID and Rick and the baby. I thought they'd turn me down at this late date, but they're definitely going forward with it. They saw the first three chapters and committed."

I looked at the screen and backspaced my latest sentence, frustrated by the interruption. "Could you take Violet downstairs, honey? Maybe get her one of those cookies to chew on?"

Violet attempted to clap her chubby hands. "Cookie!" she said, her eyes wide.

"She said 'cookie'! Did you hear that?" Maddie exclaimed. "You're such a big girl, Vi." I bit my tongue at the nickname. Maddie hoisted Violet onto her hip and left me to write.

I joined them in the living room a couple of hours later. Violet's teething biscuit had disintegrated into a drool-crumb concoction she'd smeared all over her face like a spa mask.

"I was just going to clean her up," Maddie said. "Sorry. We were busy playing with her puzzle." Violet beamed at me, the green square in her fingers crumb-coated and aimed at the correct location.

I sank into the couch, exhausted. "No, honey, that's fine. I'll give her a bath soon. Might as well let her decorate with some sweet potatoes, chicken in gravy, and Hawaiian Delight for her eyebrows."

"I'm sorry for interrupting you before," Maddie said. "I know better when you're writing. I was just curious."

"That's okay," I told her. "I was kinda stuck there anyway."

"Could I ask you something?" Maddie handed Violet the red circle and nodded at the space where it was supposed to go. Violet gazed at her and bit the puzzle piece.

"Sure, Maddie. Ask away."

"Do you know how the book is going to end? Like, do you know where it's going? Do you have it all outlined?"

"I do," I said. "Except I can't get someone I need to speak with to answer my emails or calls. All I get is voicemail. And this is a guy who used to hound me to discuss what he wanted me to write about his dad. Rick wouldn't let me call him back then, but now I'd like to add his story to the book. The novel was supposed to be based on Sam and his family, anyway." I sighed. "But I'm really curious what Gary Harris has to say. And honestly, I'd like to tell him I've found out his dad wasn't fully responsible for wrecking Violet's plans to elope in the first book."

Maddie's eyes grew round. "Violet? Like, *our* Violet? Oh, *now* I remember. You said you were naming her after a lady who'd been a big part of your life. So it's about that lady?"

"It's more about the people in her life and their perspective. That's a story that wasn't told in the original. And I have come to love these folks. Honestly, they're my found family, a family I never dreamed of. Max, Elise and Samuel have been wonderful and kind to me. Even after I moved back here and had Violet, the three of them came and brought home-cooked dinners and little presents. Well, Chef-cooked dinners, and Elise's idea of a little present is a strand of perfectly matched pearls for Violet's eventual prom. Samuel had a tiny shirt made that says 'I love Samuel more than anyone' and several more with puns like 'Taco 'bout cute' and 'Whale come, little one'—with the mama and baby whales she was wearing yesterday; you saw it. Violet just gravitates to him. They seem to have their own language. Their own little world."

I shook my head as I considered it all. "None of that would have happened without the pandemic, I guess." I picked at a spot of re-hardened teething biscuit on the couch fabric.

"Yeah, I know what you mean. It's great they've stayed isolated so they can come and be with you. Nobody gets much company these days. I think it's nice your mom spends time at my Papa's house," Maddie said. "He's been so lonely."

A lightning strike ran from my chest to my toes. "My mom? That's impossible." Surely Lee Tyler couldn't have met Jocelyn. Jocelyn didn't even know where I lived. Rick and I had been pretty deliberate about that; like any law enforcement officer, he didn't divulge his home address unless absolutely necessary.

"Yeah, Deanna. Your mom. She and Papa started spending time together a few months ago. They'd sit and talk at the gazebo at first, but now she brings him food and stuff, and they watch TV. They're good friends."

I shook my head and exhaled a mixture of relief and amusement. So Deanna had a boyfriend.

"I'm surprised she hasn't told me. And Deanna isn't my mom, though she's like a mother to me."

"Honey," Violet tugged at Maddie's sleeve.

Maddie put her hand over Violet's and guided a purple oval into place, then said, "Well, Papa kept it a secret, I guess. He didn't want anyone to know he was talking to a lady after Nana died. But he's, like, eighty. And she's old, too, and Mom saw him kiss her cheek once at the gazebo when they thought no one was looking. I think it's sweet and disgusting at the same time, like banana pudding."

Violet reached for Maddie's long hair and yanked it hard, pulling her head to one side.

"Violet, no! We do not pull hair!" I said.

Her hands flew into the air. "OKAY." She blinked at me, holding my eyes until Maddie handed her another puzzle piece.

"I've been wondering for the longest time why Deanna was suddenly so interested in her clothes and makeup and hairstyle. Maybe it's your grandfather."

"Oh," Maddie said, "I don't think there's any doubt about that. She's very pretty for an old lady. They both light up like neon signs when they're together. Like I said, sweet and disgusting." She stood and picked Violet up to kiss her goodbye.

"Bye, honey," Violet mumbled, squirming to get down. She resumed her puzzle concentration as soon as Maddie replaced her on the floor.

"Should I come back the day after tomorrow?" Maddie asked.

"Absolutely," I said. "I'm going to try to call 'Chet's' son again in the morning. Maybe I can get him to pick up."

"Or just go to his house while I'm with Violet one afternoon." Maddie shrugged. "You can Google his address."

I bit my lip. "Rick would kill me."

"If this guy meant you any harm, he'd have done it already," Maddie announced. "I watch a lot of *Dateline*. If you're really worried, add me to Find My Friends and I'll keep an eye on your location. My mom tracks me everywhere I go."

"I'll think about it." I scooped Violet up. "Ready for some supper, honey?"

She nodded her cookie-matted curls at me. "Mama supper, Wandalight."

I laughed and tapped her button nose with my fingertip. "Hawaiian Delight comes after you eat a little chicken and sweet potatoes."

"OKAY." Violet attempted to tap my nose with her finger. I couldn't escape the feeling my child was working on a teenage eye roll to accompany *OKAY*.

I felt really brave driving up to Gary Harris's house the day after Violet's birthday. It was a white ranch-style building that looked like it dated to the sixties. A semi-circular driveway bisected the front yard. It was lined with some sort of bushes in purple bloom.

I opted to park on the street, unsure of circular driveway etiquette. I pressed the video doorbell, uncomfortable knowing he could see me on camera. The white wood door opened a crack. A gray-haired woman in a floral housedress smiled slightly and nodded through the narrow opening she was clearly planning to close if I made any sudden moves.

"Yes?" she asked.

"Hi, I'm Ronni O'Shea, ma'am. I'm looking for Gary Harris. Does he still live here?"

"I recognize you now," she said. "You'd better come in." She swept the door open onto a living room straight out of a seventies sitcom. She waved at the gold-and-white floral sofa and I seated myself.

"I'm Rhonda Harris," she said, sitting well away from me in a matching gold velour chair and looping a face mask behind her ears. "Gary died two months ago."

"Oh, I am so sorry, Mrs. Harris. I had no idea." *Does he still live here? Nice, Ronni. Why does my evolution involve my foot moving ever-closer to my mouth for routine insertion?*

"Well, thank you. It's been awful hard."

I hoped she could read my sympathy around the mask I wore. "It's such an awful time for so many," I said, shaking my head.

"Yes, it is," she said. "I got my vaccinations or I wouldn't've opened that door. Wasn't that made Gary pass, though. He had a bad heart. Second heart attack he'd had, and there wasn't nothing they could do. Wouldn't even let me in the hospital to say goodbye." She sniffed. "He was workin' in the yard that day. I didn't even know what happened until the neighbor lady banged on our door. We called 911 and all. He was still awake when the ambulance drove off but he didn't make it. Honestly, it still don't seem real."

I nodded. "I know what you mean. I lost my husband last year and I'm still trying to find my way."

She rubbed her thumb back and forth across the forefinger of the closed right hand in her lap, a self-comforting gesture I'd seen in more than one Fairfield patient.

"Sorry for your loss," she said.

"Thank you." I took a deep breath. "I know this is awful timing. Your husband tried to contact me several times to talk with me about a character in my book who was based on his dad. I...well, I didn't get a chance to reach out to him until recently."

"Chet Wilson," she said. "I know what you're talkin' about. I read your book. I liked it pretty good, but Gary just about had a come-apart when he realized it was about his dad and Violet Thompson. That was a touchy subject in the family, as you can imagine." She drew her penciled brows upward.

"Yes ma'am, I know. And there are some things I've found out. For one thing, Mr. Harris's dad probably wouldn't have called the Davidsons' house about that train reservation to New Orleans if a member of Sam's family hadn't tricked him. I don't think 'Chet' would have been aware of their travel plans far enough in advance, otherwise.

I'm sure that's something your husband wanted to tell me. The thing is, I didn't know I was going to be writing a book about what happened back then until more recently. I was inspired by stories Sam's son and grandson told me. And honestly, it seems like Mr. Harris was right about 'Chet's' innocence in much of this. I came here to find out what he wanted to say."

"Well," she leaned back into her chair. "he was gonna tell you about how Dr. Tolliver Thompson died. I cain't honestly say I know all the details. Our son, Caleb, he does. And there's someone else who asked me to put them in touch if you came askin' about all this. If you'll give me your phone number, I'll get 'em to call."

"Yes ma'am, of course. I'd appreciate that."

Mrs. Harris opened a drawer in the end table next to her and extracted a legal pad and pen. "Go 'head," she said. She scribbled my number and told me, "Now, this call is gonna come from somewhere outta state and it'll look like one of them robot calls, but you need to answer it, all right?"

"Oh, yes, of course, I will. And thank you. I'm so sorry about your husband, and that I got in touch too late to talk with him."

"Thank you." She pointed at the number I'd given her. "I'm not gonna tell you who it is yet in case they don't want me to. Might have changed their mind." Mrs. Harris placed the legal pad on her table and carefully arranged the ballpoint pen across it. "And I apologize for not offering you a Coke or somethin'. I've gotten out of the habit of havin' company, ya know? I don't know what to do with myself a lot of the time. Can I get you a cold drink? A cup of coffee?"

"No ma'am, thank you very much, but I have a baby daughter at home and I need to get back to her." I stood and waved with a smile, then started toward the door.

"Oh, bless your heart! What's her name? Your little one?" she asked, right behind me.

"Her name is Violet."

"Lord," Mrs. Harris said. "Here I thought I wasn't gonna have to hear that name again for the rest of my livelong days. I'm sure she's a pretty thing, like her namesake." She patted my back and served up a polite afterthought. "And her mama, of course."

Part
Three

Twenty-FOUR

RONNI

DECEMBER, 2021

It was actually a couple of months after my visit with Rhonda Harris before my phone displayed an Atlanta number I assumed to be the not-a-robot call I was waiting for.

"May I speak with Ronni O'Shea, please?" a polished female voice intoned. It was familiar but I couldn't place it.

"This is she."

"Ronni, this is Bettina Hughes." She announced it and paused, as though theme music would accompany it shortly. "From CNN."

"I remember you, yes ma'am," I told her.

"I'm retired now, of course. You haven't seen me on-air for a couple of years."

I haven't looked. "Well, congratulations on your retirement."

"Ronni," she continued without thanks, "I would like to meet with you regarding the details of a story my nephew told me. I believe you're aware he's the late Gary Harris. Rhonda said she'd mentioned I might phone you."

"She didn't tell me it was you. Rhonda was mysterious about it. Said you might change your mind." I nodded to Maddie in the doorway, holding Violet, so she'd come into my bedroom. The two of them sat and stared at me.

Bettina ignored that and continued, "Of course, one is never really retired. I'm working on a project for a crime TV network, producing a documentary series about the impact of false accusations. Not legal charges, mind you; gossip and innuendo, things people misinterpret with grave implications. We have an interview set up with that woman from the tiger thing accused of feeding her husband to the animals. We're also talking to a man in Missouri whose neighbors became convinced he had fathered children all over town, mostly because they had the same striking red hair. It was all disproven by DNA analysis, but at that point his wife had left him and he'd lost his insurance business. We're looking into a number of similar situations across the country. Social media, the age of the internet, all that factors in."

"I thought you were calling me to discuss your brother," I said.

"Well, I'm getting there. Be patient." I heard her hiss at an assistant, then a door closed. "I do want to tell you what happened on that roof with Tolly Thompson and the man you called Chet. Rhonda says you're writing a book that could include a chapter finally reversing the damage you've done to my late brother's reputation. And as part of that, I want this series to include a pre-recorded interview with you in one of the final episodes. Your original book would lend background to the project, and if you included information that's come to light in your next novel, credibility and interest, too."

"I'm not sure—" I began.

"The episode won't come out until after your book has been in circulation for a while. It will only help your sales, not introduce spoilers." Bettina paused for my reaction.

"I'm confused. I went to great lengths to conceal both your and your brother's real names. That was really important to you, as I recall," I said.

Bettina chuckled without any warmth. "Part of this is that I don't give a damn anymore who knows I'm bedraggled little CeeCee Wilson from Anniston. That's a key component of the TV series' finale. When I open up about my childhood in this interview, the documentary's guaranteed to blow up bigger than Shephard Smith's head. Incredible ratings, watching America's most famous female news anchor's image implode on-camera. There's a lot of satisfaction in that for me."

I heard Bettina tapping something on her desk and waited as she paused. "Look, the network discarded me. My retirement was heralded everywhere, portrayed as a celebration; I had to publicly fawn over the Breaking News Barbie who replaced me. A woman can't anchor a national broadcast at my age, and it's a ridiculous double standard. Walter Cronkite could have delivered the news looking like a drooling Methuselah as long as someone wiped his chin during commercials."

I shook my head at the phone. I knew enough about documentaries and the way they're slanted to be afraid to meet with Bettina or CeeCee or whatever she called herself. On the other hand, my publisher's book publicist would be thrilled to death to have it mentioned in a national documentary with her at the helm. They'd be counting the money before it aired.

"Ronni? Are you there?"

"Yes, sorry, I was just thinking."

"Well, I'm not Oprah, but I'm probably the next best thing. If you want me to tell you these details, I'll need you to talk about Violet Glenn Thompson and my brother, too," she said.

"I understand why you're doing this. But I know how you felt about Violet. I won't say anything disloyal to her, Bettina. Mrs. Hughes. I can't do that."

Silence. Then, "It's Miss Hughes and, well, Ronni, you won't have to." She sighed. "My opinion of her has changed a bit, especially after reading your book. Before that, when you and Officer O'Shea came to see me, I was caught off guard. My mind automatically connected to all the emotions I'd stored about Violet Glenn for years and years. I wasn't particularly honest with you. Despite the way I viewed the destruction she brought to my brother's life, Violet and I did have a…well, I guess you'd call it a reconciliation."

"You did?" My jaw unhinged. "How did that happen?" My daughter was squirming in Maddie's lap, so she let her toddle over to me and pat my leg, reaching her arms into the air. I shouldered the phone and swung her up next to me on my bed, moving my laptop out of reach.

"I came to visit my brother one day at Fairfield Springs, wearing sunglasses and a scarf, of course. I can't go anywhere unless I disguise myself."

I rolled my eyes and made a face at my little Violet. She giggled. "I don't remember your visit."

"Well, I don't recall seeing you and I certainly didn't use my real name to sign in. Neither of them. When my brother began to get tired, I kissed his forehead and went to find Violet Thompson's apartment. It occurred to me as an impulse. I would go there to tell her once and for all how I felt about her. I also wanted to reveal the success I've had in this world. I couldn't wait until she realized she'd been watching me on her television all those years."

"I see," I said, my eyes widening.

"The thing you have to understand is, I'm twelve years younger than Violet Thompson. When she came to our house to babysit, my brother would transform into this charming kid who'd make her laugh. I was five years old and terribly shy. To my parents, I was invisible. If I cried, if I acted up in any way, my mother would lock me in my room for hours. I thought that was normal."

I nodded to Maddie to take the baby downstairs, afraid of the turn the conversation was taking.

Bettina continued, "She didn't hit me, she never abused me physically, but she treated me like an inconvenience, not a daughter. My dad wasn't around enough to see any of it, and I don't know if he'd have cared. So when Violet came shining through our front door like a rainbow, I'd huddle in a corner. When my brother captured her attention, as he always did, I wouldn't say a word. Violet was a grown-up to me. I was afraid she'd treat me like my mom did. Like my kindergarten teacher, who smirked at my dirty clothes and made me sit in the back of the room."

"I'm sorry," I told her. "My early childhood wasn't that different from yours."

Bettina bypassed my comment and plowed on about herself. "At that point, I didn't expect any adult woman to show kindness. I wouldn't even let Violet Glenn try."

"I understand. It's very hard to open yourself to others when you've been treated that way," I said. "It took me a long time."

"Yes, well," Bettina said. "I knocked on her door that afternoon, ready to hurl all the vitriol I'd stored into her face. She'd tormented my brother, led him on even though they were both married. I knew she'd involved him in confronting her husband. She'd ruined his life." She paused for a moment. "And I wanted her to see I'd become beautiful, too."

I heard her sniff, and she asked me to hold on. "Violet opened that door with a huge smile, looking at me expectantly until I told her who I am. Who I was. And then she reached out and put her arms around me.

"'Come in, honey,' she said. 'I've been hoping you'd visit. Gosh, you are so lovely,' Violet told me, sweeping the door fully open. I walked into her cream-colored living room and sank onto her couch, a little let down she didn't seem shocked. 'Your brother is so proud of you and I am, too. He confided in me about your career, and all you've accomplished. He thinks you're wonderful, and I do, too,' she said, with her movie-star smile.

"'I'll be right back.' Violet went off to the kitchen and returned with lemonade and Nilla Wafers. 'I seem to recall you loved this, honey.' She handed me the glass and sat across from me, shaking her head. 'I knew you'd be a star someday,' she said. 'You've always been so beautiful and smart.'"

"I sipped and stared at her for a minute, rummaging for all the nasty words I'd packed up to deliver. Instead, I set my glass down and said my coming there had been a mistake, that I only wanted to say a brief hello, I had to go…I don't remember exactly what I told her. Violet stood and reached out to hug me.

"'I know how hard you had it, honey. I'm so sorry,' she whispered. Everything inside me melted into tears and I hurried off without a word. I never went back to Fairfield. But a couple of weeks later, I got a note from Violet thanking me for my visit and telling me again she was proud of me."

"That sounds like Violet," I said, smiling.

"By the time I met you, I'd shoved her kindness to me into a dark corner of my heart. And I know now I wasn't fair to her. But I need you to be fair to my brother by telling what really happened that day with Dr. Thompson. If you'll do that, if you'll include it in your book, I'll make it part of this documentary and we'll tell the world. I have some speaking engagements coming up this week, but I'll have my assistant Kerrie contact you about setting up a Zoom interview. You won't have to worry about travel or setting up in your home, okay? I'll tell you on-camera what happened, because your reaction is needed for authenticity."

"You want to tell me what happened and record my reaction?" I frowned. "I'm not sure that's a good idea."

"It's good television, *that's* what it is, Ronni. Trust me. I'm not going to ambush you with blame, either. I know you could only offer speculation about Tolly's death when you wrote Violet's perspective."

She took a deep breath and prepared to lock down her deal with me. "Take a few days to think it over. I'm telling this story with or without you, but your participation would make it so much richer. And it's the only way you'll know what really happened, if you want to add that to your own story. My great-nephew has a few details, but not the whole picture. I'm your best bet to satisfy your readers' curiosity. And to sell a boatload of books. This would be good for both of us. When Kerrie calls you, I'm betting you'll say yes. I'll speak with you soon, Ronni. Bye for now."

She disconnected and I stared at my phone.

The next day I called Max to ask what he thought I should do. I'd come to depend on him for fatherly advice.

"Do you trust what she says?" he asked. "That she really won't try to make you or Violet look bad?"

"I think I do," I answered. "She has nothing to gain by smearing my reputation, and I think between her personal experience with Violet and what she learned through my book, she's a lot more sympathetic to her now. I mean, no one knew the abuse Violet had suffered until I made her story public. I'm sure Bettina's read every word."

"Then I think you should do it. The publicity will be great, and you handle yourself well, Ronni. You'll be great on-camera. You're smart, you're lovely to look at, and you know more big words than any normal person. Let her interview you," Max said. "But, I think I'll reach out to my attorney and have him put together an agreement to protect you, just in case. Is that all right with you? We can try to get a preview into your hands before she has permission to air."

"Oh, yes, that's a great idea! Thank you, Max. I didn't even think of that."

"Happy to help," he replied. "And Ronni, I had some things sent from our home to show you, and I'd like to do it in person. Could you leave the baby with Maddie and come over here Saturday?"

"Can you promise not to mention Peppa Pig or Big Bird?" I laughed. "I would be so very grateful to talk to grownups. I'll see you Saturday about ten."

Max answered the door in a black cashmere hoodie and jeans. "You look handsome," I told him, wishing I could offer a peck on his stubbly gray cheek, but offering a germ-free wave instead. "Why are you dressed up?"

"Thank you. Elise and I are FaceTiming Ollie after lunch. She wants us to make a good impression on his other grandparents. They act like we've gone off to the wilds of Borneo."

"Hmm," I said. "Maybe we should invite them down after the virus thing is finally over."

"Possibly someday," Max said. "But they'd act like they need a passport and currency change to visit, I'm sure." He grinned and ushered me into the living room, handing me a silver-framed photo from the coffee table. "This is from my parents' wedding reception, in 1949. It was at the Plaza."

The black and white picture showed Deborah laughing as she cut an impossibly tall cake. She stood atop a white chair with Sam at her side. Her mother, Diane, was barely visible in the background, watching her daughter balance on the chair.

"Oh, wow. It's great to see all these people I've heard so much about," I told Max. "Your mom really was beautiful. And that *dress*. My gosh!" Deborah's arms were cap-sleeved; layers and layers of ruffles bearing tiny sparkling crystal beads cascaded from the lace bodice with a sweetheart neckline. She looked like more of a confection than the wedding cake.

The next photo was of Sam and Deborah held aloft in the same white chairs, their hands holding a white cloth between them as they grinned at dancing and clapping guests.

"What's with the napkin thing?" I asked Max.

"It signifies their union." Max handed me the last framed photo, of Deborah holding a tiny blue bundle on the steps of an apartment building. "That's the day they brought me home, in 1950," he said. "Also when they started using color film for the big stuff, apparently." He chuckled. "I'm sure my dad took it. We lived there, in a small East Side apartment until my brother Aaron was born in 1952. Then we moved from 62nd Street to a brownstone on West 94th Street. We lost Mom in 2010, and Dad rattled around in that house all by himself for a few years. When his health got bad, we moved him to Fairfield, as you know. Elise and I live in that place now. I think my folks paid around twenty thousand for it. We'll never sell, but we get crazy offers every day. My wife would kill me if I even thought of saying yes."

I glanced at the stairs, wondering if Elise or Samuel might join us. "You never talk about your brother Aaron. Would you tell me about him?"

Max closed his eyes. "Aaron was shy, loved sci-fi books, hated high school, wanted to own a golden retriever someday. He was sensitive and kind of quiet, always listening to classical music instead of Zeppelin and the Stones. He was a thoroughly good soul. Actually, Samuel reminds me of him a lot." Max nodded at the stairway leading to where his son worked upstairs. "While I was safely tucked away at Columbia, where my dad insisted I enroll, Aaron had a bad breakup with his first girlfriend. He was devastated and pretty aimless for a couple of weeks; my parents were worried about him. He was supposed to go to Manhattan Community College that fall, and they kept trying to get him excited about that, about being done with high school and starting over, meeting someone else, you know? He had his whole life ahead of him."

Max shook his head slowly and lowered it to his chest, eyes clamped shut. "Then, without a word to any of us, Aaron enlisted in the army. Of course they sent him to Vietnam. You ever heard of Hamburger Hill? That's where my brother died. He lost his life trying to take a damn mountain ridge called Dong Ap Bia in the Hue Province."

Max held his hands out, palms up, shrugging. "Then the U.S. Command decided there wasn't any strategic value to the location, after all. They abandoned the camp a couple of weeks later. Aaron and about seventy other young men were machine-gunned down and hundreds were wounded so that our military leaders could stand there and decide they'd been mistaken." Max leaned forward and rapped the knuckles of both hands on the coffee table. "And my parents never spoke of it again, after Aaron's funeral. Mom had a teenager on her hands in the seventies, my brother Frank, and I think that kept her going. He was a surprise in 1960. Thank God he was too young for military service."

"I'm sorry, Max," I said. "I didn't know."

"Yeah, well, you wouldn't, like I said. I doubt my dad even told Violet about Aaron. He probably bragged about me and Frank, who is," Max looked at his watch, "probably having lunch delivered from Katz's about now. I don't think he and Janice have left their apartment since the pandemic started."

"You haven't said much about Frank, either," I mused.

"Frank is what my grandmother would've called a *shtarker*. He's been employed by the stores since he was sixteen and has never really worked a day in his life. But he makes sure everyone he meets knows he is very, *very* important at Philippe." Max laughed. "Don't get me wrong, I love Frankie, but he can be supremely annoying. Just ask Elise. She had everything set up exactly as she wanted for our wedding reception in 1979, and Frank secretly arranged to have one of the Bee Gees surprise us by popping in and singing 'More Than A Woman' for our first dance."

"What?" I laughed. "Which Bee Gee? Why wouldn't Elise love that?"

Max shrugged. "I don't know, some hairy man in a white jumpsuit; you'd have to ask Elise. She's the one who found disco tolerable. Anyway, Frank grabbed the mic and announced he'd arranged a special surprise for our first dance and introduced the guy, who stood in the corner and half-heartedly sang the song with no accompaniment. We had to go along with it, of course, with smiles frozen on our faces. The Bee Gee walked off without a word when he finished. Then the DJ played what was *supposed* to be our first dance, which was 'If' by Bread, and we first-danced all over again. That was just Frank showing he could get a celebrity to appear, even though it wasn't what Elise wanted or planned."

"That's a great story, Max. I'm sorry y'all had an accidental Bee Gee ruin your first dance, but you have to admit it's fascinating."

"Have you ever tried to move gracefully to an acoustic version of 'More Than A Woman?' To this day, no one is allowed to play that song." He glanced toward the kitchen. "Would you like to stay for lunch? Chef's making sushi."

"No, thank you; it's Saturday and I promised Maddie I'd be back soon." I met Max's eyes. "That does raise a question I've wondered about, though. It's your Sabbath day, right?"

"Yes." Max nodded. "Elise and I don't do much to mark it. Truth is, after we married, our family kinda went from Jewish to Jew-*ish*. Elise is half-Presbyterian. Our sons celebrated bar mitzvahs, but we enjoy both Hanukkah *and* Christmas every year." He nodded at the beautifully decorated tree in the corner of their living room and drew a deep breath. "We've lost touch with a lot of our heritage and tradition. My grandparents would be very disappointed."

"In what?" Elise breezed into the room and asked. She wore a chic ivory wool pantsuit and looked as effortlessly glamorous as I did frumpy in my extra-stretchy black yoga pants and baggy t-shirt. She offered me a little wave and sat down.

"Our failure to preserve the religion and tradition I was raised with," Max answered. "I feel guilty sometimes."

"We'll talk about that later, darling." Elise smiled at her husband. "Ronni, will you please stay for lunch?"

"No, thank you, Elise, I have to get home to Violet; Maddie's already been there for two hours. It was great for me to get out of the house, though. Thanks for inviting me to see those photos, Max. They're precious." I stood to go, trying to mimic Elise's perfect posture.

"Well, we'll be seeing you at Christmas," Elise said. "I have some special gifts for Violet."

I ran through the possibilities. *"Baby's First High Heels." A mink coat or diamonds or a car. Maybe a miniature yacht.* "That's so sweet of you, Elise. Violet misses her 'Eeeese.'"

"I wish I could steal her and keep her here. We haven't seen Ollie in so long, and we're going to do a video chat with him this afternoon.

I can't wait to hear his latest exploits. Jeannie promised he'd play a new violin piece."

I noted the subtle raise of Max's eyebrows as he nodded.

"Anyway, it's clear from photos our sweet grandson is growing up fast." She shook her head sadly.

"I bet he is, and I know you miss him. Well, if not before, we'll see you at Deanna's," I said, nodding at Elise and heading to the door. My mind wandered as I walked away to Deanna mysteriously insisting on hosting everyone at her house for Christmas. She'd acted all offended on the phone when I referred to her relationship with Mr. Tyler as a romance.

"He's a nice man and we talk occasionally. That's all there is to it," she'd said. "We're just two people who enjoy each other's company."

"But you cook for him and go to his house to watch TV?"

"Lord, that Maddie has a big mouth on her," Deanna had said into the phone. "Look, Ronni, have you met Lee? He's a very practical man. I'm sure he finds it practical to have a lady friend with an excellent oatmeal raisin cookie recipe. And since we both stay isolated, we can be around each other."

Elise snapped my attention back by calling after me, "Did Max tell you we're going home right after Christmas? I can't wait."

My eyes grew wet immediately and turned to look at Max. He was smiling, but with lower than his usual movie-star wattage.

He jumped up and said, "I'll walk you out, Ronni."

As soon as we exited the front door, I told him, "I'm so sorry to see y'all go. I'll miss you a lot, old man."

Max laughed, perfectly happy to be an irresistibly handsome old man. "I'm sorry, I was going to tell you. We'll come back to visit. Samuel will be here, and we're finally bringing in a construction crew in late January. That is, if they can still put together a crew. It's hard to find workers right now. These guys are out of Atlanta."

"Well, good. I know he's looking forward to getting the store open. We all are. I feel like 2022 is going to be a much better year, and I can't wait to shop at Philippe."

Max reached to open my car door and leaned over it, looking at me. He nodded his head slightly, as though reaching some decision.

"There's one more story I need to tell you for your book. I've been turning it over and over in my mind. No one knows what my dad confessed to me when he knew his time was short. But it seems appropriate to include why my Leon grandparents moved back from New York so suddenly. Not even Elise knows that."

He was frowning into the distance as I said, "Max, it's okay, you don't have to. The stories of your parents and grandparents are more than enough. I'm grateful for them."

He sighed and met my eyes. "Everything has been about the Davidsons. The Leons should have a voice, too, no matter how my father may look when they do."

Twenty-five

NEW YORK CITY

1962

Andrew Leon was a family man.

He'd met Diane Silver at Stone Mountain, Georgia in 1928, when they'd both come to see the wreckage of a small airplane that crashed into the massive granite dome the evening before. The pilot, a distant cousin of Diane's, not only survived the crash, but managed to grab his cargo—United States airmail—and walk down the mountain.

Andrew was a senior at Scheller College of Business at Georgia Tech, an honor student on full scholarship. It was unlike him to take a Saturday for something as frivolous as a sightseeing trip. He drove thirty minutes to examine the crash for one reason: though his future was in accounting, he harbored a secret wish to be a pilot. He wanted to see the small biplane, and he hoped to encounter aviator Johnny Kytle, who'd walked away from the incident mostly unscathed.

Instead, he found a beautiful young woman with her family among the crowd gazing at the wreckage, which was mostly hidden in trees and brush. Diane was nineteen, with her blonde hair cropped into a fashionable bob. She wore—and he would always remember this—tan denim trousers and a white blouse. This was both scandalous and intriguing to Andrew, and he made his way to stand near Diane and her younger sisters. They spoke about the crash, which the youngest Silver daughter, Eleanor, informed him had been survived by her cousin Johnny. Andrew told her that was astoundingly lucky, especially in the heavily clouded weather of the prior evening.

Eleanor introduced herself and her siblings, Judith, Ruthie, and Diane. "We're the Silver Sisters, which would be a good name for a singing group if we could sing. We live in Atlanta." He noticed Diane giggle a bit when she nodded hello to him, immediately returning her eyes to the plane wreckage.

"Andrew Leon," he said. "Nice to meet y'all." He mentioned he'd been fascinated by airplanes his entire life, shifting back and forth on his feet uncomfortably as he searched for things to say to the little girl, trying to keep the conversation flowing. Eleanor informed him she was a Girl Scout, and might receive a scribe badge for writing a report about her cousin's airplane accident.

"Hey," she said, "could I ask you a few questions, for my article?"

Andrew shrugged. "Sure."

"Okay." Eleanor produced a small notepad and pencil. "Tell me about yourself. I already know you're here because you're interested in airplanes. What else?"

He told her he was a student at Georgia Tech, that he was from Anniston, Alabama. Andrew pointedly mentioned, "All my fellow students are guys. It's nice to talk to a young lady reporter."

Eleanor nodded, obviously flattered. "And have you visited Stone Mountain before?"

"No," he said, "I haven't. I wish I could see the plane better, but I'm glad I came here. It's not far from Atlanta, and it's really pretty here, isn't it?" Still nothing from Diane, who appeared to be ignoring

Andrew. "I enjoyed the drive up here, too. I have a 1914 Model T Ford. I've saved money since I was seven and bought it from my parents. I keep it running myself." Surely that would impress Diane, even if his car was fourteen years old.

If only she would say something, *anything,* to him.

"And what do you hope to gain from this experience today?" Eleanor tilted her head.

Andrew chuckled. "Well, an impromptu hike is always good. I spend a lot of time sitting at a desk. And even if I didn't get a good look at the airplane, I've met The Silver Sisters. If y'all can't sing, maybe you should work on a juggling act."

"We can't do that, either," Eleanor said, slipping her pocket notebook into a small handbag. "Thanks for the interview. I'll include you in whatever I write."

"Good luck, Eleanor. I hope you get that badge," he answered. He pretended to try to look at the wreckage from various angles, though it was nearly impossible. The crowd murmured around Andrew, most of them frustrated with trying to see the airplane and turning to the mountain view, instead.

Diane met Andrew's gaze straight-on for the first time as her parents announced it was time to leave. He barely heard them all walking away, he was so entranced by the deep blue of Diane's eyes; the color of his mother's hydrangeas, he thought. Andrew heard a twig snap in the distance and noticed her mother and father moving along the wooded path with her sisters trailing like a row of ducklings.

"Mama!" Diane called. "I'll be down in just a minute."

Diane's mother stopped and turned back to look from thirty yards away. She placed her hands on her hips as she saw her daughter's reason for lagging behind. Mrs. Silver rolled her eyes, too exhausted by raising four girls to put up a fuss.

"We'll meet you at the car," she called. "Be careful on the trail. It's slippery, and there's loose gravel." She stared at Andrew for a few seconds, a warning.

Diane cleared her throat. "I hope Eleanor didn't drive you crazy with questions. She thinks she's Nellie Bly, Girl Reporter."

"I enjoyed it. She's a sweet kid," Andrew replied, and promptly ran out of things to say. He watched Diane's family disappear from sight, feeling the awkward silence envelop the two of them, a dense fog of unspoken words descending. "I guess we should get going," he said, sweeping his arm in front of him. "We can talk on the trail." He desperately wished Diane were the reporter in the family. She nodded at him, clearly disappointed.

Andrew walked in front, pulling back branches and watching for slippery spots on the trail. He reached back once to grab Diane's arm as she stumbled.

"Thanks," she said. "I don't remember it being this treacherous on the way up."

"Me neither," Andrew said. "Seems like humidity has settled on everything. The moss on these rocks is like oil. Just stay to the left and try not to step on—"

A shrill scream interrupted him. "I think that's Eleanor!" Diane said, her eyes wide. Andrew sprinted ahead and saw the little girl had tumbled to about twenty feet below the path. She sat in a shallow ditch, her back against a rock, scraped and bleeding. He climbed down as the Silvers watched, tearing his best clothes in the process, and scooped up a dazed but mostly unharmed Eleanor. Andrew carried her up and handed Mr. Silver his youngest daughter.

Andrew Leon was a family man.

Ten months later, Diane and Andrew were wed in a traditional ceremony in Atlanta. Andrew took his accounting degree and his new bride to Anniston, where began a career in the offices of the Lee Brothers Foundry. The company held him and Diane in good stead through the Great Depression and the births of Deborah in 1931 and David in 1937. Andrew doted on his children, never missing a school performance or one of David's baseball games.

Diane would have told you her accountant husband was as solid and steady as the numbers he loved, the mathematics that spoke truth and poetry to him. He found joy in his wife and children, and success in the world of business when his profit-sharing arrangement with Lee Brothers brought a new wave of prosperity during World War II. After the war, Andrew left to open a certified public accounting office of his own, investing in small local businesses along the way.

He planned his family's vacations at the beach, carefully coordinating with their closest friends, the Davidsons. Deborah and their son Sam were dear friends. Diane and Esther Davidson were practically inseparable. Andrew liked and respected Philip, too; they were occasional golf partners.

When Philip offered him an opportunity to serve as chief financial officer of his new store in New York, Andrew jumped at the chance, partially because Diane's sister Eleanor and her family lived on Long Island. His wife was thrilled by the idea of being close to her baby sister, her nieces and nephews. Eleanor's husband Rob was a reporter for *The East Hampton Star* so she was often alone with the kids. Andrew joked that Diane's daily calls to Eleanor from Alabama generated so much revenue for Southern Bell, she might as well fly up there and back each week.

He didn't mind, really.

Andrew Leon was a family man.

Now he sat in his office, head in his hands, and contemplated what he'd just witnessed. He turned his weary eyes to the window, knowing Sam had gone home to Deborah and that Philip, like he, would be working late. He pushed his chair back and walked down the hall, closing the door to Philip's office behind him.

Philip Davidson looked up from a trade exposition brochure. "Hey, Andrew. Long day, huh? Care for a bourbon?" He stood to cross to the bar hidden in a mahogany cabinet. "I'm trying to figure out if we should send buyers to this thing. It's in Chicago. Expensive trip." He returned with two glasses and deposited one in front of Andrew, who left it untouched as Philip settled back into his chair.

"Are our numbers okay? You look like the bearer of red ink," Philip said, and took a swig. He set his glass down and leaned forward, hands clasped on his desk.

"I just saw your son kissing Patricia Carpenter in a stockroom," Andrew said, his eyes on the floor.

Philip inhaled a deep breath. "Are you sure it wasn't—"

"There wasn't a damn thing innocent about it, Phil. Don't even attempt that. I know what I saw. He was all over her, and if someone hadn't made a noise, who knows what my eyes...?" Andrew shook his head and leveled his gaze at Philip. "I've been sitting in my office thinking about this for an hour. I will not tell Deborah. Your son has hurt her enough in this lifetime. More than enough. She's home taking care of three boys—your *grandsons*, Philip—and I will not burden her heart with this knowledge. You'll handle it. You will talk to your son, and you will fire Patricia tomorrow. She cannot stay in this store."

"Andrew, wait a minute." Philip held up his palm, his face a tangle of emotions. "Patricia's worked for the store her entire adult life. She not only runs Cosmetics, she *is* Cosmetics. I can't just fire her for no—"

Andrew stared. "Don't you dare say 'For no reason.' You can't possibly allow her to stay here. Either she or Sam has to go, and I'm guessing your choice will be Patricia." He crossed his arms and sat back. "If I see your son right now, I'm likely to strangle him."

Philip nodded. "I feel the same. It's just—"

"It's just what? You can't defend him, Phil. There is no defense." Andrew stood and walked to the doorway, pausing with his hand on the brass knob. "Tomorrow. That girl is gone tomorrow. This is Violet all over again, behind my baby girl's back, except it's so much worse. They are *married*, Phil. And when you're through talking to your son, you'll send him to me. There are some things I need to say, too."

Philip stood and waved Andrew back into the room. "Sit, please, Andrew. Listen. There are things I should tell you, things that have weighed heavily on me for a long time. I feel like Esther and I...well, we may have somehow set Sam up for this to happen someday."

Andrew shook his head, but he walked back and collapsed into the chair opposite Philip, choosing this time to drain his bourbon glass before nodding for him to proceed.

Philip exhaled a sigh. "When we brought Sam up here—when *you* did, actually." He twisted his wedding ring around on his finger, faltering. "Andrew, Sam didn't break up with Violet. Essie and I forced them apart. We wanted Sam to be with Deborah, knew he'd be happy with her, and you see how it's worked out all these years." He looked at Andrew, saw the anger draw his eyebrows together. "We thought we were doing the right thing, for Deborah and our son both. A marriage to Violet would have been…impossible. Esther wouldn't have spoken to them again, maybe not ever."

"He wanted to *marry* Violet?" Andrew was twisting his hands together. "You did this to Deborah?"

Philip seemed unable to stop the torrent of words that followed. "Andrew, I feel so guilty. We met that girl at the train station, where she was waiting to elope with Sam. And I gave her money, money to go away." Philip ran his hand under his eye, swiping. "We did a terrible thing, Essie and I…"

"She took money from you to go away?" Andrew shook his head, his mouth falling open. "There has to be more to this story. Violet Glenn came from a nice home, nice family. She didn't need your money, Philip." He stared at his old friend, noting how Philip's hand shook as he moved it from his face.

"I think she was pregnant," Philip said quietly. "She wasn't sure."

Andrew blinked at him. "Phil, how could you?"

"I don't know. I don't know, Andrew, but we did. And I have carried this inside me ever since. Our son was a kid; he was *eighteen*, Andrew. We did an awful thing to him. To Deborah. To Violet. Essie and I truly thought we were doing what was best. I mean, Violet went off to Florida. She's married now, to a fancy doctor in Birmingham. And they have no children, so—"

"So you think it's all fine?"

"Of course not, Andrew. I feel this eating my belly every day," Philip said.

Andrew sat for a moment, his eyes on the window, watching shadows gather outside. "Did you try to find out if she had a baby? Did you even try, Phil?"

"Of course I did. I hired a guy years ago. That's how I know she ended up married to this Dr. Thompson. But the detective couldn't find anything showing she'd given birth, no record of the child, not in Florida or anywhere else. After a week, I told him to stop." Philip ran a hand through his thinning hair and looked Andrew in the eye. "I decided to find out as much as I could live with."

Andrew sighed. "I don't really know how you've lived with *any* of this."

Philip raised his eyebrows and drank a bit from his glass. "Like I said, it's been a heavy weight on my heart. And Andrew, what you saw… if Sam is drawn to Patricia, it's likely because she reminds him of Violet. Maybe Esther and I, we created this. We made such a mess of things."

"That's a ridiculous excuse, Philip. You're trying my patience. Sam may have been a teenager then, but now he's a grown man with a family. Patricia Carpenter will be gone tomorrow, and not transferred, *fired*." Andrew's eyes flashed. "Her behavior was completely inappropriate. I'll remind you Patricia is married, too."

Philip exhaled slowly and turned his face to the ceiling, hands behind his head. "What am I going to tell Essie? I can't let her learn about this, Andrew. It would break her into pieces. Sam and Deborah's marriage is a treasure to her."

Andrew offered a small, joyless chuckle in Philip's direction. "That's for you to decide, Phil," he said. "She won't hear it from us. Not unless you fail to fire that girl. Patricia leaves tomorrow. I won't have Sam seeing her here every day."

"Yes, she'll be gone tomorrow," Philip said into the air above him. "And I'll talk to Sam. It won't happen again."

"No, it won't. Because I'll talk to him, as well. So will Diane." Andrew stood and walked to the door. "And Phil? Five percent of this company is mine. I'll calculate the value for you tomorrow morning, and you'll send me a check after I call."

"Andrew, wait, that's not—"

Andrew paused on his way to the door and held both hands up at Philip. "I've decided Diane and I are moving back to Alabama. David's made a life here and can stay if he chooses. But Phil, I never want to see your face again. Not Esther's, either."

Andrew Leon was a family man.

Twenty-six

RONNI

FEBRUARY, 2022

"It's not the same, with Max and Elise gone," Deanna said. "Samuel's a great kid, but he's not exactly a conversationalist. At least, not with me. I took some cookies to the store site yesterday and he barely spoke." She sipped her coffee and looked out the window at my backyard. "Elise promised they'll be down for a visit next month. I might even go to New York and stay with them when it's safer."

"I love talking to Samuel," I told her. "He gets my puns."

Deanna raised her brows. "Love? Is there something brewing with you and Samuel?"

"Oh, of course not. Just because you spent Christmas and New Year's Eve all snuggly with Lee Tyler doesn't mean romance is blossoming everywhere. I'm not interested, Deanna. There will never be anyone like Rick. I don't want anyone but him." I sniffed and clamped my eyes shut.

Violet walked in and held her arms up for a swoop into my lap at the breakfast table. "This little one is all the love I need." I kissed the top of my daughter's head, inhaling baby shampoo and something suspiciously like chocolate.

Deanna set her mug down. "He'd want you to have someone," she said quietly.

I shook my head, determined to change the subject. Violet did it for me, pointing her chubby finger at something in the distance.

"Cat!" she announced. She looked up at me.

"I see him, honey." I nodded. "That poor old cat." He was walking along the top of the stucco wall surrounding the backyard, the same scraggly creature we'd seen daily for a week. I'd asked the neighbors if anyone was missing a black cat with a white dot at his neck; no one claimed him. His fur was missing in a couple of places, and he was terribly skinny. I'd started setting cat food out, the most fattening kind the grocery store carried. He wouldn't let me come near. The food was always gone the next day, though, and I noticed the squirrel mafia had relocated to more relaxed yards nearby. We seemed to have developed a symbiotic relationship, the scrawny cat and I.

Violet squirmed in my lap. "Poorole cat," she said. "Go see poorole cat."

"That's not his name, honey, and he doesn't know you, so you might get scratched by the poor old cat—"

Deanna said, "No one's claimed him. Maybe you and Violet should adopt him."

"I'm happy to feed him, Deanna, but I don't think he wants an official adoption. Seems pretty feral. He runs every time I come near," I said. The cat had stretched himself along the wall, one paw hanging down. He looked asleep until a squirrel ran by on the ground, then he leapt down near it and immediately chased it up a tree.

"I don't think he's so old." Deanna chuckled. "It would be great if you could get him to a vet. I'll bet you he has worms. If it were warmer outside, he'd be covered in fleas. I wonder where he sleeps. Must get awfully cold out there."

"I know what you're doing," I told her, rolling my eyes. "He has a fur coat."

"Poorole has fur coat," Violet said, clapping her hands together.

"Honey, his name isn't Poorole," I answered, laughing. "I'll try to get him to trust me. Maybe I can lure him into a box or something without too much bloodshed. He really does need a vet." I watched the cat resume his napping spot on the wall. "But no promises."

"Violet, come sit with me," Deanna said, beckoning. "Let's watch Mommy try to pet Poorole—"

"That's not his name," I replied as Violet went to Deanna.

"Maybe it is," Deanna chuckled again. "I kinda like it." She handed me a piece of bacon. "Here's your secret weapon. Go conquer the beast."

The cat raised his head as I went out the back door. Bacon is a very seductive force.

"Hey buddy," I said in a low voice. "No one wants to hurt you, I promise. I just brought you a little bit of bacon." He didn't move as I came closer, a first. I placed a tiny morsel of bacon a few feet away from him on the wall and stepped back. The cat wandered over and ate it, then licked his paws and stared at me from a safe distance. When I stepped closer, he took off like a shot. Deanna and Violet were applauding on the other side of the window.

"That's a start," Deanna told me. "If you keep baconing him, he'll be your new best friend and squirrel herder."

"I'll try," I said. "Poor thing really needs a trip to the veterinarian. Something tore the fur off his right side, a whole patch of it."

"Poorole cat," Violet said.

"You know what, Violet, he has a round spot on his neck like a pearl. How about Pearl, instead?"

"POOROLE," she replied with a firm nod. "Him's name is Poorole."

And so him's name was, from that day on. I didn't even try to change the spelling to "Purrole," though the temptation was strong.

After a week of tasty people-food and lots of gentle talk, the cat allowed me to run my hand down his bumpy spine, which he raised in pleasure. A low rumble of a purr started in his chest. I sat there with tears running down my face, grateful to touch him. So much had been lost: the simple comfort of a stranger's handshake; a random hug. This cat unleashed a torrent of sadness by allowing me to run my hand over his soft fur. I decided right then I would do everything in the world to help him.

It took another two weeks to maneuver Poorole into one of those cardboard carriers, and more bacon than was probably advisable for any creature under a hundred pounds. He was decidedly unhappy about being enclosed. I set out to the nearest veterinary clinic with the cat trying to claw his way out, Violet in tow.

"Poorole is mad," she proclaimed from the back seat. "Him wants out."

"*He* wants out, Violet," I answered. "Not him."

"He is him!" she hollered at me, determined to convert me to her grammatical style. "Him is my cat."

"Him…he…is our cat. We're going to take him to the doctor so he'll feel better. He needs medicine and maybe an operation. We might have to let Poorole spend the night there." I met her eyes in the rearview mirror. The poor cat would need neutering. This was going to require a lot of guilty makeup bacon.

"Him not like that," she informed me.

"No, but he'll be really happy to come home to us, won't he? We'll make Poorole a welcome feast." I parked the car in front of the veterinary clinic, noting the name of the vet, Dr. Willow, who'd been recommended by our neighbor. I unbuckled Violet and helped her out to hold my hand as I retrieved the cardboard box. It was a hissing earthquake.

"Hi," the receptionist greeted us. She handed me a thick pile of paperwork to fill out. I stashed Poorole under the wood bench and resisted the temptation to spell the cat's name my way, not as Violet intended. By the time I'd finished the last page, Violet had almost fallen asleep leaning against me.

We were called back to sit in a small room with a stainless steel exam table in the center. It looked exactly like the vet's office where I used to take Halle, right down to the cheap maple cabinets and flea treatment posters.

We heard a knock and a man who was way too young to be Dr. Willow entered. "Hi, I'm Dr. Harris. I see you brought me a cat." He reached down and patted Violet's head. "Okay," he told her, "I'm gonna need you to jump up on this exam table." He patted the surface.

Violet giggled. "I am not the cat. Poorole is the cat." She pointed to the suddenly silent and still box at my feet.

He raised his brows at me. "Parole?"

"P-o-o-r-o-l-e, like the paperwork says. It's a long story."

Dr. Harris glanced down at my handwriting. "You could at least spell it 'Purr-ole.'" He chuckled, amused by his own pun. I didn't bother to tell him I'd beaten him to it. He extracted a curiously cooperative Poorole from his box and set him on the table. "You wrote 'male,' didn't you? This is a young lady cat, I'd say about two or three years old. And I think she's had at least one litter." Poorole lay on the table, gently submitting to the doctor's touch. Obviously, she liked men. "She's a stray, right?"

I was downright insulted he'd think I'd keep a cat in Poorole's condition voluntarily. "Yes, she showed up in our backyard and no one seems to know anything about her," I told him. "We're going to adopt her."

"Well," he said, "that's very kind of you. Let us run some tests and see if Poorole is in a family way, though she doesn't look like it. You want her spayed?"

"Oh, yes," I answered. "Do you think she has worms? She's so skinny."

"I think she has worms and ear mites, too," he said, flipping Poorole's ear inside out. "We'll treat her for everything and keep her for a couple of days, if that's okay with you. We can do the surgery tomorrow." He ran his hand down the cat's back and elicited a louder purr than I'd ever been awarded. Then he turned to Violet. "Are you ready to be a cat owner, Miss? It's a big responsibility."

"Mommy can," she informed him.

Dr. Harris squatted down to meet Violet's eyes. "You should help, though. Poorole will be your cat, too. I'm sure she'd love some attention from you. Just don't ever pull her tail or anything. Cats hate that." He glanced at me. "Okay if I pick your daughter up?"

I nodded yes since he was masked. He boosted Violet up onto the table. "See how happy Poorole is?"

Poorole did not look happy to me. Submissive, maybe.

He demonstrated a smooth glide of his hand down Poorole's back. "Just pet her like this and she'll really like it." He watched as Violet ran her hand along the cat's back. "Good job. And don't pick her up. Especially when she first comes home. Let her get used to you before you try that. Your mom can tell you when and if it's okay."

Violet nodded gravely. "Mommy feeded Poorole bacon."

Dr. Harris offered a tiny laugh with a shake of his head. He kept one hand on the cat as he stretched to knock on the door.

"Kay? Could you come in?" he called. A young assistant in scrubs walked in and scooped Poorole up. "We'll need a stool sample and blood tests. And please clean her ears up and start her on MilbeMite. She'll be spayed tomorrow, so set her up to stay a couple of days. Her name is Poorole."

Kay glanced at me. "Parole?"

"It's a long story," I answered.

"POOROLE," Violet told her, and chose that moment to throw both arms into the air, something she hadn't done in months. Kay regarded my bossy toddler with a look that seemed to imply she much preferred small animals to small humans. She nodded and took a mewling Poorole out of the room.

Dr. Harris went to wash his hands. "We'll take good care of her," he said. "I don't think she's pregnant, but we'll make sure." He cocked his head to one side. "You know, I saw your name and thought of that book that came out a few years ago. Are you the author?"

"Yes." I nodded, preparing to hear a veterinarian-in-Alabama book proposal. *Y'all Creatures Great and Small.*

"Yeah, that was my grandfather, the guy who inspired Chet. I read your book."

My jaw unhinged and I quickly snapped it shut. "You're Caleb Harris?"

"What? No, Caleb's my big brother. He lives in Anniston, but I just moved back from Auburn about six months ago. Stayed a few years at a practice there after I graduated." He leaned against the counter, drying his hands. "My name's Chad. Technically, it's Chadwick, but no one is allowed to live after calling me that."

I smiled at him, noticing the blue eyes and dark hair that had made the original Violet swoon so long ago. Now I could definitely see the resemblance, though I'd only known his grandfather as a very old man.

"Well, I'm writing a sequel to that book, and I think it's going to shed new light on some things. I didn't have the whole story the first time around."

He surprised me by saying, "Yeah, that's what I always told my dad. I mean, how could you have known? Anyway, it's a good book, and I'll look forward to the sequel."

"Thank you. I'm sorry for the loss of your dad. I went to your parents' house too late to meet him."

"He was a good guy," Chad said. "Seems like we've all lost someone in the last couple of years." He tugged at his mask and turned to open the door. "It was nice meeting you, Mrs. O'Shea. And you, too." He smiled at Violet, eyes crinkled at the edges.

"I am Violet," she told him.

"And please call me Ronni," I added.

"Okay, Ronni and Violet," he said, swinging the door open. "I'll see you lovely ladies about three o'clock on Thursday, and I'll have a full report on PURR-ole."

I swung Violet up onto my hip to keep her from correcting him.

Poorole was downright thrilled to see me two days later. She even allowed me to hold her, cradling her tender post-surgery parts away from pressure. She willingly went into her box and collapsed into an exhausted nap as I was still talking to Dr. Harris. Chad. I was kind of surprised he met me with the cat, rather than sending in a tech. He proceeded to tell me Poorole's surgery went well, and that she hadn't been with a male cat in a biblical way.

I laughed. "Well, that's a relief."

"Where's your beautiful daughter?" he asked.

"She's home with our babysitter, Maddie. It's just much easier to deal with a temperamental cat without a temperamental toddler. Thank you for taking care of Poorole."

"That's not a name I'm likely to hear again." He chuckled. "Poorole is a very sweet cat. She's really affectionate when she relaxes. I think she had an owner at one time who took great care of her. We'll give you meds to take home and continue, but the worms and mites should be gone. She's up on all her vaccinations, too. I suspect Poorole will have a long and happy life at your house, if you stop feeding her bacon."

I gave him an embarrassed smile. "It was necessary to lure her. I promise to stop."

"Well, she needs to gain a little weight." He smiled as he turned to wash his hands. "So, are you from Anniston originally?"

"I grew up around this area and Birmingham. I…I kinda moved around a lot. What about you?"

He nodded yes. "I grew up here, went to Donoho on a poor-kid scholarship, went to Auburn on an academic scholarship, somehow managed to get into vet school there. I worked my way through that, though I'm going to be paying off student loans until they bury me. Fell in love with Auburn and stayed for a long time. After Dad died, I talked Dr. Willow into taking me on so I could be closer to Mom."

"Do you miss Auburn?" I asked.

"You know, I do, but I was ready to move on. After a while, all those undergrads start looking like an army of twelve-year-olds. I was thirty-two and they made me feel ancient."

I chuckled. "I worked in a nursing home for a long time, and our residents made me feel young."

He met my eyes over his mask. "You are young." He paused for a second and continued, "And Mr. O'Shea is a lucky man."

I blushed and looked away. "Thank you," I murmured.

Chad cleared his throat. "Anyway, we dulled her claws a bit at the tips, just enough to keep her from eviscerating you or Violet or your husband. I'm just kidding. She's not the kind of cat to deliberately hurt you."

"I umm...I lost my husband to COVID. Not long after the pandemic started. It's been almost two years."

"I am so sorry," he said. "Truly, I had no idea. I never mentioned meeting you to my mom. She would have told me that."

I held up my hand. "It's fine. Nobody expects the thirty-year-old widow." I shook my head and took a deep breath. "My husband was a state trooper. Rick was exposed before we understood what this virus could do. He never got to meet our daughter."

"Well, I feel awful," he said. "Let me buy you dinner to apologize."

He might as well have punched me in the stomach, and he knew as soon as he saw my expression. "Oh God, I'm sorry, I didn't mean...I'm sorry. Of course you're not dating. I feel like a Neanderthal. Please accept my apology, Ronni." He was staring at me, shaking his head.

I gathered up my cat and muttered a thank you as I walked out, trying not to cry. I ran the full waiting room gauntlet, every eye upon me until I closed the door and took a deep breath in the parking lot. I deposited Poorole into the back seat and called Deanna as I drove away.

"Hey," I began, "I just reacted completely inappropriately to an invitation to dinner. An invitation from a very nice, cute, charming man, the veterinarian I told you about. He offered to buy me dinner and I acted like he'd hit me. You should've seen his face, Deanna. I'm really embarrassed. I am so far from *normal*, I don't know if I'll ever get back." I allowed the tears to flow. "I mean, it's been nearly two years. I should be better by now."

"Ronni, you're doing fine. There isn't any clear point at which you're better, honey, grief isn't like that. You've been doing what's necessary, the hard things, and you've done a beautiful job taking care of yourself and Violet. You're just not ready for this next phase of your life yet, and that's okay. Going somewhere with a date, well, that might be impossible for you right now. I'm sure you told him about losing Rick, didn't you?"

"Yes, I had just told him." I swiped at my wet face.

"Well, then I'm sure he understands. He's the one who should feel embarrassed. Don't be so hard on yourself."

I exhaled a ragged breath. "I just want to feel normal again. I've spent so long hurting. I can't stop missing Rick."

"Ronni, you never will completely. And honey, I've been through some very hard times in my life, you know that. It will get better, I absolutely promise you. We all go through sorrow, every person does." She paused. "You know, Ronni, it has to get dark enough for you to see the stars. Maybe we go through the awful times and emerge to appreciate the good ones more deeply."

"Where did you get 'dark enough to see the stars'? I heard Rick say that to Devonte on the phone one night."

"I think Dr. Martin Luther King, Jr. said it. But before that, it was Ralph Waldo Emerson. Part of a thing Sarah had to memorize in high school. I've always thought it's a lovely phrase."

"Yeah, it is." I sniffed. I was sitting at a stop light, and the lady in the car next to me quickly looked away when I turned my head toward her.

"I think what happened today was just a jolt, a reminder of your loss. If this poor guy gets his courage up enough to ask you again, maybe by then you'll be ready," Deanna said.

"I don't know if that's going to happen anytime soon," I told her. "I behaved like an idiot."

"You behaved like someone whose heart is still tender and bruised. I suspect this Dr. Harris knows that and may try a softer approach someday. In the meantime, go home and enjoy your little girl and your new kitty cat. Are y'all going to keep her inside?"

"Yes, she's still recovering. Violet and I bought her a cushy bed, and we're going to pamper her."

"Sounds like the best thing for Poorole and for you two, as well. Just make sure Violet gives her some space. The poor old cat's been through a lot to be reborn as the housecat a toddler pampers to death." Deanna laughed.

"I'll make sure. She'll only be a part-time housecat, when she's off squirrel duty. We really should change her name to Pearl, but I guess it doesn't have the appropriate weirdness for my daughter." I sighed, pulling into the driveway. "Thanks for talking me down. I love you."

"I love you, too. I'll talk to you tomorrow, honey. Bye."

Twenty-seven

NEW YORK CITY

1962

The day Andrew Leon announced his resignation, Philip took his time getting home, trying to prepare for the conversation he'd have with Esther. He hung his fedora on the stand in the apartment's foyer, where he detected the scent of his wife's delectable fried chicken. He walked into the kitchen to offer her a peck on the cheek.

"You're really late, Phil," she said, opening the oven door. "I've been keeping this warm for almost an hour. You should have called."

"Yeah, sorry." Philip rapped his knuckles on the small kitchen table. "Something came up. I have news, Essie. Maybe let's have a glass of wine before dinner. Come join me." He walked to the living room and picked up a decanter of chianti, Esther's favorite. He handed her a glass as she settled onto the sofa.

"I'm not sure this is the correct pairing with fried chicken," she said, and sipped. "But who cares?" His wife grinned at him, but her face fell when she sensed Philip's mood. "What happened? What's wrong, Phil?"

"Andrew Leon has decided to retire and move back to Alabama. The winters here are hard on him," Philip improvised. He drained half his glass and looked at Esther, whose eyes were wide.

"That's not possible," she said, shaking her head. "Diane would have told me. She hasn't said a word. Diane loves the city, and being near her sister. Surely you're wrong, Phil."

"I think it's a decision they reached very recently," Philip answered. "Maybe she was afraid of the way you'd react." He shrugged. "Andrew's cashing out his share of the business."

Esther set her glass down. "What did you do? What did you *do*, Phil? Andrew wouldn't want his share of the business unless you made him mad. Surely you can make up. Call him and apologize, Philip. You have to say you're sorry. Whatever you've done this time—"

"Whatever *I've* done, Essie? I've done nothing. This is a personal decision Andrew and Diane have made. It has nothing to do with me. The stores are fine. It's not about the business, it's personal reasons. Maybe his arthritis is bothering him in the cold. Maybe he misses Alabama. I don't know."

Esther finished her wine and walked to the decanter for more, her eyebrows asking Philip if he wanted a refill; he shook his head no. She turned her back to the console table and leaned against it, clutching the glass to her bosom.

"You have such a temper, Phil. I'm betting you offended Andrew one time too many. Maybe you got frustrated with the numbers and snapped at him. He's not a man of harsh words, but you are. You know this." She sipped her wine.

Philip was incredulous. He'd expected anything from Esther but blame. "Esther, Andrew and I have been close friends for many years. It's insulting that you would think that. I've never offended Andrew that way. At work, we're all business and I'm very professional."

Esther carried her glass into the kitchen. "That's what you think. Diane tells a different story. Face it, Phil, you can be very difficult. I'm sure Andrew's wanted to quit before. He's just never had the nerve to confront you."

Philip felt himself grow smaller with every word his wife spat at him. His hands clenched and unclenched at his sides.

"That's not true. Essie, I love you, but I don't like you right now. You're manipulative, bossy, and your constant criticism is more than any man could take. Please stop."

Esther shot him a withering look and then ignored him. She began placing chicken parts and mashed potatoes on plates as Philip settled at the table.

"You have to fix this."

Philip stared at her. "*Fix* this? There's no fixing. The man wants to retire, and he's entitled to. I'll find someone we can trust to replace him."

"Phil," Esther said, setting his dinner before him, "you have to think about Sam. He loves having his father-in-law as part of our business. And Deborah would miss her parents terribly if they moved. Think about Sam for once."

Philip smacked his palm on the table, causing Esther to jump a little. "I *am* thinking of Sam, Essie. I've always thought of Sam. Maybe we wouldn't be having this conversation if you hadn't insisted on meddling between Sam and Violet. Maybe he'd be happily married to her, living here, and I wouldn't have a hole in my gut from thinking about what we did to him. To Violet and Deborah, too. Maybe I wouldn't be writing Andrew a check tomorrow for a crazy amount of money because we made all this happen, *for Sam*. We should have stayed out of it!" He stood and threw his napkin down. "*You* should have stayed out of it."

Esther calmly began to eat her dinner. "You'd have had him marry that cheap *goy* girl. You'd have had *her* for a daughter-in-law. You'd have destroyed our family. You've lost your mind, Phil. Sit down."

"No, I've lost my appetite. My mind is perfectly clear. *Too* clear. I'm going out."

Esther watched him turn to leave, her mouth open in disbelief. She threw the drumstick in her hand at her husband's back.

"Philip, don't you dare walk out that door. You will come back here and speak to me the way I deserve to be spoken to."

Philip turned around and picked up the piece of chicken from the polished floor, placing it on the kitchen table. "That's exactly what I just did, Esther. For the first time, I spoke to you the way you deserve."

Esther blinked at her husband. "What has gotten into you? You're all *meshuggeneh* because Andrew's getting this money? Because you screwed up and you'll have to pay? Is that it, Phil?"

"It has nothing to do with money," Philip said evenly. "It has to do with what you've done to Sam. You want to know the real reason, Esther? You want the truth? Your son was seen kissing Patricia Carpenter in a stockroom this afternoon. And you know why I think that happened, Esther? Because we forced him away from the love of his life. We set Sam up to fail in this marriage."

"What a ridiculous thing to say. We did what was best for Sam," Esther replied.

"And guess who discovered them together, Essie? *Andrew* saw Sam and Patricia making out, and came to me. I ended up telling him everything about Sam and Violet, about what we did. He's furious we put Deborah in this position."

"That's a lie," she sobbed. "Sam wouldn't—"

"Yes, he would and he did. No one's going to tell Deborah about this, ever. I promised Andrew I'll fire Patricia tomorrow." Philip clutched the back of his chair so hard, his knuckles were white. "If you hadn't insisted you would disown our son unless he obeyed you, this would never have happened."

"How can you blame me?" Esther was crying and swiping at her eyes. "I only did what I knew was best for Sam. I know you feel the same way."

"All I feel is shame, Essie. Andrew never wants to see either of us again, and I don't blame him," Philip said, his voice low. "So yes, I've spoken to you the way you deserve now. And you get to live with this, just like I do. Every bit of this trouble is because you wanted to make your dreams come true for Sam, with no regard for anyone else, Essie. Enough." Philip turned to leave without a look back at his wife, who was palming tears up her forehead and into her gray hair.

"Phil!" she yelled as he reached the door. "If you hadn't brought Patricia up here…you knew Sam liked her…"

Philip paused, weighing the only burden he hadn't added to Esther's heart. He sighed and looked back toward the kitchen. Philip couldn't, he wouldn't, mention Violet's possible pregnancy. It was too much for Esther. Instead, he went to their bedroom and packed a bag. Esther followed and stood in the doorway, looking on in disbelief.

"Where do you think you're going?" she said.

"I'm going to a hotel for a few days. I need some time alone, and a neutral place to talk to our son about what he's done. Don't worry, Esther, I won't tell him what we've done." Philip closed and locked his suitcase. He brushed his wife aside as he headed out.

"But Phil, you can't leave—"

"I can. You should maybe think about the way you treat me, Essie. No husband should have to put up with this. No son, either." He left her sobbing on their bed, face in her hands. Philip made a point of slamming their apartment's door, something he'd never done in the history of their marriage. His neighbor down the hall, Mr. Etheridge, ignored the noise and hurried by without meeting Philip's eyes.

In the years that followed, Esther and Philip Davidson's marriage was never quite the same. Philip would periodically check into The Plaza Hotel, where he'd sit in silence and read or watch television, his room service order long noted and delivered each evening at precisely seven o'clock. Occasionally, he'd gaze out the window at the trees of Central Park and reminisce about a simpler life in Alabama.

Twenty-eight

RONNI

APRIL, 2022

I watched Samuel drive his new/old BMW into my driveway and park. He'd done his best to secure a new car off the lot, but there were none to be had. Samuel ended up with a disturbingly bright tomato-red 2018 BMW 440i convertible, which couldn't possibly have been more opposite his personality. That, coupled with his limited New York City driving skills, led to a lot of jokes. Today he had the top down to amuse Violet, and I noticed him smoothing his hair back into place before he walked to the front door.

"Are you sure we have to go in the Sexmobile?" I asked as I waved him in. "I don't feel like it's age-appropriate for Violet. And lord knows what's gone on in that back seat. Maybe I'll put gloves on her."

Violet ran into the room and jumped into Samuel's arms. "Hi, honey!" she said, hugging him and placing a gooey kiss on his cheek. Her curls bounced as he jiggled her up and down. Violet was wearing one of her Elise outfits, a Stella McCartney "daisy friends" white shirt and pants with yellow smiley-face flowers. She had on her matching bright yellow mary janes, which were the softest leather on earth. My daughter still loved taking them off, though, delighting in throwing them across rooms for no apparent reason. I sneaked a quick photo of Samuel holding her, Violet grinning back at him and stroking his hair carefully, like he was Poorole.

"Are you ready to see an elephant?" Samuel asked her. "Your mommy says there's an elephant."

Violet nodded and he set her down, taking her tiny hand. I shrugged and followed them out the door, a third wheel of discipline and healthy snacks. I pretty much disappeared when Samuel was nearby; my daughter stayed turned toward him like a wildflower to the late afternoon sun.

"Thanks for inviting me," Samuel said as I handed him Violet's car seat. "I really needed a day away from the store construction. Yesterday two more guys failed to show up. We're officially three weeks behind schedule and the contractor is going around looking like his underwear is twisted. The smiling assurances are long gone. We probably can't get stock in there for at least two more months."

"I know you're really stressed out. And I can use a hand at the Anniston Museum of Natural History, keeping *her* hands *off* the natural history. Are you sure Gwendolyn doesn't mind?"

"Gwendolyn's showing properties all day. She's fine with this; she thinks it'll be a good break for me. Anything but staring at construction that isn't happening. I actually wish I had paint I could watch drying." Samuel clicked Violet into place and stood waiting for me to get into the passenger seat. "You look pretty," he said.

"Thank you," I batted my eyes and closed the door. Gwendolyn McLendon was Samuel's new girlfriend, a doe-eyed brunette beauty queen who ran her daddy's real estate empire across three counties. They'd met when Samuel acquired the property next to the store for a parking lot. Gwendolyn (never Gwen) was the real deal, a former majorette and homecoming queen at the University of Alabama.

Worse, she was actually very likeable and I couldn't find anything wrong with her, especially since her vivaciousness offset Samuel's quiet side so well.

The females really do have the brighter plumage, Rick used to say. I had chosen today—two years after we lost him—for this adventure with Samuel, though I hadn't mentioned the anniversary. I had no intention of bringing everyone down with that knowledge. This was going to be a fun, much-needed distraction for the three of us. Now that the world had relaxed some pandemic-wise, it felt wonderful and exciting to go and do an ordinary thing in a public place.

Samuel slid into the driver's seat and asked if I was okay with keeping the top down.

"Not really, but I want to do it for Violet." I grinned and produced one of Rick's old baseball caps, a worn Montgomery Biscuits hat I'd adjusted to fit.

When I put it on, Samuel immediately said, "What the hell is *that* thing, peeking out from the 'M'?"

"It's a biscuit, their mascot," I told him. "He's grinning."

"He's creepy," Samuel replied.

"He is *not*, yankee. We should go to a game someday. They used to actually throw biscuits into the stands."

Samuel rolled his eyes and shifted into reverse. "You people really don't understand baseball."

Violet admonished him with a wave of her chubby finger. "No say HELL."

Samuel met her eyes in the mirror. "Sorry. I forgot there's a lady present." He glanced over at me. "And your mom."

We made it a mile or two before Samuel decided it was too hard to yell our conversation and pulled over to put the top up. Violet didn't seem to mind, anyway.

"So, what I was trying to say was, how did the interview with America's News Grandma go?"

I shrugged. "I was just glad we finally got to do it. That was the third time we've rescheduled, because her assistants keep quitting or being fired, not sure which. Bettina was polite to me. And I didn't stumble, even though I was really nervous. I was so afraid she was going to attack Violet or make me look bad, but she didn't. She's all about telling the world what happened with her brother on that roof a million years ago."

"So, *tell* me, already," Samuel said. "What happened?"

I laughed and took my cap off, fluffing my hair in the visor mirror. "You'll just have to wait for the book."

"There are zero perks to knowing the author, Violet," Samuel informed her. "Your mom is a big meanie."

Violet nodded, clutching her foot in the air and trying to remove her shoe. "Uh-huh," she agreed. "Writin' writin' writin'," she grumbled, shaking her head. Not yet two, and she'd perfected her guilt trip.

"Just...were you surprised by what Bettina told you?" Samuel looked at me, eyebrows raised.

"You could say that." I nodded and clamped my mouth shut.

Samuel sighed. "How much farther is this museum?"

"It'll be ahead on the right in about half a mile," I said.

"Elephun." Violet was straining to see out the window.

"The elephant is inside, honey; it's not like at the zoo. He won't be walking around. But you can see how big he is and we'll take your picture with him, okay?"

"FEED elephun," Violet said.

"Honey, the elephant is...well, he doesn't move. He'll just be standing there."

"Poorole elephun." Violet gave a sad shake of her head.

"You are in big trouble," Samuel told me, smirking.

"Mind if I pair my phone?" I asked him. "This is straight up magic."

"Go ahead."

Peppa Pig's perky British accent distracted Violet immediately, and soon we were singing about dancing in mud puddles. Samuel looked like he'd enjoy rolling across a bed of glass shards more than listening to Peppa Pig.

"It grows on you," I told him.

He nodded. "Like a tinkly musical fungus." He swept his longish brown hair back with one hand and I thought for the hundredth time how ridiculously good-looking he and his entire family were. Like mutants from the planet Dazzle.

Samuel slowed the car as we approached the museum entrance, reaching to extinguish the music. "Almost there, Violet! Are you ready?" he asked.

"Elephun!" she said, kicking her car seat.

Samuel extracted her and carried her in. They stood looking at the enormous twirling globe in the lobby as I bought our tickets. I heard Samuel say, "We are there!" every time North America came around.

"THERE!" Violet would giggle as he bounced her.

I hadn't counted on every display being quite so huge and toothsome. Violet stared at the pterodactyl suspended over us, but hid her head in Samuel's armpit as we passed the towering T Rex. We saw live snakes behind glass, which made *me* yearn for an armpit to hide in. There were gigantic bears, brown and polar, baring their incisors at us. She didn't relax until Africa, where she pointed to the rhinoceros and screamed "ELEPHUN," causing several museum-goers to swivel their heads.

"No, honey, the elephant is coming up," I told her. Violet strained to see ahead and I nodded at Samuel to let her down. She sprinted to the ten-foot-tall elephant and stared, speechless.

Violet took a tiny step back. "Not Emleee," she said.

I looked at her little lip poking out and finally realized what she'd expected: Emily the animated elephant on Peppa Pig.

"Oh, honey, I'm sorry. This is a real elephant from Africa. Look at him. Isn't he magnificent? See his trunk...?"

My daughter reached her arms up to Samuel, clearly disappointed.

"She's a little young for this, Ronni," he said. "In a few years, she'll love it all. This is a super nice museum, really well designed and especially impressive for a city Anniston's size."

"I know," I sighed. "I did think she'd enjoy the animals, though. The truth is, we're not really here for Violet."

"You brought me to see an elephun?" He tilted his head to one side.

"No. Let's get through the rest of Africa and the Egyptian mummies. I have a surprise for you." I noted my daughter getting sleepy on Samuel's shoulder.

"Real Egyptian mummies?" Samuel asked. "I think that's surprise enough."

I laughed. "They're a staple for every school kid in the county. Go ahead, test me on my mummification knowledge. I've field-tripped all over this place."

Violet lifted her head to gaze at the still-colorful mummies in their glass case. "Them is asleep." She yawned and rested her head again.

"A kid in sixth grade tried to convince me they wake every midnight," I whispered to Samuel. "The bad dreams lasted until I was eighteen."

He chuckled. "Thanks for the creative new nightmare inspiration."

I blinked at him. "Are you okay carrying Violet? I think she'll be out for about thirty minutes."

"Light as a feather," he said.

"Okay, then. I want to show you something next door."

We made our way through the inevitable gift shop with Violet blissfully unaware of the toys and candy for sale. Samuel and I walked over a little bridge to another building about fifty yards away.

"What's the Berman Museum?" he asked as the sign came into view.

"You'll see," I answered. I swung the door open for him and Violet, then showed our tickets to the lady at the counter.

"Welcome to the Berman Museum," she said. "Have y'all visited before?"

"I have. I know my way around, thanks."

"Y'all's little girl is beautiful," she said, nodding at my sleeping Violet, her tiny hand resting on Samuel's chest.

"Thank you," Samuel answered.

We made our way through the doors leading into a huge collection of Frederic Remington bronzes, exquisitely detailed sculptures of cowboys and Native Americans. "I've never seen so many of these in one place," Samuel said. "Is this what you brought me here for? I have a well-documented fascination with the old west."

"Not even close," I told him. We wandered through exhibits that made Samuel stop and stare, sometimes calling me over to point something out. Guns and militaria fascinated him. He tried his hand at the old telegraph machine, glancing at Violet to make sure he wasn't disturbing her with the movement.

"She hibernates like a bear," I told him. "Don't worry about waking her."

"Ronni!" Samuel whisper-screamed. "Look at this!" He was beholding a jeweled Persian scimitar that had belonged to Abbas I and had eventually been presented to Catherine the Great. It was covered in diamonds and rubies, all glittering around a gigantic emerald. "This is incredible. The collection they have here is crazy. I've never seen anything like it, not even in the city. Of course, our museums are spectacular, but this is the most interesting and eclectic thing I've ever seen. My inner history-nerd is beyond excited."

"Well, for the record, it's not *the* city, Samuel. If Anniston's going to be your new home, you have to stop calling New York that. And your history-nerd is pretty much *outer*."

Samuel goggled at the thirteenth century Bohemian crown and Napoleon's ivory dressing set. When he reached a silver tea service, he handed Violet to me and leaned toward the glass case for a closer look.

"Ronni," he whispered, "this belonged to Hitler. Like, *personally*."

"I know." I smiled. "Surreal, isn't it? There's a bit about it in the book I'm writing. But it's not why we're here."

He raised his brows and reached for a still-dozing Violet. "Are you sure?" I asked him. "She gets pretty heavy after a while."

He nodded. "You get to hold her all the time." He ran his hand up her back and patted her between the shoulder blades. "She's such a cuddler." As if on cue, Violet shifted her head closer to Samuel's neck, nuzzling in and exhaling a deep sigh.

When Samuel spotted the Nazi flag, there was a discernible shift in his posture. He walked over for a closer look.

"I did not expect this," he said quietly.

"Mr. Berman and his wife were both spies in World War II. They collected all sorts of militaria. But the reason I brought you here, Samuel," I took his arm, "is this." I led him to a glass case displaying uniforms from World War II, mostly American. But at the end of the case were three mannequins dressed as Nazi soldiers, one of them wearing an SS officer's black uniform with a bright red swastika armband.

I watched his arms close tighter around Violet's little body, clutching her to him. We stood for a minute until I said, "Your great-grandfather donated these to the museum, Samuel. He collected Nazi military uniforms for this display. But not the first ones he managed to track down. He *burned* those in his backyard, right after the Second World War. Philip thought it was cathartic to sit and watch them go up in flames, and I imagine it was. He was grieving the loss of his cousins in Europe as well as the millions of others discovered in death camps. He wanted to help Mr. Berman memorialize this for all to see, to remember."

He swiped his eyes. "How could I not know about this?" Samuel shook his head, staring at the display. "He really tracked these down and *burned* some of them?"

"In their new backyard barbecue. He did it a couple of times, then decided he was being crazy, so he and your great-grandmother decided to donate these to Mr. Berman, who was already amassing an impressive number of artifacts from the war. I think it was Philip's way of working through his pain and trying to move forward. It took him a long time, though. He finally mentioned his cousin Sophia to your grandfather, Sam, not long before he died. He said she'd lived near Berlin and was taken to Ravensbrück. Philip tried to find her after the war, but never could. She was twenty-two when they took her. Eventually records revealed Sophia was killed there in 1944. Philip didn't know it, but months ago I found out Sophia spent most of her time at the camp producing uniforms for the German Army. I'll show you the website."

"Wow. She could have made one of these." He shrugged his shoulders and Violet stirred a little, shifting her head. Samuel reached for Violet's soft hair and stroked it absently. "Does any of her family remain? Sophia's, I mean."

I shook my head. "None of them made it out of Germany, Samuel. I'm sorry."

"This is overwhelming, Ronni. I'm trying to take it all in. I can understand why he'd want to destroy them, though." Samuel stared at the case, his jaw set in a rigid line. "These uniforms must have represented the worst evil in all of mankind to my great-grandfather."

"They did. They still do," I told him. "What he did was so meaningful, Samuel. Philip Davidson was a good man, a brilliant man, and what a legacy he left."

Samuel nodded and bit his lower lip, still staring at the uniforms. "Thank you for bringing me here, Ronni."

"And also, Samuel, I feel I've come to know and love him through writing this book. One thing is sure: Philip would be incredibly proud of both you and your dad."

There were many more exhibits, but we walked right past them and headed to the exit downstairs. Violet opened her eyes as we emerged into the sunshine. She blinked at me over Samuel's shoulder. I took her from him and buckled her into the car seat without a word. Then I climbed in, closing the door more softly than usual. We were both kind of dazed by what we'd witnessed. Samuel was gazing into the distance, toward the botanical gardens, but I didn't think he was really seeing them.

"Does my dad know all this?" He turned to look at me.

"Most of it." I nodded. "He said he didn't want to burden you."

Samuel started the car. "Sounds like Max." He shook his head. "If you don't mind, I'm going to run you home now." He threw an arm up on the back of my seat to back the car out.

"That's fine," I told him. I handed Violet the least messy snack I'd brought, a bag of Cheerios. I'd pick up a bunch of them from the seat and floorboard when Samuel parked the car, but at least they wouldn't be gooey. I hoped.

"In your dad's defense, Samuel, he couldn't have brought you here during the pandemic," I said, studying his face.

"Yeah, I know. And I know my father. There are some things he finds difficult to talk about, so he pretends they don't exist." He shook his head, his mouth a tight line. "It's fine, Ronni. I'm grateful to you for telling me. For showing me." He patted my hand. "It was just kinda shocking, that's all. I have a lot to think about."

Samuel pulled out of the lot and began to drive the winding road to the park that surrounded the museums.

Violet said, "CHEERIO," and handed me one, downright gleeful. "Samull cheerio," she added, holding another out toward him. Samuel turned to reach for it and we heard a thump at the front of his car.

"What was that?" I asked him.

He hit the brakes as he put Violet's manhandled cheerio into his mouth. "I have no idea. Must've run over something."

Samuel and I spotted him at the same time: a scrawny little gray terrier mix mutt of some sort, limping as he walked back into the picnic area of the park. Samuel stopped the car and got out, calling to the dog and looking for his owners. The place was deserted. The dog began to drag his rear leg behind him, making a determined escape into the nearest pavilion. Samuel caught up to him.

"Poorole dog," Violet said. "Him's hurted."

"Yes, he is," I told her. "I think the car bumped him."

"Samull hurted him," she announced, popping another cheerio into her mouth.

"He didn't mean to, Violet. He was distracted and the dog must've run out—" I stopped talking as Samuel approached my side of the car, carrying the limp little dog. I opened the door and he held up a finger.

"Wait," he said. "I have a towel in the trunk. He's pretty filthy." Samuel walked to the back of the car and wrapped the dog in a worn blue towel, returning to place him in my lap. "He won't bite," Samuel said. "Just don't touch his leg."

The dog looked at me with his brown eyes so wide I could see the whites surrounding them. I could feel him shaking through the towel.

I asked Samuel as he got in, "What are you going to do?"

"I dunno, but I can't just leave him here. He doesn't have a collar. Doesn't look like he's eaten in a week. I'm pretty sure he's a stray and no one's going to help him."

"POOROLE DOG!" rang out like a foghorn from the back seat, making him jump so hard, the towel came off on one side.

I replaced it and said, "Violet, we have to be quiet. The dog is very scared. Shhh."

"Do you know a vet? A vet who might let us walk in?" Samuel asked. He started to drive toward the highway.

"Yeah, the guy who took care of our cat, I guess. Either he or Dr. Willow will see us, I'm sure." I gave Samuel directions and gingerly touched the fur on the dog's head. He gave a tiny, faint whimper and closed his eyes. After a minute or two, he seemed to tremble a little less.

As Samuel parked the car and extracted Violet, I hurried inside with the dog, who seemed a lot more relaxed. I didn't know if that was a good thing or not.

"Hi," I told the receptionist. "I'm Ronni O'Shea. We have a cat named Poorole who's a patient of Dr. Harris's—"

She nodded and began typing. "Parole?"

"No, not…it doesn't matter. I'm here because we think we hit this stray dog with our car. His leg seems hurt. We need to see Dr. Harris or Dr. Willow, please, if you can fit us in." I glanced around the waiting room. It was populated by four people, all of whom were holding leashes on dogs of various sizes except a lady with a giant Maine Coon cat on her lap, running her hand over its fur. The dogs had already begun barking. The ginormous black Labrador retriever was making it hard to hear anything else.

His owner yelled, "General, sit!" and the dog immediately complied and sat silent. The Maine Coon had his head buried under the lady's arm.

"Honey, we're all here for checkups. If that dog's hurt, you go on ahead of us," the lady said. I watched the mouth of Black Lab Guy drop open, but she shot him a look and he sat back without protest.

The receptionist said, "I'll be right back," and disappeared behind a door as Samuel and Violet entered hand-in-hand.

"They're checking to see if we can get in," I told him. "These nice folks said we can go ahead of them." I smiled at them all, and they nodded, if a bit grudgingly.

The receptionist reappeared and directed us to an exam room. I didn't put the dog on the table. He was clearly scared to death. Beyond the door, the black lab shouted his frustration at something. The rest of the dogs joined in the cacophony, which caused the receptionist to say, "I'd better get back out there. Ginny will be in soon." She closed the door without another word. I don't know what she did, but all the dogs stopped barking within a few seconds.

"Do you know Ginny?" Samuel asked. "Is she one of the vets?"

"No, I don't think so. And they're both men," I told him. The dog looked up at me with worried eyes, though the whites weren't as exposed. Violet held her arms up for Samuel, who obliged by swinging her onto his hip. "You're really great with her," I told Samuel.

"Well, I have lots of practice, mostly with Ollie. Jeannie and Ethan used to treat me like their built-in babysitter since I didn't go out much."

"Ah. How are they doing, anyway? Are they back in New York?"

"Yeah, Jeannie wanted Ollie to be back with Mom and Dad around. I think she was bored in Connecticut, too. She's entering Ollie in a beauty pageant in Manhattan."

"What? There are little boys in pageants? Since when?"

"I guess it's something new." Samuel shrugged. "Both girls and boys compete, and they name a king and queen. They each get a crown. Oh, and listen to this: Ollie lost a tooth and they had a fake one made to fill in his smile. He's going to wear a little tuxedo."

I frowned. "Do they have a talent competition built in?"

"No, it's just how they look, how photogenic they are, how much poise they have. I mean, Ollie loves attention. You've seen that. This is perfect for him."

"I would never, ever enter my child in a beauty pageant," I said, checking to see if the dog was okay. He looked like he was asleep. "I think it sends the worst possible message. Don't you?"

Samuel shrugged. "Violet would win any pageant you put her in. She's beautiful and outgoing. I can picture her in a pageant dress." He smiled at my daughter, who was leaning down and trying to remove her shoe again, struggling as she reached over his arms. Samuel lifted her chin with his finger. "You're very pretty, Violet," he told her.

"I know." She nodded and resumed trying to get to her shoe.

"Violet, stop it…" I quieted as I heard the door open behind me.

Whoever Ginny was, she never made it to our room. A man in a lab coat who looked to be seventyish held his hand up in a wave.

"I'm Dr. Willow," he said. "How are y'all today? Understand you had an accident with your car and a dog?" He indicated the bundle I held, pointing with his chin. "Would you place him on the table, please?" I gently put the dog on the same stainless steel table we'd used when Poorole made her visit.

Dr. Willow examined the dog for a few minutes as we looked on in silence. Violet broke it by saying, "Samull hurted him." She added a grave shake of her head.

"Looks like the car probably just tapped him and he fell funny. We'll get some x-rays to be sure. I'll get Ginny in here to take him. Y'all please be patient, because we are covered up today. But I think your dog is going to be fine. What did you say his name is?"

Samuel said, "Lucky. His name is Lucky. Will you please make sure he's up to date on shots and whatever he needs? I'll take him to a shelter as soon as you're finished with him and we know his leg's all right."

Dr. Willow nodded and opened the door. "Nice of you to bring him in. Some folks would've driven away." He smiled at Samuel as he left.

"A shelter? Really?" I said.

Samuel lifted his shoulders. "What am I gonna do, Ronni? Take him back and dump him at that park? He's a nice dog. He'll make someone a good pet."

"Just not you." I folded my arms and looked at the dog, whose head was between his forepaws, ignoring us.

"Oh, come on." He scowled. "You think I have some sort of obligation to take him home with me? That's ridiculous—"

He was interrupted by Chad Harris walking into the room. If he recognized me, he didn't show it.

"Hi," he told Samuel. "I'm Dr. Harris. Ginny's going to be tied up for a while, so I'll take Lucky for his x-rays. We should know right away if his leg's broken. I'll be right back." He scooped the dog off the table without a glance at me.

"Hiiiii," Violet sang, waving.

"Hi," he responded. "Hey, I remember you. You're the cat your mom brought in a couple months ago. Your fur's grown out some."

Violet giggled. "I'm not Poorole." She rested her head on Samuel's chest.

Dr. Harris smiled at her. "How is Poorole?"

Violet didn't answer, so he turned to me. "Hello, Mrs. O'Shea. How's Poorole?" he asked, very formally.

"She's doing really well, thank you," I answered. "We cherish every meowment with her," I added, deadpan.

Dr. Harris allowed himself a small chuckle. "Well, that's pawsitively awesome." He took a deep breath and glanced at Samuel holding Violet, who had her dimpled arms around his neck now.

Is it my imagination or has she started to look like him?

Dr. Harris nodded and held my eyes for several beats. He petted the dog's fur and handed Samuel the towel.

"We won't need this. Back in a few," he said, and closed the door behind him.

Samuel rolled his eyes. "What was *that* about?" he asked.

"Nothing," I said. "Absolutely nothing. We both like stupid puns."

"Yeah, that hurt my ears," Samuel said.

Violet threw her hands to her ears and held them there, staring at me.

"I think you should consider adopting that dog, Samuel," I said. "He'd be okay while you're at work all day, and you have that big fenced backyard. Maybe you're meant to take him home with you."

"I'm not a dog person," he told me. "We never had dogs when I was growing up in the city."

"This," I said evenly, "is a different city." I sat in the corner chair and crossed my arms again. "And you'd be doing a wonderful thing for that dog. Sometimes dogs come into people's lives just when they're supposed to. I think you need him as much as he needs you. Just give it a try. If you two don't work out, then you can take him to a shelter."

Violet patted Samuel's face. "Hurted dog," she said, looking at him. "Him is sad."

I wasn't sure if she was talking about Samuel or Lucky.

Samuel closed his eyes. "This day has been three days long." He sighed. "Okay, I'll take him home with me. But he's mostly going to live in the backyard. And if he drives me crazy barking or anything, he's going to a shelter."

"Of course." I nodded.

Dr. Chad Harris walked in, holding Lucky. "No break at all. He's bruised, and he'll favor the other leg for a while," he told Samuel. "Are you taking him home with you?"

"I guess I am," Samuel answered.

"I'll get Ginny in here to give him his shots and some flea and heartworm meds. You'll need to make an appointment to bring him in to be neutered, if that's your plan, and I'd highly recommend it. That'll give me a chance to take another look at his leg, too. Maybe in a couple of weeks?" It wasn't really a question.

Samuel said, "Okay, I'll set up an appointment on the way out. What kind of dog is he?"

Dr. Harris said, "Lucky." He laughed and added, "He has a diverse genetic heritage. I guess the strongest suggestion is the hint of Jack Russell Terrier in his face. He'll be a great dog, Mr."—he glanced at his paperwork—"Davidson." He turned to nod at me. "Nice to see you again, Mrs. O'Shea."

Samuel's phone rang and he pulled it out of his pocket. "Hey, you," he began. "Yeah, we finished at the museum and I have so much to tell you. No. Oh, yes. Umm, Gwendolyn, I'm at a veterinarian's office right now. I hit a dog with my car. No, no, he's fine. We thought he had a broken leg, though."

Violet was studying each second of this phone conversation, hanging on Samuel's every word. She turned her eyes to me and nodded, though I had no idea what that meant.

"Yes, well, the thing is, I think I'm going to take the dog home with me. No, there was no owner there. He's a stray." A brief silence and then, "In the backyard. It'll be fine." More silence. Violet reached up and began to tap Samuel's lower lip until he grinned at her. "Yeah, okay, that sounds great. I sure will. Bye, baby. I love you." He hit the phone button and I resisted the urge to comment on anything I'd heard.

Violet lay her head on his shoulder. "Love you honey," she said.

Samuel looked at me. "Has she ever said that before?"

I shook my head. "Not even to me."

"I love you, too, Violet," Samuel told her, patting her back.

She loves you more, I told myself. *She just needed to form the words. Maybe I would take her to a Peppa Pig concert. Is there such a thing? It might require drugs.*

Samuel and Violet continued adoring each other and I stared at the flea treatment chart. After what felt like a year, the elusive Ginny showed up and took care of Lucky, who was not enthused.

Ginny swung the door open and waved us out. She said, "Y'all have a beautiful daughter," smiling at Violet and walking away.

At that point, both Samuel and I were too tired to say anything other than thank you.

I caught a glimpse of Dr. Chad Harris at the end of the hall, his hand on the ginormous black Lab, his eyes on me and then Samuel as we exited.

Twenty-nine

BIRMINGHAM, ALABAMA

MAY, 1965

J erry Lee Urban looked up from an air conditioning box on the roof of Jefferson Memorial Hospital, waiting for his boss, Chet Wilson, to hand him a wire cutter. The May sun had introduced more than a hint of the summer heat to come. Jerry Lee wiped his forehead with the sleeve of his blue coveralls. Chet was taking too long, clearly distracted. He was looking at something in the distance across the roof, not the assortment of tools they'd brought.

Jerry Lee didn't stand up to see what Chet was watching. He'd already guessed. "Well," he said, "are you actually gonna say something to him? You're runnin' outta time, Chet. We'll be done here soon. No more excuses to hang around this place, and I'll be mighty glad to work in Mrs. Wiley's cool basement tomorrow. Enough of this shit. And you're not even going up to the guy. It's been *four* days."

He removed the cigarette dangling from his mouth and tapped its ash. "You chickenin' out before it's over? Why the hell are we up here? Ain't about money, the way you underbid this job." Jerry Lee put the wire cutter down and sat on the roof's hot surface, grimacing slightly. "Go on, Chet. Just say what you came to say." He rested his cigarette hand on his knee and nodded. "You want me to do it? I'll teach him a lesson he'll never forget, guaranteed. Ain't no man putting rough hands on any woman I know without paying for it."

Chet took a deep breath and clasped his hands together, twisting them as he watched Dr. Tolliver Thompson take a swig from his flask. "I said I'm gonna confront him, Jerry Lee, not beat him up on this roof."

Jerry Lee snickered and took a drag, exhaling smoke. "Can't believe you're actually gonna try this." He stubbed his cigarette out and told Chet, "Look, it's now or never. You know he'll only be up here fifteen more minutes, unless he manages to suck the last drop outta that thing sooner." He reached from his sitting position and smacked Chet's calf muscle. "Go on."

Chet took a few tentative steps toward Tolly, glancing around to be sure no one else had accompanied him to the rooftop. He was alone, as usual.

When Chet drew near, he called out, "Hey, you got a cigarette I can bum? We're up here working on wiring for the air conditioning units, and I smoked my last Marlboro an hour ago."

Tolly ran his eyes up and down Chet's blue uniform, appraising him. "Sure," he said, tapping his pack to expose a filtered Kool and extending it to Chet. "I heard about that lightning strike. Are y'all about done?" He replaced the pack in his lab coat pocket. "You need a light, too?"

"No, thanks, I have a lighter. We're finishing up replacing wires today and they can get the air conditioning guys here tomorrow," Chet replied. He lit his cigarette and watched Tolly take a deep draw on his flask. "You got something good in there?"

"Water." He held the flask out and regarded its silver shine in the afternoon sun. "Water you asking for?" Tolly chuckled at his joke. "Not that it's any of your bus…business."

Chet noted the slur in his words and thought the doctor had probably started his drinking early today, before he came for his cigarette break. He knew he'd better say what he'd come to say. Tolly had obviously almost exhausted his afternoon beverage supply.

"Dr. Thompson, my name is Chet Wilson. I'm an old friend of your wife, Violet. Known her since we were kids in Anniston."

Tolly turned to fully face Chet for the first time, swigging the last of his bourbon. He placed the flask in his pocket.

"Is that right?' he said. "Well, it's nice of you to say hello, Mr. Wilson. I'm going to get back to my patients now."

"Wait." Chet held up his hand. "This will only take a minute. I came over here to tell you that if you ever lay a hand on her again, you'll be laid out in this hospital yourself. If you survive the ambulance ride, which is doubtful."

"Lay a…who the *hell* do you think you are?" Tolly growled. "How dare you threaten me? I'm going to get security and have you removed. You can plan on being barred from working here, too—"

"Oh, we're done with the wiring. I don't plan on coming here again," Chet said.

Tolly stared at him, his bloodshot eyes popping. "You're her…have you been with my wife? That goddam whore. You have, haven't you? Oh, she's going to pay—"

"Of course not," Chet struggled to keep his voice calm. "I only know what you've done to Violet because I saw her at her parents' house. I've never believed those bruises came from any car accident."

Tolly shoved Chet aside, his strength surprising for a much older man. "They were there because my wife foolishly tried to drive my sports car. If you had any medical knowledge, that would be obvious to you." Tolly started to stalk off, then returned to add, "Are you the father of her bastard child? *That's* it, isn't it?" He studied Chet's surprised features. "Ohhhh, you didn't know. She's a *whore*, Mister…"

Tolly squinted at the name on Chet's shirt. "…Wilson. Has been all her life."

Chet swung his fist at Tolly and missed as he jumped back, stumbling but recovering his balance. Tolly laughed and wiped his mouth with the back of his hand.

"No need for blows here, Wilson. I have no intention of fighting you. And I absolutely promise you'll never hear from my wife again. I'll make damn sure of that." He started to walk to the heavy metal door that opened onto the staircase, just as Chet had planned.

Chet chased after him. "You will not lay a hand on her, understand me?"

Tolly swung the door open without a backward glance. "Security will be up in a minute. I suggest you gather your things."

Chet watched the door close, then walked back to Jerry Lee. "He's furious and he'll head to the house as soon as he can leave the hospital. That gives us at least an hour and a half. Let's wrap this up."

Jerry Lee asked, "Are you positive she's not there?"

"One thing about a man like Tolly: he keeps his wife on an extremely strict schedule. It's Friday, so Violet will be at the country club playing cards with her friends until three. I'll drive over there and meet her in the parking lot, tell her I saw her husband and he's furious. I'll say she has to let me in that house to wait for him somewhere, because he is definitely going to hurt her when he gets home. Only this time, *I'll* be there. And no, she's not gonna like it, but Violet will understand."

Chet glanced at his watch. "As soon as he moves to hurt her, I'll confront him and hit back, hard. He'll feel every ounce of pain he's ever inflicted on her, and more." Chet reached to gather screwdrivers and electrical tape they'd left atop the air conditioners, hurrying to throw everything into buckets.

"Are you sure this is the best idea, though?" Jerry Lee cocked his head. "You've thought it through? I mean, how do you even know for sure—"

"I've seen the bruises with my own eyes, and they're horrible. I saw them when they tried to explain it as a car accident, and again in Birmingham when I stopped to give Violet a notebook for her writing. That time, I thought she was going to tell me the truth, but she didn't." Chet exhaled heavily and continued, his hand clenching into a fist. "This is the only way I can think of to stop him. I'll make it very clear to Dr. Thompson I'll kill him if he ever hurts her again after today. It's time he got a taste of his own medicine."

"*If* she lets you into the house." Jerry Lee raised his eyebrows. "You ask me, that's a longshot."

"It won't be easy, but I'll convince Violet this is our only chance to put an end to his abuse. That she *has* to give me the opportunity. And I'll tell her if Tolly doesn't touch her, I'm wrong and I'll slip out a back door." Chet nodded at Jerry Lee. "But he will. You saw him."

"Guy like that, Chet, he'll press charges." Jerry Lee was twisting the final wire replacement into position and preparing to close the air conditioner's access door. "It'll be his word against yours, and I don't like your chances."

Chet shook his head. "I'm pretty sure he's never allowed Violet to call the police, and I don't think he will, either. There's a lady who's worked in their house for years, too. She has to have seen what he does to Violet. Dr. Thompson knows that." Chet gathered and threw a handful of wire lugs into a bucket, then stood with his arms crossed, leaning against the box they'd been working on.

"Why not just get Violet out of there?" Jerry Lee closed the air conditioner's access panel with a grunt and reached for a screwdriver.

"She wouldn't leave him. Hell, she won't even admit he hits her. I think some part of Violet still cares about him, which is beyond my understanding. I think she's scared to death he'll hurt her family, too. He probably makes all kinds of threats." Chet paused, thinking. "There's something he said. I don't know. Maybe Violet had a baby before she met him. Tolly made some crack about a bastard child."

Jerry Lee began gathering and packing his tools. "And you don't know anything about that?"

"No," Chet said. "Nothing at all. But maybe that's the real reason she's been so afraid of leaving him. Maybe he threatened to hurt some kid he thinks is hers."

"Maybe." Jerry Lee waved toward the exit. "We'd better get out of here before security shows up."

They each picked up a bucket of supplies and began walking toward the door as Chet continued, "Violet should've told me the truth when she was at her parents' place and let me handle it then. But now he'll see what I'm willing to do to him and he'll know I'll finish the job if he hurts her again. Maybe she'll get the courage to leave him, move back to Anniston someday."

"Are you trying to convince me or yourself? And is that the real reason you're doing it, Chet?" Jerry Lee sniggered a little. "I mean, she is a great-lookin' broad."

Chet stopped in his tracks. "Look, it's no secret I love her. I have ever since I can remember. But Violet isn't going to leave Tolly, and I have a wife and kid at home. So, no. The reason is because I believe he'll kill her someday if I don't stop him. Period."

"So, we had to take this bullshit job just so you could confront him?"

Chet fixed his eyes on Jerry Lee's and placed a hand on his shoulder, stopping him before they reached the door. "I had to get him angry enough to confront Violet and be there when he did it. That required us to be here, in Birmingham. I'm sorry about underbidding this job, Jerry Lee, but I'll make it up to you. I promise. And you have to promise *me* you'll never tell anyone about this."

"Nah," Jerry Lee shook his head. "Hell, I got a record, Chet. This could blow back on me, just bein' here."

"Okay, well, you'll get in your car and go on home. You won't be anywhere near Violet's house." Chet swung the metal door open and started down the concrete stairwell, his steps echoing until they stopped suddenly and Jerry Lee almost collided with his back.

Chet turned around and put a hand on Jerry Lee's chest. "Oh God. He fell. The damn drunk fell down the stairs." Chet pointed at Tolly's body, which lay on a landing a floor below, one of his legs bent at an impossible angle and a pool of dark blood by his head.

They stood and stared for a few seconds. Jerry Lee said, "We have to get somebody to help. What if he dies? Everybody knows we were up there, Chet. Oh God, oh God…" Jerry Lee began breathing harder and harder in a panic. "What are we gonna do?"

"I'm going to check for a pulse, Jerry Lee," Chet said. He ran down the steps to Tolly's body and carefully placed his bucket of tools to the side. He pressed his fingers to the man's neck. He shook his head at Jerry Lee and leaned back against the wall, his arms crossed.

"Chet," Jerry Lee hissed, "we gotta tell somebody."

"Everyone in this hospital knows he goes up and drinks on the roof every day. They won't be surprised he stumbled and fell," Chet said. "Let's get out of here. Somebody's gonna notice he's been gone longer than usual."

"Are you gonna go tell *her?* At the country club?" Jerry Lee's voice shook as he passed Tolly's body and avoided stepping in his blood. "Oh God, my fingerprints are all over this railing."

"Your fingerprints are everywhere, Jerry Lee. So are mine. We've been working here four days, it fits right in. Come on, we have to hurry. I'm not going anywhere near Violet today, knucklehead. I'm driving home, and you are too." Chet took the stairs as quickly as he could and they emerged onto the mostly deserted sixth floor, where they rode the elevator to the ground level and walked out the hospital's back door unnoticed.

Jerry Lee handed Chet his bucket and sprinted off to his faded blue Chevy sedan parked down the street. He slammed the driver's door closed. He gave Chet a quick wave through the window and pulled his car out, looking decidedly suspicious. His head swiveled right and left as he drove away.

Chet watched the retreating car, noting no one was around on this narrow street behind the hospital. He carried both buckets of tools to the Superior Electric van parked down the block, placing them in the back. Chet climbed into the driver's seat, still looking for anyone who might've witnessed their exit. He sat and stared at the hospital for a minute, his hands gripping the steering wheel.

Chet remembered an old saying: *man plans and God laughs*. He turned the key in the ignition and shook his head. He could not, would not call her. But maybe he'd go to Tolly's funeral, just to make sure they buried the son of a bitch.

The van seemed to want to steer itself to the country club parking lot instead of home. Maybe he could catch a glimpse of Violet as she walked to her car; it would be three o'clock soon. He wouldn't say a word, just see her safe and happy and drive away with that picture in his head.

He pulled up at 2:30 and parked in a safely hidden space. Violet's car was nowhere in sight. Chet drove to a pay phone and called the Thompson home.

"Hello?" Violet said.

He hung up the receiver and let his hand rest on it for a few seconds, then began the drive back to Anniston.

Author's Note: Please watch the upcoming television special "Disbelief," produced and presented by former CNN news anchor Bettina Hughes. This 2023 Criminal Behavior Network series will feature a re-enactment of events that led to the death of Dr. Tolliver "Tolly" Thompson in Birmingham, Alabama in May, 1965. "Chet Wilson" will be identified in Episode 8 with his given name, Eugene Crawford Harris. Harris's employee, Jerry Lee Urban, issued a written statement to Miss Hughes corroborating his testimony of events as presented here shortly before his death in 2019.

Thirty

RONNI

CHEAHA STATE PARK, ALABAMA

OCTOBER 30, 2022

Maddie reached to adjust the bow on my dress and I put my hand atop hers. "I'll fix it, honey, if you'll take care of Violet," I told her reflection in the mirror. My daughter was wearing a white knit dress with tiny crystal rhinestones along the neckline, its skirt a frothy floor-length confection of chiffon ruffles. My heart was a little fractured by how grownup Violet looked a month past her second birthday. Now she stood dangerously close to a dish of candies she could employ to destroy her outfit, watching to see if anyone caught her edging close to the custom-monogrammed M&Ms sitting around like chocolate landmines.

Maddie scooped her up and toted her to look out a window, pointing at mountains and valleys in the distance. I saw Violet shaking her head wildly, her shoulder-length curls flying.

"I'm telling her we have to be careful not to fall," Maddie said.

"It's a long way down, but there's a safety fence around the deck. She'll be fine," I answered.

"She wasn't so fine at the rehearsal." Maddie shrugged. "Boogeretta here ran off while I wasn't looking and was halfway to the swimming pool. I mean, it's covered, but still."

Violet's finger crept close to her nose. "Stop that!" I said, my voice a little too loud in the room. I would die of embarrassment if my daughter defiled that dress with something she extracted from her nostril. Violet threw her arms into the air and glared at me.

"OKAY."

Deanna said, "Did I ever tell you I figured out where she got that? When she was a baby, I'd prop her against me on the couch while you tried to sleep. There was some stupid seventies sitcom running late at night on TV, and one of the characters—I think his name was Pinball—would throw his hands in the air and yell, 'OKAYYYYY!' over and over. The laugh track made it obvious that was his signature move. I'd forgotten all about it until a week ago, when it popped up on my TV. She had to have seen it." Deanna chuckled as I placed my hands on her shoulders and regarded the two of us in the fancy gilt 'bride's mirror' in the corner of the dressing room. "It's much funnier when Violet does it."

I looked at my daughter, still in Maddie's arms. "It's funny now. Not sure how her teachers will take it in kindergarten."

Deanna giggled. "I'd pay good American dollars to see that. She'll outgrow it, I guarantee you. Enjoy her cute toddler things while you can." She sighed and patted her gray hair, which the stylist had fashioned into an updo and adorned with tiny pink and white flowers. "I feel like mutton dressed as lamb. I'm too old to be wearing this." She swept her hands up and down along her pale pink satin dress. It had glittering crystals scattered all over the bodice. The sweetheart neckline and wide sash were complemented by a full, ankle-length skirt. Deanna's shoes were dyed to match.

She looked like a beautiful fairy-tale queen, and I found myself hoping her mother was witnessing this moment from somewhere.

"The dress is perfect on you, and no one is too old to be a bride. Honestly, Deanna, you look gorgeous and I can't wait until Lee sees you," I told her.

Maddie walked up and shifted Violet onto her other hip. "He's absolutely crazy about you, Deanna, and he's going to love that dress. Some cheugy bridal suit would have been awful. We made the right choice." She nodded. "Mom has a good eye for fashion."

We both stared at Maddie. "Cheugy?" I asked.

"Yeah, you know, basic," she said, controlling the urge to roll her teenaged eyes. "We started out looking at old-lady wedding suits. This is much better."

"Your mom was very helpful," Deanna told her. "I don't mean to insult the dress. I'm just not used to wearing something like this." She smoothed the satin sides nervously in the mirror. I thought about the shopping trip from hell Deanna had described, with her daughter Sarah and Lee's daughter Darcy fighting over appropriate dresses for the bride while Maddie stared at her phone. Deanna told me she'd have said yes to a cardboard dress to get it over with.

"How much longer?" she asked.

"Not long," Maddie said. "Uncle Huel is coming to get us in a few." She set her phone on the table. "You ready, Miss Violet? Remember what we're supposed to do?"

"Walk and smile." Violet nodded, her face slack as though bored with the idea.

"I'll be in front of you, and you get to be just before the bride. *And* you get to throw these flower petals at people," Maddie held up the basket.

"Not *at* people," I corrected, with visions of Violet hurling a basket at guests. "Like this." I took two pink rose petals out and tossed them in front of me.

Violet squatted and picked up the petals, carefully replacing them in the little white basket. Only Maddie and I knew it had once been used for her Easter Bunny gift from Jinxie years ago. I liked the idea she'd be present somehow.

"So, I'll go first and then Maddie and then you and then Deanna, okay? Do you need to go potty?" I asked her.

Violet shook her head no.

"I do," Deanna said, handing me her bouquet. She rushed off just before Huel knocked on the door and poked his head in.

"We're gonna need a minute," Maddie told him.

"Hiiii, honey," Violet sang, and waved at Huel. To the best of my knowledge, they'd never met.

He looked away from the door and held up a hand. "I'll be back in a few. Natives are restless out here."

"We know. Just a minor delay." I nodded toward the bathroom, hoping Deanna wasn't having dress problems. Or worse, Spanx problems. Maddie and I locked eyes after a full three minutes and I started to walk over just as Deanna emerged.

"Okay," she said. "Do I look all right?"

I kissed her cheek and swiped my lip gloss off with a thumb. "Better than all right. You're exquisite and radiant as any bride's ever been." I handed Deanna her bouquet and dabbed at my eyes.

Huel poked his head back in and gave Deanna a wide grin. "Let's go, Mrs. Tyler. They're waiting for us." He held the door open wide and we assembled, watching for Huel to take his place next to Lee.

I walked down the makeshift aisle in Vista Cliffside Event Center, its floor-to-ceiling windows offering a view of the mountains beyond as well as the deck outside, where tables were set with flickering candles in the late afternoon sun. Over those were suspended thousands of tiny white lights.

Violet made her way down the aisle, scattering petals efficiently until she spotted Samuel. She came to a dead stop next to him and handed him the basket, holding her arms up to climb into his lap. The crowd tittered and I nodded at Samuel, who removed Violet from the procession. She'd made it a good three-quarters of the way. Not too bad. The plan had been for Maddie to take Violet's hand and sit up front, so Maddie improvised a quick wave toward Samuel and sat down.

I watched Lee's face as he waited for Deanna, jittery and excited as a twenty-year-old. He and his best man, Huel, wore black tuxedoes with pink paisley vests peeking from their jackets.

We all waited in silence—Deanna's choice—and then the opening strains of the instrumental recording of Stephen Sanchez's "Until I Found You" began to play. It was a decidedly non-traditional selection influenced by Maddie, beautifully ethereal. The original version would be their first dance at the reception.

A few seconds felt like an eternity, and then Deanna appeared on Max's arm. I heard more than a few people gasp as they stood to face the bride. Sarah, who had been less than enthusiastic about Deanna's remarriage, began crying when she saw her mother. I think we all did. Any misgivings about the future she'd had would have been melted by Deanna's radiant smile.

If Violet Glenn Thompson ever reappeared on Earth, it was at the moment Deanna began walking down that aisle, beaming at her guests, sheer happiness shining in her eyes. *My* Violet was next to Samuel, slightly out in the aisle, clapping her tiny hands. I saw Max wink at her as they passed.

Deanna and Lee stood before the assistant pastor of his church, the grandson of the man who'd married Lee and Jinxie in 1975. He told them what a gift the Lord had blessed them with.

We all knew.

Lee kissed his bride and Reverend McKinney announced Mr. and Mrs. Lee Tyler would greet us on the deck, where dinner and dancing would follow. Before they walked away, Deanna reached over and gave my hand a squeeze. *I love you.* She paused where Sarah and her grandchildren stood to hug each of them, then made her way outside. Lee's protective arm stayed fixed around her, I saw through the window, until Deanna sat down beside him.

I stepped out into the slightly cool October air on the deck. The western sky was a ballet slipper surrounded by deep blue. Tiny white lights danced over our heads, and made us all so lovely, I thought.

I saw Samuel and Gwendolyn sitting with his parents and waved. Violet yelled "MOMMY!" from Maddie's side. I took Violet's hand.

"We're going back to the room for just a minute to put your other pretty outfit on, remember?"

Violet shook her head and patted the skirt of her dress. "No. I wear dis."

"You can't, honey. It'll get ruined out here, all your pretty white ruffles could get torn. I brought your new Peppa Pig shirt and your favorite jeans. We'll be right back. Let's go before they start bringing the food."

My daughter responded by sitting on the surface of the deck, where a splinter army awaited her chiffon ruffles and tender legs. I put my hands under her armpits and carried her away without a word.

Violet seized the opportunity to yell, "BYE. Mommy take me awayyyyy. Bye, honey!" At least thirty pairs of eyes tracked us off the deck, and I'm sure they noted Violet's helpful kicks to my thighs to speed us along. I changed her clothes and touched up my lip gloss. My hair was frozen into place by half a can of spray. It moved in concert like a single unit. I patted it in the mirror and sighed.

Violet would never have admitted it, but she enjoyed her sprint in a comfortable outfit and shoes back onto the deck, waving at the crowd like she'd just been paroled from Leavenworth. We joined Maddie at her parents' table and I gratefully accepted a glass of champagne as Violet climbed into Maddie's lap, ignoring her chair next to me. Huel made a toast to the bride and groom, incorporating his version of the day they met.

"Lee walked to the neighborhood gazebo every afternoon to watch the sunset. And one night, this star appeared to him." He waved his hand dramatically at the horizon, then grinned and winked at Deanna. "And she had cookies." The crowd laughed politely and he continued, "Seriously, cookies were the least of it. Deanna, we love you and welcome you to the family." He turned to Lee, who stood for a hug. "You did good, old man," Huel added. "Congratulations on your beautiful bride." He handed the microphone to Lee and sat. I saw his wife Muffy run her hand up and down Huel's back, no doubt telling him he'd done a great job.

Lee stood looking at the crowd for a minute, clearly emotional. "I, uh…I never expected…" he glanced at Deanna and swallowed. "When I lost Jinxie, I thought I'd lost the will to go on. I climbed out of bed in the morning and immediately wanted to go back. Some days I *did*, and just stared at the ceiling. I made it through that darkness with the help of my family, especially my precious Maddie and Donnie, who brought laughter and light into my world whenever they could. But then, a little more than two years ago, I met this beautiful woman. I didn't know at first why she came into my life, but I do now. She saved me. Deanna, you and I are going to celebrate every moment we have together as man and wife. I promise you, we will make these years wonderful."

He paused and loosened the bowtie knotted at his neck, pulling at its side. "I'm old, y'all. I know it. But this lovely lady makes me feel twenty years younger." Deanna smiled up at him and sipped her champagne. "Wait, honey, there's more to my toast." Lee laughed. "Some of you know, when we really couldn't travel or go much of anywhere during the pandemic, Deanna and I made the trip up to Cheaha a lot. This place is special to us. We're going to spend our first night as man and wife in a chalet here tonight, and we want y'all to stay and enjoy this party even after the old folks have gone to bed. Deanna and I need our sleep because tomorrow, we're flying to Italy."

I watched Deanna's mouth form an 'O', which she quickly covered with her hand. Lee continued, "She thought we were going to Nassau." Deanna clutched both sides of her face, shaking her head in amazement. He grinned at her and continued, "I love you, Deanna, and thank you for becoming my wife. I will cherish you, always." He held his glass up and clinked it with Deanna's.

Darcy leaned over to ask me, "Did you know about that? About Italy?"

"No, I didn't. Lee asked me a while back to help her get a passport, but she thought it was for a honeymoon in The Bahamas. Actually, I'm not sure you even *need* a passport for that." I took a drink of my champagne. "This'll be a wonderful trip for her. She's always wanted to see Rome."

"Yeah, Daddy knows that. He's been planning this surprise for a while. He made me help him put together a suitcase of warm things for her to wear. I hope I did okay. I'm just so glad they can travel there safely now."

"Yeah, me too," I said, setting my glass down. I wondered briefly if Darcy knew about the pre-nuptial agreement Huel had Deanna sign for "Daddy," not that it was any of our business. They each had assets, and it only made sense to protect them.

I patted her arm. "Darcy, would you excuse me for a minute? I need to say hi to Max and his family. Maddie?" Darcy and Maddie both nodded at me; Violet was in Maddie's lap, tearing some rose petals she'd stashed into pieces. "I'm paying you for this," I told Maddie.

She responded by shaking her head vigorously up and down, eyes wide, but I could tell she was enjoying Violet's company. For now, at least.

Max and Elise stood to hug me, both of them healthy and shiny and pretty as ever. "I've missed you two," I told them. "Seems like a million years ago I was forcing you onto that bike."

Max patted the empty seat next to him and I sat. "Where's Gwendolyn?' I asked Samuel.

"She had to go take a call. She'll be right back," he said.

Elise reached her hand across Max and grabbed mine. "Did you come alone? Surely not," she said. "You look too gorgeous to waste it on a wedding reception with no date. Maybe there's someone here…" she trailed off as she scouted other tables.

"It's fine, Elise. I'm not really—I'm good," I told her. "I'm happy being here with Violet. She's more than enough escort for one person."

"I thought I was going to die trying not to laugh when she handed Samuel that basket," Elise said. "She is truly adorable. I so wish Ollie could be here tonight. They could have a lot of fun together."

I smiled and tried to picture that, with the colossal age gap and Ollie either playing violin or trying to cast a Spidey-web around my daughter, neither of which would impress her much. Unless he knew Peppa Pig's greatest hits.

"Yes, I'm sorry Ethan and Jeannie couldn't make the trip."

Elise cut her eyes over at Samuel, hesitating. "Well, with any luck, they'll be here for a different wedding soon."

"Mom." Samuel frowned and shook his head. "We talked about this." He continued shaking his head as he turned to me. "I have no wedding plans. It's all in my mother's head." Samuel punctuated this by mouthing the letters N O.

Servers were starting to place salads and I thought I'd better get back to my own seat, especially before Gwendolyn returned. "I'll talk to y'all later, after cake." I blew them all a kiss and returned to my table. Violet wriggled off Maddie's lap and walked over to sit in mine. I kissed the top of her head and wrapped her in my arms, hugging her little toddler belly.

"Hey, baby girl. You wanna eat salad with me?"

Violet shook her head adamantly, clearly expressing her hatred of salads and other forms of vegetation on plates.

"They're bringing her some diced fruit," Darcy informed me.

"Oh, that's perfect. She'll probably eat that." I was highly dubious. Violet shared Rick's disdain for healthy food. I stood and placed Violet in her own chair next to me, pulling it close enough for her to reach the table. Violet used the fruit like little building blocks, stacking chunks of apple atop strawberry slices, then crowning each with a sad-looking wrinkled blueberry. The small plate the servers had given her with the fruit cup was the only thing that saved the white tablecloth.

When they delivered Violet's chicken fingers, she gobbled one up and then made her way over to Elise's side to gnaw on another, standing defiant against seating charts and vegetables. I tracked her out of the corner of my eye, mindful of what Maddie had said about her wandering off. Violet loved the attention she was getting too much to wander anywhere, though. I saw her gazing up at Elise and pointing to the dais with Deanna and Lee. Within a minute, she'd been carried up there and presented for hugs.

Once we'd all finished our beef tenderloins and scalloped potatoes, I extracted Violet from Elise and made her sit next to me. Lee and Deanna cut into a three-tiered chocolate cake with pink roses that looked straight out of the 1960s, which made sense. They didn't do any of the traditional cake and icing smears on each other's faces. I was grateful for the dignity as well as keeping the idea from Violet's head. I insisted on feeding her bites of the cake until she started excavating her slice with her fingers. I gave up and fished a baby wipe out of my purse, one eye on the balance of her cake. At least it wasn't in her hair.

"Staaaaahp," she protested as I tried to clean her hands and face. "That is a hurt," she accused me.

"It is not a hurt. I had to get the chocolate off you." Violet climbed down and headed back to Maddie, her refuge when I made her angry.

"If you wait a few minutes, I'll dance with you," Maddie told her. Violet's eyes were wide with excitement as she looked back at me, then she remembered she was supposed to be mad and offered an exaggerated frown.

The adults sat back with our champagne glasses and watched Lee and Deanna walk around to the small dance floor in front of their table. "Until I Found You" played as they swayed together, Lee mouthing the words *unless it's you I fall into* to Deanna. That reminded me to look over at Max. Sure enough, he was making seated disco moves and singing "More Than A Woman" to a laughing Elise.

The next song was "Sweet Home Alabama," which may be legally required; I've never been sure. Maddie and Violet walked hand in hand to the dance floor and looked adorable enough to make the videographer follow them around. They stayed through several songs and it occurred to me I should just buy Maddie her first car in exchange for babysitting. It seemed right as she handed me an exhausted Violet and went to dance with her dad.

I cuddled my sleepy daughter and rested my head on hers; I was worn out, too. I began to plan our exit to the cabin we'd rented nearby. When the music stopped, Deanna surprised me by taking the microphone and signaling to a server.

"I want all of you to dance by candlelight, because we're unplugging the strands over your heads for a while. Take the time to look up, y'all. There isn't a cloud in the sky, and I want it dark enough for you to see the stars. I think it's time for *all* of us to do that. It's been a long two and a half years."

The crowd murmured as Deanna sat back down, smiling directly at me. Someone flipped a switch and we waited for our eyes to adjust, Violet whimpering a little. She didn't like darkness.

"Look up," I told her. We leaned back together as the DJ started playing "Sweet Caroline." Around the first BOM BOM BOM from the crowd, the darkness fully settled and our pupils dilated. We saw thousands, *millions* of pinpricks of light twinkling in the sky. For the first time in my life, the Milky Way was clearly visible to me, close enough to touch from that mountaintop. I glanced down at my daughter, the reflection of a sparkling universe in her eyes.

Maddie nudged me. "Mom and Dad are leaving and I think I will, too." I waved at Darcy and her husband as they walked away, the music a bit loud for a proper goodnight. "Do you want me to put Violet to bed? I'll stay with her in your cabin. We're just next door." My daughter's chubby little arms automatically reached for her beloved Maddie.

"Actually, I was just going to take her myself. I've been up since 5:30 and—"

A man's voice to my left interrupted me. "I'd appreciate it if you'd stay a little while," he said. "I'm sorry I'm late. Had a very sick horse to deal with." Chad Harris plunked down in the seat Violet had vacated as Maddie winked and carried her away.

I watched Violet literally dig her heels in until Maddie brought her back. "Hiiii, honey," she told Chad in her sweetest voice.

He laughed and said, "Hey, Violet. You are very pretty tonight."

"Yes," she nodded. "I am."

"How's Poorole? Is she doing okay?" Chad asked her.

Violet arranged her little features into a grimace. "Her eated a bug."

Chad chuckled and looked at me. "Her is fine," I told him. "Okay," I said to my daughter, "kiss me goodnight and I'll be there soon. I love you, baby." Maddie leaned Violet over to kiss my cheek and then they walked off toward the cabins.

Chad was dressed in jeans and a plaid shirt, smeared all over with what I hoped was mud, about as un-wedding-y as an outfit could be.

"Oh!" He glanced down and patted his clothes. "I'm not wearing this. Just didn't have time to change yet. I was afraid you'd leave before I did. Let me go wash up in the motel. I have a room."

My mouth was still kind of hanging open at the idea he'd appeared. Up at the head table, Deanna watched the two of us, an amused look on her face. It all fell into place then.

"Yeah, she invited me," Chad said. "I told her I might be late if there was an emergency, and of course there always is." Chad reached for my champagne glass and downed the rest. "I'll get us more," he assured me with a smile. "Stay right there. Please, Ronni. I'll be back in five minutes. There's so much I want to tell you." I nodded and he backed away, holding his hands up like I was a golden retriever, then turned and ran toward the parking lot.

Elise wandered over as Max went to ask Deanna to dance. Samuel and Gwendolyn were already on the floor. I noticed Gwendolyn break into a huge smile as "When A Man Loves A Woman" began to play. She unclipped her long hair and let it sway behind her in the candlelight. I laughed as Max sat down next to the bride, holding out for a different song.

Elise patted my thigh and waved, magically conjuring a server out of thin air. "Would you please bring us each another glass of champagne?" she said to him. I was pretty sure the guy would've brought her all of France if she'd asked.

"Oh, three, if you don't mind," I added.

"Good thinking," Elise said, and watched the server walk away. "I assume your young man is changing clothes and will be right back, so I'll keep this short."

"He's not my young man, Elise. He's a young man Deanna pity-paired me with tonight, that's all."

She accepted her champagne flute from the server and I saw her slip him a twenty as I took the other two. Elise sipped and set her glass down.

"That's not what I hear. Dr. Chad Harris was beyond thrilled to come here tonight as your date. Deanna used the word *giddy*, though that's not very manly. Certainly *dresses* manly, though. All he's missing is the hat."

I pictured Chad in a black cowboy hat, and it was not unappealing. "He had to go see a sick horse," I said. "I used to wait for Rick to fix flat tires and other stuff. There's no such thing as a schedule." I shrugged and looked at the space where Chad would walk back in. "But Elise, this is just a fix-up. Deanna felt sorry for me because I made a complete ass of myself the one time he asked me out. That was months ago, and I never heard from him again."

"Ronni, the fact he's here says everything. Don't be disingenuous. You're a smart woman. Chad came all the way up this mountain because he likes you, not because some old lady without a pet asked him. Now, I'm counting on you to give him a chance."

"Elise, I—"

She put her hand on my arm. "Look up, Ronni. Not backward, not forward, but *up*." I did, and almost gasped all over again at the array of diamonds set against the black velvet sky. I turned my eyes back to her and nodded.

Elise walked away with a contented smile, and I leaned my head back again. My eyes blurred as I heard the opening notes of "My Girl." The song Rick set for me and our daughter on his playlist. The song I knew he'd have had on for Violet when he danced her around the living room on top of his feet; when he drove her to kindergarten; when he danced with Violet at her own wedding. I got lost in those images as the stars merged into one soft light above me. How I wished he'd gotten to hold our daughter, to witness this beautiful tiny person we'd made together. I needed him more in that moment, surrounded by couples swaying and laughing, than I had in months. I blinked to clear my vision and saw a shooting star at the edge of the horizon, falling on Alabama as a whisper.

I drew a deep breath and sighed. "I love you," I said, "but maybe it's time."

I was wiping the tears from my cheeks as Chad walked up, dressed in a navy suit, his white shirt open at the collar. He pretended not to notice I'd been crying; he stood next to me for a few seconds before reaching to pull out a chair.

"It's a beautiful night, huh?" Chad said, and took a swig of champagne. "Umm, Ronni, I wanted to tell you that day you brought the injured dog to the office, but I never got a chance. I apologize again for the way I blindsided you. I blurted out something you clearly weren't ready to hear. And I know what that's like, not being ready. I lost my wife four years ago to—"

"Oh, Chad, I'm so sorry," I interjected. "I had no idea."

"To a tennis pro at the country club in Opelika." He shook his head. "I was attempting a joke. You make me awkward, Ronni." Chad shrugged his shoulders. "I was going to say I know how uncomfortable it can be when everyone assumes you're ready to move on. Now I'm awkward again."

"I'm not exactly smooth here, Chad." I drank a little more champagne, enjoying the fizzy buzz. "So, your love meant nothing to your wife."

"Ha. You get one love pun, and we're done. Anyway, I think part of the weirdness is, I feel like I already know you. We never met at Fairfield, but you took care of my grandfather. And reading your book was like—well, some parts are practically your diary."

"I didn't put everything in there, just so you know. It's funny, I finished writing a chapter about your grandfather the day before yesterday. I feel like I really know *him* now."

"Probably better than I did. He had a lot of health problems when he was older, so I never got to spend much time with Granddad. I mostly know him through Dad's stories and your book, honestly. How's the new one coming along?"

"It's almost done," I told him.

"That must be a relief," he said. Chad looked away as he took a drink.

"It kind of is and isn't. I get all emotionally involved with characters, and then have to say goodbye. It's good and bad."

"Why are those people all staring at us?" Chad nodded at the crowd. Samuel, Gwendolyn, Elise, Max, and Deanna all swiftly averted their eyes from our table.

"My family is dying to see if we'll dance or something." I realized it was the first time I'd used that word with an outsider. "Well, they're close friends, as you'll know from *The History of Ronni, Part I.*"

"Family's the word I'd choose. I know Violet Thompson was like a grandmother to you, and Deanna considers you a daughter. Looks to me like your hearts are connected closer than a lot of genetic families."

I nodded and drained my glass. "I think you're right." I met his blue eyes fully, and he looked so perfect in that candlelight. I remembered what Violet had said about his grandfather at about the same age. Chad really *did* make me think of a young Elvis Presley, especially his eyes and dark hair.

It was probably on the playlist Deanna and Lee chose; they were old enough to remember Elvis singing it for the first time. But maybe a particular star winked at me from the heavens above. Because at that exact moment, "Can't Help Falling In Love" began to play.

I looked at Chad and held out my hand. "We might as well, and make Deanna happy. Would you like to dance?"

"No, thank you." He shook his head. "As I recall, this song was playing at Fairfield when you danced with Rick, at the end of your book. And that's a beautiful memory, but it's not ours. I think we should dance to our own music."

"Thanks for the fresh awkwardness," I said, and tried to laugh.

"Come on," he said, "let's take a walk. Let them wonder what we're up to. I want to show you something." Chad slid his chair back without waiting for an answer. I followed him to his truck in the parking lot, which had a white trailer attached to it. Chad unlocked it and swung the doors open, waving for me to look inside.

"This is Maisie," he told me. "She's fourteen weeks old, and we lost her mother today. I'm adopting her."

I blinked into the trailer, which had no interior lights. Slowly, I could make out the form of a baby horse—a foal—standing in the corner.

"Oh my gosh, she's beautiful." The little horse was a tan color with a white stripe down her nose. She bobbed her head and welcomed us with a soft nicker. "The poor baby."

"I promise you, she'll be pampered into the most spoiled filly in Alabama. I have a mare she'd be with right now in my pasture, but I detoured up here." Chad reached and grabbed a bottle from a box by the door. "Want to feed her? She's not afraid of people. Just walk up slowly." He held the bottle out to me and I gingerly approached Maisie, who knew exactly why I was there and what to do. I stroked her mane as she drank.

"She's so pretty," I told him.

"She's a beauty queen, for sure. Do you ride?" he asked.

"Never in my life," I said.

"Well, maybe we can fix that." Chad watched in silence as I fell in love with a baby horse, patting her and running my hand down her side. When the bottle was empty, I gave her neck a little hug and walked back to Chad, his eyes shining in the starlight.

"Will she be okay in here?" I asked him.

"She'll be absolutely fine and safe. She has a fluffy bed of hay in there, and I'll check on her before I turn in." Chad closed and locked the door. "Is it okay if I hold your hand?"

"Of course," I said, and felt the warmth of his hand enclose mine like a blessing. We walked back into the reception as every head on the deck swiveled to look. I didn't care. I was still smiling at the memory of Maisie.

We sat down as Lee and Deanna prepared to exit, stopping to hug their guests and receive their well-wishes. When they got to our table, Deanna kissed my cheek and whispered, "I don't know where y'all went, but I hope it was magical."

"Actually, Mrs. Tyler," I whispered back, "it was. And thank you. Eat some wonderful pasta for me. I love you."

Deanna pulled away and said, "I love you, Ronni. See you in two weeks. And you take good care of her, Chad, okay?"

He smiled and nodded. We watched them walk away and sat back down.

"I have something for you," Chad said, reaching into his pocket. "It was in Granddad's things, and I thought you might like to have it." He extended his hand and showed me a small, glittering gold rock.

"Is this the one your grandfather gave to Violet back in the forties, when he was a kid? And she gave it back to him at Fairfield?"

"Yep." Chad grinned at me and nodded as he passed it to me. "Seems right for you to have it."

I turned the pyrite over and over in my hand. Someone had switched the white lights overhead back on while we were gone, and the rock glinted with each movement.

"Thank you, Chad," I said. "This means a lot to me. I've been immersed in their world lately. Your timing is perfect."

"I hope so," he replied. Chad waved at a server, still passing out champagne. He handed me a fresh glass, clinking his with mine. "To new beginnings, for Maisie and all of us," he said.

We both drank. The country music had everyone crowded on the small dance floor, trying to do their version of some line dance I'd never known. Every single one of them was laughing and bumping into each other. I noticed Samuel's eyes never left Gwendolyn, who was a ridiculously-good-looking match for him under those lights. Max and Elise bobbed along to the music without even attempting the steps. I saw Samuel walk over to the DJ when it was done, Gwendolyn trailing along. He smiled across the deck at me as they returned to their seats.

I didn't recognize the opening guitar chords of the next song, but Chad did. He sat and looked at me for several seconds, studying my face. Then he held his hand out to me.

"Yep, I think this is our music. Come on." We made our way to the dance floor as Chris Stapleton sang about how one of us could be a lucky penny and the other a four-leaf clover, starting over.

I slid my arms around Chad's neck and smiled at the lyrics, my head against his chest as we moved, inhaling some strange and wonderful cologne that evoked horses and sandalwood.

Maybe this could be the song we'd both dance to in our hearts, just as Violet said.

THE END

The leading cause of death
for law enforcement officers
in the United States of America
in 2020 and 2021
was COVID-19.

AUTHOR'S NOTE

Philip and Esther Davidson are fictional characters, but
Colonel and Mrs. Farley Berman (Germaine) are not.
Among The Berman Museum's Nazi effects,
you will find armbands and hats, though not a full uniform.
That is an invention for purposes of this narrative.

This gem (my word) in my hometown of Anniston, Alabama houses a 10,000+ piece collection from all over the world, ranging in dates from ancient China to the Gulf War. Its displays include weaponry, art (both paintings and sculptural), ethnographic artifacts, military uniforms and accessories, and archival photography and ephemera. It features items owned by multiple rulers, including Catherine the Great, Napoleon Bonaparte, Benito Mussolini, and Adolf Hitler.

About 6,000 of the pieces are the original donation by Farley and Germaine Berman, who were both spies during World War II.

If you don't visit The Berman Museum, you are missing out.

It's a stunning, world-class experience that will resonate long after you leave.

ACKNOWLEDGEMENTS

It takes a village.

Mine is populated by the most wonderful team you can imagine:

My early readers, Patricia Poucher, Debbie Tuckerman, Marianne Barnebey, David Boyd, Sue McKay, Savannah Duke, and Kninah Bradley, are simply the best and I love them all.

> (Picture them receiving and reading countless chapters from me under the covers with a flashlight late at night, sometimes shaking their heads, possibly pointing out I've made a character twelve months pregnant because I don't math.)

My editor, Alison Jack, has been enormously helpful and provided me with great advice. She polished *Dark Enough to See the Stars* to a sparkling shine.

> (Picture her poring over her laptop, scratching her head about some weird Southernism I employed, with a cup of tea at hand in the prettiest part of England.)

My interior designer, Rachael Gartman, made the book you're holding lovely to behold (be holding!), line by line. The artful title page and chapter headings are her unique and creative crowning touch to this story, and they take my breath away.

> (Picture her detangling all this text with a fine-tooth comb and grooming it into something sublimely legible and attractive with no weird cowlicks.)

The reason the cover of this book is exquisite is the uber-talented Rachel Lawston. I adore Rachel, who is also a very successful children's book author.

(Picture her as Leonardo da Vinci, but much, much prettier, Mona Lisa-ing books for the luckiest writers in the world.)

I am grateful to three doctors whom I love and respect: Davisson Edmond, Jacquie Tessen, and Tony Pizzo. They are not only great physicians but lovely people, as well, and provided invaluable medical advice about COVID-19 and more.

(Picture them in lab coats, looking sage, surrounded by adoring patients.)

Dave White helped me with information about photography and cameras in the 1940s, shedding a bright light onto Sam's darkroom. His expertise is much appreciated.

(Picture him holding a precious, antique Rolleiflex and knowing precisely how to create art with it.)

My husband, Saint Jay, has been designated such for enduring the construction of five novels, throughout which I am generally demanding and slightly intolerable. He's listened to several million ideas and plot twists, accompanied me on numerous research trips, and helped me brainstorm when there wasn't even a warm front in my head.

(Picture him staring at the door of the hermetically sealed writing chamber, infinitely patient, telling the dog to hush, wondering if I'll ever cook again. Also, picture him on our first date, taking me to meet an adorable baby horse.)

My beautiful book club women: you are a joy to me. My favorite part of writing is meeting readers, and I've made so many wonderful new friends. Y'all mean the world to me and *IT ALL COMES BACK TO YOU*.

(Picture me hugging you with enormous affection and gratitude.)

Thank you to everyone for reading. For you to allow my writing into your heart and mind is a rare privilege I never, ever take lightly.

Love,

Beth

(Picture me with a tiny tear running
down my cheek because I already
miss these characters.)
November, 2022

OTHER BOOKS BY BETH DUKE

TAPESTRY

IT ALL COMES BACK TO YOU

DELANEY'S PEOPLE

DON'T SHOOT YOUR MULE

Please visit www.bethduke.com

ABOUT THE AUTHOR

The Read House Hotel, Chattanooga, Tennessee
December 2021
Photo Credit: Savannah Duke

Beth Duke is an Amazon #1 Best Selling Author and the recipient of numerous honors for her fiction on two continents.

She is eyeing the other five.

The characters in *DARK ENOUGH TO SEE THE STARS* originated in her bestselling novel *IT ALL COMES BACK TO YOU* and have been loved by readers around the world.

Her book *TAPESTRY* was the Bronze Medal Winner in Southern Fiction in Publisher's Weekly's 2020 Readers' Choice Awards, an Award-Winning Finalist in the 2020 International Book Awards, and a Five Star Readers' Favorite Award Winner.

Country music superstar Randy Owen said, "Beth Duke's works are as real as grits and gravy in The South, and her usage of her Southern English has the taste of Mama's biscuits."

Beth lives in the mountains of her native Alabama with her husband, Jay, and an assortment of dogs including a recently-rescued coonhound named Daisy who has stolen her heart. Beth is the adoring and proud mother of Jason and Savannah. She is a constant reader, travel aficionado, and likes to pretend she's in baking competitions.

Her books *DELANEY'S PEOPLE, DON'T SHOOT YOUR MULE, IT ALL COMES BACK TO YOU, TAPESTRY,* and *DARK ENOUGH TO SEE THE STARS* are all love letters to her home state.

Made in United States
North Haven, CT
30 March 2023

34758350R00189